Victor Andres Triay

FREEDOM BETRAYED

The Unbroken
Circle Series,
BOOK II

12/8/15

For the world's greatest doctor, Dr. Kane,
from

PRAISE FOR THE STRUGGLE BEGINS, BOOK I OF THE UNBROKEN CIRCLE SERIES

Victor Triay's "The Struggle Begins" is a rare gem: a great novel, and, at the same time, great history. A rare and exhilarating combination of fact and fiction, this is one hell of a page-turner that draws you in and never lets go"

–Carlos Eire, Ph.D., Riggs Professor of History and Religious Studies, Yale University. Author of *Waiting for Snow in Havana* (National Book Award 2003)

"Triay is a master at plot mechanics. This novel encompasses a universal story of hope, betrayal, and fighting for one's beliefs."

–Lily Prellezo, author of *Seagull One: The Amazing True Story of Brothers to the Rescue*

"Triay has taken the facts of the takeover of Cuba by Fidel Castro and intertwined these with fictional, but totally believable characters. I started reading it one afternoon and couldn't put it down until I finished."

–Margaret L. Paris, author of *Embracing America: A Cuban Exile Comes of Age.*

"Triay is a first class story teller with a passion and a real under-standing of the background issues that surround the characters. As a seasoned historian he knows his facts extremely well and that shows throughout the entire book. The characters are so real that you can almost touch them."

--Carmen Romañach, past president, Operation Pedro Pan Group, Inc.

ALSO BY VICTOR ANDRES TRIAY

Fleeing Castro: Operation Pedro Pan and the Cuban Children's Program (1998)
"A tale of great heroism."-**Florida Historical Quarterly**

Bay of Pigs: An Oral History of Brigade 2506 (2001)
*Winner, Samuel Proctor Oral History Prize, 2001, Florida Historical Society
"The book establishes Triay as a significant researcher of Cuban-exile history." -**Fabiola Santiago, Miami Herald**

"superb" "Victor Andres Triay as well as the brigadistas should be congratulated for providing us with a most moving and interesting first-hand account of the Bay of Pigs invasion." -**Florida Historical Quarterly.**

La Patria Nos Espera (2003)
". . . debe saludarse la publicación de *La patria nos espera* (Random House Español, 2003), uno de los libros más completos sobre la invasion de Bahía de Cochinos . . ." -**El Nuevo Herald**

The Cuban Revolution: Years of Promise (2005)
"For Cubans who remember that time, this book will be like re-living it. For those who do not, it offers a good introduction to a complicated period." -**Tampa Tribune**

For my parents, Andrés and María Elena

ACKNOWLEDGEMENTS

*T*he Unbroken Circle series has been over a decade in the making. Its completion would not have been possible without the assistance of the hundreds of people who have left their mark on the final product. I am deeply indebted, above all, to the Bay of Pigs veterans and Operation Pedro Pan participants I interviewed for my first two non-fiction books. Since the publication of those works, I've met scores of additional people from these groups. Many of them have been gracious enough to share their stories with me as well, all of which served to enrich my knowledge of the period and provide me with additional insight when writing the present work. During the writing of *The Unbroken Circle* series, I also consulted, in addition to a myriad of written sources, a large number of relatives, family friends, colleagues, acquaintances, and former interviewees for additional information that proved critical in constructing a work of accurate historical fiction. Ricardo Sánchez, a family friend and a paratrooper during the Bay of Pigs invasion (1st Battalion, #3378), was especially helpful during the final phases of the present volume.

The support of my parents, Andrés Triay, Jr., and María Elena Solana, to whom Book II is dedicated, was crucial at every stage of the writing. Without their enthusiasm and assistance over the years, the completion of *The Unbroken Circle* would not have been possible. My grandmother, Elena Carrión, who passed away in 2004, likewise offered valuable information during the early days of the writing and, indeed, for many years prior. Special thanks also go out to Dr. Juan Clark, a Bay of Pigs veteran (1st Battalion, #2949) and Cuba scholar who generously shared his expertise with me on all of my projects. Dr. Clark passed away shortly before the release of Book I of *The Unbroken Circle* series. May he rest in eternal peace. I owe special appreciation to Wes Hevia, who provided the idea for the setting of Book III while he was a young student at Fordham University in Bronx, New York.

My lifelong friend Roberto Allen, the son of Bay of Pigs veteran Carlos Allen Dosal (6th Battalion, #3865), has been part of this work since its inception. His unflagging moral support, counsel, energy, and enthusiasm for the story were, without question, the most critical contributions any individual made to the work. To count the number of hours he sacrificed from his personal and professional life to help bring the series to life would be an impossible task. As a tribute to his late father, as well as to his late mother, María–a beautiful person who was the single greatest source of inspiration in his life–he poured an incalculable amount of personal energy into assisting in every way possible. In my previous non-fiction book about the Bay of Pigs invasion, I referred to Roberto as my "secret weapon." It is a title he has once again earned.

Over the years, various individuals from my inner circle have read excerpts from the series and provided valuable feedback. Although a complete list would be impossible to provide within the confines of this brief introduction, it would be remiss of me not to mention at least a few of them. My mother-in-law, Migdalia Garí, was generous enough to read through many early versions, as were my close friends Tony Varona, Judith Felton, Francisco Izquierdo, Jan Youngblood, Sally Walton, and Judith Mérida.

My wife, Emilia, as with my previous projects, has been a constant source of patience and encouragement and likewise deserves my unending thanks. And, as always, I owe a special debt of gratitude to my mentor, Dr. William Rogers of Florida State University.

Special thanks likewise go out to my editor and proof-reader, Joseph Childs, whose efforts have improved the work immeasurably.

HISTORICAL INTRODUCTION TO THE UNBROKEN CIRCLE SERIES (REVISED)

On January 1, 1959, Cuban dictator Fulgencio Batista was driven from power by a revolution comprised of a diverse collection of democratic organizations. The group that ultimately reigned supreme in the Revolution, however, was the 26th of July Movement, led by the young lawyer and veteran political activist Fidel Castro. The 26th of July's mountain-based rebel army, through its top rate propaganda machine abroad, had enchanted the international press. Foreign journalists made regular wartime pilgrimages to the rebel camps and gushed over the bearded rebels, depicting them and their dynamic leader to the world with all the romantic imagery of a modern-day Robin Hood legend. Upon Batista's flight, the Cuban public, weary from years of civil war and government corruption, eagerly awaited Castro's promise to restore Cuba's democratic Constitution of 1940. The young leader validated the nation's hopes upon taking the reins of power by appointing a cabinet composed of highly esteemed, anti-Batista Cuban liberals.

But Castro soon disappointed. He quickly banned political parties, postponed the promised elections (they were never held), and essentially began ruling by decree. With an eerie resemblance to the terror of the First French Republic,

public trials of Batista officials were held before frenzied mobs shouting *¡Paredón!* (To the execution wall!). Hundreds of political executions were carried out within just a few months. Ernesto "Che" Guevara, Castro's Argentine under-boss, justified the use of unbridled state power to satisfy public bloodlust by stating, "The executions by firing squads are not only a necessity for the people of Cuba, but also an imposition of the people."

The appalling executions and the accompanying demagoguery were not the end of the story. More jarring shocks awaited the Revolution's democratic supporters.

Within weeks of Castro's assumption of power, Marxist commissars were quietly sent to indoctrinate soldiers of the Rebel Armed Forces. In the ensuing months, members of Cuba's Communist Party, which had maintained decades-old ties to the Communist International, began receiving appointments to a variety of important government posts. This development perplexed a large number of Cubans, as Castro had never belonged to the Communist Party and the party had played virtually no role in Batista's ouster. Some of Castro's most ardent supporters, unable to conceive of their leader betraying the Revolution to Communism, naively believed for a time that the Communists were somehow infiltrating and subverting the Revolution behind his back. Suspicions of Castro's true intentions hardened, however, when he systematically purged the liberals he had originally appointed to his cabinet and replaced them with Communists and close political allies. As these developments unfolded, the first large-scale expropriations of private property began. When some of Castro's former comrades opposed or questioned these moves, they were jailed, exiled, or killed. Castro, meanwhile, vehemently denied any allegiance to Marxism.

Castro's intention to create a Communist dictatorship was confirmed when a scientific exhibition from the Soviet Union was invited to Havana in February, 1960, to demonstrate the wonders of the Communist superpower's achievements. During the exhibition, Soviet First Deputy Premier Anastas Mikoyan made his landmark visit to the island. Diplomatic ties and trade agreements between the two nations followed, and Castro began importing shiploads of weapons and armies of advisors from the Communist bloc. Meanwhile, the Revolution's anti-American pronouncements increased in both frequency and intensity, while its flattering comments about Communism became disturbingly commonplace. At this point, the United States, which had initially lent its political backing to Castro, began more actively supporting the fledgling pro-democracy opposition on the island. Cuba, to the astonishment of most Cubans, quickly became ground zero in the Cold War.

Cuba's independent institutions soon found themselves in the Revolution's crosshairs. The island's vibrant free press, its independent labor unions, its professional organizations, and its arts community were obliterated and replaced by Revolutionary associations in ideological alignment with the regime. The University of Havana's historic autonomy was stripped, and Cuba's business sector was gradually eliminated. Religious institutions, especially those of the Roman Catholic Church, were assaulted in an explosion of anticlericalism encouraged by the government. As the radicalism spread, thousands of Cubans, most of whom had initially supported the Revolution, began fleeing the island, the majority of them finding refuge in nearby Miami, Florida.

By mid-1960, domestic opposition to the Castro dictatorship was widespread. As the island became increasingly communized, several covert anti-government groups emerged, led in many cases by Castro's former comrades and allies from the anti-Batista struggle. Their shared goal was to rescue Cuba and the Revolution from the Communist subversion that Castro and his faction had so masterfully engineered. Underground groups organized guerrilla armies that fought Castro's forces in Cuba's mountains and woods, as well as networks of urban resistance cells made up, to a significant extent, of university-based organizations and Cuba's democratic political parties.

A political alliance was ultimately forged among several opposition groups called the *Frente Revolucionario Democrático Cubano* (Cuban Democratic Revolutionary Front; later reorganized as the Cuban Revolutionary Council). Its exiled leaders in Miami, composed largely of Cuban liberals (some of whom had served in Castro's first government), created a Cuban Liberation Army, christened Brigade 2506, to invade Cuba, overthrow Castro, and free their homeland from Communist rule. The alliance received the financial and political backing of the United States government, the latter assigning the task of training Brigade 2506–as well as overall responsibility for the military operation–to the CIA. The aim of the exile coalition was to carry out the Revolution's original stated goal of restoring democratic, constitutional rule in Cuba. Accordingly, Communists and former Batista associates were banned from both the *Frente* and the Brigade.

Brigade 2506 was recruited from the expanding exile community in the United States and trained primarily in Guatemala. Although made up of a cross section of Cuban society, it was disproportionately middle class. Young, former military cadets in Cuba with no previous ties to the Batista dictatorship assumed leadership positions, but the vast majority of Brigade members had no former military experience. The Brigade's largest single group (although by no means the majority) consisted of ideological university students.

Just weeks before the Brigade's planned invasion of Cuba, John F. Kennedy was sworn in as President of the United States. Anxious about arousing negative international reaction to a U.S. sponsored invasion of Cuba, and firm on maintaining American "plausible deniability" in the whole affair, the new administration sought to conceal the U.S. role in the operation to the greatest extent possible. It thus rejected the CIA's original plan to land Brigade 2506 near the city of Trinidad (the ideal location) and instructed the agency to find a more remote spot. Planners then proposed the area around the Bay of Pigs on Cuba's southern shore, a site that met with the administration's approval. In the days leading up to the invasion—and, indeed, after the operation was already underway—the new administration, fearing international condemnation as well as a Soviet response to what was obviously a U.S. backed operation, sought to conceal further its involvement by ordering disastrous changes to the air plan, thus dooming the Brigade's April 1961 invasion. To the very end, the men of Brigade 2506 believed the United States would never abandon them. They were wrong.

By the spring of 1961, Cuba's fate was sealed: the long-awaited, large scale military operation had ended in disaster; Castro openly declared Cuba to be "Socialist;" and, in a pivotal moment for middle class Cuban families, the island's numerous private schools were expropriated. The entire Cuban school system was subsequently shut down, as the regime designed a new, compulsory educational program intended to re-educate and re-program Cuban children along Marxist lines and mold them into an army of impassioned, atheist militants devoted heart and mind to the Revolution and to the person of Fidel Castro; in short, the Revolution's future "New Men" and "New Women." Opposing the regime or dissenting from its official ideology, even peacefully, would, by this point, almost certainly earn the citizen social ostracism, a lengthy term in one of Castro's gulags, or an appointment with the execution wall. In the coming years, countless thousands would become victims of such draconian measures.

The flight of Cubans into exile grew from a trickle to a veritable tidal wave. A significant portion of those fleeing were families who sought to prevent their children from being raised in Fidel Castro's totalitarian state. Many parents who wanted to protect their children, however, were unable to leave Cuba. Their reasons ranged from family responsibilities that kept them on the island to the delays they encountered in obtaining exit documents following the break in diplomatic relations with the United States. The solution for these parents came in the form of a semi-secret program, dubbed Operation Pedro Pan by the American press, which provided special exit documents for children to depart the island expeditiously. The program, approved by the U.S.

Department of State, had been initially designed in late 1960 to help the children of underground operatives leave Cuba; it was nevertheless open, from the very beginning, to any parents who sought to rescue their offspring from the clutches of Cuba's Communists but could not leave the island themselves. After the developments of the spring of 1961, the number of parents who opted for the program skyrocketed. Launched by the combined efforts of Father Bryan Walsh of Miami's Catholic Welfare Bureau, Mr. James Baker of Ruston Academy (an expropriated American school in Havana), and the anti-Castro underground, Operation Pedro Pan helped more than 14,000 unaccompanied Cuban refugee children reach freedom in the United States between December 1960 and October 1962. Roughly half of the Pedro Pan children had no relatives to care for them in the United States. These children entered the Cuban Children's Program headed by Father Walsh.

As in many historical novels, I have superimposed fictional characters on actual historical events. This was done especially in scenes depicting both air and ground battles during the Bay of Pigs invasion, which include an extra B-26 bomber in some of the aerial attacks and an additional squad in the Second Battalion. Each was inserted in order to integrate the characters into the events portrayed. The work also takes, in a few places, some minor liberties with the historical record. When this was done, it was solely to strengthen the story's plot and narrative flow as well as to heighten drama.

In Book II, for instance, Che Guevara is depicted as the head of La Cabaña prison. Guevara indeed held that post for several months, but did so at a time earlier than depicted in the story. Perhaps most significantly, however, the briefings of the Brigade pilots in Book II were written so as to give readers a broad picture of the specific–and very real–changes to the air plan for the Bay of Pigs invasion, rather than to depict literally any interactions between Cuban pilots and U.S. personnel in Central America. Information that was, in reality, disseminated by different people at different points over a few days, was neatly fused into fictional briefings on April 13 and 14. This was done so the reader could more readily comprehend the actual plan and how it was so disastrously altered at the last moment. It is important to note, moreover, that the American delivering the briefings and the Cuban pilot repeatedly questioning him are *not*–in any way, shape, or form–intended to depict actual people. They, like the scenes in which they appear, are simply literary tools meant to convey information to the reader. The scene depicting the cancellation of the critical D-Day air raids, on the other hand, is based, as closely as a fictional account could be, on the actual history as related in numerous works. Readers may wish to consult the bibliography at the end of the book for a more detailed history.

Moreover, the characters in the story, as they appear in relation to the battle at the Bay of Pigs, are probably better informed as to the invasion's overall military and political strategy than the average soldier, in reality, was. Like the briefings described above, these parts were written in this manner so that readers could gain a comprehensive view of the invasion through the experiences of the characters and the dialogue between them, rather than through a disruptive historical narrative during the story. The locations of some Brigade units during training were also slightly altered and the Cuban Children's Program facility mentioned in Book III was actually opened a few months later than it appears in the story. Again, these changes were made in order to bolster the overall story.

Although the history behind the story is based on actual events, and some of the situations depicted are inspired by the numerous stories I have heard and recorded, the characters, including the main characters, are purely fictional. Any similarities to real-life individuals, including names, are purely coincidental. There are a few exceptions in the brief appearances of obvious historical figures such as Rogelio González Corzo, Manuel Artime, Erneido Oliva, Hugo Sueiro, Alejandro del Valle, José Pérez San Román, Maximo Cruz, Bryan Walsh, Ernesto Guevara, Osmani Cienfuegos, and a handful of others.

Please visit the author online:
Website: http://victortriayauthor.com/
Blog: http://www.victorandrestriay.blogspot.com/
Facebook: https://www.facebook.com/victortriayauthor
Twitter: @vtriayauthor

LA CABAÑA FORTRESS
Havana, Cuba
January, 1961

I srael Muñoz woke up with a start, his lungs drawing rapid, shallow breaths. He lay upon the floor of the large dungeon-like cell, his shoulders and chin trembling, the nightmare's closing images still taunting him from the edges of his mind. Around him slumbered scores of other political prisoners in *galera* (cellblock) number 10 in La Cabaña, the 18th century fortress and prison across the Bay of Havana. He turned his head and stared down the vaulted *galera's* tunnel-like hall, toward the iron bars facing outward to the fort's dried-up moat. The bars at the other end faced the prison yard. He was fully awake now, the stillness of his surroundings arousing an empty, lonely feeling in the pit of his stomach. He pulled his prison shirt, its large stenciled P on the back for "prisoner," tightly around him and closed his eyes again.

Memories of his first night in La Cabaña assailed him. He shuddered. Christ, he thought, the kid was only nineteen, a university student. He'd been casually marched outside, tied to a stake, and put before a firing squad. He'd cried, "*¡Viva Cristo Rey!*" ("Long Live Christ the King!") the moment before the bullets tore into his flesh. The memory of his shrill, defiant voice made Israel's flesh crawl. He could still hear the crackling of the rifle fire, followed seconds later by the thud of the pistol shot delivering the *coup de grâce* behind the boy's ear. A ghastly banging of hammers had followed. "The coffin," one inmate explained. It was the first of many executions Israel would witness.

Israel opened his eyes. He figured it was around three o'clock in the morning. The January wind howling through the open end of the *galera* was biting and cold. He sat up and pulled his prison shirt around him more tightly. He put on his glasses, the nose bridge held together now by strips of tape. He stood and made his way to the excrement-laden hole the prison authorities had the audacity to call a toilet.

A couple of guards suddenly started banging on the iron bars with their flashlights, the sharp metallic sound rousing the prisoners. "Prisoner Israel Muñoz. Present yourself."

Everyone looked around for Israel. One of the guards shined his flashlight on him. "Come with us." Israel, already standing, froze for a moment and then walked over. The other guard unlocked the gate. A prisoner took a step toward the opening. The guard swung his flashlight at him and shouted, forcing him back.

Israel was handcuffed and marched across the prison yard by the guards. His legs felt weak and cramped; he hadn't walked this much in days. They entered a passageway and reached a set of doors flanked by two Cuban flags and two sentries. They stopped. One of the sentries knocked twice, went in, and shut the door behind him. A few seconds later, the door opened again and Israel was escorted inside. The long rectangular room had a wooden ceiling that rose at a 45-degree angle and met the top of the near wall. The floor had checkered black and white tiles. An oak desk sat along the far end. At the desk, in the light of an office lamp, sat a man with a wispy beard; a Revolutionary beret pressed down a mass of long, unkempt hair. Israel recognized him immediately. Ernesto "Che" Guevara looked up from his papers and motioned to the guards to bring the prisoner before him.

Ernesto "Che" Guevara, the Argentine political radical who'd joined Castro's invasion of Cuba in 1956, was one of the Revolution's most iconic figures. His trademark beret, revolutionary beard, and long hair had made him a hero of radicals across the globe. The image he projected as a dashing, beatnik freedom fighter had created a cult of personality that rivaled that of Fidel Castro himself. When Israel had gone into the mountains to join the 26th of July rebels in late 1957, he had admired Guevara's zeal to rescue Cuba's poor from their misery. He was somewhat taken aback, however, by the ease with which Guevara had ordered the executions of suspected traitors. At the time, though, Israel had naively attributed the killings to the savage rules of guerrilla warfare.

Guevara now only aroused repugnance in him. Once in power, the beloved Che had continued on his murderous path. He'd excelled primarily in organizing Revolutionary tribunals, which followed no legal procedure, that sent a countless number of men to their deaths at the *paredón*, the execution wall. The sadistic executions during the war, Israel realized too late, had been merely a prelude to the bloodbath to come. Perhaps the world's leftist activists viewed Che Guevara as a dashing rebel hero, but to pro-democracy Cubans he became known simply as the Butcher of La Cabaña.

Guevara waved Israel over. "Come closer," he ordered, signaling the guards to back away so he could speak to the prisoner privately.

Israel, sensing grave danger, stopped a few inches before the desk.

"Well, Israel," said Guevara, leaning back in his chair, "how perfectly ironic it is that we find ourselves like this. We were once allies."

"It's not so ironic," Israel said. "If you're looking for allies from the struggle against Batista, your *galeras* are overflowing with them."

"Correction," Guevara snapped, leaning forward and pointing his finger at him, "the *galeras* are filled with traitors; traitors to this Revolution, traitors to this country."

Israel drew a deep breath. Did he just say "this country," as if he were Cuban? Who does this arrogant Argentine think he is, accusing *Cubans* of treason? Israel said nothing and just stared blankly at a set of doors behind Guevara.

"Do you disagree with me?" Guevara asked, baiting him.

Israel resisted the impulse to seize Guevara by the throat.

"You do disagree, Israel, don't you?" Guevara said jovially. He jammed a cigar into his mouth and lit it slowly. He leaned back in his chair again, propping his dirty boots on the antique desk. He looked up at the angled ceiling and took a long draw from the cigar.

"Yes," Israel said. "I disagree."

"Why?" Guevara asked, his palms opening in a pleading gesture. "Please, help me understand, why you, of all people, have betrayed the Revolution."

Israel's jaw hardened. "We promised democracy to the people of this island, a return to the Constitution, and now–

4

and I realize that I risk my life for saying this–you have created a dictatorship more insidious than this hemisphere has ever seen. So, *comandante,* if anyone is guilty of a betrayal, it is the current leadership of the Revolution." He held his breath.

Guevara laughed. "Israel, Israel, are you so blind? I think perhaps you've fallen under the influence of those rich capitalists who were educated by the priests. You've become disconnected from your roots as the rural peasant that you are. The fact is that we have done more for the people of Cuba in two years than any government in history."

Israel glared at him. "You rule this country without the consent of the people. Hold an election, and you can claim legitimacy."

Guevara chortled. "An election? My goodness, Israel, you *are* naïve."

"As you say, *comandante.*"

"Israel," Guevara said patiently, "this is a *Revolution.*" He swung his feet to the floor and sighed, shaking his head like a parent explaining a math problem to a thick-headed child for the tenth time. He rested his cigar in a glass ashtray and folded his hands on the desk. He spoke in a hushed tone. "Didn't you feel it in the mountains, Israel? This thing became bigger than all of us, all under its own energy. The forces of historical evolution seized this Revolution and led it to its inevitable conclusion. The entire world felt it, that's why it supports us. Can't you see that? You can call it Communism if you'd like, but it's much bigger than any single ideology. No one can stop it. The world is at a turning point, and Cuba is leading the way. You're a man of great learning and intelligence, Israel. Why can't you see that?"

Israel shrugged his shoulders and arched his eyebrows in feigned simple-mindedness, "Then why don't you just hold an election and see if the people of this country share your point of view?" Then he narrowed his eyes at him. "Or don't you trust those you claim to represent?"

Guevara slapped the top of the desk and pointed at him menacingly. "You have been *brainwashed* by American imperialism and by the priests! You talk about elections. Well, just look at how the Revolution is validated day after day by the peoples' marches and rallies. Or haven't you seen the hundreds of thousands of citizens filling the public squares? That's democracy–direct democracy, *Revolutionary* democracy–not the sort of bourgeois democracy you speak of, the type that manipulates elections and puts puppets of the rich into power so they can continue to commit the worst sorts of abuses against the people. This Revolution, Israel," he said, jabbing the tip of his forefinger on the desk, "which with our help will inevitably sweep the rest of the world, is self-sustaining and run by the masses it represents, the masses who are now being educated by Revolutionary leaders about their role in such a great society."

Israel had to use all his powers of self-control to keep from laughing out loud. Public rallies as validation for a government? Did he just say Cuba was run by *the people*? Yes, he did, just before he said the masses were being "educated" by the Revolutionary leadership about their "role." He let out a low, sarcastic chuckle.

"You'll never understand," Guevara said, taking another long pull from his cigar, propping his boots on the desk again, and crossing his feet. "Not everyone does." He glared at Israel sternly. "But the historical forces propelling us toward an ideal society—one without priests and imperialists—will just as inevitably produce enemies who will resist, either out of ignorance or self-interest. And, unfortunately, we must deal with them."

Guevara looked at the nearest guard and then hunched back over his papers. The audience was over.

When Israel returned to his *galera,* he stood before the outward facing gate so he could feel the cold wind coming in off the ocean. He tried to imagine for a moment what he must look like: dirty, unshaven, undernourished, and physically battered; a man forced to live in a cage, his life hanging by a thread.

He closed his eyes. His mind clicked to images of his boyhood in his father's palm thatched *bohío.* The feel of the dirt floor underneath his bare feet, the smells and sounds of farm animals just outside the window, the crow of roosters at dawn, and the comfort of the crude furniture, all rushed back to him in a cascade of blissful recollections. He smiled.

The only article of value his parents had possessed was a small, ceramic statuette of Our Lady of Charity, Cuba's patron, which his mother had displayed on a tiny makeshift altar in a corner of the home. Although he couldn't recall a single time his family attended Mass, his parents were devotees of Our Lady of Charity, their beloved "Cachita." He leaned his forehead on the cold iron bar and remembered the 17th Century legend associated with Her, that of rescuing the two Indians and the slave boy in their tiny canoe during a violent storm in the Bay of Nipe. His mother's ceramic statuette depicted the trio in the boat, the two on either end rowing feverishly, the one in the middle looking to the heavens in prayer, the Virgin hovering above them majestically, protecting them, and guiding them to safe harbor.

Israel felt like those men in the boat, tossed about in a storm, unable to direct his own course, powerless against the capricious waves threatening to drown him. He took a deep breath, imagining that the Virgin of Charity now hovered above *him*, protecting him, guiding his course. He grabbed the iron bars tightly. He was not afraid.

MIAMI BEACH, FLORIDA
January 3, 1961

The rotund female tourist barked at the hotel towel man. "Boy, hey boy!" She pulled at the seams on her wet bathing suit, making a suctioning sound. When she let go, the suit snapped back tightly on her cellulite dimpled skin. "Good grief! I'm waiting here for a damned towel!"

Goyo turned, sported a fake smile, and nodded toward her curtly. He went into the laundry room and pulled a toasty warm towel from one of the dryers. Had that bovine just called him "boy?" He felt like urinating on the towel.

Goyo hung the towel over his arm and reemerged on the pool deck. He offered it to the woman. Her husband, a white whale of a man, was sprawled shirtless on a lounge chair under an umbrella, his hand wrapped around a tropical drink of some sort with a miniature parasol mixer. He huffed at his wife, "Service here ain't what it used to be. Why they ever started hiring all these Ricky Ricardos, I'll never know." He smiled at Goyo. "Hey boy, you speeka da English?"

Goyo shrugged apologetically and held his forefinger and thumb an inch apart. "A leettle beet."

The man sipped his drink and smacked his lips. "Well, tell me something, Ricky, why is it that bastard Castro's still in power? Way I see it, if all you people just stood up to him, instead of runnin' to our country with your tails between your legs, he'd be gone by now. You afraid to fight or something?" He turned to his wife. "Honey, can you imagine George Washington runnin' to *Cooba* after writing the Declaration of Independence?" They both snickered.

"Well, I certainly can't," Goyo said, dropping his fresh-off-the-boat accent, "especially since it was Thomas Jefferson who wrote it." He turned and strode toward the lobby. He heard the man muttering behind him, "Ought'ta send *all* these damned spics the hell back!"

Goyo punched his time card and walked out through the hotel's front entrance. He said hello to his father's old friend, Dominguez, who was manning the valet parking station. Dominguez, one of Cuba's most distinguished legal scholars, waved his tip jar at him. "For groceries!"

"Can't do without that," Goyo laughed as he walked to the bus stop. The bus pulled up after a few minutes. Some members of the hotel's night crew got out, all of them recently arrived Cubans. At least they were all lucky in one respect, Goyo thought: it was the tourist season and there was work for them on Miami Beach. Goyo boarded the bus and took a seat. He stared through the window at the Cuban workers lumbering up the hotel entrance. The bus departed. He took off his stupid name tag and put it in his pocket.

Goyo still hadn't gotten used to being an "exile." Yet, there were tens of thousands now just like him, and countless more arriving every day—entire Cuban families who'd leave everything behind and arrive in this country with only the three sets of clothes and the fifty dollars the Cuban government allowed them to take. He rested his head on the window and watched a vacationing American family taking an evening stroll. One of the kids was licking an ice cream cone. He shook his head; "exile" was the stuff of radical French philosophers and Russian revolutionaries, not quiet, unobtrusive, middle class people, like the majority of Cubans coming now. As the bus crossed the bridge into Miami proper, he looked across Biscayne Bay, the fading evening sun painting its waters a soft orange. The most ironic part was that most of the exiles had supported Batista's ouster and at one point had even backed the Revolution. He rubbed his eyes and sighed. Now, two years later, Cuba's most talented professionals, intellectuals, artists, and entrepreneurs were cleaning swimming pools, washing dishes, and scrubbing floors at Miami Beach hotels. He thought of Dominguez parking cars and grunted in disbelief. He imagined they all looked like a family standing on the sidewalk watching its house burn down. His chest suddenly felt like it was weighted down with lead.

Goyo tried to shake himself out of his melancholy. He smiled at an old lady across from him. She smiled back. Everyone here in Miami said this period of exile was only temporary, a few months at the most. There was simply no way–*no way*–their beloved Cuba could ever really join the ranks of the world's Communist hellholes. It was among the most prosperous nations in Latin America and possessed one of the region's largest middle classes and highest standards of living, surpassing that of even some nations in Europe. Immigrants from all over the world flocked to it. In any event, everyone knew the day would come when news arrived that someone had assassinated Castro, or that some general had launched

a coup d'état, or that the public had risen up in rebellion, or
. . . *something;* and, at the end of the day, all else failing, the
world understood that there was simply no way the United
States would allow a Communist dictatorship to take root in
a neighboring country with which it shared deep historical
ties, much less tolerate a Soviet satellite ninety miles from its
shores. Would it?

Goyo picked up a discarded newspaper and mindlessly
scanned the headlines. He flipped a page and saw an article
about Fidel Castro. His stomach contracted; a burst of anxiety radiated throughout his body. He closed the newspaper,
folded it, and put it down. He shut his eyes, reminding himself that the exiles weren't just standing by idly waiting for
something to happen. Cubans of all ages had responded to
the call-to-arms and had thrown themselves into the cause
of regaining Cuba's freedom. Men who'd never fired a gun
in anger joined groups training for the fight against Castro;
others ran arms and supplies to comrades combating the dictator on the island; a large number joined political associations and attended patriotic ceremonies and rallies. Cuba's
feuding pro-democracy groups had even set aside their differences and formed a political coalition known as the *Frente
Revolucionario Democrático Cubano,* known simply as the *Frente.*
Its leaders in Miami were working directly with the U.S. government to free Cuba. Indeed, Goyo thought smiling, Castro
would not last long. He started to breathe more easily.

The *Frente* was now openly recruiting men in Miami and
elsewhere for the Liberation Army that Antonio de la Cruz
had spoken to him about in Cuba. According to what he'd
heard, the exile army called itself "Brigade 2506." Although

technically under the *Frente's* authority, it was common knowledge that the United States government was in charge of the Brigade's training and that the Americans had promised military support when it was sent into action in Cuba. The close alliance with the world's foremost democratic power was what ultimately closed the deal for many of the exiles who had volunteered. The Americans, after all, had never lost a war or abandoned an ally—or so everyone believed. Goyo thought about Castro's Soviet alliance and the Russians training soldiers in Cuba. He sighed nervously; something told him that it wouldn't be as easy as some people thought.

He leaned his forearms on his thighs and folded his hands. His thoughts drifted to the young family he'd seen strolling on the sidewalk a few minutes ago. He tried to picture his own family on a leisurely evening stroll. He wanted to go home; above all things, he just wanted to go home. The leaden feeling spread from his chest into his throat.

The bus finally reached his stop on Southwest Sixth Street and Ninth Avenue in Miami. He walked the remaining block home, went up the moldy staircase, and entered the miniature apartment he shared with Tony Méndez, a friend from the *Agrupación Católica*. He went into the bedroom, reached under his bed, and took out a shoebox where he saved his tip money. He put that day's earnings into it.

He took a quick shower and went out into the small garden behind the building. He sat on a rusted patio chair and lit a cigarette. It was almost dark. He started thinking about his family again. His original plan for all of them to leave Cuba together if the Catholic schools were shut down had been thwarted by his unexpected solo flight from the island. So, after arriving in Miami, he and Raquel had spoken over the telephone in an improvised code and hastily amended their strategy: Raquel and the kids would stay in Cuba and hope for regime change before the government expropriated the schools; when the Castro government fell, Goyo would return to Cuba and the family would resume its normal life. But, if Castro stayed in power long enough to shut the schools down, Raquel was to go immediately to the U.S. embassy in Havana and acquire visas for travel to the United States. She was then to buy airline tickets with the cash he'd hidden in the house, fly to Miami with the kids and his mother, and ask for political asylum upon arrival—something thousands of people were now doing weekly.

Goyo suddenly felt someone grab his shoulders from behind. He spun around and was surprised to see Manuel Artime, an old friend from the *Agrupación Católica*, standing there. Tony, Goyo's roommate, was with him.

Goyo excitedly sprung from his chair to embrace Artime. "Manolo! My God, what a surprise!"

"I needed to get away from all these politicians in Miami for a little while," Artime said smiling. "The fighting here is worse than in Cuba." A medical doctor, Catholic activist, and former rebel, Manuel Artime had defected from the Revolution when it turned to Communism. Despite his youth, he was the exile head of the opposition group MRR (*Movimiento de Recuperación Revolucionaria*), the same group Rogelio González Corzo and Antonio de la Cruz were part of in Cuba, and one of the *Frente*'s top leaders. "Plus, Tony here tells me he's become quite a chef, so I thought I'd take him up on his kind invitation to supper."

Over supper, Artime told them that he was leaving the next day for Brigade 2506's training camps. Goyo, who dared not inquire where the secret camps were located, asked him, "How did it get that name—Brigade 2506?"

Artime sipped his water. "It was named in honor of Carlos Rodríguez Santana, a university student who was the first member to die in training, back in September. His serial number was 2506."

Goyo felt a twinge of guilt. He picked at his food. "You know, I've thought about joining the camps myself, Manolo, but right now I need to make sure my family is all right. I may have to bring them over any day now. I can't think of anything else."

"Are you the only one from your family here?" Artime asked, wiping one side of his mouth with a napkin.

"Well, two of my cousins–both of them were students at the University–got out through Mexico; they were connected to the MRR as well, although I didn't know about it until they fled. They called me from New York City a week ago. They received scholarships to Fordham University in the Bronx; apparently, a Jesuit there is familiar with Belén." Goyo neglected to mention that they hadn't called since then.

"What are their names? Do I know them?"

"Roberto León and Emilio Hammond."

"Emilio *what?*"

"Hammond. Emilio Hammond."

Artime nodded and looked down at his plate for a moment. He checked his watch. "Brothers, it's late."

Goyo walked Artime to his car. Artime embraced him. "You take care of yourself, Goyo. You stay here in Miami, and be ready to reunite soon with your family in Havana. We have more than enough men at the camps, and we'll need your talents when this is all over. OK?" Goyo smiled and nodded. Artime got into his car and drove away.

Goyo didn't feel like going back into the apartment. The mere thought of sitting there brooding for the rest of the night depressed him further. He walked over to Southwest Eighth Street, the neighborhood's main thoroughfare, and stopped at the coffee window outside a Cuban cafeteria that had opened only the week before. He leaned on the counter. The waitress motioned toward him with her head. He indicated coffee with his fingers. He wondered what Raquel and the kids were doing at that moment. Having supper? Sitting on the portico? He sighed sadly. The heaviness in his chest and throat came back and spread into his gut.

He stared blankly at the counter as he sipped his coffee. He felt as though an internal parasite was gnawing away at his heart, devouring his soul.

He suddenly froze; all at once, a sense of revelation overcame him.

He took a deep breath and stood erect. He spun to face the street. Everything became obvious to him in an instant; that which had been obscured by the shock of leaving Cuba and the subsequent day to day struggle emerged in a sudden flash of clarity. The decision for his family to stay in Cuba had been an utter mistake. What had he been thinking? He realized at that moment that he and Raquel hadn't yet fully appreciated the massive shift that had occurred in their lives. Why were they persisting in carrying out parts of a plan they'd designed under completely different circumstances? To hell with the plan, he thought; tomorrow, first thing, he would call Raquel and tell her to get the visas and to bring everyone to Miami immediately. They would all just have to start over again in this country. The Cuban government, of course, would take their home and everything in it, but it was ludicrous to persist with this ridiculous arrangement any longer. Maybe they could all return to Cuba one day, but that was a secondary consideration. He had to reunite his family. Now.

He finished his coffee in a single gulp and, emboldened by the resoluteness of his decision, slammed the small cup down on the counter. He threw some coins on the counter and thanked the waitress with a nod. As he turned to leave, he saw a Cuban man about his age walking hurriedly down the sidewalk toward the cafeteria. He held a stack of the evening newspaper in his arms. He shouted, "Did you hear? Did you hear?"

"Hear what?"

"The United States broke off diplomatic relations with the Castro government today!" He gave Goyo a copy of the newspaper and ran into the cafeteria to share the news. Goyo read the headline three times. The meaning of the announcement sank in more profoundly with each reading: the break in relations meant that the Americans were now free to back the Cuban opposition leaders and Brigade 2506 more openly and decisively, unencumbered by all the diplomatic niceties that had heretofore impeded full-blown support. The die was cast. The United States would act. Castro was done for. It was, indeed, cause for celebration.

He tucked the newspaper under his arm and started walking briskly back to his apartment, intending to read every detail of the article as soon as he got there. His thoughts drifted back to his family as he walked. The combined effect of his recent decision and the news he'd just received made his head swirl with new possibilities. "Should I still bring my family over, now that we know the Americans are determined to help us oust Castro?" he asked himself. "After all, breaking off diplomatic relations is sending the strongest possible signal." He nodded to himself. "Yes, I'll still bring them, because you never know what will happen. And if Castro is overthrown after my family is already in Miami, we'll all just go back together. I'll call Raquel tomorrow and tell her to start the process, regardless of the new situation." He started calculating how long it would take Raquel to get all the documents in order. Maybe she could be here by next week, but there was no telling, he thought, given the number of people petitioning for visas at the U.S Embassy.

He stopped abruptly. He pulled the newspaper out from under his arm.

"My God," he gasped as he read the first paragraph over and over. "My God, my God, my God . . ." He dropped the newspaper on the sidewalk and pulled his hair. It suddenly dawned on him that the break in diplomatic relations meant that the Americans would be shutting down their embassy in Havana and pulling out all diplomatic personnel–and it was only through the embassy and consular offices that a person could obtain a visa to travel to the United States. Although the United States would probably grant asylum to any Cuban who reached its soil, Cuban authorities would certainly not authorize a legal departure from the island without an exit visa. Thus, Raquel and the kids were stuck in Cuba with no way to get the necessary exit documents to leave. In an instant, the bridge linking Goyo to his family across the Florida Straits had imploded right before his eyes.

Goyo bent over and rested his hands on his knees to catch his breath. His heart was racing. After a few seconds, he calmed down enough to pick up the newspaper. He walked the rest of the way home as if in a funeral procession. He went into his room and lay down on his bed.

Tony came in a little while later. "Did you hear the news?"

Goyo held up the newspaper without looking at Tony.

"What's the matter?" Tony grabbed the newspaper and read a few lines. "Oh, my God, that's right," he said, covering his mouth with his free hand. "I didn't think about that; no one can get visas now." He blanched.

Goyo nodded.

They sat silently for a few minutes. Tony's parents and younger siblings were still in Cuba, too. Tony said, "I guess everything now hinges on Brigade 2506's success." Goyo nodded again. Tony left the apartment.

Goyo sat up all night smoking cigarettes, imagining ways to get his family out of Cuba: daring maritime escapes, getting third country visas, seeking asylum at a foreign embassy. Perhaps, he thought, the United States would figure out some other way to grant visas to Cubans who wanted to leave the country. Just before dawn, Goyo gave up. His mind rejected every potential solution as impossible. He concluded that Tony was right: the reunification of his family was now tied to the success of Brigade 2506.

As the sun's first rays peeked through the morning clouds, Goyo picked up the telephone and called in sick to work. He went to Mass, and then walked to a local bank to open an account with his shoebox money. Without knowing exactly why, he tossed his cigarettes into a garbage can outside the bank and vowed never to smoke again. He hailed a taxi and gave the driver an address. A few minutes later, he arrived at his destination and walked into a building.

"Can I help you, sir?" asked a young man behind a desk.

"Yes," Goyo said. "I'm here to enlist for Brigade 2506."

3

oyo was taken into a back room where a lanky official at a small desk took his information. A secretary came in and offered him a cup of Cuban coffee. He took it and thanked her. An hour later, he was driven to a safe house not far from his apartment building. There were ten other new recruits there, all of them younger than Goyo. He didn't know any of them and he spoke to no one. From the safe house, the group was taken in three separate automobiles to a building in Coral Gables for medical exams. Goyo met a recruit his own age there, Fernando Miyares, a fellow teacher who hailed from Pinar del Río. They struck up a pleasant conversation. When the doctors were done, a middle-aged Cuban in a dark suit sent them home, telling them that they'd be contacted soon.

Goyo went back to his job at the hotel. He worked overtime every day and accepted every odd job he was offered during his off hours. Living with the frugality of a monk, he soon piled up substantial savings. He never once doubted his decision to join the Brigade, even when he'd heard about the different means people in Cuba were now using to acquire the necessary documentation to leave the island. In the back of his mind, he wondered if he'd felt all along that volunteering for the Brigade was his duty. Was that why he'd decided to join so impulsively? Had the break in diplomatic relations and the closing of diplomatic offices simply given him the pretext he was waiting for? Well, it didn't matter now.

Finally, on the morning of January 17, he received a call telling him to report to a safe house at five o'clock that afternoon. His hands trembled as he wrote down the address. Then he called the hotel to say he wouldn't be going back to work.

After hanging up, he sat at the table, pondering what to tell Raquel. She had no idea that he'd enlisted in the Brigade, and there was no way he could tell her. All calls to Cuba were tapped by the G.2 and mail was being screened. If the authorities in Cuba found out that he'd joined an invasion force to overthrow Fidel Castro, Raquel would get thrown out of the house and probably arrested. It was a miracle she wasn't thrown out after his flight from the island last month. At any rate, he reasoned, telling her would only send her into hysterics. He figured this would all be over in a few weeks anyhow, when the Brigade–now with virtually guaranteed American support after the break in diplomatic relations–defeated Castro and marched triumphantly into Havana.

He got up and started packing his personal belongings. When he finished, he sat at the table again and took out some paper. He wrote to Raquel about a job he'd received teaching English to the children of migrant workers at a remote Jesuit mission in California. He wouldn't be able to contact her for several weeks, he said, but he would be safe and earning good money. He would send the money to Tony in Miami, he told her, and Tony would forward it to her. Whatever letters she had for him, she could send them via Tony. She needn't worry. He sealed the envelope, stamped it, and put it in the mailbox.

Goyo then wrote out some instructions for Tony, the only one who knew, outside the people at the *Frente*, about his enlistment. Tony was to wire a fixed amount of Goyo's bank savings to Raquel every week through a bank in Spain, and forward to him any letters from her through the *Frente*'s Miami office. Goyo would send Tony his letters to Raquel, and he would forward them to her. Finally, Goyo would entrust to his friend a letter for his family in case he didn't come back alive. That one took him two hours to write.

When Tony came home for lunch, he instantly read Goyo's expression. "You're off to the camps, aren't you?" Goyo nodded and gave Tony his instructions, adding that he not tell Roberto and Emilio–from whom he still hadn't heard since they'd first arrived in New York–about what he was up to. If they knew, they'd be sure to follow him to the camps. Tony promised he'd do as instructed and volunteered to drive him to the safe house.

When Goyo arrived at the safe house at five o'clock that afternoon, Fernando Miyares, his friend from the medical exams, was outside with his family. Fernando called out to him, "Hey, Goyo, wait up!" He was bidding farewell to his three children, all girls, ranging in age from three to eight. The little one he held in his arms clung to his neck; the other two had their arms wrapped around his waist. His wife was sobbing uncontrollably into his shoulder. Fernando gave them all a last round of kisses, his head bobbing like a chicken.

He put down his little daughter and jogged over to Goyo. His eyes were wet. "So, did you ever think your life would come to this?" Goyo chortled and shook his head.

After a two-hour wait, Goyo, Fernando, and three other recruits were driven from the safe house to a building off Twenty-Seventh Avenue. They were put into a room with a group of other recruits. Everyone sat quietly. Half an hour later, a fifty-year-old Cuban came in, thanked them for their service, and left. Almost immediately thereafter, an older man in a gray suit and horn rimmed glasses walked in with some khaki uniforms for them to change into. "New uniforms," one of the recruits, a student, joked as he held out the shirt, "just like at the beginning of a new school year." After they'd changed, an American entered the room and ordered them in stern English to board the back of the covered military truck parked outside. The men grabbed their belongings, jogged into the early winter night, and piled into the vehicle, sitting on benches along the sides of the truck bed. Goyo sat by the open canvas flap on the end. The American came over and tied the flap shut, plunging them into darkness. Goyo's heart fluttered as the truck rumbled away.

Fernando leaned over and whispered, "What's with all this secrecy?"

"Security," Goyo said. "This town is full of Castro spies." Fernando grunted his agreement. Less than an hour later the truck stopped. The American driver spoke to someone outside in English. The truck lurched forward again, only to stop a couple of minutes later. They heard the roar of a large engine nearby. "That's an airplane," someone said. The

American driver got out of the cab, walked to the back of the truck, and unfastened the rope shutting the canvas flap.

"Let's go, on the double," he barked as he threw back the flap. The recruits jumped out of the truck. A C-54 transport plane, engines roaring, lights flashing, was parked a hundred yards away. "On that airplane, now! No looking around!"

Trotting to the plane, Fernando asked loudly over the din of the engine, "Where are we?"

One of the recruits answered, "Opa-Locka Airport."

Two blue-eyed pilots, conversing in what Goyo guessed was a Slavic tongue, were hovering near the cockpit door as they boarded. The recruits staked out spots on the metal seats running along the sides of the oily-smelling fuselage. The back of the airplane was neatly packed with boxes of supplies held down by large cargo nets. Fernando nervously ran his fingers across one of the airplane's windows before sitting down. He told Goyo, "Look, the windows are taped over and painted black so we can't see outside. They don't want us to know where we're going!"

Goyo tried not to look alarmed. He asked his friend, "Where do you think we're going?" Fernando shrugged his shoulders. "I don't know, but if what I've heard is true, I'd say the camps are in Guatemala."

"Oh, come on," Goyo said, shaking his head. He sat, stretched out his legs, and folded his arms. "Now, I've given this a lot of thought. Do you really think that's the case? I'm sure those were just rumors they spread, part of a misinformation campaign to confuse the enemy. They did that a lot during World War II, you know."

"Thanks for the history lesson, professor," Fernando said, retying his shoe laces. "But I'll stick with Guatemala. I'll bet you a beer."

"A beer it is," Goyo laughed, resting his head on the window behind him.

The other men, all younger than Goyo and Fernando, had no trouble sleeping during the long, uncomfortable flight. Goyo and Fernando could only sleep for a few minutes and spent most of the night talking about their families. When the sun started shining through the cracks on the taped windows after several hours, everyone was sore and hungry. A little later, the airplane's wheels pushed out from its belly and they landed, coming to a quick stop on a runway. One of the Slavic pilots opened the door and waited for some stairs to be rolled over. As the recruits began exiting the aircraft, Fernando asked one of the Slavs where they were. The Slav answered in a thick accent, "Guatemala." Fernando looked back at Goyo with a joyful expression and pointed at him, saying, "You owe me a beer."

Goyo froze for a moment in disbelief. "So much for secrecy," he thought, and went down the stairs.

A Cuban in military fatigues assembled the new recruits on the tarmac. "Good morning, and welcome to the Brigade 2506 air base at Retalhuleu, Guatemala."

"A Tropical beer," Fernando whispered to Goyo, "nice and chilled." Goyo smiled wryly.

"You can all go over to the mess area and eat to your heart's delight. Afterward, you'll board a truck that will take you to the training camp."

Goyo reared his head back. He raised his hand. "Sir, isn't this the camp?"

"As I stated, this is the base for the Brigade Air Force," the man said. He turned and pointed to the mountain peaks behind him. "The infantry units are at Base Trax, way up there on a coffee plantation." Goyo looked up at the misty mountaintops. His shoulders dropped.

Goyo sat at a table in the mess area with the rest of his group to eat breakfast. All of a sudden, a thick arm ferociously wrapped itself around his neck and squeezed, forcing him to spit the food out of his mouth. His assailant shouted in his ear, "*Guano*! You have been tricked! You are at a G.2 base in eastern Cuba! You are under arrest for conspiring with American agents against the Revolution!"

Everyone started laughing. The arm uncoiled itself. Goyo whirled around and saw that it was his old friend Bernardo Cuervo. He was attired in full flight gear. Goyo hadn't seen him in fifteen years, but had heard that Bernie had become a pilot for *Cubana de Aviación*, Cuba's national airline.

Goyo stood and shook hands with him. "Bernie, what are you doing here? Christ! You almost choked me!" He slid down the bench to make room for his friend.

"I should be the one asking you that question, old friend," Bernie said as he sat down.

"I'm on my way to the camps," Goyo answered.

Bernie took off his pilot's glasses and stared deeply at Goyo. He shook his head. "I've seen a lot of things these past few months that have given me hope. But seeing you here . . . a guy who went through an illness like you did, a guy with a family; now I know we'll win!" He slapped Goyo's back and turned to face the rest of the group.

Goyo blushed at Bernie's words. "So how did you end up in this thing, Bernie?"

Bernie shrugged his shoulders. "Well, when I saw that Castro was turning Cuba over to the Soviet Union I decided to go into exile like everyone else. One morning, I very casually boarded my family on a small private airplane and flew it to Miami. We asked for asylum when we got there. The next day, I got a call from one of my colleagues who'd also defected, and he told me they were recruiting an exile air force to fight Castro. I told him that I had never flown military missions, but he said that was OK, that they would train me." Bernie was now talking to the whole table. "Anyhow, get this: I had to take a bunch of medical exams and some psychological tests. One of the American shrinks asks me if I was a homosexual, and I told him that he should go ask his sister if I was or not. Can you believe that shit?" Everyone laughed. "Anyhow, they shipped us out here a few days later and we joined a group of former air force pilots and began training. We flew some missions to drop supplies to the guerrillas in the Escambray Mountains, but conditions there made that impossibly difficult. Very few of the supplies made it to our men."

Bernie looked around and lowered his voice. "I don't know how much you boys have been told, but that was the end of the original plan for the Brigade, which was to expand the guerrilla war against Castro on the island. The Americans had trained entire guerrilla units here, in Miami, in the Panama Canal Zone, and other places to penetrate Cuba as guerrillas. But Castro was receiving too much help from the Communist countries and his counterintelligence capacity had gotten too sophisticated. So, a couple of months ago they changed course and decided on a frontal assault instead–an invasion–and that's what we're training for now. That's also why they've started recruiting more heavily in Miami–an invasion would need more people."

"Do you know where they're going to land us?" one of the recruits asked him.

Bernie shook his head. "No one knows for sure, but all bets are on the southern coast, in Trinidad. It's the only place that makes sense. There are good, sandy beaches nearby for landing craft, a great port a few miles away at Casilda for the supply ships, and a landing strip that could quickly be lengthened for the airplanes. Plus, remember that the people in Trinidad have always hated Castro. We could take the city and the bridges that give access to it from the outside. If Castro's air force is destroyed like it's supposed to be, our B-26 bombers can use the landing strip there and knock the hell out of any ground forces moving toward the city. They'd be sitting ducks; hell, they'll probably run home or join us. We can set up a new government right there in Trinidad and thousands of new men would join us, including the guerrillas fighting in the Escambray Mountains, which as you know are right next to the city. Anyway, if Castro can't dislodge us from Trinidad, he's done for, especially if the Americans give us the help they've promised." Bernie sighed. "But in the end, this is all speculation."

The Cuban who'd met Goyo's plane waved the group over. It was time to go. They all stood. Goyo shook hands with Bernie again. "I've got to leave, Bernie. Listen, I want to see you alive at the end of this."

Bernie shrugged his shoulders. "Who knows who'll be alive? Remember, 'to die for the *patria* is to live,'" he said, quoting the national anthem's most iconic line.

The group was put into the back of a Guatemalan military truck. For several hours the truck wound its way up mountain roads so narrow the recruits were certain they'd fall right over the edge. When the road finally flattened, they passed a sign that read "Base Trax" and stopped. The men jumped out of the truck and scanned the desolate, muddy camp consisting of a handful of wooden structures and several rows of tents.

"This is it?" one of the recruits asked the Guatemalan driver incredulously.

"This is the place. Welcome to Base Trax," the truck driver chuckled. He pointed at one of the wooden buildings. "You guys go to that building over there and they'll tell you what to do." He drove off singing a tune.

A Cuban inside the small building took their names, assigned them each a four-digit serial number, and sent them to the infirmary for their inoculations. As the medics were poking them with needles, they heard a fleet of trucks rumble into the camp. The medic looked up. "That's the Second Battalion. They've just returned from a training mission. We should get busy in here real soon."

As if on cue, a member of the Second Battalion strutted in and asked to have his hand bandaged. Goyo, facing away from the door, recognized the voice. He turned. The boy was already staring at him, his mouth curved into a shocked smile. "Mr. León?"

Goyo gasped. "Pedro Vila!" He shook his head in utter perplexity. "After all I went through to get you out of Cuba?

What are you doing here? Your father is going to kill you!" He knew Pedro wasn't yet eighteen and had probably lied about his age.

Pedro laughed gleefully. He came over and threw his arm around Goyo's shoulders. "Don't worry, Mr. León, now that you're here, I'm safe. Hey, what battalion are you in?"

"I don't know yet. We just got here."

"Listen, my commander in the Second Battalion, Hugo Sueiro, is a really good guy. I'm sure he'll let you be with us. Come look for me outside when you're done in here."

"He's done now," said the medic.

Goyo and Pedro Vila went outside to look for the battalion commander. Goyo brought Fernando Miyares along with them.

"There he is," Vila said, pointing out a slight, but strongly built, young man. He was talking to a taller youth with a thick Mexican-style mustache.

They walked over. As Pedro made the introductions, Goyo exchanged a long stare with the tall, mustachioed young man standing next to the commander. After a few seconds, he snorted at him, "You! I can't believe this!"

NEW YORK CITY
Late December-Early January, 1961

Because of the Christmas holiday, it had taken Roberto and Emilio over a week to receive their passports and money in Mexico City. Upon obtaining them, they booked a flight to New York City, as they wanted to be up close to the Cuban exile political activity centered at the United Nations. If events dictated, they decided they'd proceed to Miami, the anti-Castro nerve center. New York was frigid cold and shrouded in a thin layer of fresh snow when they arrived on December 27. Shivering, they hired a cab at the airport and stopped at the first department store they saw in Queens, where they purchased winter coats, hats, socks, and gloves. They took a different taxi into Manhattan, checked into a hotel on Lexington Avenue, and telephoned Cuba. Lorenzo told Roberto that Goyo had fled the island soon after their departure and that he was in Miami. He gave him Goyo's telephone number and told him to call.

Roberto hung up with his father and walked over to the window. Staring down at the traffic on Lexington Avenue, he touched the window pane with his hand to feel the cold. "You know, I'm wondering if we should even call Goyo." He turned to Emilio, who was sitting on one of the beds. "Give me a cigarette. He'll just pester us to get jobs and go to school and stay away from Miami." He took the cigarette, lit it, and plopped into the chair next to the window.

Emilio stretched out on the bed. "At least we have to let him know where we are. Just tell him that we're enrolled at Fordham University . . . Christ, this bed is comfortable . . . anyhow, it's a Jesuit school; he'll like that. Then we can just do whatever we want."

Roberto called Goyo at the Miami number his father had given him. He fed him the story about Fordham. "Yeah, Goyo, as soon as we got here today we went straight down to Fordham University in Brooklyn . . . no, no, no, you're right, you're right, in the Bronx, sorry. Anyhow, we met with a Father O'Malley there. And do you know what? He's familiar with Belén and is a great admirer of the school." Emilio rolled on his stomach and buried his head in a pillow to muffle his laughter. Roberto waved his hand at him to shut up. "Anyhow, Goyo, so we told this Jesuit that we were graduates of Belén and that we were now university students who'd fled Cuba in exile. He left the room all of a sudden and, you know, we got nervous and everything, we didn't know what was going on. But you want to hear something? You're going to be amazed. Ten minutes later he came back telling us that we'd been given scholarships to attend Fordham." Goyo was too swollen with school pride to doubt the story. He told them to stay in school in New York and to get jobs there. Roberto didn't argue with him.

When Goyo finished with his admonishments, Roberto's tone turned more somber. "Cousin, listen, I really need your help with something." He told him about Sonia. Knowing that his cousin was connected to the resistance on the island at a higher level than he and Emilio, he pleaded with him to send someone from the underground to tell her what had happened to him. Goyo was sympathetic, but said, "Ask someone under deep cover to relay a love message?" He paused and sighed. "I can't make any promises." He took some information from Roberto and told him he would see what he could do.

The next day, the cousins rented a one-bedroom flat on East 85th Street near Second Avenue in Manhattan's Yorkville neighborhood, agreeing to pay a weekly rate. That afternoon, they got jobs bussing tables at a supper club near Times Square. The money was garbage, but the nighttime hours left them free during the day to engage in political activities with other Cuban exiles in the city. They immediately made contact with some people from the MRR and other organizations, and for the next few days attended political meetings and participated in a couple of anti-Castro rallies in front of the United Nations building.

The day after New Year's Day, they took the subway to work. There were only a few other people aboard the train: two college girls and a drunk, a bottle of booze resting between his legs as though he'd just given birth to it. Roberto leaned back in his seat and shut his eyes, settling in for the ride. An image of Sonia came into his mind. A dull throbbing erupted in his throat as he thought of her waiting for him at the park. Had Goyo sent that message yet? He knew his cousin would at least try; that was his nature. He sighed sadly, thinking she had probably moved on with her life by now. His thoughts wandered to his parents, old and alone in Cuba, and then to

Israel Muñoz, the leader of their underground cell, rotting in prison. He'd never anticipated that his flight would affect so many people.

He opened his eyes again. Emilio was flirting with the college girls; a few more minutes and they'd be his. Too bad their stop was coming up soon. Roberto started thinking back to the rallies and meetings they'd attended here in New York over the past few days. He recalled that José Martí, the father of the Cuban nation, had himself been exiled in New York; but Martí had returned to Cuba to fight for the homeland, and ultimately met a martyr's end. Martí, in turn, made him think about Sixto Abril, his old tutor in Switzerland. He wondered how the old patriot would react if he saw Cuba today. Roberto's face turned red hot with shame. He rested his head against the window behind him. He imagined Abril galloping past Martí's fallen body on a swift horse, machete in hand, ready to decapitate the first Spaniard that crossed his path.

He turned sideways and rested his foot on the seat next to him. The lights flickered a few times and then went out, plunging the rumbling train into pitch darkness for a few seconds. They came back on. He looked over at Emilio again. The girls were gone. Emilio was giving the drunk a cigarette. He saw Roberto looking at him and came over. "What?"

Roberto moved his foot off the seat. "Martí was in New York too, you know."

Emilio sat down. "Huh?"

"Nothing." Roberto bit his bottom lip. "Cousin, what are we doing here?"

Emilio shrugged. "I don't know. The girls are nice. You think we should go to Miami?"

Roberto backhanded the air. "What for? So we can attend more rallies?"

Emilio shrugged again.

Roberto stared into the dark subway tunnel through the window opposite him. His face hardened. "What do you think about these camps people keep talking about? You think maybe we should go?"

Emilio thought for a second. The lights went out again and came back on. "I don't know," he said. "It would be a lot more useful than shouting and holding signs out there on First Avenue, that's for sure."

Roberto looked down at the floor and nodded his head. "We owe it to Israel." He looked back at Emilio. "You know, our family will kill us if we enlist."

Emilio waved his hand. "Ah, they'll forget all about it when we march victoriously into Havana. Listen, the hell with work, let's go enlist right now if that's what we're going to do."

"No," Roberto said. "We'll let Mr. Papadopoulos know this will be our last night."

When they got to work, they went to see Mr. Constantine Papadopoulos, the Greek owner of the supper club where they were employed, in his office. He listened with interest as they told him about their intention to join the Liberation Army. A bejeweled Orthodox Madonna oversaw the proceedings from a perch upon the wall. Papadopoulos suddenly slapped his hands on his desk, making the cousins flinch. "It is important to love America," he declared in his thick accent, "but it is just as important to love your mother country." He put his right hand on his heart, saying, "I am moved." He reached into a drawer and took out two small stacks of cash and handed one to each cousin. "Something to help you along the way. Consider it my contribution to the cause. Now, go. My nephews will cover for you tonight!"

Early the next morning the cousins went to the *Frente's* New York City office and enlisted. That afternoon, they were put aboard a flight to Miami. From the Miami airport, they were taken for medical tests and then to a safe-house for the night. The news that the United States had cut off diplomatic relations with Cuba produced a wave of hope that ran through everyone they encountered. During their brief stay in Miami, the cousins remained as inconspicuous as possible, worried that they'd run into one of Goyo's friends–their older cousin would have a heart attack if he found out they'd joined the camps. The following night, they were transported to the Brigade air base in Retalhuleu, Guatemala. They landed the next morning.

Roberto and Emilio sat alone as they ate their breakfast at the Guatemalan air base. Emilio stretched and yawned when he finished eating. "I've got to piss," he said. He left the mess tent and looked around the base for the latrine. Turning a corner, he slammed into someone walking the other way.

"Emilio!" the young man he'd rammed into exclaimed. It was Angel Villanueva from his building in Havana.

"Damn, Angel, you joined the camps?" They shook hands.

"Yeah, you too, huh?"

"We just got here a little while ago," Emilio said.

"Where are they sending you? Not to that awful infantry camp in the mountains–that's been a mess with political problems and God knows what else!"

"I don't know where they're sending us," Emilio said with a shrug.

Angel lowered his voice. "Listen, stay with me. I joined the First Battalion, the paratroopers. It's a great outfit. I can introduce you to the commander, he's a guy around our age, a real military type. I'm sure I can get you in."

Emilio felt his spine tingle and a rumbling in his chest. "Let me use the bathroom. Wait for me here." As he walked away, his legs suddenly weakened and his vision blurred. He was thinking suddenly about his father's death in that frightening way he knew brought on his "episodes;" and at that moment he could feel one coming–a bad one, too. He tried to escape it by changing his thoughts, but he couldn't stop it. For over ten years he'd tried to pinpoint what triggered this horrifying chain reaction in his mind, but there was no pattern; a song, a word, a gesture someone made, a barking dog, just about anything could do it. What had Angel said just now that had done it?

The bathroom was empty. He took a deep breath and leaned against the wall furthest from the door, still struggling futilely to fight the imminent emotional onslaught; but he knew it was past the point where he could put the brakes on it. He finally shut his eyes in surrender. The familiar image of his dead father formed vaguely at first, accompanied by a sudden infusion of warm memories from his early childhood with him; then, as always, the joyous memories were washed away by the approaching, unstoppable torment, like a sandcastle in the face of a tidal wave.

He was transported back to the first moments after he'd learned of his father's death, the moments that had redirected the course of his life. The darkness within him took him over with terrible force. He became blind and deaf to everything around him, suddenly feeling as though he was lost in a vast, dark cave; dangerous beasts he could hear, but not see, lurked all around him. His scalp broke out in sweat. He managed to stumble into a toilet stall and closed the curtain. He sat on the toilet seat and rested his elbows on his knees, holding his face in his hands.

Feelings of guilt and shame began consuming him now, as they always did during these episodes. Why such feelings? The shrill voice in his head, as if on cue, answered for him: his father had given him all of his love, had even given him his name, but he, Emilio, had failed his father utterly and tarnished his name by growing into an underachieving screw-up, a degenerate playboy, the mischievous family mascot; anything he'd ever done of note had been following Roberto's initiative, including his presence here at the camps of the Liberation Army. Emilio could almost see the words "mediocre" and "shiftless" stamped on his forehead like the comment section of a bad report card. He felt as though he had no right to feel anything but profound shame.

His entire body quaked as his father's face came into sharp focus, the ghost slowly straddling his back, shoulders, and neck. Feelings of longing, guilt, and shame–all merged into a single, overwhelming emotion–washed over him. He pressed the heels of his palms into his eye sockets, hardly able to breathe. Maybe he'd never deserved his father, he thought; maybe God had taken his father from the world to spare the man the humiliation of having such a bungling fool for a son.

Then, the dark feelings unexpectedly started to recede. He looked up at the ceiling, his jaw locked tight, his eyes shining. He exhaled slowly and came out of the toilet stall. He washed his face in the sink and went back outside. Angel was still waiting for him. "So? What do you say?"

Emilio found Roberto still sitting alone in the mess area, smoking a cigarette. He sat down across from him.

"Where in the hell were you? The food wasn't *that* bad."

Emilio silently scanned the mess area.

"Anyhow, listen," Roberto said, "when we get to the camp, we have to make sure they put us in the same unit." He looked over Emilio's shoulder to the other side of the mess area. "Hey, I recognize that guy over there." He looked back at Emilio, "Anyhow, listen, we probably know some of the people there so I think we can arrange it. You know how these things work."

Emilio's mouth was drawn downward, his eyes bloodshot. Roberto suddenly noticed and stopped talking. Emilio folded his hands on the table. "Cousin, I'm not going with you."

Roberto reared back. "What? Are you backing out?"

"No. I've joined the First Battalion, the paratroopers."

Roberto opened his mouth to speak. He closed it again, realizing all of a sudden that Emilio was in one of those weird moods he got into now and then. They sometimes lasted for hours or days. Goyo said it had something to do with his father's death, a recurring trauma, some crazy shit like that.

Roberto leaned forward and snuffed out his cigarette. He propped his elbows on the table and looked at Emilio for a long moment. His voice was soft. "Well, maybe we can join the paratroopers together."

Emilio shook his head. "I asked the commander. There's no more room."

"I see," Roberto said. He leaned back again and toyed with his fork.

Emilio reached his hand out. "It's nothing against you, cousin. You're my brother. You'll always be. You know that. This is just something . . . something I have to do on my own. I don't really understand why, but it is."

Roberto compressed his lips tightly and laid the fork down on the table. He looked away. "Well, sometimes we have to do things no one else understands, or that sometimes we don't even understand," he said. Emilio's eyes misted. Someone called for the group going to Base Trax to board the truck outside.

Roberto stood. Emilio got up with him. They embraced. Roberto squeezed hard and cried into his cousin's ear, "You're my brother, Emilio, remember that." He let go and walked away. Emilio waved at him as he fell in with the group.

Before leaving the mess area, Roberto turned to take a last look at his cousin: there he stood, tall, confident, as good looking as ever–and alone. In that moment Roberto understood that Emilio had been alone all along, and he was filled with great pity.

* * *

"How long have you been here?" Goyo demanded of Roberto. They walked a few feet away from Pedro and

Sueiro, the battalion commander. "You guys told me that you were enrolled at Fordham University. What happened to that priest who thought so highly of Belén that he gave you scholarships? Father O'Malley, indeed! This is the second time you guys pull something like this. I specifically told you to stay away from all of this! You lied to me, Roberto. You *lied* to me!"

"I didn't lie about being in New York. Besides, I've only been here a short time."

Goyo pleaded, "Roberto, you're too young to be here."

Roberto snarled, "Are you blind, Goyo? I'm almost twenty-one years old. There are guys here who are younger. Anyhow, you can't stop me."

Goyo looked away and grumbled angrily. After a few moments, his face muscles began slowly to relax. He looked back at his cousin, his face still hard. "When did you grow that ridiculous mustache?"

Roberto smiled, stroking the top of his mouth. "Does it make me look older?"

"You look like Pancho Villa. Where's Emilio?" He looked around.

"He isn't here."

"Thank God," Goyo sighed. "Is he still in New York?"

"No."

"Where then? Miami?"

"No. He's here, in Guatemala."

Goyo narrowed his eyes. "What?"

"He joined the paratroopers."

"Oh, Christ! How did that happen?"

"I don't know. He went to the bathroom and came out in one of his dark moods, you know the ones, and then he told me that he'd joined the paratroopers. I haven't seen or heard from him since." He shrugged his shoulders.

"Listen, Goyo," Roberto continued, "I'm with the Second Battalion. I can get you into the battalion if you'd like."

"So I've heard," he said, pointing a thumb at Pedro Vila, who was still huddled with the commander.

"So, what do you say?"

"Roberto, I'm not going to take my eyes off of you until this whole thing is over."

"Let's go, then. But first, I have a surprise for you. Follow me."

They walked across the camp and stopped in front of a tent. Roberto called inside, "Hello?"

"Yes? Come in," said a voice. Roberto opened the flap. A man inside was lying on a cot reading a book. A gilded crucifix gleamed on a side table.

"Goyo!" The man bolted up. "I don't believe it!"

"Father Hidalgo!" Goyo said, surprised. "You're a long way from the school. When did you become a soldier?"

"I got here a couple of days ago. I'm one of the Brigade chaplains."

"Then this mission is indeed blessed!"

"God wills it," beamed the priest. "God wills it."

5

HAVANA, CUBA
Miramar Section
January 1961

Raquel hated doing dishes. She didn't mind cooking, or even doing the laundry, and she never minded not having domestic help like all the mansion dwellers in the neighborhood. But doing dishes–*that* she hated. She held one of the dishes in front of her face and contemplated smashing it on the floor. Teresa, Emilio's mother, came over and gently nudged her away from the sink, taking over the chore.

After Goyo's departure, Teresa had moved in to help Raquel, and Raquel was glad for it. Everyone loved Teresa, and she understood firsthand what it was like for a home suddenly to lose a husband and father. It was like being stripped naked and thrown into a busy street filled with traffic.

Teresa had adapted well to life with Goyo's family. She relished being the doting aunt, and she especially enjoyed her long conversations with Raquel. Last night, they were sitting on the portico after the children had gone to bed. It was a dark, windy night; the air smelled of rain. Raquel asked her, "Teresa, what was it like to be the baby of the family?"

Teresa smiled distantly. "Well, I lived a charmed life when I was little. I was the only girl and my parents had me late

in life. Lorenzo was fifteen years my senior. He and Gregorio were very protective of me, especially after Father died
young. A few years after his passing, of course, Lorenzo went
off with the Foreign Service and Gregorio opened the bank.
Gregorio looked after me then. My God, when I became a
teenager, he wouldn't let any boys near me. They were all terrified of him. He was awful with them!" They both laughed.

Raquel rested her chin in her hand. "So, what happened?"

"Well, after a while the young men stopped calling altogether. By the time I was twenty-two, I thought I would either
grow old living with Gregorio and María del Carmen–he was
already married then–or become a nun. Back then you were
considered an old maid by twenty-five. Anyhow, I'm boring
you with these old stories."

Raquel crossed her arms and rested them on her thighs.
"No, no, don't stop. How did you meet Emilio's father?"

Teresa sighed and smiled. "Well, one day I was walking
to the church for Mass. I remember I had it in mind to talk
to the priest that day–Padre Orozco, an old Spaniard–about
possibly entering a convent. I don't know if I really thought
I had a vocation or if I just needed something to do with my
life. Anyhow, on the sidewalk outside the church there stood
the most handsome man I had ever seen. Raquel, he had
the shiniest brown hair and the most beautiful green eyes."
She paused and stared dreamily across the shadowy sea. "He
looked vaguely like an American, but somehow you could tell
he was Cuban. Our eyes met for just a second." She laid her
hand heavily on her chest and sighed. "I swear to you, my
heart stopped beating. Anyhow, I went to Mass and pushed
him out of my mind. I never talked to Padre Orozco that day

about the convent. Well, the next day the man was standing in the very same spot, only this time he was dressed in a white linen suit, a *dril cien*. Can you believe that he had the nerve to tip his hat to me? Gregorio would have killed him!" They both laughed again.

"Well, the next day when I went to Mass, he wasn't on the sidewalk. I was furious with him. Can you imagine that? I'd never even spoken to this man and here I was reproaching him for standing me up! At any rate, I went to my regular pew. I looked across the aisle, and there he was, on the opposite side, the man in the *dril cien* suit. I remember imagining that he had a closet full of *dril ciens*, one for each day of the week." Raquel giggled. "Anyhow, our eyes met again, but this time we held our gaze for a few seconds. Then, after Communion, he was gone." She swept her hand in front of her when she said "gone."

"I became flustered. 'Where did he go?' I asked myself desperately. I nearly went into a panic. Anyhow, when the Mass ended I stayed with a group of ladies for a recitation of the Rosary, but it was really to see if he would come back. When I was getting up to leave, Padre Orozco poked his head out the sacristy door and waved me over, which was very strange. I'd never been inside a sacristy. 'Teresa, come here, please,' he said. When I walked in, there he was, the man in the *dril cien*." Raquel gasped.

"Padre Orozco said, in his thick Spanish accent, 'Teresa, I would like to introduce you to a good friend. His name is Emilio Hammond.' Emilio took my hand and kissed it. Well, at that moment I knew I wasn't ever going to enter a convent." Raquel rolled back in her chair and grinned.

"Then Padre Orozco said, 'Mr. Hammond would like to call upon you at your home tonight, with your permission, of course. I will accompany him to guarantee the good intentions of his visit.' All I could think was that Gregorio would kill both of them. I think Padre Orozco read my mind, because he waved his finger and said, 'And don't worry about that brother of yours.' I was shocked to know that Gregorio's reputation had reached even the ears of the parish priest. I just nodded and left. I never said a word.

"I was terrified when I got home. I should tell you that my brother was never anything but generous and kind and gentle with me. But still, I was scared. I was in the patio reading a book when he got home. He came over and said, 'I had a visit from Padre Orozco today. I assume you know what it was about.' Then he thundered, 'That priest! Playing matchmaker! The audacity!' I couldn't tell if he'd accepted the invitation or if he'd thrown Padre Orozco through a stained-glass window! But then he smiled and said, 'The priest told me I've been too protective of you. He's right, but I just don't believe there's a man on this island worthy of my sister.'" Teresa wiped her eyes.

"It was a magical night, Raquel. Emilio brought over his guitar. Padre Orozco, who liked to drink, had a little too much and started telling stories about his childhood in Spain. Eventually, Gregorio and Emilio sat in a corner and talked alone. I could tell Gregorio liked him. He found it especially interesting that Emilio's grandfather was from the United States. He'd come here after the Civil War, as you know. Later, when the priest started rambling on with Gregorio, Emilio and I talked alone for the first time. He was the most charming and witty man I'd ever met. I was in love with him after ten minutes." She sighed happily at the memory.

"Later on, we all went out to the front porch. Emilio took out his guitar and asked if we wanted for him to play something. I said, 'Play something we've never heard.' He said he knew a song in English, a kind of hymn. His grandfather had taught it to his father, who taught it to him. It was a terribly sad song, but lovely all the same. I forget the words now, but after he was born little Emilio loved to hear his father play it. The song said 'by and by' in it so we just called it the 'by and by song.'

"Anyhow, after that night Emilio and I secretly exchanged love letters. Some of them were very passionate. We married six months later and moved into a small house in the Santos Suárez section. We were so happy, Raquel. Emilio was a fun-loving, joy of a man. We had lots of friends and went everywhere—parties, soirees, formal galas. I had never felt so free. A year later, I was pregnant."

Raquel's smile disappeared. She'd heard disjointed pieces of what happened next. Teresa looked down, her eyes vacant. "As you know, seven months into the pregnancy the child died. I lost two more children in the womb, and then María Teresa was born, my little baby . . . oh, Raquel, we loved her so much." She covered her face, which had started to twitch. Raquel reached out and rubbed her shoulder.

With a sad sigh, Teresa recovered and continued. "Well, in late 1939–it seems like yesterday, really–I found out I was pregnant again. Sara and Lorenzo, who were still in Europe, were also awaiting a child after two decades of frustration. But I wasn't happy. I thought I would lose this child as well. I prayed to the Virgin constantly, and the boy, thank God, was born healthy the next year. Naturally, we named him after his father.

"The next ten years were pure heaven. The hole in my heart for María Teresa and the memory of her death were still there, and I had a Mass said in her memory every year on her birthday. It was the one day of the year that I mourned openly for her. But otherwise, everything was pure joy. My husband had received an executive position with an American tobacco company, Emilio, Jr., was thriving in school, and we were looking to build a new home near Gregorio's in Miramar. Emilio was such a good father, Raquel, very much like Goyo. He loved that boy, and spent all his free time with him. And the boy worshipped him."

Teresa's face hardened. "Then, one day, the police showed up at my front door telling me that my husband had been killed in an automobile accident along the Central Highway. It was my fate, Raquel." It was Raquel's turn to wipe her eyes.

"Gregorio, of course, looked after Emilio and me. And it was a great relief when Lorenzo and Sara moved back to Cuba with Roberto. Emilio finally had a brother. But I'll tell you, I felt more pity for Emilio than I did for myself. He adored his father; strangely, though, he never talked about him after his death, even to this day he doesn't mention his name. Sometimes I think he's forgotten him. But I know that deep down he never has. I know he thinks about him a great deal." Teresa looked at her hands.

"I don't know how you did it alone all those years," Raquel said. She bit her thumb nervously.

Teresa reached out and grabbed her hand. "My husband died, Raquel. Your husband is still walking and breathing, just ninety miles across the water there. Don't be discouraged. You have reason to hope." Raquel smiled. Teresa continued, "We must both have hope, Raquel. My son is also somewhere beyond that sea. But unlike your husband, my son is reckless and impulsive."

"Oh, he's a good boy," Raquel said, smiling more broadly.

Teresa lifted her eyes. "Yes, at least according to half the women of Havana!"

They both laughed.

"But I do miss him," Teresa said, shaking her head sadly. "As perfectly wicked as he is, I do miss him."

Raquel looked at her tenderly. "You have us, Teresa, and we love you as though you were our own mother. Emilio is going to be fine. You'll see. Besides, he's with Roberto."

They both froze for a moment and then burst out laughing again.

"Roberto!" Teresa cried, throwing up her arms. "Well, the judge probably won't give them more than twenty years of hard labor."

They talked into the night. Every few minutes, Raquel felt the tickling sensation of new life jumping inside her womb. She laid her hand flat across her stomach and couldn't help but to smile.

Meanwhile, across Havana Bay, Israel Muñoz awaited his fate.

6

LA CABAÑA FORTRESS
Havana, Cuba

The worst part about Israel's stay at La Cabaña was witnessing the family visits of his fellow political prisoners. Despairing families delivered their loved ones care packages containing whatever meager provisions they were permitted to bring into the prison. Some families showed up only to be told by the other prisoners that their son or father or husband had been executed; the Revolution often had more pressing matters than to inform the relatives. Israel's poor father had come once from Matanzas. He told him, in hushed whispers, that Anita had reached her husband's guerrilla base camp. That was a relief. But the old man couldn't stop crying. His strength and vitality were sapped, his old spirit gone. Israel felt as if his heart was being ripped out just looking at him. He begged his father not to come again.

A few weeks later, Israel was called out of his *galera* by the guards. He was marched to a separate building, where a makeshift courtroom had been set up. He was ordered to sit, and for the next few minutes watched the closing moments of a trial. The tribunal sat at a raised, rectangular table, all of its members bearded and dressed in olive green uniforms. Israel thought, with dark humor, that they looked as if they were going to a costume party dressed as Fidel Castro. They were trying a young man around his own age. Chomping on cigars, they accused the youth of sabotage and sedition against the government. The tribunal delivered its verdict without hesitation, stating that it was the "moral conviction" of the court that he was guilty. Israel knew that meant that the prosecution had no evidence. He was also aware that many of the verdicts were decided by the secret police, the G.2, long before the cases even went to trial.

A lawyer by training, Israel shook his head in disgust when the young man was given a twenty-year sentence, all without so much as a shred of evidence. As the verdict was being read in language rife with Revolutionary demagoguery, a middle-aged man in a white, long-sleeve *guayabera* shirt sat down next to him. He was holding some legal documents.

"Are you Israel Muñoz?"

"Yes."

"My name is Martínez." He shook Israel's hand. "I've been appointed as your attorney. I received the brief just a little while ago. Your trial is next."

Israel nodded and closed his eyes. Nothing surprised him anymore. This was the first and only time he would meet his court-appointed lawyer, seconds before trial.

The lawyer's eyes scanned the brief. "According to this, you were the head of a CIA-supported underground cell and that you coordinated acts of sabotage. It also says that you assaulted a building manager in Old Havana and were an accomplice in the murder of a *miliciano* at a boarding house near the University. Is this true?"

Israel blanched. "I killed no one. I know nothing about a murder." He looked away. Did Anita kill a *miliciano* at the boarding house? Christ, Anita! He looked back at the attorney. "And I don't fight for the CIA or for the Americans. I fight for Cuba."

His case was called next. Israel and his lawyer sat at the small table before the kangaroo court. Besides the charges of which his lawyer had informed him, the government's prosecutor accused him of illicit association with counterrevolutionary former bank owners who, to make matters worse, were educated by the priests. They seemed never to be short of incendiary language, Israel thought. When they paused, Israel, seeing there was no real procedure, stood up. "You say I was working with the CIA and that I was an accomplice in a murder. I demand evidence! And please state the legal precedent for establishing 'illicit association' as a punishable offense."

His lawyer squeezed his arm and stood up next to him. "I ask that my client be shown leniency. He knows nothing of this murder. The record clearly shows that he was not in the room when said murder was committed. I plead the court's mercy. He is remorseful of his actions and asks that he be spared the death penalty and be instead given a sentence of thirty years in political prison."

Israel swiveled his head at his lawyer. A guffaw popped from his mouth. His own lawyer had just asked the court to give him thirty years on a charge with no evidence.

Israel turned back to face the tribunal. "These proceedings are a mockery!" He pounded the table. "I demand a fair trial with an attorney of my choice and time to prepare my case."

The tribunal burst into laughter. "Son," one of them said leaning back in his chair, "I think you have a very bourgeois sense of justice. This tribunal is charged with protecting the people of Cuba from terrorist elements such as you and your confederates. We will not permit procedural niceties to stand in our way."

Israel looked at each of them in turn. "I am a citizen of this country, yet this court treats me like a prisoner of war." The lawyer sat and tapped Israel's arm lightly for him to sit as well. Israel didn't budge.

"You are a traitor and a violent counterrevolutionary," shouted the tribunal leader, taking off his glasses and pointing them at Israel. "Legally speaking, you are an enemy combatant."

This is too easy, Israel thought. "If that's the case, then I demand my rights under the Geneva Convention, to which the Cuban Republic is a signatory."

The leader of the tribunal bolted up, knocking over his chair. He shouted, "You will sit down and speak no further. You are a traitor to your country. This court finds you guilty on all counts."

Israel sat and let out a frustrated sigh. He thought about his father. He felt faint. Tears formed behind his eyes. He wanted his mother. The head of the tribunal put his glasses back on and looked down at his papers. "This tribunal hereby sentences you to thirty years in prison."

Israel's head dropped. The lawyer stood quickly and clumsily gathered his papers, muttering his thanks to the tribunal. He spirited Israel out of the courtroom. Once outside, he explained that he had not disputed the charges because it would have been futile. He told Israel that he was lucky he hadn't been executed.

BRIGADE 2506 PARATROOPER TRAINING BASE

Near Retalhuleu, Guatemala
January, 1961

Jimmy Strickland hated being drunk. But he usually drank himself into oblivion three nights a week, usually by himself, and usually with Tennessee whiskey, "the only good thing to come outta that shit ass state." But he'd never missed a single roll call, never shirked his responsibilities, and never lost the life of one of his men because of it. It was his own business, something he did on his own damned time.

He sat up on his cot and looked around his quarters, the half empty whiskey bottle and shot glass resting on the turned up footlocker he used as a nightstand. It's really kind of cozy in here, he thought, at least compared to outside, where the Guatemalan wilderness teemed with all sorts of nasty critters and Lord-knows-what-else. He grabbed a small mirror and looked at his reflection. His eyes were bloodshot. He had his daddy's eyes. He frowned and ran his fingers through his short-cropped hair. He turned his head slowly to look at the left side of his head, checking to see if his disfigurement had somehow miraculously healed. It hadn't. He tossed the mirror aside and grabbed his guitar.

He absentmindedly started caressing the guitar strings with his fingers. His voice wailed and meandered in his throat, looking for a tune. He caught a hymn from childhood. He closed his eyes and rocked back and forth as he played and hummed and sang to himself.

Jimmy stopped playing and opened his eyes. He could hear some of the Cubans talking and laughing outside in the distance. He put the guitar down and filled the shot glass. He knocked it back and slammed it back down on the foot locker. He stretched and lay down again on his cot. There was a lot of good about the Cubans, he thought, interlacing his fingers behind his head, but there was a whole lot of danger, too. They were the most motivated men he'd ever trained. That was good. A whole bunch of them were educated, a lot of them even spoke English. That was good, too. Still, he worried sometimes that they knew too much about what they were fighting for. Back when he'd served, the Army pretty much told you who you were fighting and why; shit, they'd show you a film about it and everything. A soldier's mind was completely malleable. But the trainees here knew the enemy first hand. Some of them had already fought against it in some capacity or another. Worst of all, they viewed this army in training as *their* army and the coming battle as part of *their* war. He'd even heard about a strike among the infantry units training higher up in the mountains over some political grievance. Soldiers on strike? He grabbed a Camel cigarette and popped it into his mouth. Well, he was an airborne instructor. Whatever happened up there wasn't his problem.

He sat up and lit the cigarette. He took up his guitar again and started plucking the strings, the Camel dangling from his lips. It wasn't just *their* war. It was his, too. He knew about Communism: mass executions; political prisons; peoples' property and livelihoods seized; children forced to renounce their families and religion; a free people herded against its will into a collective mass with no individual rights or personal freedom. Shit, it was scary enough when Communism took root in parts of Europe and Asia after the war, especially in China, but now it had secured a foothold on the doorstep of his country. Damn it, it *was* his war.

Jimmy flung the Camel to the floor and stamped it out with his boot. He closed his eyes and kept playing his guitar. Images from home surfaced from the depths of his mind, like they always did when he was drinking. He saw Daddy, a minister, up preaching a fiery sermon. "Asshole," Jimmy thought. His chest tightened. He saw Momma in the kitchen and his chest loosened and warmed. Momma was an angel, and he loved her more than anything in the whole world. He shook his head from side to side, plucking the strings more vigorously, muttering some lyrics. Sundays were the best. The aroma of Momma's fried chicken hung in the air all afternoon, while he and his sister took turns on the swing hanging from the Spanish moss-covered live oak whose branches shaded the yard and house. Grandpa and Grandma, Momma's parents, would be on the front porch wearing their Sunday best, Grandpa always with an instrument in his hands. Jimmy loved his grandparents almost as much as he loved Momma. He liked sitting at Grandpa's feet and listening to him tell stories about how his ancestors had come to this land and built this house and how he gave it to Momma and Daddy when they were married. Grandpa also taught him to play the guitar and all the old ballads and hymns.

After a couple shots of whiskey, Jimmy could feel his mouth water at the thought of Momma's Sunday chicken. It took three shots before he could smell the cotton fields surrounding the house and see the little Flicker birds hopping on the grass. By the fourth shot, he could remember all the words to the songs Grandpa had taught him and feel the rush of swinging from the live oak, the clumps of Spanish moss dangling from its branches like curly beards. By shot number five, he'd remember the day Momma collapsed in the kitchen, back when he was thirteen and his sister Eleanor was fifteen. Shot number six. He was so frightened that he'd sprinted down the dusty dirt road until he reached the church two miles away. He told Daddy about what had happened to Momma, and they both raced to pick up Doc Peters in the truck. Shot number seven. Momma was still lying motionless on the floor, her skin pale and clammy. Eleanor sat next to her, shaking. "She ain't dead, is she Doc?" Shot number eight. Doc Peters felt Momma's wrist and under her chin. He bowed his head. "She's gone." Shot number nine. The people from the funeral home came over, lifted her onto a stretcher, covered her face, and took her away. Shot number ten. All he could hear now was his sister, "She ain't dead, is she Doc?" over and over in his head like a siren.

Daddy didn't say much of anything for months after the funeral. Eleanor quit school to try to make things more comfortable for him. Daddy barely noticed. Daddy met Ms. Dorothy a year later and married her. They all moved to a new state and started a new life. Grandma and Grandpa stayed back home and both died less than a year later, before Jimmy could ever see them again. He hated Ms. Dorothy and he hated Daddy for marrying her and ripping him away from home.

Jimmy graduated high school in 1941. He planned to return to his home state for college and started working at a local mill to save money for tuition. He could go back to his roots, he thought, maybe even buy the old family homestead after he graduated. He'd be back in the place his soul had never left, the land where Momma and Grandpa and Grandma now rested. Then Japan bombed Pearl Harbor.

Jimmy enlisted at the nearest recruiting station. He had no doubt that it was the only right thing to do, and it was what Grandpa would've expected. Grandpa always told him about how their ancestors had been in almost every war this country had ever fought. One ancestor had fought at King's Mountain during the Revolutionary War, and another had fought under General Jackson at New Orleans in 1815. Even Daddy had fought in the Great War, although he never talked about it. Jimmy's most glorified military ancestor, though, was Grandpa's Uncle Edward who'd fought for the Confederacy during the Civil War. Standing in line at the recruitment center, Jimmy remembered Grandpa telling him about how, after the war, his Uncle Edward had gone to seek his fortune in South America with a bunch of other former rebels. Grandpa remembered meeting Uncle Edward back when he was a kid, during his uncle's visits home from South America; but after Grandpa's father died, Grandpa never saw Uncle Edward again.

Jimmy was assigned to the old 82nd Infantry Division, the "All Americans," re-designated in 1942 as the 82nd Airborne Division. He fought in Sicily, Salerno, Normandy, and the Ardennes. He earned a Silver Star. During a skirmish late in the war, a fuel tank exploded next to him. The flames seared off most of the skin on the left side of his face and head. It was now permanently twisted into an obscene spider web of scar tissue.

By war's end, Jimmy's dreams of going to college had evaporated. He had no wife, no children, and a father and stepmother he had no desire to see. Ever. His sister had moved to California when the Marines shipped her husband there before his deployment; when he lost his life in the Pacific, she lost her mind. She was admitted to a mental hospital near Fresno where they tried electro-shock therapy, but that only made her comatose and she died six months later. Jimmy visited his childhood home once after the war–his only visit since he'd left it as a boy–and spent time with Momma and his grandparents at the cemetery. All his blood connections to them were gone now. He was alone.

Because jumping out of airplanes and fighting were the only things at which he had ever excelled, and because the injury to his face didn't preclude him from doing it, he reenlisted and remained part of the 82nd Airborne. He received a commission, and for the next fourteen years trained U.S. paratroopers in different environments for the inevitable war with the Communists. In late 1959, having achieved the rank of captain, he was given an honorable discharge. Several months later, he was quietly approached by the CIA about working for them. They needed men like him to help train foreign soldiers fight Communist insurgency in their home countries. Of course his work would all be off the books, his name would not officially appear in CIA records, and he would always be paid in cash. The Internal Revenue Service, he was assured, would never ask questions about his income. He accepted the job.

In the late fall of 1960, Jimmy was called to Washington for a briefing on the Communist disturbance brewing in Cuba. A group of anti-Communist Cuban exiles, he was told, had been organized into a "Liberation Army." It was currently being trained in Central America to invade Cuba and overthrow Fidel Castro. The Army's Special Forces would do much of the training, but they needed some help with the airborne arm of the mission.

And so, here he was, on a cot, three sheets to the wind, in the Guatemalan wilderness helping to train a bunch of Cubans to be paratroopers.

His bunkmate, Willie Young, came into the quarters. Willie was a tall, muscular, dark-skinned African American. Jimmy nodded a greeting. He wouldn't have accepted this assignment unless he could bring Willie along. He'd trained Willie himself back in the day, soon after they'd desegregated the armed forces, and he was the best damned paratrooper ever under his command. Best of all, Willie was from back home, even though Jimmy didn't know him until he was in the Army. Willie was like a brother to Jimmy and the closest thing he had to a family.

Willie sat down on his bunk and glared at Jimmy. He'd seen him drunk plenty of times and knew better than to say anything about it. He started unlacing his boots. "Remember, country boy, we start early tomorrow, 5 a.m. There's a new batch of Cubans got here tonight, and I'm not sure if any of them speak English."

Jimmy stopped playing his guitar. "Don't tell me what to do," he snarled. He stared at Willie for a few seconds with glassy eyes. Then he pointed his finger at him. "And I'll be goddamned if I'm gonna start taking orders from a fuckin' slave boy!"

"Hey, who do you think you're talking to?" Willie shouted back harshly. "I'll be goddamned if some inbred, pale-assed redneck calls *me* a slave!" Willie flung his boot at Jimmy's head with terrible speed.

Jimmy blocked the boot with his right arm and laughed hoarsely. He picked up the boot and tossed it back.

"Hey, hayseed," Willie said, throwing the boot aside and taking off his socks, "why don't you put your head down and dream about Hank Williams or something? We both need to sleep."

Jimmy gave him a sideways glance. "Don't you ever kid about Hank Williams. He was from our hometown, y'know." Everyone from around those parts knew that.

"Now, white boy, we both know that there wouldn't be a Hank Williams if it wasn't for Rufus Payne, a.k.a. 'Tee Tot,' a *black* man. Tee Tot showed that good ol' boy everything he knew, right there on the streets of that goddamned one-horse town."

Jimmy put the guitar aside and rested his forearms on his thighs. He nodded sentimentally. "That's right, Willie, 'goddamned one-horse town,' that's right." He looked up and smiled at Willie. "But it is home, ain't it?" Jimmy felt a wind blowing inside his chest. There was no home anymore. He filled his shot glass and held it high. "Here's to ol' Tee Tot. God bless him." He downed the drink and pitched back on his pillow, fast asleep.

BRIGADE 2506 PARATROOPER TRAINING BASE
Next Morning

E milio lined up with the other new paratroopers. It was 5 a.m. Last night, someone told him that the paratrooper unit had been recently moved to this camp on the coastal plains above San José from a base up in the mountains. The Cubans had nicknamed this base *Garrapatenango*, for the millions of cattle ticks they encountered there. Before Emilio and the new group, in the semi-darkness, stood the Cuban battalion commander, a twenty-two-year-old dynamo named Alejandro del Valle. Next to him was a wiry American with a large nasty burn scar that covered the left side of his face and head. A tall black American stood behind them.

"Gentlemen," del Valle announced, "welcome to the First Battalion, the paratrooper unit of Brigade 2506. The training here is tough and the atmosphere highly disciplined. If you feel you cannot handle the rigors of training, or if you suddenly develop a fear of heights, please indicate so and we will assign you to a different battalion. But for now, I will introduce you to two of your trainers, Fred and his assistant Sam." The two Americans nodded toward the group.

Jimmy Strickland still wasn't used to being called by a phony name; "Fred," for Christ's sake. He stepped forward and looked to the left. A Cuban translator emerged from the shadows. Jimmy spoke. "Now, you boys have come a long way to free your country. Last night, I told my assistant Sam," he nodded toward Willie, "that I have never, in all my years, trained a group of men more motivated to fight than y'all. That said, neither I nor any of the other trainers will allow any new recruit to inject laziness into this unit, nor will we permit anyone to play politics. Because if you do, you'll be out of here faster than a bull clamps his ass shut during fly season." The translator hesitated, guffawed, and translated. The men laughed. "This is an elite unit," Jimmy continued. "You must decide right now that you will train and fight as a single man. As paratroopers, you will be dropped into dangerous combat zones and be the first to encounter the enemy. You will likely be outnumbered, so you must not be outperformed."

Jimmy started pacing before the group. "Now, it wasn't too long ago when the great evil seeking to devour the civilized world was the Nazi movement. We defeated it, but that war unleashed upon the world another dark force–you boys know it well: Communism. This darkness has already consumed free peoples around the world: Russians, Poles, Czechoslovaks, East Germans, Hungarians, Romanians, Bulgarians, Yugo-slavs, Chinese, Vietnamese, Koreans, and others. Our side of the world, by the grace of God, had been spared; but now . . . *now* this pestilence has entrenched itself right here in our hemisphere, right under our very noses. And, unfortunately, it was in your country where it gained its first foothold."

Jimmy stopped pacing and turned sharply to face the men. He stayed quiet for a full five seconds. He wasn't a preacher's boy for nothing. He breathed sharply through his nose and raised his voice, proclaiming, "And *you*, gentlemen, are the ones who have been given the honor and privilege of removing this cancer. *You*, the First Battalion of Brigade 2506, will be the first unit of the first assault wave thrown against it; and not only will you free your country, but you will save this hemisphere, and perhaps the rest of the world, from falling under its odious shadow."

Jimmy took a clipboard and walked up to the first recruit. "What's your name, son?"

Emilio was wide awake now. He hadn't needed the translator; he'd followed the English perfectly. He normally rolled his eyes when people employed such melodramatic rhetoric–too many corrupt political types in Cuba over the years had mastered the skill–yet he couldn't help but to feel completely uplifted. The front line troops in a war to save the hemisphere, and perhaps the whole *world*, from a dark force. Wow! Before he knew it, Fred stood before him. Behind Fred were Sam, Alejandro del Valle, and the translator.

"What's your name, son?" Fred asked, looking down at his clipboard.

"Hammond. Emilio Hammond," he said, not waiting for the translator.

"Hammond?" Fred snapped his head up sharply. He paused. "I ain't never heard of a Cuban with a name like that." He looked Emilio directly in the eyes. He seemed annoyed.

"My great-grandfather was from the United States, sir," Emilio said, thinking, "What's the big deal? There are plenty of Cubans with Anglo names."

Fred's eyes narrowed. "Where?" he asked slowly.

"I'm sorry, sir, but, 'where' what?"

Fred gritted his teeth and snorted, "Where was he from?"

"Alabama," Emilio responded quickly.

Fred's shoulders dropped. "Exactly *where* in the great state of Alabama, son?" he said slowly and menacingly.

Emilio racked his brain trying to recall the name of the town scribbled in his great-grandfather's book. It came to him. "He was from Georgiana, in Butler County. He went to Cuba after the Civil War."

The ends of Jimmy's mouth slanted downward. He took in a deep breath. His stare stabbed into Emilio like daggers. The scar tissue on his head started crawling like a thousand maggots. He let out his breath and handed Willie the clipboard. "You finish up here, Sam." Willie took the clipboard and watched Jimmy disappear into the darkness.

Jimmy sat hunched over on his cot. He downed a shot of whiskey and lit a Camel as a shaft of morning sunlight began shining in through the window of his quarters. Those eyes, he thought, they were unmistakable. Someone knocked. Jimmy lifted his head. "In!" he cried, in a gruff military tone.

Emilio came in and stood before him at full attention. "You asked to see me, sir."

"Relax, son, sit down," Jimmy said amiably. He pulled a stool over before the cot. He pointed at the bottle. "Have a drink."

Emilio glanced over at the open whiskey bottle and declined the drink with a polite wave. Fred's pistol, in its leather holster, was lying next to the bottle. Emilio sat on the stool, his pulse racing.

Jimmy stood up. He patted Emilio on the shoulder and walked past him. "Don't worry, son, there's nothing wrong. I just had a question."

Emilio turned to follow him with his eyes. "What is it, sir?"

Jimmy leaned on the wall behind Emilio, crossing his feet and arms. "You wouldn't happen to know the name of your ancestor from Alabama, would you?"

"Yes, sir. His name was Edward Billings Hammond. Why do you ask?"

Jimmy stayed quiet for a few seconds. "Glory be," he muttered, pushing himself from the wall.

"Excuse me, sir?"

Jimmy walked over and poured himself another drink. He drank it and sat on the cot again to face Emilio. "Edward Billings Hammond, your great-granddaddy, was my granddaddy's uncle."

Emilio knitted his eyebrows. "What?" Sweat started forming at the base of his skull.

"Edward Billings Hammond, your great-grandfather, was my grandfather's uncle, *my* great-grandfather's brother."

Emilio's voice shook. "What? How do you know this?"

"Well, I don't think there was but one Edward Billings Hammond who came out of Butler County and left after the war." He poured himself another shot.

Emilio thought this might be some kind of CIA mind game. He took a long, hard look at Fred. Fred stared back at him. Something told Emilio that he wasn't lying. "Uncle Edward was in the First Alabama Cavalry during the Civil War."

Emilio nodded. "Yes. We had a book at home that said that."

"The way I figure it, we share the same great-great-grandfather, you and me," Jimmy said. He scrunched up his nose. "I think." He looked at the whiskey bottle and shuddered. "Anyhow, Momma's family on her daddy's side was called Hammond. It was Momma's maiden name. I grew up in Butler County until I was fourteen, in the same house Uncle Edward did. He was a war hero, they say, a real gallant soldier too. Grandpa met Uncle Edward a bunch of times when he was a kid, back when Uncle Edward would visit from South America—or I guess now it was Cuba. Grandpa never knew what happened to him after that."

Emilio sat on the stool as if stapled there. He looked closely at Fred. The haunting familiarity intensified by the second. He thought back to when he'd arrived in Guatemala, when Angel had prodded him to join the paratroopers. The subsequent episode he'd experienced in the bathroom had been intense, but, unlike all the other times, it had been mysteriously short-circuited by the irresistible pull he'd felt to join the paratrooper unit. And now here he was, the very next day, sitting before the only blood link to his father that he knew of.

"Lord have mercy," Jimmy said. "I thought I'd never see a Hammond again." He stood and stared out the window. "Now, I can't tell you my real name because of security regulations—but you know damn well it ain't 'Fred,' although you're gonna have to call me that for the time being. Hammond is Momma's family name, and I guess that's OK for you to know. Still, I don't think anyone else around here should know about this coincidence."

Emilio stood up unsteadily. "Yes, sir." He had a million questions, but they'd have to wait. He saluted and left.

* * *

Emilio's training was intense from the first day at the camp. Physical conditioning, comprehensive weapons training, maneuvers, and simulated jumps filled the rapidly passing weeks. He'd never worked so hard in his life. He was intrigued and fascinated by the new muscle that began bursting out from his formerly gentle frame. His stomach hardened like a tree trunk. He slept like an infant at night and was infused with irrepressible energy every dawn.

One day in early March, his unit was given the late afternoon off to unwind and relax. Emilio still had plenty of energy to burn off, so he went for a run along one of the dirt paths running through the surrounding area. He increased his speed incrementally as he ran, and after several minutes reached his target pace. He came to a fork and went left, uncertain of where it led. Several hundred yards later, it cut into a stretch of dense, dark jungle. Thick vegetation surrounded him on both sides, a canopy of tangled branches and vines covering him from above. The path, rockier now, became gradually steeper as he ran. He pushed his legs harder into the ascending gradient, welcoming the strain on his muscles. After a mile or so, the trail turned to the right and came out into a clearing.

He stopped abruptly and glanced about him. He stood atop a low hill, looking west toward the red setting sun. A small valley carpeted by wildflowers—a variety of flower he hadn't seen until now–sloped downward from where he stood. A soft, warm wind ruffled his hair. There wasn't another soul in sight. He took slow, deep breaths, conscious of the air moving in and out of his lungs, the oxygen nourishing all his muscles and organs. Using his shirt, he wiped the sweat from his eyes and forehead, but left the rest on his face, finding the sensation pleasing. He walked over to a fallen tree and sat on its trunk, absorbing the resplendent landscape through all his senses. He noticed that even the trees and shrubs looked different here.

In this state of isolation, his heart rate slowing, the wind rushing over him, he became reflective. He thought about Roberto and wondered how he was. He remembered the last time he saw him, back at the air base, and how he'd told him that he was his brother. He had said it with such conviction in his voice. God, he missed him. He couldn't remember the last time they'd been away from each other for so long. Then he recalled his "episode" in the bathroom just before that. He hated when that happened, when that dark, mysterious force emerged from deep within him, without warning, and took possession of his mind; when those poisonous feelings of guilt, shame, and self-loathing would slither from inside to strangle him.

Emilio stared at a bird flying overhead for a few moments. He then turned his eyes back to the landscape and the sunset before him. He had never really made an effort to understand why he had those episodes; he had always just endured them and hoped that he'd outgrow them or that they'd simply go away by themselves one day. But they never did. Now, in the tranquility of his surroundings, he asked himself, for the first time ever, where those tormenting feelings of guilt associated with his father truly came from. "Do I really believe that my father, from wherever he is, considers me a disappointment because of my grades and my behavior?" Deep down, he instinctively knew that the answer was no. At some level, he now realized, he had always known that that wasn't the case. His father hadn't been the type of parent to judge his child so harshly or to express such a level of disapproval over relatively trivial matters. What was it then? Where did those feelings come from?

Taking a deep breath, he focused his attention on recalling all of the emotions that passed through him during his episodes. Then, he consciously stepped outside himself and observed the emotions closely; he accepted them as real and made no effort to deny their existence. After several minutes of complete stillness, his eyes fixed unwaveringly on the hill sloping down before him, his attention turned completely inward, a powerful awareness overtook him. All at once, he felt intricately connected to everything in his surroundings. The flowers, the trees, the vines, the dirt, the rocks, and himself–not merely his body, but the universe of spirit that dwelt within his every cell–all blended into a single, living entity. It was the most honest moment he'd ever experienced.

And, in this state of mind, the true cause of his ten-year torment unfolded itself before him.

He saw, with absolute clarity, that the guilt he carried had nothing at all to do with what he imagined his father thought about his grades or his underachievement or how he measured up against his peers; rather, it was that he, Emilio, believed, somewhere deep in his heart, that *he* had somehow been the cause of his father's death. As irrational and disturbing as it seemed to him, he now saw that it was this deeply buried, unconscious thought that had been haunting him for over a decade.

He sat in complete silence with this new-found knowledge. After a little while, he shook his head and asked himself, "How could I have ever believed such a thing? My God, I was just a kid when he died." He thought about those things to which he had previously attributed his dark feelings, and wondered, "How could I have ever believed that my father, the gentlest and most loving person I've ever known, would so brutally torture me from beyond the grave?" In silence, he asked his father to forgive him. Then he put his hands on his knees and sat up straight. He remained still, as if waiting for something to guide him.

Finally, he stood up, looked across the small valley, and planted his feet firmly on the ground. He took a deep breath and sensed a powerful wave of energy emanate through him from the earth, entering first through his feet, and then rumbling through his legs, his torso, his arms and hands, his throat and head. On an impulse, he stretched up his arms, palms facing skyward, and took another long, deep breath. It seemed as though the energy was now pouring forth from everything around him, flushing the poison from his spirit. His senses sharpened like a razor's edge. A chorus of birds singing in the trees filled his ears; the wind cascaded across his face; the smell of leaves and earth filled his nostrils. His body shaking with rapture, he felt as if he was holding the sun in his outstretched hands.

He lowered his arms, closed his eyes, and took in another deep breath. He felt a powerful sense of relief and a rush of energy flow through his abdomen, as if a path there, formerly obstructed, had been suddenly cleared.

He exhaled, opened his eyes, and looked at the wild-flowers springing up from the hillside before him. He bent down and picked a few with shaking hands. He beheld them carefully. They had come into the world not unlike him, he thought, starting out as an idea, as invisible energy, and then emerging into physical form in absolute perfection. And as they grew and lived out their physical existence, these exquisite creations of nature did so only in the truth of the present moment, brilliantly fulfilling their divine purpose in creation. How much even the greatest minds could learn from a simple wildflower.

Emilio jogged back the way he had come. He felt stronger, more awake, and more alive than at any time in his life.

* * *

Emilio and Jimmy Strickland (Emilio still knew him as "Fred") got the opportunity to talk alone only in brief snippets. The days at the training camp were so busy, and their need to keep their connection a secret so great, that they rarely had a chance to be together alone for more than a few minutes at a time. "Psst, cousin," Jimmy would say to Emilio at night sometimes when he walked past his quarters, "c'mon in for a quick nip." Jimmy would pour the whiskey and they'd take a shot together. He'd compliment Emilio on his development as a paratrooper and inquire about the other aspects of his training. Even though Emilio hardly knew "Fred," he felt a connection with the American that he'd never felt with anyone before, knowing his father's blood coursed through Fred's veins.

One afternoon at the end of March, Jimmy told Emilio to come by his quarters in the evening. By this time, the units from Trax that had come down to *Garrapatenango* earlier in the month for several days of training had gone back to their mountain camp. Everyone knew that D-Day was around the corner. When Emilio got to Jimmy's quarters at around eight o'clock that night, he found him and Willie lounging outside on a couple of old lawn chairs around a roaring campfire. Jimmy was strumming his guitar and humming. He pointed at an empty chair with his chin for Emilio to sit. Emilio glanced at Willie, and then back at Jimmy. "Don't worry, Sam's my brother," Jimmy told him. "He knows about you being my cousin and all."

Emilio brushed some dirt from the empty chair and sat down.

Jimmy stopped playing, laid the guitar across his thighs, and stretched out his legs. "My goodness, cousin, we finally get a chance to sit down together. So, listen, tell me about your Daddy. I need to know what the Hammonds in Cuba are like."

Emilio stared into the fire. "He died when I was ten."

Jimmy leaned forward and started poking the fire. "Well, I bet you miss him a whole lot."

Emilio shrugged his shoulders. "It was a long time ago."

"You don't ever talk about it, do you?"

"Not really," Emilio said. He lit a cigarette and melted into his chair. "Like I said, it was a long time ago."

Jimmy poured Emilio and Willie each a shot of whiskey. They drank them. "But you do think about him a lot, I bet."

Emilio had never spoken to anyone about his father, not even his mother. But this American was a blood relative of his father, the only blood relative he'd ever met, and for reasons he would have been at a loss to explain, that made a difference to him. He furrowed his brow and sighed. "Yeah, I think about him all the time; and, yeah, I miss him a lot. We were very close." He felt a flutter in his chest. He took his asthma inhaler out of his pocket, looked away, and took a puff.

Jimmy leaned over to refill his glass. "I know what you mean. My momma died when I was thirteen. God, I loved her. My life was never the same after that." He put the bottle down and reached inside his pocket. He pulled out a couple of photographs and held one of them out for Emilio to see. "Look, here's a picture of Momma, Edward Billings Hammond's grand-niece, in Georgiana, Alabama."

Emilio took the picture and scrutinized it. He smiled and looked up at Jimmy. "She's got the same eyes as my father."

Jimmy nodded. "And you. First time I saw you I knew you was one of ours." He showed him the other picture. "Now, look here, this is a picture of Grandpa. He was your Great-Granddaddy Hammond's nephew and your grandpa's first cousin." The eyes weren't as clearly visible, but the resemblance to his father was uncanny.

"Was this in Georgiana too?"

"Yes, sir. Georgiana, Alabama. Butler County. Home."

"Home," Willie echoed.

"Tell me about it," Emilio said. He flung his cigarette into the fire.

Jimmy leaned back in his chair. His gaze shifted to the heavens. Above them, the sky was a starlit dome. The fire snapped on a large branch. "Well, any place a man considers home is always going to be beautiful to him, I guess. But I'll tell you, Butler County is just about the prettiest place you'll ever see. That house in the picture? It was built by the Hammond family when they came to Alabama. Grandpa's father and Uncle Edward were raised in that house. When Uncle Edward came home from the war he stayed around for a while, and then went to Cuba, although Grandpa always said it was South America. I guess Grandpa could've used a geography lesson." They all laughed.

"Anyhow, Grandpa told me that when he was a kid, Uncle Edward came back every few years to visit. He said Uncle Edward and his daddy–the two brothers–would spend hours on the porch singing and playing music, and a lot of times Grandpa would play with them. He said Uncle Edward was always interested in the new songs; he even knew some of them already from some of the other Americans who'd settled in South America after he did–sorry, I mean Cuba."

Jimmy sighed and shut his eyes. "But, man, Butler County was just beautiful. Lots of cotton fields all around, the land so fertile that folks grew watermelon, cantaloupe, corn, all sorts of things. The whole area was filled with woods and streams and deer, and most of all good folk; lots of them poor, but good folk. And it just smelled good. You know what I mean? When the spring would come and all the dogwood trees would be in full bloom . . . Lord have mercy." Jimmy opened his eyes and looked up into the sky again. "And the magnolia trees, my goodness, some of them had leaves a foot long, and when they'd blossom in the spring with their huge white flowers; well, you just have to see it to believe it."

He turned his head toward Emilio. "You know who was from Georgiana?"

Emilio folded his arms. "Who?"

"Hank Williams."

Willie rolled his eyes.

"Who's that?" Emilio asked.

Willie jumped in. "Some white boy taught to sing and play guitar by a black virtuoso named Rufus 'Tee Tot' Payne, that's who."

"Now don't get started Sam," Jimmy said, giving Willie a sideways glare. He turned back to Emilio. "Hank Williams was the best goddamned musical genius in America. He died some years back. I can't believe you ain't never heard of him, cousin. Boy we've just got to bring you back to Alabama."

Emilio looked into the fire again and frowned. "My father and I were going to visit and track down our relatives there, but he died before we could ever go."

Jimmy laughed roughly. "Well, I'll bet you never thought you'd track down an Alabama relative in the Guatemalan wilderness, now did you?"

Emilio chuckled and shook his head. "No, I could have never imagined that." Then he thought for a moment. "But somehow, I'm not surprised."

Jimmy smiled and poked the fire again. "There any other Hammonds in Cuba?"

"Not that I know of; I don't remember my father ever mentioning any extended family. I grew up with family on my mother's side."

The three of them looked silently into the crackling fire for a few minutes. The wind blew, sending some sparks aloft.

"Maybe you're right, maybe it ain't a coincidence," Jimmy said suddenly. "Maybe we were meant to meet this way. Life has a funny way of working out. At least that's what Grandpa used to say."

Emilio nodded and hoisted up his empty glass. "Here's to Grandpa!"

"I'll drink to that!" Jimmy said. He poured them each another shot. The three of them downed it immediately.

Jimmy picked up his guitar again. "You ever hear any of the old songs your great-granddaddy sang?" Jimmy asked.

"No, not really," Emilio answered.

"Well, I'll play you a real old hymn from way, way back. Grandpa taught it to me. I don't hardly sing it no more, though, too damn sad." He played a few soft chords and started humming. Willie started tapping his foot and bobbing his head. Jimmy sang in a slow, mournful cry.

"There are loved ones in the glory,
Whose dear forms you often miss;
When you close your earthly story,
Will you join them in their bliss?"

Emilio knitted his brows, the tune sounding vaguely familiar. His eyes burst open when Jimmy and Willie started singing the chorus.

"Will the circle be unbroken
By and by, by and by?
In a better home awaiting
In the sky, in the sky?"

Emilio had started mouthing the chorus with them, the words coming back to him in a rush. It was the "by and by" song his father used to sing to him, the same one his father sang the night he'd met his mother. Jimmy looked directly into his eyes and said nothing. He just smiled at him and sang.

"In the joyous days of childhood,
Oft they told of wondrous love,
Pointed to the dying Savior;
Now they dwell with him above."

Emilio took the cue and sang the chorus with them.

"Will the circle be unbroken
By and by, by and by?
In a better home awaiting
In the sky, in the sky?"

Jimmy winked at Emilio and gave him a slight nod. Emilio felt a jolt.

"You can picture happy gatherings
'Round the fireside long ago,
And you think of tearful partings,
When they left you here below."

Emilio felt as if he was hovering above the fire now. He sang:

"Will the circle be unbroken,
By and by, by and by?

In a better home awaiting
In the sky, in the sky?"

Emilio closed his eyes and listened to Jimmy sing the final verse. He felt as though his father was there singing along with him.

"One by one their seats were emptied,
One by one they went away;
Here the circle has been broken—
Will it be complete one day?"

The three of them sang the chorus one last time, more slowly than before:

"Will the circle be unbroken
By and by, by and by?
In a better home awaiting
In the sky, in the sky?"

Jimmy stopped playing and stared at Emilio. His voice sounded as though it came from a distant realm. "You see, Mr. Hammond, it's no coincidence that we met."

Emilio stared back at him, his mouth slightly ajar, his eyes glistening.

Jimmy started to pluck some notes. He kept his eyes on Emilio. "Now, my grandpa was a very religious man. He always told me that life was nothin' but a series of broken circles. We love certain people, or we love where we're from, and we become attached to them in a circle that binds us.

They define who we are on this earth, down to our very core. But, inevitably, we lose them–sometimes slowly, sometimes all at once, by death, by separation, by whatever–and the circle breaks; it *always* breaks, because all earthly things, without exception, pass: every object, every person, every place, and every relationship that make us who we are. And when they do, we're filled with longing, with that feeling that we just want to go to them, like we just want to go *home.*"

Then Jimmy smiled.

"But those things, you see, also have an existence that isn't physical, but spiritual, and that part of them never dies. It lives in our hearts. The beautiful thing is that when *we* pass into the next life, those broken circles close for us again, only this time it's permanent; and, at some point–I think, at least– we see that they were really unbroken the whole time."

Jimmy stopped plucking and looked at Emilio deeply. The reflection from the fire danced in his eyes. He touched Emilio's arm. "You're fightin' for your country, son, for your people's freedom, and that's the greatest single thing a man can do in this life." He nodded once. "Make no mistake about it: your daddy's right proud of you, *right* proud of you."

Emilio's mouth curled downward into a little boy's frown. He wiped the sides of his eyes and nodded.

HAVANA, CUBA
Miramar Section
April 15, 1961

Raquel lay in bed, her heart pounding, eyes wide open. She hadn't slept a full night since Goyo had left Cuba back in December, almost four months ago now. Fear, hopelessness, and disaster fantasies of every variety seized her mind as though they were living, malevolent spirits. It was worse–far worse–when she closed her eyes. She waited desperately for the dawn, for the first rays of sunlight to pierce the dark sky, knowing that only then would her head clear and her confidence return. She gently ran her hand across the empty space in the bed next to her and wanted to cry. She turned suddenly, grabbed her Rosary off the bed post, and made the Sign of the Cross.

Emptiness and longing gripped at her heart like iron claws as she began the opening prayers. She stopped, took a deep breath, and started over again, this time trying to focus on the prayers more intensely. Her distress, however, was like a concrete wall, resisting the power of even the most fervent supplications. She stared at the Rosary for a few moments and decided to stop. She hung it back on the bed post and sat upright. She looked out the window: it was still dark. She lay down again. "What if the children never see their father again? What if they're already orphans and just don't know it yet?" she wondered, the new thought joining the noxious stew in her heart.

After Goyo left home, she felt as though the family oxygen supply had been cut off. Goyito had hardly spoken, and on some days he seemed frightened for no reason. Her mother-in-law had given them her television set so he could watch the baseball games on it, but he had yet to turn it on. Ana Cristina had grown more irritable with each passing week and never talked about her day at school anymore. Both children had withdrawn into their own private worlds. For their own protection, she couldn't even be candid with them about the real reason Goyo had to leave Cuba. At first, she'd told them that he was taking some courses at a university in the United States. After his letter in January, she'd explained to them that, having finished the courses, he was now teaching children from poor families at the school in California he'd told her about. They weren't stupid, however. They'd been home when Paquito's thugs searched the house that day.

She ran her hand across her belly. She still hadn't told Goyo about her pregnancy in her letters, fearing that he might lose his characteristic common sense and do something rash, like trying to sneak back into Cuba. He'd probably get arrested, and possibly even executed, if he did. He would know about his new child in God's good time. She couldn't, however, hide the pregnancy from her adult relatives. She'd told them about it last week. The women didn't seem at all surprised. She didn't tell the children, though. They were under enough pressure and, so far, they seemed oblivious to her expanding belly.

She looked outside again and saw the first signs of daylight. She sat up and spun toward the floor to put her house slippers on. One of them had slid under the bed. She reached for it and felt one of the suitcases under there. Goyo had instructed her to be packed and ready in case of a military strike, and, if it came, to go immediately to his mother's relatives' home in their small town in the Camagüey interior. There, they'd be far away from the shoreline, the cities, and the mountains where the fighting would likely take place. She pushed the packed suitcase further under the bed.

She went into the kitchen and put the coffee on. She was slicing bread when a groggy Goyito came in. "Good morning, dear." She kissed his forehead. "You're up early today."

Goyito sat at the kitchen table and yawned. Mickey, the dog, wagged his tail and rubbed his nose against his leg. He scratched the dog's back.

"It's hard to believe we're half-way through April," Raquel said, trying to sound cheery. "School will be out before you know it and you'll have all summer to play."

Goyito yawned again. "When is Papi coming back?"

"Like I've told you, son, he's working with the fathers helping the poor children in California. He'll be home soon enough."

Goyito laid his arms on the kitchen table and rested his head on them. Silence engulfed the small kitchen.

Suddenly, a deafening explosion rang out in the distance. The walls of the little house shook to the foundation, rattling the glass in the windows. Goyito jumped up to his feet and gasped. He and Raquel looked at each other, their mouths and eyes frozen open. Moments later they heard another large explosion, and then a series of smaller ones. Air raid sirens began wailing. A large, low-flying airplane passed overhead. Raquel, regaining her senses, ran to Goyito and wrapped her arms around him. They heard the rat-tat-tat of machine gun fire and the reverberation from the anti-aircraft battery positioned down the shore from the house.

"What is that? What's happening?" Goyito cried. Mickey barked wildly and circled them protectively. Ana Cristina screamed hysterically in her bedroom. Aunt Teresa ran to her.

Raquel squeezed Goyito and whispered excitedly through heavy breaths, "It's coming from Campamento Columbia. It's started! It's started!" Then, releasing him, she grabbed his shoulders and looked squarely into his eyes. "Go get dressed, now! Tell your sister and your aunt that we're leaving right away! And stay away from the windows! Go!"

Raquel flew into the living room and turned Radio Swan, the exile radio station, on full volume. She didn't care who could hear it from outside now.

The day of liberation was at hand.

10

DAWN, APRIL 15, 1961
SKIES OVER THE CARIBBEAN SEA
(A short time earlier)

Bernie Cuervo recited a Hail Mary as he flew his B-26 bomber north over a darkened Caribbean Sea. He'd already been in the air for a few hours and was awaiting the early signs of daybreak. He inhaled deeply as the first rays of sunlight appeared on his right, the eastern horizon becoming slowly discernible. As he took in the majesty of the early sunrise, he felt his pulse quicken. He looked over at the three other Brigade B-26s, flying in formation next to him, and wondered if their pilots felt as he did. As they prepared to enter Cuban airspace, all four aircraft dropped their altitude until they were flying just above the sea's surface.

Their odyssey had begun ten days earlier when the Brigade Air Force was ordered to pull out of Retalhuleu in Guatemala and redeploy to the operation's staging area: an airfield outside a small coastal town in Nicaragua called Puerto Cabezas. The Americans had code-named the air base "Happy Valley." Then, just a couple of days ago, officials from Washington, D.C., arrived at Happy Valley. Bernie and the other B-26 bomber pilots were separated from the transport pilots and gathered inside a large tent surrounded by a barbed wire fence and armed American guards. "Security," they were told, "for the good of the mission."

"The invasion is a go," was the first thing one of the Americans who'd come from Washington announced to them, "and you guys are going to deliver the opening salvo." The Cuban pilots were almost lifted out of their seats. They settled down to listen. Sixteen Brigade B-26s were to depart Happy Valley during the predawn hours of April 15–that is, on D minus 2, two days before the main invasion–and attack three of Castro's airfields at first light: the Santiago de Cuba airport, the San Antonio de los Baños airfield, and the airfield at Campamento Columbia, a.k.a. Ciudad Libertad, Havana's main military base, and fly back to Nicaragua. Sixteen more B-26 attacks were to be launched at last light on the same day, making for a total of thirty-two sorties on D minus 2. Their objective: to destroy Castro's small air force while it was on the ground in order to guarantee complete air supremacy when the Brigade's ground forces landed in Cuba on D-Day, April 17.

"Excuse me, sir," Bernie interrupted the American, "wouldn't flying bombing raids two full days before the invasion give away the element of surprise? Wouldn't it warn Castro that the invasion was coming, giving him a chance to lock up the opposition that's supposed to rise up when the Brigade lands? Now, I'm not a career military man, I'm an airline pilot by profession, but–if you'll kindly excuse my insolence–wouldn't it make more sense to launch an all-out air attack at the same time the Brigade is landing, and order the underground to rise up simultaneously, thereby catching Castro totally by surprise on multiple fronts?" The American gave him an impudent grin and explained that the decision makers in Washington had good reasons for wanting the first aerial attacks to be launched two days prior to the landings. "We have a lot of experience in these matters," he said, and turned around to set up a map.

The man from Washington continued outlining the mission. "The D minus 2 strikes will be followed by a second wave of strikes the following day, D minus 1, the day before the invasion. These will again involve sixteen B-26s, attacking both at first and last light, for a total of thirty-two sorties that day as well. And finally," the American said, pointing his finger skyward, "the last blow: an aerial attack on Castro's airfields at first light on D-Day, around six hours after the ground units begin landing in Cuba."

Bernie did the math in his head. Thirty-two strikes on D minus 2, thirty-two strikes on D minus 1, and a strike on D-Day. "Not bad," he thought, his doubts surrendering to the sheer volume of the numbers.

The man from Washington was almost giddy when he explained the D-Day strategy. "Now, during the pre-dawn hours of April 17, just hours before your final D-Day sorties, the Brigade's amphibious units will land at three spots in the vicinity of the Bay of Pigs, which I'm sure all of you know is on Cuba's southern shore, in the area of the Zapata Swamp." He used his pointer to trace the bay, which ran a straight eighteen miles into the island from its southern shore like a giant, slightly bent finger puncturing a funnel shape into Cuba's underbelly. "The ground forces will land amphibiously and secure a forty-mile-long and approximately twenty-mile-deep beachhead. The center of operations will be the town of Girón." He placed the tip of his pointer on Girón, located on the coast, slightly east of the Bay of Pigs' ten-mile-wide mouth. "Now, there's an airstrip at Girón long enough to accommodate B-26s. Therefore, after the D-Day air strikes on Castro's airfields, you will commence air operations from Girón, joining the Brigade's land and sea units there. At this point, an entirely new mission begins for the B-26s."

The man from Washington cleared his throat and checked that he had everyone's undivided attention. "With Castro's airplanes destroyed and uncontested Brigade domination of the air, your main responsibility will now be to help seal off the beachhead from Castro's approaching ground forces. The Brigade ships anchored offshore will carry everything you need to operate from Girón–mechanics, spare parts, fuel, .50 caliber rounds, rockets, bombs, napalm, you name it–and an endless stream of incoming supply ships will replenish the equipment."

The American saw that he had the Cubans mesmerized. "Now, sealing off the beachhead from advancing enemy ground units will be a simple matter, since the only way for them to reach the beachhead would be to come down three narrow causeways, miles apart from each other, and each cutting across several miles of solid swamp. Paratrooper units will be dropped at strategic points along these roads at first light to set up fortified roadblocks and engage any arriving enemy troops. Units from the battalions landing amphibiously on shore will move up the roads to support them at these roadblocks." He outlined each road with his pointer. One road went north to south, ending at the bay's northern tip at a place called Playa Larga, code-named Red Beach. Two other roads, well to the southeast of Playa Larga, meandered roughly south and southwest in the direction of Girón and linked up a few miles north of the town at a place called San Blas. It continued on as a single road until it reached Girón. Girón was code-named Blue Beach. An area east of Girón, several miles down the coastal road, was code-named Green Beach.

"We call these narrow stretches of road cutting across the swamp the 'shooting galleries,' since enemy forces cannot seek refuge from your aerial attacks off road, therefore making them the proverbial 'sitting ducks.' Once you guys start hitting the enemy there, the roads will become clogged by heaps of destroyed tanks and trucks; they will also be cratered by bombs, rendering them totally impassable. Under those circumstances, the roadblocks established by the ground and paratrooper units, with your constant support from the air, could resist any advances by enemy troops *ad infinitum.* Now, once the roads and thus the beachhead are secured, you will begin to concentrate on enemy troops amassed along Cuba's exposed highways en route to the battle zone, on bridge crossings, and then on military and economic targets farther away."

The Cuban airmen started to stir excitedly in their seats again. The man from Washington continued. "Now, here's the most important part. After the beachhead is sealed off, a pro-democracy, provisional Cuban government-in-arms will be flown into Girón and receive diplomatic recognition from nations across the Americas as well as U.S. assistance. The provisional government will be made up of members from the Cuban Revolutionary Council; some of you might remember the group as the *Frente,* the group's former name. In any event, with an impenetrable beachhead on Cuba's southern shore under the control of an internationally recognized, U.S. backed, pro-democracy government–'free Cuban territory,' if you will–the Castro brothers will be on the run and things will begin to happen, such as a significant increase in the size of the Brigade from volunteers in Cuba and abroad, as well as the underground uprisings some of you have mentioned. The regime will undoubtedly crumble under these conditions." The man from Washington threw Bernie a smug look. He refocused his eyes on the table before him. "Of course, all of this will succeed, *unless . . .*"

The Cubans stopped breathing.

"Unless," the American repeated, looking up, "Castro is left with even one airplane. Castro has a few B-26s himself and, of far greater concern, a handful of faster Sea Furies and T-33s. If even one of them is left operational, if even one of them can get into the air after the invasion commences, the whole operation could quickly become a fiasco. The faster Sea Furies and T-33s can easily down our B-26 bombers and prevent them from even landing at the Girón airstrip, making your mission to seal off the beachhead all but impossible. Even worse, they could target our supply ships anchored offshore, sinking them or forcing them to flee. In this worst case scenario, the Brigade, even if it manages to land, would be left on the beaches alone–no supplies, no air support, and facing an enemy of tens of thousands marching unimpeded into the beachhead. In short, men, everything hinges on the Brigade air force's success at destroying Castro's planes *on the ground before the invasion.*"

On the evening of April 14, the day before the first air strikes, the American who'd come from Washington gathered the Cuban pilots and informed them of some important changes. First, the second strike on April 15, D minus 2, the one scheduled for last light, had been canceled. The strike at first light on D minus 2, though, was still a "go." But, the American pointed out, the number of planes to be used for that strike was reduced to around half of what he had told them before.

"Just a minute, sir," Bernie said incredulously, "why are we reducing the number of sorties on D minus 2? You told us that the entire mission 'hinged' on the success of the pre-invasion strikes. Reducing them just seems stupid, doesn't it?"

"Well," the American said, perturbed by Bernie's brazenness, "it was believed that in order to ensure maximum military *and* political success, one reduced strike on D minus 2 was more advisable."

Someone mumbled in Spanish, "Not even *he* believes that. Washington's just trying to conceal its hand in this all of a sudden."

"I beg your pardon, sir," Bernie said in a sardonic tone, "are we also reducing the number of strikes planned for D minus 1? After all, the Brigade will land the following day."

The American paused for a moment and swallowed. "As a matter of fact, the sorties on D minus 1 have been canceled entirely."

A shock wave reverberated across the room.

"So, sir," Bernie said sharply over the other voices, "we are going from *sixty-four* planned strikes over the two days before the landings, down to, what, eight or nine? And . . . and . . .," Bernie shook his head searching for the words, ". . . and we're going to give Castro a full forty-eight hours of peace to recuperate after that first watered down attack? Excuse me, but that's insanity. Are you sure the people in Washington want us to win?"

The American from Washington held his hands up for quiet, his tone suddenly collegial. "Gentlemen, gentlemen, remember that you will *still* launch an all-out attack on Castro's airfields at first light on D-Day, the day of the invasion, and that's by far the most important strike. The Brigade's B-26s, no matter what, will be operating from Girón on D-Day, sealing off and protecting the beach-head and enjoying complete air supremacy." Everyone seemed reassured by the American's words. They spent the rest of the day studying maps and aerial photographs of their targets.

Bernie was part of the group slated to attack Campamento Columbia (also known as Ciudad Libertad), near the Miramar neighborhood where Goyo León lived, on the morning of April 15, D minus 2. He was in high spirits that evening when he went out and watched the ground crew preparing his B-26. The airplane was being loaded with 500 pound bombs, fragmentation bombs, rockets, and thousands of rounds for its .50 caliber machine guns. It was painted with the insignia of the Cuban air force, a little deception they worked in to confuse the enemy.

Bernie napped until around midnight. He woke up and sought out the chaplain. He roused the clergyman from his sleep. "Father, please hear my confession, grant me absolution, and give me your blessing." Just before 2:30 a.m., he and his navigator boarded their B-26 bomber. After strapping himself into the cockpit, Bernie looked up and saw that the runway was lined with over a hundred personnel–Cubans and Americans–who had gathered to witness this historic moment. He taxied his airplane into the line of B-26s in take-off position on the main runway. One by one they took off into the dark sky toward Cuba, their blue exhaust flames–the only light visible on the aircraft–were torches of freedom to

Bernie's eyes. A few minutes later he was in the air setting a course for Havana.

And now, at the crack of dawn on April 15, D minus 2, as Bernie approached his homeland low from the south, he blinked his eyes to clear them of the salty tears that had started to fill them. In a few minutes' time, he would experience the first–and perhaps the only–combat mission of his life. The Cuban coastline came into view before him, the glorious event heralded by the rising sun. He began humming the National Anthem. He and his navigator shared a nervous chuckle.

Flying across Cuba's southern shore, Bernie felt his jaw tighten, his mind now keenly focused on the mission. It seemed as though only a few minutes had passed before he realized that they'd flown across the narrow width of the island. He saw the outlines of Havana's buildings quickly take shape before him. He was soon flying over the capital's outlying farms and towns, and then over the sleeping city itself. Campamento Columbia came into view. He checked the time: it was just before 6:00 a.m. Within seconds, he was flying fifty feet over Columbia's structures. He saw the camp's airfield laid out before him. Castro's aircraft were all lined up like little metal toys in a display window. His finger caressed the release button. He counted, "five, four, three, two, one . . ."

The plane jerked up violently the moment he released the 500-pound bomb. A second later, he heard the deafening explosion below and felt a powerful tremor reverberate through the cockpit. He looked back and saw a colossal black cloud. The adrenaline surging through him like a wild river, he let out a savage roar, "Wooooooooooo!" His navigator was also cheering.

Bernie shook with euphoria as he soared away from the base, all the pent up tensions from the past two years released in the energy of that single bomb. He circled over some of the rooftops in the surrounding area at low altitude, radioed the other B-26s, and circled back over the base. As he came over the airfield for a second pass, he heard machine guns firing at him from below. He came straight in on the enemy position and sprayed it with his .50 calibers. He dropped more bombs and fired his rockets before flying out of range again. He suddenly heard anti-aircraft guns booming; he looked around and saw the shells exploding all over the sky in popcorn-like balls of black smoke. He turned back for another pass. The skies above the base were now choked with black smoke. His visibility reduced, he dropped the remainder of his payload.

Bernie headed north, out over the safety of the sea. He saw that his B-26 had been hit by machine gun fire, but he and the navigator figured they could make it back to Nicaragua in one piece. One of the other B-26s pulled alongside him. Bernie radioed the pilot and asked him about the other two planes. The pilot told him that he saw one heading east; smoke was pouring out of one of its engines. It didn't look good. The other one radioed that he was going to make an emergency landing in Key West. Bernie set a course for Nicaragua.

After a few hours in the air–the fastest hours of his life– Bernie and the other pilot landed their B-26s safely at Happy Valley. An American jeep went out to the tarmac to collect them and the navigators for debriefing; but before they could be whisked away, the Cuban ground crews, violating all protocol and in direct violation of orders, swarmed the returning airmen, cheering them, welcoming them back with an emotionally-charged heroes' welcome. They had delivered the first blow against the enemy.

The liberation of Cuba was officially underway.

11

CARIBBEAN SEA
ABOARD THE FREIGHTER *HOUSTON*
Daytime, April 15, 1961

The men aboard the cargo ship *Houston,* carrying Brigade 2506's Second and Fifth Battalions to Cuba, cheered when they heard the news of that morning's air strikes. Goyo, lounging atop an equipment crate on the *Houston's* deck, bolted straight up. He didn't share in the exuberance. His family was only a short distance from one of the targets. He wrung his hands nervously, remembering the anti-aircraft guns positioned just down the shore from his house. A chill settled on his shoulders and behind his ears. He shook his head, trying to dispel his anxiety. "Don't worry," he told himself calmly, "Raquel is probably en route to my relatives in Camagüey by now." He suddenly felt a spasm in his stomach. His right hand flew to his forehead "Damn it," he thought, "the government probably declared martial law after the air raids and shut down the Central Highway! God curse me! Why didn't I anticipate that?" He buried his elbows into his thighs and covered his eyes with the heels of his palms, feeling all of a sudden as though he was imprisoned on the ship. He looked up for a second and scanned the deck. His eyes fell on one of the lifeboats. Stealing one of them and rowing home flashed across his mind.

He stood up and walked over to the edge of the ship. He stared across the expanse of open sea. The other Brigade ships were nowhere in sight. They had each taken a different course and would rendezvous off the Cuban coast somewhere near the landing zone–wherever the hell that was–just before the invasion. They weren't entirely alone, however. Each Brigade ship was being shadowed by an American naval vessel, like cubs protected by their mothers. Just last night the men aboard the *Houston* watched in speechless wonder as an American submarine circled around them. Goyo shaded his eyes and searched for the silhouette of the American destroyer he'd seen shadowing them earlier that morning. He couldn't see it.

As he looked to the horizon, Goyo pushed back against the screeching panic inside him. He closed his eyes and breathed slowly and deeply, letting himself feel the full emotional force of his disquietude. He felt the strain most acutely in his chest and stomach, he noticed. He focused on it until it subsided. Everything was going to be fine, he told himself. He was here for them, for his family. The Brigade would carry the day. He would be with his wife and children again soon, in their little house on the shoreline, living in a free Cuba. He opened his eyes and gazed toward the horizon again. He spotted the American destroyer in the distance. He smiled and lay back down on the crate. He covered his eyes with his right forearm to block out the sun and tried to sleep.

His thoughts wandered back to the weeks he'd spent in training. When he'd first arrived at Base Trax, things there were a political mess. A large group of trainees had declared themselves on strike and refused to continue training, claiming that some of the Cuban military commanders at the camps were conspiring with the CIA to launch a *coup d'état* against the civilian leaders of the *Frente* in Miami. They were there, the striking trainees had said, to fight for constitutional government, not to install another military regime in Havana. *Frente* leaders were flown in from Miami to reassure the men–especially the idealistic university students–that the camp commanders enjoyed their complete support and that they could continue training without fear of a *coup*. The atmosphere cooled off and soon hundreds of fresh recruits–a large number of them family men who'd left wives and children behind, and in some cases arriving as father-and-son pairs–began pouring into the Guatemala camp, injecting a much needed boost to morale. Manuel Artime being permanently stationed with the Brigade further helped abate suspicions and cool tempers.

Goyo ran his left hand over his flat, hard stomach. His training had brought out new, lean muscle; the thin layer of fat that had started to encase his body over the last few years had all but disappeared. He smiled inwardly, thinking about how he could now scale steep hillsides, advance for miles through dense vegetation with a heavy pack, and shoot an M-1 rifle with deadly accuracy. Who would've ever thought? A soft, dry breeze blew. He felt a light sleep coming over him.

Suspended between consciousness and sleep, his mind drifted to the final weeks of training. Normally, that many Cubans in a political setting would have produced nothing but perpetual infighting, power struggles, and schism; and, at the beginning, it was like that. But, almost as soon as the political crisis ended and the flood of new recruits joined the camps, everyone had, almost miraculously, fused into a single man pursuing the common goal of freeing Cuba. After crossing that threshold, the men no longer identified themselves primarily as being from one group or another from the Castro opposition; no longer did they identify themselves as anti-Batista university students, former military cadets, or former Castro rebels; nor were they country club aristocrats, private school *bitongos*, taxi drivers, or *güajiros*. They had become *Brigadistas*—men of the 2506, the spearhead of Cuba's freedom. Perhaps they would all start fighting again after the liberation, Goyo thought, but they would undoubtedly stand as a single man during the upcoming battle.

A large cloud blocked the sun. Goyo welcomed the cool break. Of course the energy at the camps had affected Roberto even more deeply, he thought. In his own grave, hyper-nationalistic, melodramatic style, Roberto had declared, "Never before in the history of the Cuban nation has such a diverse group of men pulled together for the achievement of a single patriotic goal. Cuba will, no doubt, be reborn as a beacon of justice, democracy, and freedom in America." Roberto's physical prowess, his fluency in English, and his proficient marksmanship (he had learned to handle firearms in Switzerland) had earned him an appointment as a squad leader in the Second Battalion. The new responsibility had brought out latent leadership qualities in him; Goyo quietly believed that being away from Emilio had helped that happen. Pedro Vila, whom Goyo made certain would be in their squad, had come to idolize Roberto. Goyo thought that perhaps freeing the *patria* from an oppressor was a role for which Roberto had been preparing his entire life. Still, it bothered him a little that he had to defer to his little cousin's authority; still, in the end, he was proud of him.

Goyo remembered that day in late March when the battalion returned to Base Trax after a period of training at *Garrapatenango,* joining the other units who were stationed there. It was right after that when large shipments of weapons began arriving at Trax, and the Brigade commanders began conferring more frequently with the Americans in private. The invasion was near, there was no doubt. Everyone in the camp was buzzing, dying to get to Cuba already, and speculating as to where they would land.

"My money's on Trinidad!"

"Trinidad? You're crazy! Everyone knows that the key to conquering Cuba is in the east, in Oriente–just ask Teddy Roosevelt or Fidel Castro, they'll tell you."

"Teddy Roosevelt? He's still alive?"

"Are you stupid, or what?"

"No, no. The key is to land at the narrowest point in Camagüey, and cut the island in half."

"I don't give a damn where they land us, I just want to go! I can't stand this waiting any longer!"

On the afternoon of April 9, as Goyo was resting in his quarters during a break from training, he heard a commotion outside. For a moment, he thought there was a *coup* in progress. He went out to see what was going on. He looked closely at the men's faces as they moved quickly past him. Their faces registered elation. Roberto suddenly crossed a few yards in front of him. He stopped and flashed Goyo a satisfied grin. The sun, low in the sky behind him, made Roberto's Arab features seem more pronounced. "What is it,

Roberto? What's going on?" Goyo asked. "You look like Saladin entering Jerusalem."

"Cousin, we've just been given the mobilization order. We leave for the staging area tomorrow."

Goyo's breath stopped.

That night, the Brigade priests celebrated Mass for the men in the rustic chapel at the camp. The next day, April 10, Brigade commander José "Pepe" Pérez San Román assembled the men on the parade ground. In solemn, inspiring tones, he announced that they would be moving out that very day. He admonished them, "Always protect the civilians and treat prisoners with respect and decency." Then he paused and shouted, "On to victory! Freedom is our goal, Cuba is our cause!" The Brigade responded with a righteous, bellicose roar. As Goyo cheered along with the others, it struck him how young the Brigade's top leaders were. San Román was only thirty-one, his second-in-command, Erneido Oliva, as well as Manuel Artime, hadn't even reached the age of thirty. Hugo Sueiro, his own battalion commander, was only twenty-one.

That afternoon, the Brigade said goodbye to Base Trax and boarded a fleet of trucks bound for the Retalhuleu air base below. Despite inclement weather, a celebratory atmosphere prevailed. Under pouring rain, the men issued a litany of *vivas*, and sang the national anthem over and over. After all this time, after all their sacrifice, they were almost home. Local peasants, Indians mostly, lined the dirt road under the torrential downpour to wave goodbye. Goyo wondered briefly how many Castro spies there were mixed in among the innocuous looking natives.

Over the next two days, the men were ferried on C-54 transport planes from Retalhuleu to the Happy Valley air base outside Puerto Cabezas, Nicaragua. The paratroopers remained at the air base, while the rest of the troops traveled by train and truck to their ships at the waterfront. As they passed through the town of Puerto Cabezas, Roberto's squad caught a glimpse of the obscure coastal town. It was only a mile long and a few blocks wide; its unpaved main street was flanked on either side with wooden plank sidewalks. Some of the storefronts had hitching posts. Roberto looked around, saying, "I think we're going to see John Wayne pop out of a saloon any minute now." Everyone laughed.

The journey ended at a long commercial pier, where they at last saw the vessels that would deliver them to Cuba: rusty cargo ships embarrassingly unfit for war. Goyo's heart sank. Then he took a deep breath and reminded himself not to worry, that the Americans were in charge of this operation, and the Americans always win wars. Just before his mind extinguished its last scintilla of doubt, one of the older squad members, a former policeman and World War II veteran named David Ramirez, blurted out incredulously, "Those are the ships taking us to Cuba? My God, they don't even have protection. Look, no heavy guns! Are we going to war or shipping bananas?"

Roberto patted his shoulder and reassured him. "Don't worry, Ramirez. I'm sure this is part of the plan. They'll probably transfer us to better ships at sea."

Goyo peered dubiously at his cousin.

Roberto shrugged his shoulders. "That's what I heard someone say."

The squad boarded the *Houston* with the rest of the Second Battalion, the sheer excitement about departing for Cuba quickly overcoming whatever reservations the men had about the ships. Looking out over the port of Puerto Cabezas, they watched as P-51 fighter jets and B-26 bombers zoomed across the sky. They saw the other battalions boarding different ships. Besides the *Houston*, which carried the Second and Fifth Battalions, were the cargo ships *Rio Escondido, Atlántico,* and *Caribe,* which carried the other ground units. The two LCIs (landing craft, infantry), the *Blagar* and the *Barbara J*, would act as command ships. The *Blagar* carried the headquarters staff and both LCIs carried Brigade frogmen; rumor had it that CIA personnel were aboard both vessels. Goyo waved at a rubber raft zipping by the *Houston* carrying some of the frogmen, having recognized a young man he knew from Camagüey.

Captivated by the spectacle, Roberto turned toward Goyo and grabbed his arm. He had tears in his eyes, "Cousin, can you believe all this?"

Goyo smiled at him and nodded, reminding himself that Roberto, despite his current position as a squad leader, was still an impressionable youth.

The ships were loaded to the brim with war materiel. The holds, as well as the decks, were packed with explosives, ammunition crates, food, medicine, and large drums of aviation fuel. The men had to find places on deck to sit or lie down as best they could. Some lay on the equipment bundles, others sat right on the deck or in one of the life boats; the braver ones sat on top of the fuel drums. Smoking was strictly prohibited, lest a match blow them all to hell. Many smoked anyhow.

In the late afternoon of April 14, after three days in conference with the Americans, the Brigade commanders were seen aboard small outboard motor boats speeding toward the invasion ships. The men of the 2506 leaned over the railings and cheered them like a home crowd welcoming their team back on opening day. A few hours later the ships pulled out of port, each in a different direction, the plan to meet again in a few days' time at a rendezvous point off the Cuban coast.

And now, here they were, April 15, stealthily crossing the Caribbean Sea en route to liberate Cuba. Goyo got up again after a little while and walked about the deck. The excitement over the bombings had died down, and a quieter, more reflective mood had settled over the men. He found Pedro Vila standing alone near the prow, staring at the sea before them. Goyo walked up to him. "How are you, Pedro?"

Pedro sighed and looked at Goyo for a moment, and then returned his gaze to the horizon. "I know you'll probably be angry with me for saying this, Mr. León, but I've made the decision to give my life for Cuba." Goyo's stomach turned. He felt like slapping Pedro for saying such a thing, but somehow the words got trapped in his throat. "Pedro, don't talk like that," he finally muttered lightly. Pedro kept staring out as if he hadn't heard him. Goyo walked away.

That afternoon, the men were briefed on their mission. They were to meet the other ships at a rendezvous point code-named "Point Zulu," approximately thirty miles off Cuba's southern shore early the next evening, April 16. They were to land during the pre-dawn hours of the following morning, April 17, in the Bay of Pigs area near the Zapata Peninsula, home of the million-acre plus Zapata Swamp. They would land, under an "umbrella" of protection from the skies, at three strategic points code-named Blue Beach, Red Beach, and Green Beach. Blue Beach would be at Girón, the command center, just off the eastern end of the bay's mouth. Landing there would be the command staff aboard the LCI *Blagar*, as well as the Sixth Battalion, the Fourth Battalion, the Heavy Weapons Battalion, and a tank unit. The units landing at Blue Beach would also seize the nearby airstrip. Most of the Third Battalion would land at Green Beach, several miles east of Girón, to guard the coastal road from Cienfuegos. Landing on Red Beach, around twenty miles northwest of Girón and at the innermost tip of the Bay of Pigs, would be the battalions aboard the *Houston*–the Second and the Fifth. The LCI *Barbara J* would lead them in. They were to secure the isolated coastal village of Playa Larga and set up their base of operation there. From one end of the front to the other, the Brigade would control approximately forty miles of coastline.

Once the ground forces had secured their respective beach positions, units from Blue Beach and Red Beach were to move up the narrow causeways that connected the shoreline to points inland. They were to link up with First Battalion paratroopers, who would be dropped at strategic points along the roads at first light. Together, they would set up fortified roadblocks, bottling up Castro's only access to the beachhead. Primary responsibility for securing the roads, however, would fall to the Brigade's B-26 bombers which would be flying out of the Girón airstrip by that morning. The Brigade ships carried all the equipment the B-26s would need to carry out a prolonged air campaign, and more supply ships were in other ports loaded and ready to be moved into the battle zone.

They were then told about the provisional, democratic government-in-arms that would be flown into the beach-head.

When the briefing broke up, Roberto and Goyo looked out over the stern of the *Houston*. It was nearing dusk and the sun was slowly descending in the western Caribbean sky.

"What a coincidence, huh?" Roberto said.

"What is?"

"That we should be landing in Las Villas Province."

"Why?"

"Why? Because of the *Himno Invasor*," Roberto said. The Hymn of the Invader.

Goyo shrugged his shoulders.

Roberto recited the first few lines:

"A Las Villas valientes cubanos (To Las Villas brave Cubans)
a Occidente nos manda el deber (to the West duty sends us)
de la Patria arrojar los tiranos (from the Homeland we shall expel the tyrants)
a la carga a morir o vencer (charged with winning or dying)

Goyo pointed over the portside of the *Houston*. "Look!" In the distance, the American destroyer came into view.

"We can't lose," Roberto said solemnly. "We may die in the process, but in the end Cuba will be free. Freedom has always had its price."

Goyo rolled his eyes. Well, he thought, Roberto was a 19th century romantic at heart; he couldn't help it. Goyo patted his cousin's shoulder. "God will keep us, Roberto. Have faith."

HAVANA, CUBA
April 15, 1961

It took Raquel longer than she'd expected to get the children, the dog, and Aunt Teresa ready. She dashed about the house remembering a hundred items she'd neglected to pack, while frantically calculating how long it would take to drive to Goyo's relatives' home in Camagüey. They'd all be safe once they got there. Three different people telephoned within fifteen minutes to tell her that Castro's troops had occupied Belén and to stay clear of the school. Mickey, sensing a crisis, paced up and down, intermittently stopping at the window to scan the family's territory as though he were a sentry.

Raquel kept her eyes glued to the sky when she went outside to pack the car, praying that no more war planes flew by before they made their escape. Her legs trembled with excitement and fear. She entered the house again and went into the bathroom to finish packing a toiletries case, all the while muttering last minute reminders to herself.

Someone started pounding wildly on the front door.

Raquel's limbs froze; her throat contracted. Mickey barked and growled feverishly at the door, his hackles straightening like porcupine quills. She heard Teresa open the door.

A male voice thundered across the house. Mickey's barking became lethal.

Raquel ran into the living room. Two *milicianos* were parading in with rifles slung over their shoulders. Goyito was doing his best to hold back the enraged dog. "Stop, Mickey! Stop!" But the stronger Mickey, baring his front teeth, a wet, primordial growl emanating from his throat, broke away. He lunged at one of the *milicianos,* knocking him off balance and sending him headlong over the coffee table. The dog pounced on the incapacitated man, towering over him and growling ferociously, daring him to make an aggressive move. The *miliciano* blanched and curled his head and body into a protective ball. The other *miliciano,* a teenager, slung his rifle off his shoulder, aimed it at the side of Mickey's head, and pulled the trigger.

Ana Cristina had seen it from the hallway. All the color drained from her face. She opened her mouth to scream, but nothing came out. She fell to the floor like she was going to crawl, her eyes transfixed all the while on the dead dog. Goyito simply stared at the *miliciano's* smoking gun barrel, his face frozen.

Everything inside the home had gone still, except for the reverberation from the gun shot that still rang in everyone's ears. The smell of gun smoke filled the room. The young *miliciano* breathed heavily. After a few moments, he strapped the rifle back over his shoulder and snorted, "Dogs: the ultimate symbol of bourgeoisie decadence. Feeding them like princes while the people starve. We should do here what Mao did in China and kill *all* the mangy pests!"

Raquel was watching him, her mouth agape. She felt like fainting. She finally found the strength to plead, in a meek, bewildered whisper, "Why did you do that?"

The teenage shooter sneered at her. "That mutt attacked my comrade. Just be thankful it was only your dog. I would've killed one of your spoiled kids if I had to." Raquel noticed his hands were trembling.

The other *miliciano*, indignant and embarrassed, got up from the floor and stood before Raquel. "Raquel González de León, we are here to detain you."

"What?" Raquel cried, taking a step back. "You can't take me away from my children. What have I done?" Her knees began to buckle.

"All suspected counterrevolutionaries are being detained. The imperialists attacked this morning and the nation is preparing for war."

"But I've done nothing, and I don't know anything about any *imperialists.*"

"Then perhaps, madam," came another man's voice from the front door, "you can explain why you're preparing to flee at such a time." The man stepped inside the house, a Czech submachine gun slung over his shoulder. He dropped one of the suitcases Raquel had packed in the car at the entrance.

"I should have known," Raquel snarled, her fear instantly turning into rage. It was the goddamned bank teller.

"I hope you enjoy each and every one of your years in prison," Paquito Vega responded wryly. He shifted his beret to a jaunty angle, turned, and left in his own car, leaving the rest of this job to his lackeys.

The two militiamen dragged Raquel into the backseat of a 1959 Studebaker. Two other alleged counterrevolutionaries sat there handcuffed: a university student whose parents lived in the neighborhood and a priest from a local Catholic parish.

A middle-aged militiaman was sitting behind the wheel. The teenage militiaman slid into the middle of the front seat, while Mickey's "victim" knelt on the passenger seat facing backward, his rifle pointed at the prisoners. The car drove off and stopped a few minutes later at the front entrance to Miramar's Blanquita Theater.

When the militiamen alighted, the university student quipped, "How kind of them. They're taking us to a performance at the Blanquita; the Russian ballet no doubt."

"Or perhaps it's the Moscow Symphony," the priest chortled.

"Shut up! No talking!" one of the *milicianos* yelled as he swung open the back door on the sidewalk side. The three prisoners were marched into the theater lobby, where a host of militiamen and G.2 agents swarmed about, all of them looking agitated and nervous. Most of them were smoking.

Passing the ticket booth, the student said, "Three tickets please, orchestra." The *miliciano* behind him shouted, "Shut up," and struck him in the shoulder with his rifle butt.

They were escorted into the gigantic main theatre, where several thousand "enemies" of the Revolution were being detained, the whole place illuminated with excruciatingly bright klieg lights. Taking in the surreal spectacle, Raquel's eyes fell on Dolores Gómez, an old school chum. Dolores made eye contact a second later. She ran over and threw her arms around Raquel. "Oh, Raquel, this is awful. These people are animals!"

Raquel squeezed her tightly, relieved to have found a friendly face. "What's going on, Dolores? They dragged me here from my home."

"Raquel," Dolores whispered into her ear, "the invasion is coming! Those airplanes this morning was just the beginning. Castro's people are terrified." She stepped back. "Since early this morning they've been rounding up everyone on lists the G.2 has been compiling for a year. Anyone they think may be in the resistance, or their relatives if they can't find them, are being detained all over Cuba. The say the prisons are overflowing; they've even started concentrating people in baseball stadiums and parks. Rumor has it that thousands more will be detained by nightfall. And they've surrounded the Catholic churches, the Catholic schools, and even convents with the nuns inside."

"How do you know this?" Raquel asked.

Dolores lowered her voice, "I'm part of the resistance."

"You, Dolores?"

Dolores nodded.

Raquel looked at the bright lights, feeling suddenly dehydrated. "Where can I get something to drink?" she asked.

Dolores's mouth bent in anger. She shook her head. "They give us nothing, not even water." Raquel felt even thirstier now. Someone grabbed her shoulder from behind. She turned and saw a thin, pale girl of around twenty.

"Help me, please, kind lady," she said, leaning on Raquel. Her other hand was wrapped around her protruding, pregnant belly.

"Oh, my," Raquel said, turning to help the girl stand. "Are you in labor?"

"I'm not sure . . . I think so," she answered in shallow breaths, "it's my first."

Raquel reached down and felt the girl's skirt. It was soaked. She laid the girl down gently on the floor and shouted, "Somebody tell the guards that this woman needs a doctor!" The crowd began calling for a doctor.

The girl screamed through a contraction. When it passed, she said, "I've already told them. They said they couldn't help me. They said no one can come in or go out."

A gentlemanly looking fellow in his mid-fifties, one of the prisoners, was brought over to the girl. "I'm a doctor," he said. Everyone moved back to make room for him.

Raquel knelt next to the girl and held her hand while the doctor took her pulse. "Is your husband here?" she asked her.

"I'm here alone."

"Then I'll stay with you," Raquel said, patting the girl's hand to soothe her. She noticed a Miraculous Medal around her neck. "Would you like to pray to Our Lady?" The girl nodded, her pale, perspiring face contorted with gratitude and pain. Raquel pulled out the Rosary she always carried in her skirt pocket, kissed the crucifix, made the Sign of the Cross, and began to recite the prayers.

* * *

Ever since the aerial raids that morning, Lorenzo had kept vigil near the telephone and listened closely for a knock at the front door. After a while, he went upstairs to his bedroom and knelt on the floor next to a sofa bed he kept there. Several weeks before, he had disposed of the folded bed inside and filled the hollow interior with small bombs, pistols, ammunition, grenades, radio equipment, and propaganda leaflets. He–and thousands of others across the island–had agreed to hide such items for the underground-led uprisings that were supposed to break out across the island when the military operation from abroad ensued. He had screwed in a perfectly cut board along the top of the sofa frame in order to cover the stash, and topped it with a thin layer of foam and solid green upholstery. The sofa cushions were laid on top.

Lorenzo made sure everything was secured, and then sat heavily on the sofa. He looked across the room and saw that his bed was still unmade, not an unusual occurrence now since most of the servants had been dismissed after the bank was taken over.

For over a year now, Lorenzo had been in direct contact with important people he knew that had lined up against Castro—mostly liberal democratic politicians, the sort he'd built his diplomatic career with, the sort the Americans were now supporting. But for a long time he went no further than simply networking and keeping himself informed. He'd been waiting for the "right" moment to get involved more directly, a moment he could use to his own best advantage and which would entail the least risk to his personal safety. If he played his cards right, he'd figured, he could gain an ambassador-ship from the new government. But everything changed in December when he found out that his son, Roberto, had been part of the anti-Castro insurgency and had been forced to flee the island. Despite a lifelong preference for patient, careful, political calculation, Lorenzo admired the valor his boy had demonstrated by disobeying him and risking his life for the cause. His son had understood things with such great clarity.

Lorenzo looked out the window as a military truck packed with soldiers sped by. He sat in silence, remembering how he'd felt after Goyo told him about Roberto's involvement with the resistance. Shame had ripped at him; he, Lorenzo León, the great ambassador–who, to that point, had done nothing but bide his time while others did the dirty work–looking to see how he could best manipulate the situation for his own aggrandizement. Roberto had proven himself the better man; not that his son had set out to do that, but his actions had, nevertheless, had that effect. So, within a week of Emilio and Roberto's departure, Lorenzo made contact with the underground and offered himself as a soldier. He quietly thanked God that Roberto had made it out of Cuba alive and was now safely in New York.

But now, after the first bombings, his sharp political instincts told him that something had gone awry–terribly awry. He was assured that mass aerial bombings would be launched simultaneously with the Liberation Army's landing on Cuban soil, taking the regime by surprise. The confusion caused by the synchronized attacks would temporarily paralyze the government and give the democratic insurgents on the island the window they needed to launch an armed uprising, take to the streets, and seize the momentum–and Lorenzo knew that in these fluid revolutionary situations it was always momentum that carried the day. To his utter consternation, however, nothing was proceeding as he'd expected. The rather minimal aerial bombings had come and gone without the underground so much as being informed; then, nothing but peace had reigned since: no landings, no subsequent aerial attacks, and still no word to the underground. He knew the window had probably closed for good, as the government had already regrouped and placed the armed forces, the militia, and the G.2 on high alert. It had asserted undisputed control of the street and started rounding up suspected rebels by the thousands. He rubbed his temples, thinking that perhaps the bombings that morning weren't at all connected to the invasion, that maybe they were simply carried out by exile pilots operating independently from Miami. But three coordinated strikes? In B-26s? No, they had to have come from the liberation forces. Why had they stopped, then? Where was the invasion? Why wasn't the underground given the signal to rise up?

Lorenzo flirted with the idea of going into hiding, but decided that such an action would be cowardly. Plus, what if, by some miracle, his underground contact called and he wasn't there to give him the equipment and weapons? No, going into hiding wasn't an option. "Maybe there's some angle I haven't considered," he told himself over and over as the minutes ticked past as slowly as a melting glacier.

Lorenzo went to the radio and turned the dial to Radio Swan. They were delivering messages to the underground using secret code words he didn't recognize. He recalled listening to allied radio broadcasts to the French Resistance while he was in Switzerland during the war. He hadn't been able to make out any of them, either.

The telephone rang.

He grabbed it. "Hello."

"Lorenzo!" It was his sister, Teresa. She was hysterical.

"What is it? What's wrong?" Teresa was the only one in the family who knew he was involved with the underground; not even his wife knew.

"They've taken away Raquel!"

"What? Who did?"

"Some *milicianos*, and Paquito was leading them, but he left in a separate car. Lorenzo, you've got to get out of there! If Paquito used the bombings this morning as a pretext to arrest Raquel, he'll probably come after you as well."

"Was anyone hurt?"

"They killed Mickey."

"Who?"

"Mickey. The dog."

Lorenzo thought for a moment. "Teresa, can you drive?"

"Of course I can," she answered, mildly offended.

"OK. Call Raquel's parents to let them know what happened, and then do as Goyo had instructed Raquel. Take the children to his mother's relatives' home in Camagüey. Go now!"

"I will, I will," Teresa said impatiently, "but you need to go too, this instant!"

Lorenzo hung up and screamed for his wife. "Sara!" No response. Trepidation began creeping up his legs, visions of the G.2 bursting in at any moment now invading his mind. He heard the shower running.

He went into the bathroom. "Sara! Get out, right away! We have to leave! The G.2 may be on its way here to arrest me!"

"What?" she asked, turning off the water.

"Teresa called and told me that Paquito has just detained Raquel. They're probably on their way here now. Sara, I'm with the resistance, and I've been hiding bombs and weapons in the house. I'll explain later, but right now we have to get out!"

"Then go now!" she shouted, wrapping herself in a towel and yanking open the bath curtain, her eyes burning with terror, "You can't waste time waiting for me! Run! Now! Go out the back way!"

Someone started pounding on the front door. They listened in frozen stillness as Patricia, the maid, opened it. A second later they heard the sound of boots moving rapidly across the marble floor. They were trapped. They looked at one another as if in a final farewell.

The bathroom door burst open. Paquito had Patricia by the hair. She was screeching, "Don Lorenzo, I tried to stop them, but . . ." Paquito pulled her back and shoved her onto the hallway floor.

He stared at Lorenzo and Sara for a moment and then pointed his Czech submachine gun straight at them. Behind him stood two *milicianos* and one female *miliciana,* all of them in their twenties.

"Comrades," Paquito said to them, "you see how well the Fifth Avenue millionaires lived on the backs of your parents? Can you believe there are still people in this country with marble floors in their homes?" He snickered at Lorenzo and Sara. "Both of you get out of the bathroom."

"I'll appeal to your sense of decency by asking you to allow my wife to dress," Lorenzo said firmly.

"Dress hell!" Paquito snorted. He walked over to Sara and ripped her towel away. She stood there naked, covering her breasts and pubic area with her hands. Paquito raised his gun and pointed it at her head. "Hands up, on your head!" Sara's jaw dropped. "Now!" Paquito shouted. She slowly lifted her arms and folded her hands on the top of her head. She held her chin up defiantly and stared back at the bank teller. "Into the bedroom, both of you!" Paquito barked.

Lorenzo and the bare, dripping Sara stood in the middle of the bedroom, hands on their heads like common criminals. Patricia was forced to stand with them. Paquito looked icily at them. "Our country was attacked this morning by imperialist forces. We are detaining all enemies of the Revolution, including you, Lorenzo León. But first, we will carry out a thorough search for weapons." He narrowed his eyes. "Ambassador León: you'd better hope we don't find any." He pointed at the bed with his gun. "The three of you may sit on the bed, but keep your hands on your heads."

The *miliciana,* whom Lorenzo guessed was around twenty-one years old, stood guard as Paquito and the two young men carried out their inspection. Her male colleagues out of the room, the militia girl's shoulders slumped. She let out a sigh and lowered her gun to her waist. She went to the armoire and pulled a nightgown off a hanger. "Here, put this on," she said, tossing Sara the garment.

"Thank you," Sara said gratefully.

"Don't thank me, you privileged old shrew. I loathe people like you." She sniffled and raised her gun again. "I just don't like to see another woman humiliated like that."

For the next hour they listened as Paquito and the two militiamen tore apart the house. They came back into the bedroom, Paquito flushed with frustration. "Search the bedroom," he ordered, stopping in mid-stride when he saw Sara wearing the nightgown. He glanced over at the *miliciana.* "You don't have the stomach for this, dear, do you?"

The *miliciana*, sniffling again, kept her attention on the prisoners.

The two young militiamen searched under the bed, in the armoire, and behind the drapes. By now it had become obvious they were bored and growing weary of Paquito.

"That's it," one cried, a dash of insubordination in his tone, "nothing here."

Paquito was writing something down in a notebook. He shouted over his shoulder, "Check the sofa."

Lorenzo's stomach went cold. They would probably execute him right here in his own bedroom, he thought. Somehow he managed to keep his face impassive. The *miliciano* lifted the cushion and pushed down on the upholstered foam atop the slab of wood that concealed the weapons.

Lorenzo held his breath.

The *miliciano*, made lazy by the tedious turn the inspection had taken, simply flung the cushion back on top of the sofa. "Like I said, nothing."

Paquito finished jotting down his notes as if no one had spoken. He closed the notebook and shoved his pen into his breast pocket. "Ambassador and Mrs. León," he said, turning to Lorenzo and Sara, "it seems your son Roberto vanished without a trace a few months ago, didn't he? Would you care to tell me his whereabouts?"

"He's abroad," Lorenzo said curtly. Then he pleaded, "Please, Paquito, why don't you leave my family alone?"

"You arrogant old bastard," Paquito snarled, leering at Lorenzo, "you have no idea what I can do to your family. Get on your feet, Lorenzo." He shook his head at him in disgust. "*Milicianos*! Take the ambassador to La Cabaña; and take the wife, too. I've got business to attend to elsewhere. Mrs. León, you may dress properly before going to prison."

Sara wailed and threw her husband a panicked look.

"Easy, Sara, everything will be OK. You'll see," Lorenzo reassured her.

A few minutes later the militiamen led Sara and Lorenzo at gunpoint down the stairs and into a waiting car.

Within the hour they were in La Cabaña's prison yard with hundreds of other people who'd been rounded up that morning. Militiamen stood guard, terrorizing the detainees with machine guns and tormenting them verbally. The prisoners included people of both sexes and of all ages and social classes. There seemed to be a disproportionate number of Catholic clergy and university students among them. There were no toilets, no water, and no food. Surely people will die here before this is all over, Lorenzo thought gloomily. When no more detainees could be squeezed inside the packed prison yard or in the *galeras*, the authorities simply began putting them into the dried up, grassy moat that snaked around the fortress and surrounded them with machine gun posts. All Lorenzo could do now was to hope and pray it would all be over soon.

POINT ZULU
1800 HOURS
Sunday, April 16, 1961

A wave of excitement broke out across the deck of the *Houston* when the dark green camouflage uniforms were distributed to the men. A patch sewn onto the left sleeve of the shirt bore the Brigade emblem: a shield depicting a Cuban flag and a prominent Christian cross crowned by the numbers 2506. Goyo changed into his new uniform, relieved to be discarding his khakis, painted a dusty red by the ship's rust. A few feet behind him, one of the men was reading the label inside the collar of his new combat shirt. "Hey, look," he laughed, "it says, 'Happy Hunting.' These things were made for hunters!" Someone nearby called out, "Yeah, except we're going to hunt for Communists, not ducks!" Goyo proudly strutted up and down the *Houston's* deck, wearing his uniform as though it should have had a cape attached to it. He stopped and looked around at the jubilant men. The realization that their landing on a remote beach in Cuba would be world news suddenly dawned on him. A sharp vibration rumbled in his chest.

A little later, one of the commanders announced that in a few minutes they'd be joining the other Brigade ships at Point Zulu, the rendezvous point fewer than thirty miles offshore from the Bay of Pigs. The men, charged up for the fight they knew was now only hours away, leaned over the railings in their new uniforms, scanning the horizon for the other ships, the fading sunlight casting them in a beatific glow. Someone screeched, "Look! There they are! There they are!" The *Caribe*, the *Atlantico*, the *Rio Escondido*, and the command ships *Blagar* and *Barbara J*, awaited them, bobbing on the waves in the distance. One man shouted, "We're late. You see? That proves that we're the most Cuban ship!" Everyone laughed. Then someone started singing the national anthem; the others joined him with voices at full throttle. Goyo felt a tingling in his chest and arms. Roberto bounced on his toes like a child waiting to start his summer vacation as the final minutes ticked by on the last day of school. His chin was trembling; thick teardrops gathered in the corners of his eyes. Goyo squeezed his cousin's shoulder and nodded. Roberto sighed and nodded back at him.

The mood on board quickly turned deadly serious. Everyone stood by in silence as the invasion ships, engines churning, lined up behind the *Blagar* in single file. Within minutes the small armada commenced its slow, silent trek toward the Bay of Pigs. When darkness finally fell, the ships were completely blacked out, save for a masked light on each stern to guide the ship behind it. It was a moonless night.

Deep in the night, the ships came to an abrupt halt. The men nervously beheld the shadow of an alien vessel approaching from the starboard side. Goyo thought it was a Cuban naval vessel. His back tensed; his hands squeezed his rifle. One of the officers standing nearby whispered to him, "Don't worry. That's the *San Marcos*, an American dock landing ship. They're delivering the landing craft, the tanks, the trucks, and some tractors for the Blue Beach landing. This is a good sign. We're only a few miles from the coast and the Americans are still with us." The *San Marcos* disappeared back into the darkness after delivering its cargo. The small fleet carrying the 2506, now augmented by the landing craft carrying the tanks, trucks, and tractors, proceeded on to the Bay of Pigs.

Before long, Goyo could discern lights on a distant, amorphous shoreline: Cuba. His hands started shaking. He was acutely aware of his pulse pounding in his temples. When the flotilla neared the bay's mouth, the *Caribe,* the *Atlantico,* the *Blagar,* and the newly arrived landing craft quietly peeled off to the east, in the direction of Girón, "Blue Beach." The *Río Escondido,* lagging a few miles behind because of a damaged propeller, would join them promptly. The *Houston* and the LCI *Barbara J* continued straight into the Bay of Pigs, toward Playa Larga, "Red Beach," eighteen miles north.

Just before midnight, the men aboard the *Houston* watched with bated breath as comet tails from tracer bullets being fired from sea to shore lit up the beach just east of Girón. "It's started," Goyo thought. He swallowed and reached inside his shirt. He squeezed the St. Jude medallion his son had given him as a birthday gift. Roberto, his face muscles taut, was humming the *Himno Invasor.*

Happy Valley Air Base
Puerto Cabezas, Nicaragua
Evening, April 16, 1961

Emilio popped a cigarette into his mouth and lit it as the First Battalion's briefing wrapped up at 6:30 p.m. They had assembled under a giant tent made–appropriately enough–out of a parachute. They would be dropped, at first light, at strategic forward positions on the three causeways cutting through the swamp that led to the beaches at the Bay of Pigs. The forty-mile beachhead behind them was to be secured by the Brigade's amphibiously landing ground troops.

One of the paratrooper units would be dropped along the road connecting the coastal village of Playa Larga, on "Red Beach," at the innermost tip of the Bay of Pigs, to Jagüey Grande and the Central Australia sugar mill seventeen miles to the north. Specifically, they were to land near the small village of Palpite on the main road and set up a roadblock with elements of the Second and Fifth infantry battalions moving up from Playa Larga. An advance unit would engage the arriving Castro troops and tanks and draw them into the "shooting gallery" that ran across the swamp for the Brigade's B-26 bombers. Meanwhile, a detachment would seize the town of Sopillar and its airstrip.

The rest of the paratroopers would land on the eastern front along the roads leading to Girón, "Blue Beach." The main body would be dropped into the village of San Blas, eight miles northeast up the road from Girón, where they would set up a command center. From San Blas the road forked: one fork went slightly southeast and then straight northeast to the town of Yaguaramas, twenty-two miles away; the other went north-northeast toward the town of Covadonga, twelve miles distant. Smaller advance units would be dropped on the roads near each of these towns to set up defensive forward positions, with support coming in from the paratroopers at the San Blas command post and ground units moving up from Girón. Along the two roads forking from San Blas there also ran several miles of "shooting galleries" for the B-26s. Emilio was assigned to the command center at San Blas.

After the briefing, the paratroopers were given their Brigade uniforms, with the 2506 patch on the left sleeve and an airborne patch depicting a parachute on the left breast. They were each issued a blue neckerchief, a blue jump helmet, and a "Texas" hat for their march into the capital. After a brief weapons inspection, they were given a light dinner of steak and salad. They were issued a few apples for breakfast the next day. During the pre-dawn hours of April 17, everyone was told to stand by: H-Hour was approaching.

As they awaited the call to board, Jimmy Strickland strolled into the departure area. He saw Emilio alongside a C-46 transport plane. He was holding his blue jump helmet by the chinstrap. A cigarette dangled from his lips.

"Hey, cousin," Jimmy called to him, walking over.

Emilio's face lit up. He tossed away his smoke and thrust out his right hand for Jimmy to shake. He embraced him with his left arm. "Fred, I knew you'd come. How'd you get in here?"

Jimmy winked. "I got my connections." He sighed and bit his lower lip. Then he smiled. "Now, don't you be afraid of nothin.' Just remember everything I taught you."

Emilio nodded. "I will, Fred, I will."

Jimmy glanced around and then turned back to Emilio. He muttered, "Boy, I really feel like going over there with y'all. There's nothin' an old soldier wants more than to fight just one more battle."

"I can get you a parachute, and we can probably swipe a rifle somewhere."

"Hah! Don't tempt me. Besides, the brass issued a warning that if any instructors snuck aboard we'd be arrested or some damned thing like that."

An officer speaking through a megaphone ordered Emilio's squad aboard their airplane. The distant cousins looked at each other, possibly for the last time ever. Emilio started to sway playfully. He put on his best drunken voice, "Will the circle, be unbroken . . ." Jimmy joined in, the mock inebriation in his voice matching Emilio's, "by and by, by and by, in a better home awaiting, in the sky, in the sky." They laughed.

Jimmy said, "Hey, cousin, I almost forgot, I got something for you." He pulled an Alabama state flag pin out of his pocket and pinned it on Emilio's collar. "That's so you don't forget your Alabama roots and your redneck American cousin."

Emilio rubbed the pin, his lips bent downward. Then he reached inside his shirt and removed a gold chain and crucifix from around his neck. "I know you're not Catholic, but take this to remember your Cuban cousin." Jimmy nodded his head in thanks and put the chain around his neck, the scar tissue on his face and scalp darkening.

Emilio said, "How can I find you after all this is over, Fred?"

Jimmy looked around again and leaned toward Emilio. He whispered, "Listen, you know my real name ain't Fred, right?"

"Yes, of course."

"It's James, James Strickland. Folks call me Jimmy. I'm listed in Fayetteville, North Carolina. You can find me there."

Emilio nodded and touched the flag pin again.

Jimmy looked into Emilio's eyes. Momma and Grandpa were there. He hadn't felt them this close since he was a boy.

He felt his eyes moistening. He shook his head and looked away. "I'm sorry cousin, but it's like . . . Lord have mercy . . . it's like a hole in my heart being filled, you know what I mean?" He looked back at Emilio.

Emilio nodded. "Me too, James Strickland Hammond," he said, employing the Spanish custom of using both parents' surnames. He wondered what his father would have thought of Jimmy.

The commander made a final call for the paratroopers. Jimmy tapped Emilio's upper arm. "Enough of all this silliness, you've got a war to fight. Go on, now!"

Emilio squeezed Jimmy's shoulder and turned to go into the aircraft. Reaching the door, he turned back to Jimmy. They waved at each other. Emilio entered and took his seat.

When they reached cruising altitude, the commander, Alejandro del Valle, went up and down the fuselage speaking to each man individually, imparting words of encouragement. When he got to Emilio, he asked him about the flag pin on his collar.

"Alabama," Emilio said.

Del Valle wrinkled his nose. "Alabama?"

Emilio smiled at the pin. "Yes, sir, Alabama."

Del Valle shrugged, let out a hearty laugh, and went on to the next man.

14

BAY OF PIGS
PLAYA LARGA, "RED BEACH"
April 17, 1961
Pre-Dawn Hours

R oberto and his squad stood battle ready aboard the *Houston,* the ship now halted less than a mile from shore. Across jet black waters they watched in silence as the frogmen aboard the *Barbara J* sped toward the beach on an eighteen-foot catamaran to reconnoiter the area and set up marker lights for the landings. Only the gentle waves slapping against the *Houston's* hull could be heard. Roberto tapped Goyo's shoulder and pointed southeast toward Girón. Goyo swallowed when he saw the sky flashing red.

Roberto gathered his 12-man squad around him. "Remember, Second Battalion will land first and secure Playa Larga and the beach before it. Different squads will then advance in three directions: one group will go west toward Buenaventura, where there's a resort construction project underway; another will go northeast toward the Sopillar airfield; the rest of the squads, including ours, will go north up the causeway where we'll link up with a paratrooper unit and help man the main roadblock. The Fifth Battalion will land after us and take our places on the beach. Once it's secured, they'll move up to reinforce us. The *Houston* will leave us here with plenty of ammo, and then sail to Blue Beach at Girón to drop off more equipment. After that, we'll be supplied by trucks coming in from there."

Roberto saw Pedro Vila shivering. He put his arm around the boy's shoulders. "Don't forget, we'll have complete air supremacy and will operate under an 'umbrella of protection' from above. Castro's air capability has been eliminated. Our B-26s will be operating from the Girón airfield by morning. They'll obliterate any Castro forces coming down the roads probably before they even get near us. And remember that no matter what, our allies are a few miles right offshore, watching our backs and ready to help."

Happy Valley Airfield,
Puerto Cabezas, Nicaragua
Pre-Dawn Hours,
April 17, 1961

Bernie Cuervo looked on as the ground crews filled the fuel tanks of his B-26 bomber. He felt the plane with his hands; it was warm. In just a few minutes, he and the other pilots would make their D-Day sorties to Cuba to finish wiping out Fidel Castro's small air force. Though he was excited, consternation nevertheless plagued him. He wondered continuously why the Americans had canceled nearly all of the pre-invasion air strikes. The Brigade air force had flown eight sorties forty-eight hours earlier–that was *it!*–the rest called off by some pinhead in Washington, D.C. Although the watered-down D minus 2 air attack had reportedly destroyed around half of Castro's air combat capabilities, Bernie knew that a surviving T-33 here and a Sea Fury or two there could spell disaster for the Brigade. The American's words a few days earlier rang over and over in his mind like a scratched record, "If even one of them is left operational, if even one of them can get into the air after the invasion commences, the whole operation could quickly become a fiasco. The faster Sea Furies and T-33s can easily down our B-26 bombers and prevent them from even landing at the Girón airstrip, making your mission to seal off the beachhead all but impossible. Even worse, they could target our supply ships anchored offshore, sinking them or forcing them to flee. In this worst case scenario, the Brigade, even if it manages to land, would be left on the beaches alone—no supplies, no air support, and facing an enemy of tens of thousands marching unimpeded into the beachhead. In short, men, everything hinges on the Brigade air force's success at destroying Castro's planes *on the ground before the invasion.*"

This morning's mission was the last chance they were being given to do just that.

Bernie shook his head from side to side, put aside his misgivings, and focused on the mission. Besides, he told himself, American jets were right offshore, ready to take care of any Castro airplanes they might miss. Why else would they have so casually canceled the pre-invasion strikes, especially when everyone understood the importance of eliminating Castro's air force? The Americans were, after all, their allies. He rubbed the plane's belly for luck. Everything would work out.

Bernie checked his watch and looked around for his navigator. He spotted him approaching their B-26. "Are you ready?"

"Yeah, let's go finish this thing."

Bernie nodded and climbed aboard the loaded bomber. He strapped himself into the cockpit, checked the instruments, and gave a thumbs-up to the pilot in the plane next to his. Some of the other pilots were still having their fuel tanks filled. Just a few more minutes and they'd be in the air. He made the Sign of the Cross.

A jeep sped toward the flight line; it stopped abruptly before the B-26s. An American–one of the leaders of the trainers they'd known for a while and with whom they got along well, not one of the Americans who'd come recently from Washington, D.C–jumped out of the vehicle. He ran his hand across his throat in a slicing motion, the universal signal to cut engines. He stood for a moment in earsplitting silence. Then he threw his cap to the ground, shouting, "There goes the whole fucking war!"

There goes the whole fucking war? Bernie's hair stood on end. He sat in the cockpit, waiting as the American in the jeep went from B-26 to B-26 talking to the pilots. When the American came to his plane, he said, "The D-Day strikes have been called off, canceled. We just got a cable from Washington." It took a few seconds for Bernie to process the information.

"Canceled?" he asked softly.

"Yeah, canceled," the American said, obviously furious over the order.

Bernie exploded into a raging fury. "What the hell do you mean canceled? How is this possible?" he demanded.

"Are American jets being sent to destroy Castro's airplanes instead?"

"We don't know . . . we can't believe it either." He shook his head, looked away, and grumbled through gritted teeth, "Damn it!" After a second, he looked at Bernie again. "You're authorized only to provide air cover over the beachhead later."

Bernie shouted, "Provide air cover in B-26 bombers in a sky dominated by Castro Sea Furies and armed T-33s? They'll blow us sky high! That wasn't the plan!" Bernie's cheeks turned hot. "Castro's fighter planes were supposed to be destroyed on the ground *before* the Brigade landed and *before* we flew into Girón. We were supposed to interdict ground forces from the air, not engage in air to air combat against fighter planes!" He looked over at his navigator, who bore an expression of utter disbelief. "First they don't let us destroy Castro's fighters on the ground when we had the chance, and now they want us to fly suicide missions against them!" Then he groaned and closed his eyes. He pinched the bridge of his nose and said in a low, despondent tone, "My God, the men aboard the ships are landing as we speak, and the paratroopers have already departed." He opened his eyes again. They were bloodshot. "Our guys think they're liberating their country. These people have sent them to their deaths."

After a few minutes, Bernie and some of the other pilots began haphazardly plotting a takeover of the base and carrying out the mission on their own. They concluded that there was no way they could overpower the heavily armed American guards. They were helpless. Bernie excused himself, went to a discreet spot, and vomited.

Playa Larga, "Red Beach"
April 17, 1961
Pre-Dawn Hours

As the frogmen prepared the landing zone, eight small, fiberglass boats with outboard engines were lowered from the *Houston* by noisy, rusted winches. One of the men grumbled, "Christ! They can hear us all the way in Florida!" Roberto's squad was ordered to climb down the nets that were hung alongside the ship and board two of the boats. They would go ashore as part of the first wave. The boat Roberto boarded had a skull and bones painted on the hull. The frogmen on shore were radioed when the boats were ready. The frogmen flipped on the landing lights. Within moments, they came under small arms fire from some local militia near the beach. The frogmen responded with their machine guns and a BAR, a Browning Automatic Rifle. The enemy retreated and blacked out the village after taking out one side of the landing lights.

As the squads of the first wave pushed away from the *Houston,* the man piloting Roberto's boat started swearing. "What's wrong?" Roberto asked.

"The damn engine won't stay on, it keeps sputtering out." He looked up and pointed at the other boat carrying the rest of Roberto's squad. It was drifting aimlessly in the bay. "Look, they're having the same problem! What the hell is this?"

Roberto slapped the side of the boat in frustration. Like Lazarus at Christ's command, the engine came alive. Roberto told the pilot to pull alongside the other boat and threw it a rope. The two boats headed slowly toward the landing lights, pulled by the power of a single engine.

The dark outline of the beach gradually came into focus. To Goyo, the distant shore seemed like the interior of a dimly lit cathedral, the small landing lights little more than feeble votive candles. Several hundred yards from shore, they heard machine gun fire from behind them. They looked back. The *Barbara J* was firing on a spot west of the landing lights. The frogmen on shore were shooting in the same direction. The guns fell silent after several seconds; a line of Castro trucks coming in from Buenaventura was left in a blazing heap.

Goyo turned back to face the shore, feeling as if he was in a dream; the tormenting darkness, the cool salt water splashing lightly on his face, the night wind blowing across his cheeks, the piercing buzz of the engine, the oily smell of his M-1 rifle, all seemed utterly unreal to him. Roberto suddenly shouted, "Down! Everyone down!" Goyo bent over quickly. Tracer bullets were whizzing overhead like a thousand shooting stars. He shut his eyes, now deaf, dumb, and blind to the world around him, sensing only his heart pounding madly.

When they were a few dozen yards from shore, the boats suddenly crashed violently into a rock formation concealed just underneath the water's surface. The men were hurled forward. The landing lights were nowhere in sight; Goyo guessed they had been thrown off course by the tracers. Roberto barked, "Out! Out! Everyone wade ashore!" Goyo rolled over the side of the boat and fell into the water with a splash. He braced his legs to absorb his weight when they hit what he'd expected to be a shallow bottom; instead, he started plunging like a ship's anchor. He touched bottom ten

feet down and desperately pushed himself back up to the surface, cutting his arm on some coral rock, remembering only
then the fifty pounds of extra ammunition he was hauling
ashore. He struggled to the beach, shaking like a leaf in a
gale. Out of breath and spitting out salt water, he stumbled
on the dry sand and collapsed.

The two landing boats went back to the *Houston* to
retrieve more men. The squad scoured the shoreline in the
pitch darkness, Roberto calling out the code-word, "*Águila,*"
(Eagle), over and over. They had no idea where they were in
relation to the landing zone. They moved in every direction,
calling, "*Águila,* "*Águila.*" After what seemed like an eternity,
they finally heard the response, "*Negra,*" from the west. "This
way," Roberto ordered.

When they got to the landing area, the squad was ordered
to take up a position between the shore and the town and
await further instructions. Some of the squads had already
moved north beyond the town toward the roadblock. Roberto's squad was supposed to be with them, but they were being
held at the beach for the time being. Roberto looked around
and saw that Erneido Oliva was ashore. Oliva, an Afro-Cuban
and the Brigade's second-in-command, was in charge of the
Playa Larga front. San Román, the top commander, had
landed at Girón with the headquarters staff.

It took a few hours for the Second Battalion to be ferried
from the *Houston* to the beach on the small boats. Roberto,
eager to start down the causeway to join the squads already at
the roadblock, was told that his squad was being held on the
beach until the Fifth Battalion came ashore. Growing impa-
tient, he walked over toward Oliva, who was standing with an

American–presumably the CIA man from the *Barbara J*–to ask for a status report. When he was within a few feet of them, he noticed they were fuming about something. Roberto stopped in his tracks. A few seconds later, the American and the frogmen got into the catamaran they had landed in and dashed back to the *Barbara J*. Roberto turned around and returned to his squad. Dawn had started to break.

Just minutes after Roberto reached his men, they heard the unmistakable sound of an airplane engine buzzing overhead. They looked into the sky and saw it a few seconds later: a B-26 flying from north to south, shining in the early morning sun.

"There's our air cover! Look!" Roberto shouted ecstatically, pointing skyward as the airplane passed overhead.

"Thank God," Fernando Miyares sighed. The airplane dipped its wing in salute; some of the men waved their hands and hats in return. Flying out over the bay, the B-26 circled around the *Houston* and the *Barbara J* in the glory of the early morning. The men on the beach beheld the beautiful sight.

Then the B-26 started firing at the Brigade ships.

"What the hell?" Roberto muttered. All around him, voices rose in astonishment.

Goyo, apoplectic, grabbed Roberto's sleeve, "That's a *Castro* B-26! And it's attacking *our ships*! What happened to the 'umbrella of protection' they promised?"

"I don't know, cousin, I don't know," Roberto said in a stunned whisper. The B-26 seemed suddenly to have grown poisonous fangs.

The troops on the beach looked on as the Castro aircraft battled the Brigade ships and the catamaran carrying the frogmen, the plane strafing them mercilessly, the vessels returning fire with .50 caliber machine guns. Smoke began pouring out of the Castro airplane. It turned away sharply, fleeing in a northwesterly direction, and finally exploding and crashing into the swamp. Some of the men on Playa Larga cheered the destruction of the enemy airplane. Roberto and Goyo gave each other an ominous look: if Castro had that airplane, he probably had more.

The men's joy at the demise of the Castro airplane turned into shock a short time later as they watched the *Houston* and the *Barbara J* turn southward and sail away with most of their ammunition and equipment, as well as the entire Fifth Battalion and a squad from the Second, still aboard. Roberto's stomach started reeling.

They soon got word that the ships were merely sailing to Girón to land the remaining men and supplies under anti-aircraft protection from the ships there, which included the well-armed *Blagar*. Everyone relaxed. But when the *Houston* and the *Barbara J* had sailed only a few miles, while still in plain sight of Red Beach, a Castro Sea Fury and a T-33 descended from high altitude like birds of prey. The Communist-manned airplanes, ignoring the troops on the beach, flew straight at the ships, their engines sounding like carpenters' drills. The troops on Playa Larga watched in complete helplessness as the planes dove over and over at the ships, strafing and firing rockets at them.

One of the rockets made a direct hit on the *Houston*, ripping open a large gash in its hull. The ship's captain, Luis Morse, skillfully steered the vessel onto the sandy sea bottom a few hundred yards from the bay's western shore in order to prevent it from sinking with everyone aboard. The troops still on the *Houston* were told to abandon ship. They jumped into the water and tried to get ashore however they could. Some clung to floating debris and kicked their way in; most simply swam. Castro's airplanes, which now included another Sea Fury and a B-26, strafed them without mercy, easily picking off the few who'd managed to get into the small life boats. Several men drowned before ever reaching safety. The survivors regrouped on a desolate beach at the edge of a mangrove forest, cut off permanently from the rest of the war.

At Playa Larga, the men of the Second Battalion now prepared to face the inevitable enemy assault without the Fifth Battalion and minus a squad from the Second. They possessed only the days' worth of ammunition they'd managed to unload.

Roberto's squad was at last ordered up the road. They moved quickly along the narrow causeway and finally reached the roadblock. It consisted of a few squads concealed on either side of the road armed with rifles, .75 mm and .57mm recoilless rifles, .30 and .50 caliber machine guns, and other weapons. The company commander at the front, a man named Maximo Cruz who was just a couple of years older than Roberto, directed the new men into their positions. Someone told Roberto, "Castro is amassing a force at Central Australia and he's going to attack right through here. He's got airplanes, so tell your guys to get ready."

Roberto asked, "Where are the paratroopers?"

A man in a paratrooper uniform, his face and arms covered in blood, turned around. "Our plane was thrown off course by a Castro B-26. Weren't they supposed to be destroyed? Anyhow, because of that we missed our drop targets and got scattered all over the damned swamp. Our equipment was dropped off target too, and we lost most of it. We also lost radio contact with both Playa Larga and Girón. We fought Castro's troops in small groups and set up a roadblock for a while, but there wasn't much we could do without ammunition. I got separated from my unit and headed down the road; but the rest are still out there somewhere. I don't know how long they'll survive."

Roberto asked, "Do you know of Emilio Hammond?"

"He's with the group that jumped into San Blas, on the eastern front."

First Light
C-46 Transport Aircraft
Skies above Girón, "Blue Beach"

The warning light on the C-46 transport plane went on. A few seconds later, it started pulsating like a heartbeat. The paratroopers sprang to their feet, checked their equipment one last time, and hooked into the static line. Emilio checked his helmet and took a deep breath. The man next to him made the Sign of the Cross no fewer than fifty times in quick succession. "*In nómine Patris, Filii, Spiritus Sancti; In nómine Patris, Filii, Spiritus Sancti; In nómine Patris, Filii, Spiritus Sancti . . .*"

Emilio felt good. A short time earlier, they'd flown over a U.S. aircraft carrier, its warplanes lining the flight deck, and a couple of other U.S. war ships. Their allies had their backs. He was fully confident of victory.

The rear side doors opened, filling the inside of the fuselage with a powerful gust. They were over Girón a moment later. Alejandro del Valle beheld the spectacle below. "Look down there! It's like Normandy!"

The green light came on a couple of minutes later. The paratroopers gave the airborne cheer one last time and one by one jumped into the skies over San Blas, eight miles northeast of Girón. Emilio stood at the open door for less than a second, his clothes rippling, the early morning wind cutting across his face. He pushed away from the airplane, freefalling like a giant, wingless bird until his body was jerked to a halt by the resistance of the opening parachute. During the brief descent, he looked below and saw Cuban soil coming ever closer, thinking that in a few seconds at least one spot on his homeland would be free.

He hit the ground with a thud, his momentum carrying him forward several yards. He unhooked his parachute like it was on fire, grabbed his weapon, crouched, and scanned the area around him. The landscape throbbed with danger. An impulse made him gaze upward. His shoulders slumped and his eyes relaxed as he beheld a host of paratroopers dropping softly to the earth like angels sent from Heaven.

They began setting up a perimeter around San Blas, the village on this dry patch of land in the swampy region even smaller than Emilio had imagined it. Someone started shooting at them. "There, in the brush, militia," someone shouted. The Brigade men respond with their rifles and a BAR, scaring them off. After quickly securing the town, they set about recovering the equipment that had scattered around the area after the drop. They set up a command center and began digging trenches. Bewildered local residents brought them food and water. Other locals helped carry supplies and volunteered as nurses. A handful of them even asked for uniforms and weapons to fight alongside the Brigade.

After things were arranged at San Blas, Emilio and a few others were called over by del Valle. "The advance unit dropped outside of Covadonga is under heavy attack, and I've lost contact altogether with the nineteen men near Yaguaramas. Last I heard they were under fire as well."

"Where's our air cover?"

"Who knows? Listen, some mortars are coming by truck soon from Girón. You guys need to break up into two groups and go up the roads to find a place to set them up."

Emilio's group marched several miles down the road toward Yaguaramas. They found a suitable spot for the mortars and reported back to San Blas. By then, reinforcements had arrived from Girón, which included the mortars, a tank, some heavy weapons, and infantry. A guy from the Fourth Battalion who was with the group gave Emilio the bad news: not all of Castro's planes were destroyed; the groups landing at Girón had come ashore safely, although under fire, and took the airfield as planned; they still held it, but the fact that Castro still had fighter planes made it impossible for any of the Brigade's B-26s to land. "So basically, the whole plan as originally conceived is *kaput*."

The news only got worse: Castro's war planes, now uncontested, had gone after the Brigade ships. The *Houston* was hit and beached a few miles south of Playa Larga, putting tons of equipment and the entire Fifth Battalion out of commission. Off the coast of Girón, the *Río Escondido* was hit by a rocket from a Castro airplane; laden as she was with explosives and fuel drums, she exploded into a giant mushroom cloud, which explained the mystery of the explosion they had heard earlier. The men aboard the *Río Escondido* had evacuated the ship in the nick of time, "because God is great!" The other ships, seeking to protect the remaining equipment and avoid the fate of the *Río Escondido*, had fled into international waters. They would try to return later under the cover of darkness. As things presently stood, the Brigade had virtually no air cover, no naval support, and roughly a day's worth of ammunition and supplies, maybe two if they stretched it.

Panic slithered up Emilio's spine. "But there has to be an alternate plan. The Americans have war ships nearby carrying a fleet of combat planes. I saw them with my own eyes," he said incredulously. "They're supposed to have our backs. They're our allies. They wouldn't just abandon 1,400 men here!" The man held up his hands in a helpless gesture.

Emilio and his squad were ordered down the Yaguaramas road again, this time to help set up the mortars at the spot they'd chosen earlier. The tank that had come up from Girón went ahead of them to make the link with the nineteen-man advance unit near Yaguaramas. When Emilio returned to San Blas later, he followed the action through radio transmissions sent to the command center: the nineteen paratroopers on the Covadonga front were under heavy artillery attack and requesting air support. The unit at Yaguaramas, led by Nestor Pino, was back in radio contact and facing an entire battalion; except now, with the tank sent from Girón, they had counterattacked and advanced, extending their perimeter by several hundred yards. Emilio felt a jolt of hope. "Advancing? My God, we're advancing!"

15

ISLE OF PINES
MAXIMUM SECURITY PRISON
April 17, 1961

Israel Muñoz pushed himself off his bug infested cot and stretched his emaciated body in the early morning chill. He felt a cramp in his abdomen. He pressed his hand down on his belly and marveled again at how much body mass he'd lost since entering prison. The cramp subsided. He turned his gaze outside his cell and looked across the vast, silent interior of the prison building. He'd lost track of exactly how many days had elapsed since he was transferred from La Cabaña to this place, the "Model Prison" on the Isle of Pines off Cuba's southwestern shore, Castro's own "Devil's Island" for political enemies. The prison buildings in the sprawling complex consisted of two six-story rectangular structures and four multi-storied circular ones.

Israel had been flown to the small island with a large group of prisoners from Havana. They were met at an airfield by a pack of bestial guards from the prison who pummeled them with truncheons, rifle butts, and chains when they exited the plane. Handcuffed together, the new arrivals had cowered and tripped over each other under the hail of blows. After this official welcome, the bloodied prisoners were put on a truck under heavy guard and driven to the prison, where a new contingent of guards awaited them. The prisoners were shoved off the truck while still handcuffed together, the guards slapping them, kicking them, and shouting, "Good for nothing worms! Welcome to Hell!"

Bewildered and terrified, the prisoners were marched to a room at the headquarters building where they were un-cuffed, forced to strip naked, and lined up against a wall. Their personal possessions were confiscated. Items of senti-mental value–family pictures, religious objects–were thrown out or destroyed before their eyes by mocking guards. Com-pared to this place, Israel's time at La Cabaña seemed like a weekend at the Havana Hilton. They received their prison uniforms and were taken into the main prison area.

When he came into the Circular to which he was assigned, Israel was appalled by the spectacle of over 1,300 emaciated political prisoners welcoming them with cheers and applause. The cells and railed walkways that ran before them lined the round building's walls like giant, stacked rings, all of them facing the cavernous interior. In the center of the Circular's ground floor was a prison yard, and in the middle of the yard a concrete guard tower, four stories high, topped by a balcony from which the guards kept watch. The building was capped by a massive roof, giving Israel the feeling of being inside a gigantic cooking pot. The noise inside was overwhelming, a deafening babble of 1,300 voices all speaking at once, careen-ing randomly off the roof and walls, and coming together to form a single, appalling howl.

After a couple of months, though, Israel was no longer overwhelmed by the prison. Veteran status in the Circulars was achieved rather quickly by most prisoners. He'd learned to cope with the lack of food and the overall degradation to which he and the other prisoners were subjected daily. Still, he hadn't gotten accustomed to the unchecked sadism of the guards, the uniformed gorillas never missing an opportunity to demonstrate their savagery. Israel had concluded that, for this job, the regime actively recruited only documented sociopaths, their depravity being so beyond anything that could ever be brought out in a normal human being. The worst atrocities, though, were reserved for the prisoners sent to the punishment cells. Many had been locked in coffin-like drawer cells for weeks at a time; others had been stripped naked and sealed for months in tiny cells whose barred doors had metal sheets welded to them, giving the prisoner inside the sensation of being trapped inside a box. Israel shuddered every time he thought about it.

Walking across the floor of his third-story cell that morning, he stopped to kneel next to a cellmate who'd been burning with fever for three days, yet was repeatedly refused medical attention. He squeezed his hand. "How are you feeling?" The prisoner groaned. Israel could tell from his coloration that he'd taken a turn for the worse. "I'll talk to the guards again later about sending you to the infirmary." Then he smiled. "For now, I'll go upstairs to see if I can find you some food." The sick prisoner nodded his thanks.

Israel stepped out onto the walkway that ran before the cells, the hush of the early morning still hanging in the air. He stopped for a moment to savor the blessed stillness, knowing that the daily racket would soon commence. As he walked up the staircase, the silence was abruptly shattered by an explosion of cannon and machine gun fire from the nearby hills.

Israel's mouth went dry. His heart pounding, he rushed up the stairs to the top floor and went into the nearest cell. The prisoners inside were already pulling themselves up to the iron-barred windows to look outside. Israel joined them. The cannon continued to roar. He could see small, black clouds of exploding anti-aircraft shells filling the sky.

A B-26 bomber came into view. It circled the area and exchanged fire with a Cuban navy frigate at the mouth of the Las Casas River, indifferent to the barrage of shells and bullets being shot at it. When the B-26 flew away, the prisoners took out the pieces of a radio they had hidden in different parts of the prison and assembled it. They listened for news about the attack. All but the most pessimistic believed that the long-awaited war of liberation had begun.

As they struggled to find a radio signal, they heard jeeps and trucks screeching to a halt outside the Circular. They looked out the windows and saw soldiers and militiamen taking up battle positions, aiming their weapons at the prison buildings. They fired at the faces peering through the windows. Everyone jumped away. Minutes later, a group of guards burst into the Circular and fired their weapons indiscriminately at the cells through the main gate. Bullets punctured walls and ricocheted off iron bars and railings. An officer announced that anyone who went to the windows would be shot by the guards stationed outside. He turned on his heel and left.

That afternoon, a military unit came into the Circular bearing boxes filled with sticks of dynamite rolled into bunches. The frightened prisoners watched as the dynamite bunches were placed into the tunnel running to the central tower and into the building's foundations. More dynamite was laid the following day. The regime's message could not have been clearer: the inmates would be blown to bits if there was a landing on the Isle of Pines.

That evening, they learned that a liberation army had landed in the area of the Bay of Pigs. Despite the dynamite that threatened to blast them into a million pieces, a wave of excitement ran throughout the Circular.

Their day of liberation had finally arrived.

16

BAY OF PIGS
ROADBLOCK NORTH OF PLAYA LARGA, "RED BEACH"

Noon, April 17, 1961

The midday sun shone brightly on the detachment of the Second Battalion camouflaged at the roadblock north of Playa Larga. They had received word about the *Río Escondido's* obliteration and the flight of the other ships from the Girón coast a little earlier. The men nevertheless remained optimistic. They believed the United States would still support them, especially if they held the line. Goyo and Pedro Vila were crouched side-by-side, camouflaged among the others at the roadblock. Roberto was just ahead of them near Maximo Cruz, the company commander at the road-block, holding a pair of binoculars to his eyes, waiting for the first sign of enemy troops.

Shortly after noontime, an excited voice crackled over the radio. The radio operator listened carefully. He nodded. "Our forward observers report a Castro truck and a column of militia moving toward us." With the precision of a field mar-shal, Cruz adjusted the men's positions. "Wait for the order."

A truck and infantry column appeared a few hundred yards down the causeway. Goyo watched them grow larger every time he blinked. A chill ran through his limbs. Roberto, following them through his binoculars, felt as though he could reach out and shake hands with them. Castro's men kept marching into range, oblivious to the death trap into which they marched so smartly. Goyo's stomach tightened.

When the Castro soldiers were approximately seventy-five yards away, they stopped and pulled together in a tight formation. The order was given.

The Brigade's guns exploded like a burst of rolling thunder. One of the heavy guns made a direct hit on the truck. A split second later, a white phosphorus round landed in the middle of the infantry column, instantly killing several enemy troops; the rest shrieked maniacally, their skin burning as if they'd been dipped in acid. The survivors disappeared into the brush and retreated.

Brigade 2506: 1

Fidel Castro: 0

Goyo shook with both excitement and abhorrence. He didn't know for certain if he'd killed anyone. He'd just shot continually into the melee. His heart was racing with so many different emotions, he couldn't tell what he felt. "It's started," he told himself over and over. Bullets had been exchanged. Castro knew they were here. He thought his heart would explode.

He turned to Pedro Vila. The boy was beaming. "We really let them have it, didn't we Mr. León? Just look at how they ran away!"

Goyo was irritated by Pedro's cavalier attitude. Did the boy think this was a game? He was in no position, however, to reprimand him. He looked up at the sky, remembering the Castro airplanes that morning. "We have a long way to go yet, Pedro."

Around 2:30 p.m., the forward observers, who'd been stationed around six-hundred yards ahead, retreated back to the roadblock. A Castro force of hundreds was now rolling down the road, they reported. Roberto picked up his binoculars and saw it a few minutes later: an armored car at the head of a dozen or so other vehicles– commandeered civilian buses among them–packed with troops. Roberto squinted into his binoculars, finding it inconceivable that they would just come straight down the road like that again. The sheer stupidity of it made him wonder if the column was a diversionary force and that the roadblock would be attacked from behind or on its flanks.

As they waited for the enemy to come into range, reinforcements sent from Girón arrived at the front: an M-41 tank and some additional troops. The new arrivals took up their positions.

The Castro convoy stopped several hundred yards from the roadblock. The soldiers dismounted the vehicles, slung rifles over their shoulders, and began to form up in the middle of the road like a group of boy scouts at a trail head. They set up some mortars in anticipation of their advance and began forging down the road around the armored car. It sounded as though they were singing battle hymns as they marched into the 2506's bull's eye. Roberto, his mouth agape, peered at them through his binoculars. Unless this was a trap, he thought, the road would soon become a graveyard.

The order was given. The exploding shells fired from the Brigade's heavy weapons sent enemy soldiers flying through the air; but for their hideous screams, one would have thought it was a performance of Chinese acrobats. The

159

Brigade's machine guns and rifles found their targets with lethal precision, mowing down enemy troops in quick succession. Goyo fired round after round, knowing for sure that *this* time he'd shot a man.

As the guns blasted away, impossibly good news reached the roadblock: air support was on the way. They heard the engine noise a minute later. They turned. Three B-26 bombers with phony Cuban air force insignia painted on them flew in from behind the Brigade position, going south to north.

Bernie Cuervo was in one of those bombers. After the air raids were canceled that morning, the Brigade pilots were permitted to fly limited missions to protect the beachhead. Since Castro still possessed combat aircraft, the Brigade B-26s couldn't hope to land at the Girón airfield; and even if they could, it would have been pointless: almost their entire battlefield supply of bombs, ammunition, rockets, spare parts, and fuel were on ships that had been either destroyed or forced into international waters by Castro's fighters. The Brigade air force had no choice but to fly back and forth from Nicaragua. This arrangement gave them only enough fuel to spend half an hour or so over the battle zone–if they were lucky enough not to get shot down by the fast fighter planes first.

The pilots made a pass over the battlefield to get a closer glimpse of the enemy before commencing the attack. They dipped their wings in salute. Bernie sighed sadly as Castro's people, fooled by the fake Cuban air force insignia, cheered and waved their hats at them. The B-26s circled back to approach the road again from the same direction, reporting as they did so to the Brigade leadership on the ground: behind the enemy vanguard were more than sixty other vehicles carrying hundreds of additional troops into the battle zone.

The pilots were given the order to fire.

The Brigade men at the roadblock looked back over their shoulders and saw the B-26s coming over them for the second time, only this time they were flying fewer than a hundred feet above the road. The airplanes' bellies buckled as they released the first rockets. Some of the Castro men were still cheering and shouting "¡Vivas!" when they were hit.

The B-26s repeatedly swept over the battle zone in perfect synchronicity, relentlessly strafing the enemy with nose-mounted .50 caliber guns, dropping bombs, and firing rockets; the line of Castro vehicles was turned into a heap of burning rubble. The Brigade's ground units, meanwhile, overwhelmed the enemy with heavy guns, rifles, machine guns, bazookas, and the tank. Nearly the entire Castro force was wiped out. Corpses and scorched vehicles stretched along hundreds of yards of road. Only a few survivors who melted into the swamp lived to tell the story.

Brigade 2506: 2

Fidel Castro: 0

Bernie was sweating profusely. After half an hour, he was out of ammunition and had barely enough fuel to make it back to Nicaragua. It was time to go. As the B-26s prepared to exit the battle zone, a silver flash appeared on the horizon. And then another.

"Oh, damn it!" Bernie shouted over the radio. "A T-33 and a Sea Fury, take evasive action! Now, damn it, now!" Before they could make another move, the faster enemy planes were upon them. One of them scored a direct hit on the B-26 nearest Bernie, blowing it into a burning heap and sending it careening into the water. The other Brigade airplane was also hit. Smoke pouring from one of its engines, it disappeared over the horizon at low altitude, the Sea Fury in hot pursuit. Bernie knew the crew would probably never make it back to Happy Valley.

His options exhausted, Bernie pulled up and banked southwest over the Zapata Peninsula to try to escape.

It was no use. The T-33 buzzed all around him like an angry hornet, firing its machine guns. Several rounds ripped through the fuselage, one of them finding the back of his navigator's head, killing him instantly. A subsequent hail of bullets hit one of the engines; the next round knocked out the navigation equipment. The B-26 started losing altitude quickly; the cockpit filled with smoke. Bernie grabbed the radio. Gagging from the smoke, he spoke to the Brigade radio operator on the ground: "My name is Bernardo Cuervo García, previously of *Cubana de Aviación*. Please tell my wife, my children, and my parents in Miami that I went to my death fighting for Cuba's freedom and that I love them more than anything in the world." He dropped the microphone, let go of the controls, and ripped off the crucifix hanging around his neck. Holding the crucifix tightly in his fist, he crossed his arms over his chest and closed his eyes. The B-26 tilted head-long toward the earth, crashing nose-first into the swamp.

Back on the ground, a cry suddenly went up from the Brigade position. "Hold your fire! Hold your fire!" An enemy vehicle was advancing down the road. One of the commanders announced to the men, "They're ambulances! Orders from Playa Larga are to hold your fire to let them pick up their wounded!" Roberto pulled out his binoculars and saw two ambulances followed by a white truck with a Red Cross emblem painted on it. Armed troops suddenly began pouring out of the vehicles. A few seconds later, a column of troop-carrying trucks pulled up behind the ambulances. Roberto lowered the binoculars. Someone said, "They're advancing! They're using the ambulances as cover!" They reported the situation to headquarters and received the order to fire. The Brigade guns opened fire once more; the remaining Castro troops finally retreated.

The commanders learned from some prisoners the Brigade had captured that Castro was amassing a large force at the Central Australia sugar mill to the north and would try to make his breakthrough down the road that night. The men at the roadblock were ordered to fall back and join other units of the Second Battalion at the "Rotunda," a crude traffic circle northwest of the beach, where they would set up a fortified line. The prisoners asked for weapons to fight alongside the Brigade, making Roberto ponder glumly how many of those dead men and boys lying along the road had fought on the other side against their will. Part of him was crying.

Goyo had briefly seen the Rotunda when they passed through it earlier that day. Now he got a more detailed look as they dug in for the coming offensive. It was plain to see, even to his civilian eyes, that the Rotunda was the ideal place to entrench themselves, for it negated, at least to a limited degree, Castro's crushing numerical advantage. The main road going to the beach passed through the Rotunda; to get to the coast and continue down the road to Girón, the enemy had no choice but to break through it. The Rotunda's dimensions allowed for a far greater number of Brigade men and weapons to aim fire at the approaching enemy than the roadblock did; it gave the small Brigade force a definite tactical advantage over the much larger and better equipped Castro force. Pedro Vila, staring at the narrow road that entered the traffic circle and at the Brigade force settling into position, said to Goyo reflectively, "You know? This whole strategy of meeting a larger enemy in a narrow gap reminds me of Thermopylae, Mr. León, like you taught us in class." Goyo slapped a mosquito on his cheek and wiped his hands on his pants. "You forget, Pedro, that the Greeks were betrayed and that those who stayed behind to fight at the gap were all killed. Let's just hope we're not betrayed, too—because from what we've seen so far, I think we've probably been." In the middle of the Rotunda a large wooden sign promoting Castro's National Agrarian Reform Institute stared at them ironically.

While the tank, machine guns, recoilless rifles, bazookas, mortars, and rifle companies were settling into position, some welcome reinforcements arrived from Girón: a large part of the Fourth Battalion, a company from the Sixth Battalion, an additional mortar platoon, two more tanks, and extra ammunition. Despite the help, the Brigade force at the Rotunda still amounted to fewer than four-hundred men. Miyares kicked a rock. "The reinforcements are nice, but this would've been over by now if we'd had the air support we were promised."

Roberto overheard the comment. He gazed up at the sky, knowing Miyares was probably right. When he had seen the Brigade B-26s perform earlier that day, he was convinced they would have won had the Americans followed through with the original plan. A miniscule contingent of Brigade B-26s– that had flown in all the way from Nicaragua–had destroyed an entire Castro battalion in less than *thirty minutes*. He closed his eyes and tried to imagine what it would've been like to have had all *twenty-two* B-26s permanently stationed at Girón, infinitely supplied by ships stationed offshore, flying *twenty-four hours a day,* with no enemy aircraft to oppose them. It would have become unsustainable for Castro within hours. His militia and Rebel Army would've deserted or faced anni- hilation. The Brigade's ranks would have swelled and the guerrilla bands across the country would have gone on the offensive. With a provisional democratic government on the ground at Girón, as well as diplomatic and military support from abroad, the regime no doubt would've collapsed like a house of cards.

But it was not to be. They were here alone, a few hundred hopelessly outnumbered men with a day's worth of ammu- nition in a harsh, desolate corner of Cuba, facing a well- equipped military force of tens of thousands. The Brigade's unprotected B-26s, flown by pilots with nerves of steel, were being downed one-by-one by Castro's undestroyed fighter planes. Still, Roberto felt a duty to maintain the troops' morale. He sighed heavily, walked over to his men, and stood before them.

"Listen to me," he said, holding his rifle in his right hand, "we can't focus on what could have been or should have been. The situation is what it is. In a little while a force of thousands is going to come right down that road and they don't give a shit if we think we've been betrayed. Our only option is to make a united stand." Roberto had captured the attention of another group nearby. He studied them closely for a few seconds. Their faces were smeared with dirt and blood. Some of them wore bandages on a variety of body parts. They waited for him to say more, but nothing came to him. He turned to look across the Rotunda and down the road through which Castro's forces would soon try to break through. He pointed to the ground. "Here, on this spot, on this night, the destiny of the Cuban nation will be forever determined. God and fate have blessed us with the honor of fighting here. For freedom! For democracy!" He silently chided himself for being so melodramatic. He considered shutting up, but a raw impulse was driving him now. He proclaimed in a voice wet with nationalist passion, "And on this patch of sacred ground, we'll make our stand and fight to the *death*!" The men nodded, grunting their agreement. All conversation ceased.

By 7:00 p.m., everything was ready. The heavy guns and tanks were carefully positioned around the Rotunda, the machine gunners and riflemen strategically placed all about. A palpable wave of tension ran up and down the lines. The men of the Brigade waited in silence for Castro to throw his best at them. Goyo and Pedro Vila lay side-by-side, lined up with the rest of their squad on one of the flanks. Goyo squeezed his St. Jude medallion. Pedro pulled out a Rosary, kissed the crucifix, and hung it around his neck.

Shortly after 7:30 p.m., the silence was broken by a thundering barrage of artillery fire from Castro's Soviet-made 122mm howitzers. The ear-splitting explosions were followed by the bloodcurdling whistle of shells traveling at high speed. They exploded "POW! POW! POW!" into the ground with a sound so fearsome no Hollywood studio could ever hope to reproduce it. The shells were landing several hundred yards ahead of the Rotunda, as Castro's people were combing the area until they found the Brigade position. The order from the command post at the beach was, "Keep silent, and don't move!" Goyo didn't know if he could stay riveted in place while the shells inched closer. The vibrations from the explosions were making even his clothes buzz with their power. Lying face down on the ground, he wrapped his fingers tightly around his M-1 rifle, flinching with every heart-stopping explosion.

Roberto came over and crouched next to him. "A few men have gone into shock, but no one has run. I think a lot of us are going to die here tonight."

Goyo squeezed Roberto's forearm. He whispered, "Faith, cousin, faith." They heard an airplane overhead and looked up. They had seen it earlier, just before the artillery attack had commenced. Roberto said, "That's probably a Castro airplane trying to find our location so they could direct the artillery. Let's hope it doesn't spot us."

At 9:30 p.m., after two hours of ceaseless bombardment, the first shells landed at the Brigade position. Shrapnel showers cascaded down on the men, the fragments pinging against the metal of the tanks and guns; flashes from the explosions bathed them intermittently in red light. Goyo's back muscles contracted when he heard grisly screams from the men who were hit. He wanted to help them, but his orders were to stay put. Shuddering spasmodically, he imitated Pedro by putting his Rosary around his neck. At one point, the squad, along with a few others nearby, was ordered to move quickly to another spot at the Rotunda. Seconds later, artillery shells landed on their original position; apparently, the headquarters staff at the beach had tapped into the Castro radio frequency and was able to anticipate where the shells would land. A little later, the squads went back to their original positions. Goyo thanked God that the troops at Playa Larga were so well led by their young commanders, Oliva and Sueiro.

In one of the momentary flashes of light, Goyo caught a brief glimpse of Pedro. The kid was observing the artillery barrage with complete serenity, lying flat on his stomach, his chin propped up on folded hands like a ten-year-old watching a fireworks show. The young man who'd been so frightened of being captured by the Communists a few months earlier now faced them with complete equanimity. Goyo recalled the seemingly ridiculous comment Pedro had made to him aboard the *Houston*, "I know you'll probably be angry with me for saying this, Mr. León, but I've made the decision to give my life for Cuba." The memory again made Goyo want to slap him. But suddenly, he stopped shaking. He aimed his rifle toward the Rotunda's entrance.

By 11:30 p.m., the shells were flying over their heads and into the Bay of Pigs behind them. Around midnight, the guns went silent. An obsessive-compulsive named García declared that he had been counting the shells and that nearly two-thousand had been fired over the four-hour barrage. Despite this accurate figure, fewer than ten Brigade men had been killed and only thirty were wounded.

A ghastly silence now engulfed the darkened Rotunda. Everyone understood what the stillness meant. Orders went up and down the line to be ready. A sudden paternal impulse compelled Goyo to make sure Roberto and Pedro were safely on either side of him. At 12:30 a.m., they heard the petrifying din of tank engines and the heavy metallic grinding of their treads. The units closest to the front reported three enemy tanks rolling in, spaced twenty yards apart, each followed by a company of infantry.

The first Castro tank entered the Rotunda.

The Brigade's guns opened fire.

A hail of rifle and machine gun fire rained down on the enemy column pushing through the gap; the recoilless rifles, bazookas, and other heavy guns simultaneously unleashed a lethal volley of shells, grenades, and rockets. Tracer bullets and exploding shells illuminated the area as if with a stroboscopic light. The Brigade's M-41 tanks, firing at their Communist counterparts at point blank range, knocked out the first two Castro tanks, a Soviet T-34 and a Stalin III. When the third tank tried to move around them, one of the Brigade tank drivers, out of ammunition, charged at it like a bull, brazenly crashing into it as though it was demolition derby day. When the Communist tank tried to turn its gun on him, the Brigade tank driver maneuvered back and forth, ramming into it repeatedly until he split its gun barrel. Its gun destroyed and its caterpillar tread damaged, the enemy tank limped from the Rotunda. The Castro troops withdrew.

Goyo, out of breath, felt nervously to his left and right again to check on Roberto and Pedro. They were both still alive. Roberto got up and checked on his squad. One of the men, a bazooka man, had been shot through the shoulder. Roberto laid the bazooka down and ordered the man down to the beach post where there were medics and a doctor.

A second tank/infantry force started rolling into the gap just as the injured man started heading back to the beach. With the two wrecked tanks blocking the way, it was only with great difficulty that the new round of enemy tanks moved into the Rotunda. Blinded by the darkness and beset on every side by Brigade fire, the overwhelmed Communist tanks began running over their own wounded; terrified screams emanated from the injured men as they were crushed under the treads. One of the tanks suddenly broke past the congestion and began rolling deeper into the Rotunda; it stopped abruptly and pivoted in the direction of Roberto's squad. Roberto showered it with a hail of tracer bullets, illuminating it briefly as it rolled directly at them.

Pedro Vila jumped to his feet.

He grabbed the bazooka Roberto had placed on the ground before them and ran, lumbering, toward the tank. Goyo's shouts for him to come back were drowned out by the sounds of battle. Goyo went after Pedro, watching the boy's silhouette before him in the light of the explosions. When Pedro was fifteen yards before the tank, he went down on one knee and positioned the bazooka on his shoulder. He took aim. The tank rumbling directly at him, he held his ground, firing when it was only ten yards away. He landed a direct hit. As he stood to jump out of the way, a shell exploded next to where he stood. He landed several feet back, face up on the ground.

The injured tank, with some life still in it, slowly kept moving forward. Goyo, still a few yards away, saw it approaching Pedro motionless body. He reached the boy a second later, quickly wrapped his arms around him from behind, and just barely pulled him out of the tank's path. Dragging Pedro's limp body, Goyo slithered across the dark battleground on his belly. Shrapnel fell like hellish raindrops and bullets whizzed overhead as they rolled into a crater made earlier by an artillery shell. Goyo cradled Pedro between his thighs and let the back of Pedro's head drop on his chest.

A series of explosions went off in quick succession near them, lighting up the area for a few seconds. Goyo took a quick look at Pedro. He saw instantly that the boy was dead, his belly and chest blown apart by the blast. He could see the mass of wet, snake-like intestines and internal organs pouring out of Pedro's shredded torso. Goyo went into shock, his jaw and lips convulsing. He repeated, "No, no, no," over and over.

He looked over the edge of the ditch and saw Roberto drop a grenade into the tank's hatch, killing the crew inside and stopping its forward motion once and for all.

Goyo, still in a state of shock, began combing Pedro's hair with his muddied fingers. He reached toward Pedro's waist, an unconscious impulse to push his exposed intestines back into his body cavity. He caught himself and stopped. The battlefield went silent to him. An image of Pedro's father suddenly came to him. "Mr. León, why didn't you look out for him? Why didn't you go out and face the tank? Why did you let a boy do a man's job?"

Roberto rolled into the ditch a second later. He saw Pedro and forced Goyo to let go of him, ordering him out with a shove, "Come on, move! There's nothing we can do for him. Get back into position!" Goyo, completely numb, complied.

For the next hour, tank after tank rolled into the Rotunda, each accompanied by infantry. One after another, the Brigade force repelled them. By the time a momentary lull came in the dead of night, six Castro tanks lay destroyed in the Rotunda, surrounded by heaps of dead and wounded enemy troops. A thick cloud of acrid gun smoke had settled in the eerily silent traffic circle. The enemy wounded cried out in hoarse, fading voices, "Help me! Somebody come for me! For the love of God, please!"

A short while later, the first wave of Castro's heavy infantry assaults charged into the Rotunda. The men of Brigade 2506 fired at the attacking troops in pitch darkness, aiming their guns in the direction of the enemy's sounds, shouts, and screams. The Brigade mortars, having heretofore been held in reserve, were now unleashed, wreaking havoc on the enemy. The infantry waves came in unrelenting succession; soon, there were more tanks. With each attack, Castro's casualties mounted. Roberto yelled to his men, "Keep shooting! We're holding the line! The line is holding!"

At 5:30 a.m., the fighting finally ceased. Goyo watched as the darkness lifted at early dawn, casting the Rotunda in a gray, smoky light. It was the morning of April 18; the Rotunda was a grotesque arena of death. Corpses lay everywhere; those who'd been flattened by tanks provided the most gruesome spectacles. His eyes scanned the seemingly endless number of enemy combatants lying dead throughout the traffic circle. There were many Pedros on the other side as well, he thought. Goyo avoided looking in Pedro's direction, although he was determined to bury him at some point. His head collapsed on the ground. For the first time since he'd been aboard the *Houston*, he fell asleep.

A few minutes later, a lone enemy tank rolled into the Rotunda. This time, Oliva himself grabbed a .57mm and knelt to face it. To the astonishment of everyone who witnessed it, the hatch popped open and the Castro driver climbed out. He announced that he and his crew wished to surrender. He informed Oliva that the Brigade force of fewer than four-hundred men and a few tanks had faced a Castro army of over 2,100 troops and twenty-two tanks. Castro had suffered a casualty rate of over 70 percent—around five-hundred dead and one-thousand wounded. The Brigade had suffered roughly fifty wounded and twenty dead in the battle. The 2506's training, discipline, bravery, and, especially, its leadership, had won the night, had won the Battle of the Rotunda. And to Roberto, "The most important thing is that the line held! When the Americans find out what happened here last night, they can't deny us support!"

Brigade 2506: 3

Fidel Castro: 0

Before Roberto could finish piecing together the significance of the victory, an order came: all troops were to retreat back to the beach and prepare to evacuate to Girón, where they would link up with other Brigade battalions. Roberto protested, "Why are we retreating to Girón? Why are we giving up Playa Larga? We've just defeated the enemy! We've destroyed everything they've thrown at us since we landed yesterday! What's going on?" Another squad leader pulled him aside and explained that they were virtually out of ammunition, having used nearly all of it the previous night. "And Castro is amassing a giant force at Central Australia, many times larger than what he hit us with last night. To stay here would be suicidal."

Goyo, Roberto, and their squad gathered quickly to bury Pedro before heading back to the beach. By now, everyone knew about Pedro's death and sensed the guilt that was consuming Goyo. A medical student who'd given Pedro's remains a cursory examination reassured Goyo, "The explosion from the shell killed him instantly. He was dead by the time you reached him. There was nothing you could do to save him."

They buried Pedro in the same shallow trench into which Goyo had dragged him the night before, sparing them the unpleasant task of having to move his remains. They poured dirt over him. Goyo, overcome with soul-searing anguish, fell to his knees. How could he ever look into Pedro's father's eyes and tell him how his son had died? That he, revered teacher, exemplary family man, the cool, heroic underground agent who'd earlier rescued his beloved son, had allowed his boy's body to be blown apart and then buried what was left of him in an artillery crater on a desolate roadside.

Goyo got up. The squad stood silently for a moment. Miyares placed a makeshift cross atop the small mound of dirt covering Pedro. No doubt Castro's men would pluck it off when they came through. Pedro's final resting place would nevertheless have a symbol of his Catholic faith, if only for a little while. Buzzards flew overhead, ready to swoop down, as April 18 at the Rotunda provided the scavengers with an unusually bountiful feast.

They heard gunfire in the distance. Someone warned them that Castro snipers had already infiltrated their position. The squad stayed with Pedro until Father Hidalgo finished the Rite of Committal, commending Pedro's soul to Jesus Christ. The priest finished the rite in record time. They picked up their weapons and joined the other clusters of men heading back toward the beach. Someone began singing the national anthem. Everyone joined in. Roberto looked up at the sky, part of him still hoping that their air support would materialize. Then he looked at the ground, spat, and cursed.

The squad boarded one of the trucks leaving for Girón. They looked on as the two hundred prisoners the Brigade had held at Playa Larga were freed. They scrambled to get away. The truck carrying Roberto's squad jumped on the road that ran along the eastern rim of the Bay of Pigs toward Girón. Half-way into the journey, they passed an overturned Brigade truck. Someone explained that it had been carrying a mortar platoon and extra ammunition to the men at the Rotunda last night, but in the darkness it had hit a ditch and flipped over. Goyo buried his head in his hands as the truck continued its slow journey to Girón.

Just before 9:00 a.m., they arrived at their new position at the western end of Girón. They took shelter in a partially-built vacation resort Castro had begun developing there. Goyo plopped down inside one of the structures and fell into a fitful sleep on the concrete floor. Pedro appeared to him over and over in his dreams, his dripping intestines in hand, asking, "Why didn't you get me Mr. León? How could you let this happen to me?"

Bay of Pigs
San Blas Front
Night, April 17, 1961

On the evening of April 17, as the men on the Playa Larga front were digging in for the Battle of the Rotunda, reports coming into San Blas from the paratroopers' forward positions near Covadonga and Yaguaramas indicated an irreversible deterioration of the front lines. Heavy concentrations of enemy troops had amassed opposite each position and had started to plow forward. The tiny Brigade force near Covadonga had made a heroic stand, but the overwhelming pressure had forced them to begin falling back. Shortly before midnight, del Valle ordered a truck to go evacuate them.

Del Valle called Emilio over shortly afterward. "Hey, Alabama, come here." He ordered Emilio and another paratrooper to join some men from the group that had come from Girón earlier that day. They were to go down the now undefended road to Covadonga with 4.2 mortars to slow the Castro march toward San Blas for as long as possible. Forward observers would direct their fire.

The group headed down the dark road until they estimated they were within range of the enemy. They stopped and set up the mortars. The forward observers reported that scores of enemy troops, accompanied by a fleet of trucks and armored cars, could be clearly seen moving in their direction. The drivers were foolishly driving with their headlights on. The forward observers gave the coordinates. The men set their weapons' angles and waited until the enemy came into range.

Emilio closed his eyes, his heartbeat racing. He steepled his fingers over his nose and mouth and took a deep breath, contemplating that he was about to kill fellow human beings for the first time in his life. Jimmy Strickland suddenly came to mind. Emilio knew what the American would say to him: "Damn it, this ain't no time to think! You have a duty; now stop dilly-dallying and *fulfill* it!" His thoughts traveled back to that night around the campfire. An enigmatic look had emanated from Jimmy's eyes when he sang the "bye and bye" song; yet, somehow, the look was strangely familiar. Jimmy's words afterward, which came out in a voice that was equally enigmatic, suddenly flashed back to him. "Make no mistake about it: your daddy's right proud of you, *right* proud of you." Emilio opened his eyes in immediate comprehension.

There was now no doubt in his mind that everything that had happened to him since leaving New York had been guided by an external force. He curled his steepled fingers into fists and shifted his eyes upward toward the darkened sky. He perceived his father's unseen presence all around him.

The order came to fire. The Brigade unit unleashed its barrage. For the next several hours, the small group fired wave after wave of mortar shells at the advancing enemy. With every launch Emilio felt stronger, his motions becoming more automatic, crisp, and efficient. The pitch darkness and the repeated mechanical motions made him feel detached from his immediate surroundings, as if his mind and body were floating around separate planetary systems. The small Brigade group, hopelessly outnumbered, stopped the advance of thousands in their tracks.

Throughout the fight, Emilio nevertheless remained acutely aware that the minuscule mortar unit couldn't stop an entire army forever. They had only a limited number of shells–the rest of them were sitting on the sea bottom or on ships that had fled into international waters. Castro had thousands of men coming down the road along with God-knows how many tanks, howitzers, and armored cars. If the Brigade didn't get air support by morning, and if the ships carrying their equipment and ammo didn't return, they were finished, no matter how well or how heroically he and the others fought.

The next morning, the unit was ordered back to San Blas. When they got there, Emilio collapsed under a large tree. He felt as if his blood had been drained. Someone brought him some food and water. He ate and fell asleep for a little while. Later on, he helped dig some trenches. The nineteen men who'd fought outside of Yaguaramas, meanwhile, were brought back to San Blas by a truck with a mounted .50 caliber. Emilio fell asleep again, this time in a trench, and was awoken a little later by the sound of arriving trucks behind him. Startled, he reached for his rifle, but quickly saw that the trucks were carrying men in Brigade uniforms. He stood up slowly, the inside of his head spinning like a top. He looked again at the men on the trucks. They weren't paratroopers. He spotted a guy he knew from the University called José Antonio, and walked over to him. He gave him a playful shove from behind.

José Antonio turned. "Emilio?"

"José Antonio!" Emilio shook his hand and patted his back. "Where are you guys coming from?"

"We're the Third Battalion. They stuck us on the coastal road east of Girón, facing Cienfuegos, waiting for an attack that never came. Anyhow, the commanders replaced us with some guys from the Fourth Battalion who fought at Playa Larga last night and moved us here to support you. We've been desperate for some action."

"Well, I think you'll get it soon enough," Emilio said, motioning with his chin toward the Covadonga road.

José Antonio's battalion was ordered to entrench itself south of the town. He wished Emilio well and marched away.

Emilio scanned San Blas. It was utterly desolate. He squatted and unconsciously played with some of the dirt at his feet, wondering why Castro hadn't sent his army barreling down the roads yet, attacking them head on. The roads leading to San Blas from Covadonga and Yaguaramas, after all, were wide open now. Nothing could now stop Fidel Castro from converging on them from both directions. He stood up and, taking a puff from his asthma inhaler, thought that maybe, after last night's fight, Castro's people believed the Brigade contingent in San Blas was composed of thousands of well-armed men. He laughed to himself. "If they only knew!"

Castro's troops eventually started probing the town. While Emilio and some other paratroopers sat in shallow trenches waiting for an attack, they heard a truck approaching down the Yaguaramas road. Some of the paratroopers went out to meet it in a small truck. Before anyone knew what was happening, the two vehicles started circling each other and exchanging fire like two gunboats. The driver of the Brigade truck was hit several times in the arms. The Castro truck eventually retreated. A little later, a couple of paratroopers who'd been sent to lay out panels to identify their position for their non-existent air support were shot at and nearly killed. Within minutes of their return, the troops at San Blas heard the whistle of artillery shells flying at them, followed by their nightmarish concussions.

The paratroopers still in and around San Blas were eventually ordered to retreat south of the town, near where the Third Battalion had been sent earlier. As they gathered their gear to make their exit, someone found a radio and flipped on Radio Swan. The announcer was proclaiming, "The successful invasion troops are now on their march across Cuba!" Emilio shook his head, grabbed his rifle, and headed to the new position. The Brigade men looked on as an empty San Blas was razed by Castro's artillery.

HAVANA, CUBA
April 15-18, 1961

Teresa never took the children to Camagüey as Lorenzo had instructed her on April 15. When she hung up with Lorenzo she had called José María González, Raquel's father, and he had told her that it was no use. "The highways are jammed with military vehicles, you'll never make it. Plus, Castro's people are all very nervous, and that spells danger for everyone on the street." When Teresa told him about Raquel's arrest, the old man raged with fury and spent the rest of the day trying to find out where his pregnant daughter was being held. He ran into a stone wall wherever he went. Everyone was in war preparations. He went to Goyo's house in the evening with his wife and buried Mickey in a shallow grave in the backyard. He and his wife stayed with Teresa and the children at the house: doors locked, curtains drawn, and with as much food and supplies as they could gather. Fearing the island was about to enter a state of civil war, he kept a revolver on him at all times.

When the Brigade landed a couple of days later, Fidel Castro's militia poured forth from every corner of the capital. They jumped aboard trucks, tanks, and buses, singing Revolutionary songs, ready to defend Fidel against the "Yankee" threat. José María knew there were possibly even more people in Cuba like himself, whose loyalties ran with the Liberation Army. The pendulum would swing in the other direction if the liberators were victorious; and from what he'd been hearing that morning, it appeared as though they were soundly defeating the Communists. He firmly believed it would be only a matter of days before Havana was freed.

* * *

Inside the Blanquita Theatre, stress and dehydration had turned Raquel's skin the color of coconut meat by April 17. Eight thousand detainees were packed into the theatre. Sitting on the floor for two days, her back against the wall, she felt certain that she and her unborn child would die in this place. Her friend Dolores scrambled with the zeal of a missionary to find her food and water, but found little. She sat next to Raquel and kept her cool with a makeshift fan. They talked about old times and prayed the Rosary together.

* * *

Meanwhile, in La Cabaña fortress, Antonio de la Cruz also prayed the Rosary. Goyo's old friend from the *Agrupación* and his contact with the MRR had been arrested by the G.2 two days earlier. A five-minute trial before a Revolutionary tribunal was all it took for him to be sentenced to death. He sat in a cell with nine other men, eight of them, like himself, waiting to be taken to the execution wall—the dreaded *paredón*. He thanked God for giving him the foresight to send his wife and children out of the country the week before.

He began the First Sorrowful Mystery, "The Agony in the Garden." As he recited the prayers, he thought of Rogelio González Corzo, the MRR's leader in Cuba. He'd been arrested back in March at a secret meeting of democratic underground leaders that was betrayed to the G.2. The authorities at first didn't know they'd captured the hunted "Francisco," and underground members abroad did everything they could to prevent the Castro government from learning the truth. They even gave local newspapers in Miami pictures of a hooded man they claimed was the famous "Francisco" training at a secret location in the United States. It was all for naught, the G.2 figuring out rather quickly they had captured the heavily pursued clandestine agent. Now Rogelio, like Antonio, was awaiting execution somewhere in the bowels of La Cabaña. Their crusade had come to an end, making martyrs of them both. It was a fate Antonio did not relish.

When he reached the seventh bead of the First Sorrowful Mystery and repeated the words of Christ before His own execution, "Father, if it be possible, let this cup pass from Me; yet not My will but Yours be done," he felt as though he'd been stabbed in the heart. When he reached the ninth bead, "Judas's betrayal," he let out an ironic laugh.

The guards came in and gave the prisoners paper and pens to write their families a final letter. Antonio's hand shook as he held the pen. His mind drew a blank. How can a man tell his wife, his ten-year-old daughter, and his seven-year-old little boy, "goodbye" for the last time in a letter? How could a son, in writing, thank his parents for raising him as they did while he was waiting to be called out to face a firing squad? When the tears came, Antonio's pen began to move. He told his family that he loved them dearly, and that he had sacrificed his life for God and for Cuba. He asked them to be brave, and to know that, "I am dying as I lived: for the Faith." With forced fearlessness, he urged them to live their lives in the same manner, for when their inevitable end came, they would leave this world with the same peace as he would. The prisoners gave their letters to the guards. They all sat down to wait.

Antonio looked closely at the young men sitting with him in the cell. Their demeanor expressed nothing but complete inner peace. They bore no remorse about what they had done to make Cuba a free and democratic country. Within minutes, they heard a series of rusted metal gates leading to their cell open. The guards entered solemnly and called out the first prisoner. The man jumped to his feet and nodded farewell to the others. He followed the guards through the gate. A few minutes later, the men in the cell heard the crackle of the firing squad's rifles, followed by a single shot, the *coup de grâce*, behind the young victim's ear. Antonio's chest and shoulders tensed with each blast. The rusty gates creaked open again, and the guards called out the next victim.

Antonio's stomach turned to liquid. He crawled to a corner, knelt, and started praying the Rosary again, picking up where he'd left off earlier. He made it his sworn mission to finish it before his turn came. He recited the prayers fully but quickly, his scalp wet with sweat. When he reached the first of the Glorious Mysteries, "The Resurrection," the guards came and took away the third victim, a University student leader. They came next for another student, who died the same death as the others.

As Antonio finished reciting the last Hail Mary of the final Glorious Mystery, "The Coronation," the guards came in and ordered him to stand. Antonio ignored the order. He shut his eyes tightly, cocked his head toward the ceiling, and recited the final prayer out loud in an even, sturdy tone, "Hail, Holy Queen, Mother of Mercy, our life, our sweetness and our hope. To thee do we cry, poor banished children of Eve; to thee do we send up our sighs, mourning and weeping in this valley of tears. Turn then, most gracious advocate, thine eyes of mercy toward us; and after this our exile, show unto us the blessed fruit of thy womb, Jesus. O clement, O loving, O sweet Virgin Mary. Pray for us, O Holy Mother of God, that we may be made worthy of the promises of Christ."

The guards stepped toward him. He opened his eyes and made the Sign of the Cross, slowly and deliberately. The guards allowed Antonio this final indulgence. When he lowered his head, they ordered him to his feet again. Antonio obeyed this time and walked out of the cell surrounded by the guards. Images of his wife, his children, and his mother and father overwhelmed him with every step. Would his children forget him as they grew older? Would they understand his reasons for dying? He begged their forgiveness for not being part of their lives in the years to come, for not being there to guide them, protect them, and provide for them. He asked his wife to forgive him for leaving her alone to raise their children as a young widow exiled in a foreign country. He implored his parents to forgive him for making them live through the unspeakable agony of losing a child; the little boy who once stole their hearts so many years ago now walked stoically to his death at a Communist execution wall.

He would have given anything to embrace them all, to hold them, to kiss them, once more before this, his final journey.

The guards stopped at the wall and ordered him to stay in place. They walked away. Antonio looked up. The firing squad stood before him.

At that very instant he saw, faintly, through tear-filled eyes, three graceful figures drifting upward behind his executioners. In their place, the outline of a radiant, angelic female face was revealed. When the order came for the firing squad to take aim, the face reshaped itself into a hand. It stretched out to him. He reached out to the hand with his heart, grasping it tightly, the feel of it warm, undeniably a mother's. From deep in his chest, he shouted, *"¡Viva Cuba Libre! ¡Viva Cristo Rey!"*

Looking at the scene from above, held up by the maternal hand, he saw, lying in a pool of blood, a young man's lifeless body. He now knew for certain what he had always believed: his body, like all bodies, mortal and finite, was merely a temporary vessel for the immortal, eternal, universal soul. He watched as a bearded man delivered the corpse a needless *coup de grâce.*

18

BAY OF PIGS
GIRÓN
Mid-Morning, April 18, 1961

A commotion outside awoke Goyo. He pushed himself up off the bungalow's concrete floor. He felt like he'd been stampeded by a herd of cattle; every muscle, every joint, every tendon, swollen and tight. With the inside of his head pounding like a jackhammer, a layer of dried sweat and dirt caking his skin, he peered outside the door to see what the uproar was about. Everyone was pointing excitedly toward the southern sky. "What is it? What's going on?" he asked someone.

"They're coming! They're coming!"

Roberto came to the door. "Who's coming?"

"American jets! The order just came to lay down marker panels for them!" Official word came from the Girón headquarters a few minutes later confirming the news. The *Blagar* had apparently come back into radio range a little earlier and had relayed the message from Washington, D.C. The news got even better: the supply ships would return that night under the cover of darkness. Everyone was told to be ready for a possible engagement.

Goyo glanced at Roberto in disbelief. Roberto looked back at him, speechless. Someone walking by was outlining the latest hypothesis. "You see, the Americans didn't betray us. They just wanted us to draw Castro's forces toward Girón in order to expose them on the road and destroy them." Goyo felt that he'd once again come back from a near death experience.

Roberto's rifle was leaning against the door jamb. He picked it up. "Well, the best part is that our ships can return." He checked the clip. "Our ammo is almost gone."

For what seemed hours, the Brigade men looked at the sky like children waiting for a parade to come around the corner. Castro's forces, meanwhile, were slowly advancing from Playa Larga; his war planes flew over periodically and strafed the Brigade position. The Brigade's patience finally paid off. Two fast moving, unmarked American fighter jets burst into view from the southwest. Goyo wanted to fall on his knees in homage. They zoomed overhead, rocking their wings in salute to the 2506. The men cried and cheered as the jets headed toward the Castro positions. One man pumped his fists over his head, shouting, "God bless the United States of America!" Everyone started chatting excitedly, no longer hungry or thirsty, tired or achy or depressed.

A short time later, the men, looking northward, saw the jets flying back in their direction. "Here they come again." The jets roared overhead and disappeared back out over the ocean. They never fired a shot. A few seconds later, Castro's aircraft, little more than winged bicycles compared to the mighty American jets, came at them from the same direction. The Brigade men exchanged bewildered looks.

When the Castro planes reached the Brigade position, they attacked the men with machine guns and rockets, scattering them in all directions. Goyo, Roberto, Miyares, and Ramirez fled to the safety of one of the concrete structures and took cover—Roberto and Goyo on one side, Miyares and Ramirez on the other. Within seconds the roof was punctured by a hail of hot .50 caliber rounds.

When the planes flew away, Roberto got up, shouting, "Is everyone OK?" Miyares was kneeling next to Ramirez. He shook his head glumly. Roberto and Goyo rushed over. One of the rounds had caught poor Ramirez square in the back of the neck, killing him instantly. Goyo made the Sign of the Cross. Roberto ordered, "Go get the priest!"

Roberto strode outside furiously, righteous indignation radiating from him like heat from a brick oven. Looking to the south, he shaded his eyes and searched for the jets. "Bastards! Where did they go?" No one on the ground quite knew.

Castro's planes strafed the Brigade units in the vicinity of Girón throughout the day. The Sixth Battalion, meanwhile, was ordered to take up the front position guarding the road that connected Girón and Playa Larga. The Second was held in reserve and spent the rest of the day digging trenches and waiting. Castro's artillery began pounding them.

Happy Valley Air Base
Puerto Cabezas, Nicaragua
Afternoon, April 18, 1961

Jimmy Strickland paced up and down the air base searching for answers. Why had the D-Day air strikes been canceled? Why had *nearly all* of the pre-invasion air strikes been

189

canceled? No one could tell him, but the skies over the Bay of Pigs were filled with Castro fighter planes that weren't supposed to be in the air.

The Brigade pilots had nevertheless fought bravely. Undaunted, they'd flown their B-26 bombers into skies dominated by fast-moving fighter planes that were supposed to have been destroyed before the invasion. They were fully aware that they had virtually no chance of landing at Girón and little chance of even making it back to Happy Valley. Still, they'd hit Castro's troops however and wherever they could in the half-hour or so they had over the battle zone on each mission. They had even removed their rear guns to make room for extra fuel tanks. Inevitably, many of them were killed by Castro's fighters, their empty bunks a living testament to their sacrifice.

One pilot who had crash landed at the Girón airstrip was still there, severely injured. Some others had flown transport planes to the beachhead to airdrop supplies. One group had even received permission to attack Cuban airplanes on the ground at the San Antonio de los Baños airfield at first light on April 18–permission they'd been denied on D-Day–but could not do so because of the thick fog they found there; in any event, even if successful, it probably would have been too late to change the course of battle. The pilots who remained had endured unimaginable physical and emotional stress and many were fatigued from the repeated seven-hour round trips to Cuba.

When Jimmy found out that a couple of the Americans at the base were going to be part of a group flying one of the missions on Tuesday afternoon, he was determined to tag along. As luck had it, some of the Brigade air force's trainers were members of the Alabama Air National Guard. Jimmy had become friendly with them and, through them, had met some of the other American aviators. Jimmy snuck into the pilots' quarters. He told one of the aviators who was slated for the mission, "Hey, now, I need to be part of this. Y'all take me along for the ride; I can man a machine gun or something."

The airman, not an Alabaman, glanced around the quarters and checked the door. He whispered, "All right, you can fly with me; just don't say anything until we're in the air." Two of the mission's B-26s were piloted by Americans, the other four by Cubans. When they lifted off from the runway, Jimmy counted the number of years since he'd been in an actual battle zone. His mind froze momentarily when a flash of combat trauma seized him.

In late afternoon, after a few hours in the air, the navigator turned to Jimmy. "It'll be only a few minutes now. We've received word that Castro is moving a major force down the road between Red Beach and Blue Beach." He looked at a map, "Playa Larga and Girón." Five minutes later, they spotted land and descended to just a few hundred feet above the surface. Flying directly into the Bay of Pigs, they could see clouds of white dust rising from the ground along the bay's eastern rim, a sure sign of a vehicle convoy on the move. The B-26s turned toward the dust. The Castro column, clearly visible now, was strung out along the coastal road, moving slowly south, fully exposed. Thankfully, there were no Castro fighters anywhere in sight.

The pilot received instructions over the radio. He turned to Jimmy. "Here we go!" Within seconds, the six B-26s swooped down on the column. They took out the lead and rear vehicles first. With the sea on one side of them and the swamp on the other, the Castro force was trapped. The B-26s pounded the Castro convoy with impunity. Within twenty minutes, the B-26s left behind a seven-mile stretch of burning tanks, armored cars, and troop-carrying vehicles.

They flew back to Nicaragua flush with victory. Exhilarating though it was, Jimmy knew that it meant little in the long run. If they'd stuck with the original plan–if Castro's planes had been destroyed, if the Brigade air force had been able to operate from the beachhead, if the supply ships hadn't been forced to flee–the Brigade would have had a fighting chance. Jimmy figured that Castro's forces would clear the road within a few hours and just keep moving. He hoped that the raid had at least slowed the Communist advance long enough to help the men on the ground. He prayed that his cousin was still alive.

Bay of Pigs
Late Afternoon, Tuesday, April 18, 1961,
through Wednesday, April 19, 1961

By Tuesday afternoon, the Brigade troops entrenched south of San Blas felt the weight of the world pressing in on them. Castro's artillery pummeled the area without pause, combing the area in search of the Brigade's new location. Only when they were certain the way was clear did Castro's commanders advance, slowly and cautiously.

In the late afternoon, the men received word that a major force was coming at them down the main road. The men concealed themselves along the road's flanks. A .57mm recoilless rifle and a bazooka were placed in the middle of the causeway; behind them, one of the Brigade's tanks, and behind the tank the 4.2 mortars. Emilio hunkered down on the right flank, rifle in hand.

They heard the vehicles approaching: the sound of death. Someone next to Emilio handed him a pair of binoculars. He looked through them. Armored trucks followed by infantry were passing San Blas and rumbling right toward them. When the column came within range, the Brigade was given the order to fire. The Brigade's .57 and bazooka destroyed the first two vehicles; the riflemen and machine gunners repelled the infantry. Castro's column retreated, chased by the fire of the tank and the 4.2 mortars. Emilio thanked God it had ended so quickly.

Castro's howitzers began battering the area again. The bombardment lasted throughout the night. The men on the San Blas front nevertheless held out hope for victory–a hope that rested entirely on their faith in their American allies.

Along the Playa Larga road northwest of Girón, the Sixth Battalion guarded the front and skirmished with infiltrating enemy units throughout the night of the eighteenth. Behind them, Goyo, Roberto, and the Second Battalion settled in for the night in Girón. They tried to rest, but were harassed incessantly by the small, irksome crabs that snapped at them all night. The tiny crustaceans were colored red and black, the colors of Fidel Castro's 26th of July Movement.

* * *

As dawn broke on Wednesday morning, April 19, the men south of San Blas were alert and ready. They heard American jets overhead that quickly disappeared. As they dug in and awaited the Castro push, they heard the distinct sound of a B-26 bomber coming in from behind at low altitude. Emilio squeezed his rifle and braced himself. The new position provided them almost no cover from the air. The plane sped over them towards San Blas and started firing its .50 caliber machine guns at Castro's troops north of the town. The paratrooper next to Emilio screeched gleefully, "It's one of ours! It's one of ours!" The B-26 came back for a second pass, dropping two bombs on the enemy position, the explosion making the ground shake with the force of an earthquake. The B-26 disappeared over the ocean.

"Where the hell did that come from?" the paratrooper next to Emilio shouted.

"I don't know; Heaven, maybe?" Emilio said, stunned.

The men on the ground learned much later that three B-26s had flown to Cuba that morning as part of a mission approved by the White House. They were supposed to receive a one-hour "air umbrella" from American jets aboard the carrier *Essex*. The objective was to attack enemy targets and create conditions for the remaining supply ships to return. Two of the three Brigade B-26s were piloted by American trainers from the Alabama Air National Guard, the other by a Cuban. The "air umbrella" from the *Essex* never materialized as planned (the reasons remain shrouded in mystery) and all of the Alabama Air National Guardsmen were shot down and killed by Castro's forces. The Cuban-piloted B-26, the one the men near San Blas had seen that morning, was the only one to make it back to Happy Valley.

Minutes after the surprise attack, Emilio heard a rumble from behind. He turned to look. It was Alejandro del Valle. The paratrooper commander was riding atop an advancing tank, the Third Battalion and parts of the Fourth in tow. He was shouting, "Advance!"

They rolled past. The paratrooper next to Emilio shook his head. "This is insane! Who does he think he is, Don Quixote?" Emilio instantly saw the logic: del Valle was obviously using the brief chaos caused by the air strike to push the enemy back in order to buy the Brigade more time. Emilio's unit was ordered to stay behind. Emilio obeyed at first, but then he thought for a moment, said, "What the hell," and joined the attack.

The exhausted, hungry, battered men of the 2506 pushed forward toward San Blas, some of them running from the sheer thrill of advancing. Emilio, on the right flank, saw Castro men by the hundreds jump from their hiding places like roused quail and scamper away. Some of them tore off their shirts and waved them in surrender. Emilio ran out of ammunition after a while and retreated back toward the Brigade line. He saw other men pulling out as well, his friend José Antonio from the Third Battalion among them.

"I'm out of ammunition!" he shouted.

"Me too!" Emilio responded. "Let's go!"

They heard del Valle trying to rally the troops forward, but the shortage of ammunition ultimately forced them to abandon the charge. The entire Brigade contingent regrouped a couple of miles back from its previous position and formed a new defensive line just beyond a bend in the road, where an airdrop of supplies was expected. Emilio borrowed a few bullets from his squad mates and reloaded his rifle.

As they awaited the next assault, a lone jeep carrying two men suddenly came around the bend, down the same road by which they had just traveled. A high ranking Castro officer sat in the passenger's seat next to a driver. Brigade men stopped the jeep at gunpoint and detained them. José Antonio said to Emilio, "That's Major Félix Duque, one of Castro's top commanders; I guess he took a wrong turn! Can you believe it? Can this get any crazier?" Del Valle drove the new prisoners back to the command post at Girón. The airdrop finally arrived. It contained the wrong type of ammunition.

Later that day, the dreaded rumble of approaching vehicles reached their ears again. The Brigade men got into position.

The first Castro tank came around the bend. A Brigade bazooka instantly knocked it out of commission. A second Castro tank came forward, and then a third. Both were quickly destroyed. A minute later, a wave of Castro ground troops began charging from around the bend, as scores of others pushed through the vegetation and attacked the Brigade's flanks like a swarm of bees. Emilio shot one of them in the shoulder with his last round.

The enemy troops pulled back finally, and it was quiet for a while. Then, a fresh line of Castro tanks rumbled around the bend. They formed a line and began firing. The Brigade had nothing left to shoot back at them. Little by little, the men of the 2506 peeled away from the front line and began retreating south in small groups toward Girón. Emilio and José Antonio joined the retreat. Castro's Sea Furies strafed them relentlessly as they fled, sending them repeatedly headlong into the vegetation.

A couple of miles from Girón, Emilio and José Antonio stopped at a *bohío* to look for some water. They found a group of paratroopers inside. One of the medics was tending to a small child of around five years of age. Emilio gasped when he saw a gaping hole in the little angel's chest. A paratrooper turned to him, saying in a whisper, "He was hit by a bullet from a Sea Fury." The medic told the distraught *güajiro* father that his son was dead. A look of ineffable horror spread across the man's face. He pulled his hair, gasping, "No, no! My little boy! It can't be! It's impossible! My God!" He picked up his boy with shaking arms and hugged him tightly, smothering his soft, still face with kisses, pressing his wet, weatherworn cheek against his boy's. He started to stagger and hyperventilate. "Oh my . . . oh, my God . . . no . . . no . . ."

The paratroopers gently took the child and laid him on the bed. The father's shirt was stained with his son's blood, his empty arms still bent as if holding him. One of the Brigade men placed a Rosary in the father's hand and embraced him. The disconsolate *güajiro* sobbed uncontrollably into the Brigade man's shoulder.

Emilio and José Antonio quietly stepped out of the *bohío* and continued toward Girón. Emilio couldn't purge the image of the man kissing his dead son. The man loved his son deeply, but the child was dead . . . just like their cause . . . just like their country. Pressing down the road, Emilio felt his knees buckle and his eyes sting with tears and sweat. Everything became a haze. He was suddenly consumed by a desperate longing for his own father to lift him up and hold him, kiss his cheeks, and press his warm face against his. He knew only too well what that poor *güajiro* had in his heart: an agonizing, unattainable desire for his son to be alive, a frantic yearning for life to return to the body of he whose love and warmth and companionship his own life depended.

A mile from Girón, they saw black smoke rising eerily from the direction of the beachhead.

* * *

Roberto and Goyo had awoken in Girón that morning to the sound of mortar fire. They jumped up and instinctively grabbed their weapons. A nearby radio operator started relaying transmissions between the front line–two miles ahead along the Playa Larga road–and the central command post near the beach in Girón. The cousins listened in: Brigade mortars had hit the lead vehicles of the Castro column as it began its final push toward Girón. Sixth Battalion, manning the front since yesterday, was positioned at a curve on the road, ready to face the Castro onslaught. Three tanks were sent from Girón to support them; they were lined up on the left of the road, also pointing toward the curve.

Second Battalion was brought up to the front and held in reserve as the Sixth Battalion, together with the Brigade's tanks and mortars, held off Castro's advancing ground forces throughout the morning. Later that day, Second Battalion was ordered to the line. The stench of blood and gunpowder filled the air. On the rocks near the water's edge, they could see the corpse of a dead militiaman roasting in the sun. By now, the few hundred Brigade men on the Playa Larga road understood that this would likely be their last stand; they were all that stood between Girón and Castro's army.

No one even suggested a retreat.

Led by Erneido Oliva and supported by deadly mortar fire, the miniscule Brigade force withstood ceaseless attacks. Castro forces advanced on them down the road and through the thick foliage between the road and the bay, from where they tried to breach the Brigade's left flank. Facing the seemingly inexhaustible wave of enemy forces–and with more of their own men falling around them–the hopelessly outnumbered men of the Brigade nevertheless continued their lonely, desperate fight, determined to stand to the end.

By early afternoon, their ammunition supply nearly depleted, they were in a death grip. Enemy artillery began falling on their position; hand-to-hand fighting had broken out against the hundreds of Castro troops advancing on them through the trees. The front line was on the verge of collapse. In a desperate move, the thirty-five men of Second Battalion's Company G were ordered to advance through the thick foliage between the road and the shoreline, an area a hundred yards wide, to push back the Castro advance there. The company charged ahead through the dense trees for a mile and a half, fiercely battling a large number of militia units at close range. The company, to everyone's relief, was able to fight its way back, fourteen of them wounded, with the help of a tank that provided cover for them from the road. The effort temporarily stopped Castro's momentum, and the men on the front–their mortars and most of their heavy guns now completely out of ammunition–fell back several hundred yards.

By the time they took up a new position, Castro's howitzers began saturating the area. Endless shelling spewed sand into the air like oil geysers and pockmarked the ground with shallow pits. Goyo, fearful that one of the shells was bound to make his children orphans, sat with Roberto and Miyares in one of the artillery craters off the main road. With Cuba, and possibly his life, slipping away with every explosion, he implored Almighty God for a miracle. A little later, they fell back further, this time to the western part of Girón, where the artillery shells started falling on them in an unceasing barrage. Castro's fighter planes, meanwhile, strafed them from above. The end was at hand.

Then, all of a sudden, the shooting stopped.

Goyo and Roberto looked at one another with puzzled expressions. Miyares ran out of the ditch and pointed excitedly toward the waters off Girón's shores, shouting, "Look! Look! My God! It's the Americans! They're here!" Two U.S. Navy destroyers were quickly approaching the coastline. Goyo gasped, believing his prayers had been answered. The war ships eventually stopped offshore; Goyo knew that, with a single order, the destroyers' guns could have obliterated the entire Castro army on the road advancing toward them. After a short time, however, the ships turned and departed without firing a shot, just like the jets had done the day before. Roberto, his eyes dancing with fury and confusion, shouted in a shrill, hysterical voice as they sailed away, "These people are mocking us! Damn it! They're *mocking* us!" He fired a round in the ships' direction, even though they were well out of range. He shouted at them futilely, in English, "Go to Hell, John Kennedy!"

During a brief respite that followed, they joined a large group of men heading in the direction of the command center. Castro's artillery began pounding them again.

Emilio and José Antonio arrived at Girón via the road from San Blas; the defenses on that front had completely collapsed and Castro's forces were now only a few miles behind them–and advancing fast. Emilio and José Antonio were carrying a wounded paratrooper they'd found on the roadside. His left leg and foot had been shot up in a Sea Fury attack. Instead of the organized command center they'd hoped to find, they entered a scene of utter chaos and destruction, the ground marked by so many artillery craters it looked like the moon's surface. Buildings had been reduced to rubble; many of the palm trees were cruelly scorched by fire. Black smoke hung in a low cloud. Abandoned tanks, armored cars, and machine guns were scattered all about. He asked a Brigade man hurrying past where the Headquarters Staff could be found. The man answered, "Headquarters Staff? Are you joking? Didn't you receive the order? We're supposed to break up into small groups and go into the swamps to wait for supplies and reinforcements."

Emilio and José Antonio stared at each other for a moment, thunderstruck. Emilio turned and shouted after the man as he jogged away, "We have a wounded paratrooper here! Where are the doctors?" The man shook his head and held up his arms, pantomiming, "I don't know."

A Brigade soldier fifty yards away was waving his arms at them. "Over here!"

They carried the wounded man into a hospital tent. Inside, they found a grotesque spectacle of bleeding stumps, missing eyeballs, and gaping chest wounds. The air was thick with the smell of blood, entrails, and sweat. They sloshed through pools of blood and found a doctor. He was tending to a man whose belly had been torn up by shrapnel. They could easily see his intestines. "Put him down, there on the ground!" the doctor shouted over his shoulder. "We can't stay long. We have to stabilize these men and get out. The enemy's tanks are going to break through any minute. You two get out of here right now and take to the swamps!"

Emilio and José Antonio looked down at the wounded paratrooper. He saw their expressions. Through his pain, the injured man sputtered, "Do as he says . . . get out of here, save yourselves . . . no, no, don't look at me like that . . . just go!"

They strode out of the tent, glad to breathe fresh air. They walked towards the beach. Ahead of them, they saw a large group of men gathered from the battalions that had been pushed back from Playa Larga. They headed towards them. The three hundred or so bloodied, battle-worn troops were listening to Oliva, who was waving his torn-off T-shirt, shouting, and pumping his fist into the air. By the time they reached the group, Oliva had ended his speech and the group was dispersing. Emilio asked someone what was going on. "A group of us is going to go down the coastal road toward Cienfuegos and try to get to the Escambray Mountains. It's the only road that doesn't have a Castro army coming down it. We're going to try to link up with the guerrillas there."

The crowd kept moving past Emilio and José Antonio. Most of the rest of the Brigade had apparently already taken to the swamps. Looking out to sea, Emilio saw that some Brigade men had jumped on small boats and were trying to reach the American ships. Suddenly, a couple of men broke away from the group on the beach and started trotting back down the Playa Larga road, saying that they were going to die fighting. Their comrades chased them down and brought them back.

Emilio looked around at the battle-weary men and shook his head in bewilderment, knowing that, soon, tens of thousands of Castro troops would be converging on Girón from both the Playa Larga and San Blas roads.

Then, he saw them, not five feet away.

Roberto made eye contact a second later. "Cousin!" He leaped at Emilio, taking him in a bear hug. Goyo looked up, saw Emilio, and joined in the embrace. "Sweet Jesus, you're alive!" They stood like that, in a circle, in complete silence.

After a few seconds, they broke the embrace. Roberto sniffled. His eyes were glassy. "Let's go. We're taking the coastal road toward Cienfuegos."

Emilio wiped his eyes and scanned the sky. "OK, but we'll never make it with those goddamned Sea Furies flying around."

"Well, we may as well try."

They joined the small column assembled on the road, helped some of the injured men get up on a surviving tank, and fell in. They began moving. Within minutes, two Castro T-33s and a Sea Fury appeared overhead and began strafing them. The Brigade men jumped off the road and dove into the vegetation. A few of them remained on the road to shoot their last bullets at the airplanes, eventually falling where they stood. The march east along the coast was over before it ever started.

Roberto, Goyo, Emilio, José Antonio, and Miyares stayed together and joined a group of ten other Brigade men in the swamp. Father Hidalgo was among them. When Goyo saw him, he squeezed the priest's arm, "Father, you stay with me." The group ventured as far away from the coastal road as possible, trying to stay under the cover of low-hanging trees to conceal themselves from the strafing airplanes. Enemy helicopters now hovered overhead as well, firing wildly into the swamp, trying to flush out the Brigade.

The men of Brigade 2506 never surrendered to Fidel Castro. They had fought to the end of their ammunition supply, hoping their ally would, in the end, fulfill its promises to them. Now they fled for their lives across the Zapata Swamp, hunted fugitives in the land they had come to liberate.

19

GUERRILLA BASE CAMP
NEAR JOVELLANOS, MATANZAS PROVINCE
Evening, April 20, 1961

Macho shut the radio off with a violent flourish. "This thing is over," he lamented to Anita. He put his hands on his hips and sighed. He stared at her silently.

Anita shook her head, adamantly refusing to believe it. The rebel teens had been following the battle over the radio since it began on the seventeenth. As late as yesterday morning, clandestine radio broadcasts had been describing glorious victories, claiming the Liberation Army was preparing its march on Havana. The little group, like so many resistance cells across Cuba, was ready to join the invaders, their bellicosity swelling in proportion to their hope with every passing hour. But Macho didn't let his boys listen to the Castro radio broadcasts, which painted a very different picture. It wasn't until late yesterday, after the collapse of Girón, that Macho hinted that things hadn't gone quite as planned.

Then, earlier today, some of Macho's contacts sent word that a large concentration of Castro troops was closing in on the area. With the larger battle now behind it, the government was concentrating on flushing out the remaining pockets of resistance on the island.

"I wish we'd never gotten that stupid radio," Anita hissed, pushing the device over, sending it to the ground with a thud. She huffed, spun around, and stared into the dark woods. She remembered the day the radio had arrived at their little base camp. It was February, and they'd been visited by a small group of university students who had been sent there by someone from the resistance. She'd expected them to be as green as the two students who'd ventured out with her brother a few months earlier; to her surprise, however, the group was highly skilled in guerrilla warfare. They told her they'd received training in Florida, Guatemala, and the Panama Canal Zone from the Americans.

The group had brought all sorts of supplies with them, including the radio. A couple of them were members of the *Agrupación Católica Universitaria,* which none of the rebel boys had ever even heard of. They showed the boys who were interested how to pray the Rosary. One night after supper, they told them about *alzados* like themselves who were fighting all over Cuba, and about their brother *Agrupados* who'd faced their executioners shouting, *'¡Viva Cristo Rey!'"* The *Agrupados* made an especially deep impression on fifteen-year-old Alfonsito, who promised them that at the first opportunity he'd make his First Holy Communion.

Macho glanced over at Anita. Her face was outlined in the moon's glow. "What do you think, Anita, what do we do?" He bent down and picked up the radio. "The invasion was a failure. The militia will be here sooner or later and we'll all be killed if we don't get out."

She shot him an angry look. How could he even think about abandoning the fight with her brother Israel in prison?

What was she supposed to do? Get a job in a factory and for-get about him? Go to Miami? She looked away. "What if the Castro radio is lying? What if the Liberation Army is actually winning and the Castro people are broadcasting false propa-ganda?"

Macho looked at her deeply, but said nothing. Her eyes became glassy. Macho walked over and smoothed her hair with his fingers. "OK, Anita. We'll stay one day more and see if there's a change. But we'll have to break camp and get out tomorrow after dark at the latest."

Anita wiped her eyes and nodded silently. She buried her face in his shoulder and wept.

Macho addressed the boys later that night. "The course of battle in the area of the Zapata Swamp is still unclear. But it seems there's a possibility that the invasion has failed. I've also been informed that militia units have been spotted in this vicinity. We'll spend the night here, as well as tomor-row. If there's no change in the situation by then, we'll break camp tomorrow night and leave this place under the cover of darkness. We'll make camp at the Flag and decide what to do then." The "Flag" was a hidden fort Macho had built at the edge of a small, remote creek that ran through a dense forest four miles away. Made from roped-together boughs cut from nearby trees, Macho had built the fort as a rendezvous point if they ever had to flee. It was so well hidden that he'd marked it by painting a Cuban flag on a nearby rock; hence, "the Flag."

One of the boys, a seventeen-year-old nicknamed "Pesca-dito," "Little Fish," because of his agility as a swimmer, spoke up. "If that's the case, why don't we just go now? Tonight?"

Macho wasn't accustomed to being second-guessed. He bristled at Pescadito's query and wondered, briefly, whether or not he should answer. The boy was right, though; he was extending their stay only for Anita's sake. "We want to be certain that the Liberation Army was truly defeated. It might just be a Castro trick to flush us out. If the liberation forces are still viable, we have to be in a position to support them. I think we owe them at least one more day." The boys all nodded their assent, except for Pescadito, who looked at the ground warily.

Anita nudged Macho awake at the crack of dawn the next morning. She was crouching next to him, a pistol in her right hand. She held her left index finger to her lips, miming "Shush." She lightly tapped her ear, instructing him to listen. He heard it: dozens of footsteps approaching from the distance. Macho got up to rouse the boys.

"Get up, someone's coming," Macho told them in a loud whisper. He looked around nervously. "Who's supposed to be on watch?"

"Pescadito," one of the boys answered as he got up and shouldered his rifle.

They all looked at one another in disbelief, realizing instantly that Pescadito had betrayed them. "We should have known last night when he questioned Macho!"

The footsteps were more audible now and coming from all directions. Macho felt a knot in his chest. He drew the boys into a tight circle. "Listen, we're surrounded. All we can do is to try and fight our way out of here." He looked into their young faces. Some of them hadn't even started shaving regularly yet. He felt the bottom drop out of his stomach. He took an uneasy breath. Sweat dripped down his temples. Until now, the boys had never seen anything but resolute courage in Macho. They patted his back and shoulders tenderly. "It's OK, Macho, you're our leader, just like a father." Macho swallowed and nodded.

Alfonsito said, "I think we should say one of the prayers the students taught me." Macho nodded his approval. Alfonsito quickly recited a Hail Mary. They all made the Sign of the Cross. One of them pleaded, "Sweet Virgin of Charity! Rescue us!"

Macho pointed toward the west. "We'll try to break through in that direction, it's our only chance. When we get past the encirclement, everyone scatter in the cane fields; we'll meet up at the Flag tonight."

Within seconds, Macho, Anita, and the boys were at the western edge of the base camp clearing, concealed in the thickets. All of them held their rifles in their hands. A wall of twenty-five armed militiamen was plowing straight toward them through the brush and trees like a giant human comb. Macho looked behind him into the clearing; another militia contingent was closing in from the other side. The boys all looked to Macho. He drew a deep breath and pointed toward the militia line approaching from the west. The boys aimed their rifles. Macho shouted, "Fire!"

The boys leapt to their feet and opened fire on the militia line. Alfonsito made the Sign of the Cross at lightning speed and broke away from the group, running straight at the enemy line, firing and bellowing, *"¡Viva Cristo Rey!"* His body was riddled by a hail of bullets; with each shot, tiny fountains of blood gushed and misted into the air. He fell. The militia roared and rushed at them like a pack of wild dogs.

The panicked boys broke ranks and retreated back to the base camp clearing, falling into the hands of the militia units that had converged from the other side. Anita, still with Macho at the western edge of the clearing, turned around and watched as the militia began shooting the terror-stricken boys like penned animals. Macho was still firing at the militia unit charging from the west. A second later, a round caught him in the forehead, splitting his skull. Anita collapsed on top of him and wrapped her arms around his chest. She shook him and screamed hysterically, "No! Macho! No!" She shut her eyes tightly as the charging militia, eager to take part in the massacre in the clearing, ignored her and sped past.

Anita lifted her head and looked into the clearing again. She watched as the surviving boys surrendered to the militia. They were forced to kneel, all in a row, with their hands folded on top of their heads. One of them, a sixteen-year-old called Pepito, was sobbing uncontrollably. "Please! Don't kill me! Please! I have a mother and a father!" A militia captain patted the boy's shoulder. "Don't worry, son. The Revolution is just. You'll be treated with the fairness you deserve." The panicked boy let out his breath. His head bobbed in grateful relief, the militia captain suddenly his best friend. Then, as calmly as if he were switching off a light, the captain put his pistol against the boy's left temple and pulled the trigger. Skull fragments and pieces of brain splattered all over the boy kneeling next to him. The boy's lifeless body fell face first into the dirt. The captain shouted, "Worm!"

The other boys were crying and trembling. The militia leader holstered his pistol and circled them slowly, as if taking a victory lap. "Well, my little juvenile delinquents, your

friends the Americans have failed to bring down the Revolution. Playa Girón is flowing with the blood of their mercenaries! You've been abandoned and defeated. We won." He
enunciated the last words with particular relish. He nodded
to his men. Each of the kneeling boys received a bullet in the
back of the head; they each fell face-first into the earth before
them. The giddy militia captain turned one of the corpses
over. He unzipped his pants and urinated into the dead boy's
eye sockets. His comrades laughed raucously.

The laughing died down after a few seconds. The militia
unit then heard a female voice from the edge of the clearing.
"Cowards! Child killers!" They spun quickly toward the voice.
Anita was standing by the prostrate Macho, her shirt torn and
bloody, a pistol in her hands aimed at the captain. She fired
once, hitting him in the chest. He fell where he stood. She
began shooting indiscriminately into the group of *milicianos*.
They immediately returned fire. One round hit her in the
belly, another in the face, and another in the chest. She collapsed on top of Macho.

20

HAVANA, CUBA
BLANQUITA THEATRE

Morning, April 22, 1961
Three Days after the Fall of Girón

Raquel was roused by her friend Dolores. "Raquel, wake up. They've called your name, they're releasing you." Raquel rubbed her eyes and inhaled sharply through sandpaper dry lips. She hadn't had any water to drink since yesterday. Dolores helped her to her feet and walked her to the entrance. "What about you, Dolores?" Dolores shook her head. "Not yet." Raquel ran her hand gently across Dolores's shoulder.

An older, smiling militiaman escorted Raquel to an office and deposited her at the end of a long queue. Finally, her turn came and she sat before the official charged with overseeing the releases. He asked her about Goyo. "He's in the United States. I haven't seen him since December," she told him truthfully. He saw her protruding belly, finished quickly, and sent her home.

Raquel was blinded by a blast of morning sunlight when she walked into the street. Shading her eyes, she ducked into a small cafeteria a few blocks away and poured herself a glass of water from a pitcher on the coffee counter. The owner studied her closely. "Were you in the Blanquita?" Raquel nodded. "Don't drink it all at once," the man told her, "it'll make you sick." He turned and walked away.

Raquel thought of calling her father or Lorenzo to come pick her up. She looked through an open door behind the counter area and into a small living room. She guessed it was the owner's home. Someone in there was watching television; Raquel could see the set from her angle. As usual, Castro was on the screen delivering a speech. The broadcast then switched to images of captured Brigade prisoners arriving on trucks and buses at Havana's Sports Palace, where they were being detained. The screen then showed scenes of parading Revolutionaries jamming Havana's streets and squares, pumping their rifles into the air, celebrating their victory at the Bay of Pigs. "None of my people should be on the street today," Raquel thought, and decided that she would walk home. Just as she was leaving, the owner put before her a plate with some rice and beans and a few slices of roast pork.

"I'm sorry, I have no money," Raquel said to him apologetically.

"My wife sends it, there's no charge. Eat it. It'll restore your strength," he said.

"Thank you."

"Do you have a means to get home?"

"I was going to walk."

"No, no. I'll give you a ride." He glanced at the Revolutionaries on the television screen, shook his head sadly, and sighed. He looked around his small eatery and said in a low voice, "After this disaster, it's only a matter of time before the government takes this away from me. The little guys are next. I've worked my entire life to build this business, to be my own man; and now they're going to take it from me." His eyes misted. Raquel was at a loss for words. She just looked at him sympathetically.

Raquel thanked the cafeteria owner profusely when he dropped her off at home a short while later. When she reached her front door, it was locked. She groaned in frustration, remembering that Teresa had probably taken the children to Camagüey after her arrest. She looked back into the street for a moment. The cafeteria owner had driven off. She slapped the door futilely and rested her forehead on it. She felt like crying. Suddenly, she heard a male voice coming from inside. She looked back again into the street and saw her father's car parked nearby; and then she saw her own family's car. She began slapping the door again. "Please . . . open . . . it's me!" When the door opened, she fainted, collapsing into the front entrance.

She woke up in bed an hour later to the smell of rubbing alcohol. A blurry image of Dr. Mendoza slowly came into focus. She looked around and saw her parents and children in the room. She smiled. Dr. Mendoza asked her how she felt. She nodded and grunted that she was all right. Ana Cristina jumped into the bed and curled up under her arm. Goyito just stared at her and blinked. She kissed the children. "For a moment, I thought you'd be in Camagüey, but you're here. I'm so happy," she said, her voice hoarse and weak. Her mother, Adriana, standing a few feet from the bed, sobbed quietly and wiped her eyes with a handkerchief. Her father sat at the foot of the bed and stared at her tenderly. "Where did they have you daughter? I've been looking for you for days."

"At the Blanquita."

José María gritted his teeth and shook his head fiercely. "I went to the Blanquita three times!" He held up three fingers. "They told me you weren't there." His nose twitched angrily. "Sons of bitches!"

"Father, the children!"

A few seconds later, Lorenzo strode into the room with Teresa. The doctor whirled on him. "Lorenzo, I specifically told you to stay home until you were stronger. Remember what happened to your brother! You're not far behind!"

Lorenzo brushed aside the doctor's words with a dismissive wave. "Doctor, please, one wife is enough." He pulled up a chair and sat next to Raquel. "Raquel, dear, tell me, how are you?"

José María said to her, "Lorenzo and Sara were detained right after you, daughter. They were held at La Cabaña."

"Oh, Lorenzo," Raquel said, squeezing his hand. "Are you both all right?"

"Sara is very weak, but she'll recover. Me? I'm fine, as you can see, despite what the doctor here thinks." Dr. Mendoza shook his head and packed his stethoscope away in his medical bag.

Raquel kissed her children again and sent them out of the room. They showed Dr. Mendoza to the front door.

"So," Raquel told her parents, Teresa, and Lorenzo, "we heard about the invasion while in the Blanquita. What have you learned?"

"Some facts and some rumors," Lorenzo said, frowning.

José María shook his head furtively at Lorenzo.

Raquel noticed the signal. "Tell me what you know, please . . . don't treat me as if I were a little girl, Father . . . I have children. Tell me, now."

José María sighed. He paused for a second before speaking. "Well, I should first tell you that when Teresa called to tell us you'd been detained, she told us she was going to take the children to Camagüey. I told her to stay at the house, as it was too dangerous and simply impossible to travel. We all stayed here throughout the whole episode. Apparently, hundreds of thousands of people were detained after the air attacks on the fifteenth and a lot of them never made it out of the detention centers. It's a miracle you're alive, as well as Lorenzo and Sara."

"The Virgin protected us."

"Indeed," José María sighed, glancing at a small image of the Blessed Mother that Raquel kept in the bedroom. He slid over and sat closer to her. He folded his hands. "Daughter, Goyo's friend, Rogelio González Corzo, was executed at La Cabaña the day before yesterday."

Raquel bit her bottom lip. She looked at Lorenzo. He nodded. She covered her mouth with her hands. Her face muscles went taut; her eyes and temples instantly reddened.

"Raquel, dear, let's save this ugly news until you feel better."

"No, Father, tell me now," she sobbed.

José María took a deep breath. "Antonio de la Cruz was executed as well."

Raquel lowered her hands and stared up at the ceiling. Her lips disappeared into her mouth. Purple veins bulged from her temples. She lay motionless. "And the schools?" she finally blurted out in a tight, wet voice.

"They've been closed since the air attacks last week, and it's a virtual certainty they won't be permitted to reopen next year."

Raquel lowered her gaze and swallowed. She gave everyone a slight nod. "Then the moment has come. We must leave Cuba and join Goyo. I'm sure he's called—hasn't he?"

José María's eyes started to dance wildly. He stood and circled the bed. "No, he hasn't. Frankly, we're all surprised. We were sure he'd telephone or somehow get in touch after the invasion. His mother is coming in a little while and I don't know what to say to her." He stood next to the window and folded his arms.

Lorenzo said, "We haven't heard from Emilio or Roberto either. In fact, we haven't heard from them since January, except for a couple of letters telling us they're still in New York."

Raquel looked at them in disbelief. Certainly the invasion was big news in the United States.

Her father turned and looked at her squarely. "Raquel, we should start making arrangements for you and the children to leave Cuba, whether Goyo is there to meet you or not. The American Embassy is closed, but I've heard that the Americans have been waiving visa requirements for travel to the United States as long as you somehow get the appropriate documents. I'm not certain of the procedure, but we'll figure it out. You can ask for asylum once you arrive there. As soon as you're there safely, your mother and I will follow."

Raquel stared at her father like a frightened child. The old man hardened his jaw and pointed his finger at her. "The floodgates have opened, Raquel. The Communists are firmly in power now. Your children are in grave danger. Remember that Castro has declared this to be the 'Year of Education,' and that all children will soon be forced into Soviet-type schools where they'll be brainwashed in Marxism. There are even rumors that parental rights are going to be transferred to the state. Hundreds of Cuban children have already been sent to Russia for 'training.' Try and imagine that, daughter, because it's coming."

Raquel's hands started shaking. She hid them under the covers. She needed to talk to Goyo–right now. She hadn't spoken to him since he'd left for California. His letters, coming through Tony Méndez in Miami, bore no return address, and he never specified where he was in the state. When she called Tony in Miami a few weeks ago and asked him if he knew if Goyo had a telephone yet, he was strangely elusive. "Uh, not yet . . . you can just keep sending me your letters and I'll be sure he gets them." The call was cut off before she could ask him for Goyo's address.

A terrifying suspicion that recently had begun forming in the back of her mind now leapfrogged to the forefront. Goyo wasn't in California: he'd found another woman. She was certain of it. That explained all the mystery. Her ears started to burn. She was probably Cuban, too; a young, desperate, lonely refugee who'd found a rock of support in Goyo. The whore had probably dangled herself in front of him like a slab of meat before a starving man. Everything in Raquel's line of vision took on a reddish coloration.

She pushed herself out of bed.

"Daughter, stay in bed," her father scolded.

"I'm all right. I'm going to call Tony to see if he knows if Goyo has a telephone yet."

Raquel went to the living room and picked up the telephone receiver. Her hands were still trembling, an image of her adulterous husband and his young mistress setting up house in her mind. She went cold inside. As she dialed the first number, someone knocked at the front door. Her mother opened it. Raquel looked over. A young man in his early twenties wearing a dark suit stood in the doorway. Raquel recognized him as one of Goyo's former students from Belén. She thought for a moment. Alberto was his name. She hung up the telephone and walked over.

Alberto bowed to her nervously as he stepped inside. "Mrs. León, I just wanted to tell you how sorry I was to hear about Mr. León. He was a great man and the best teacher I ever had." He looked down. "I still can't believe he's dead."

Raquel's jaw dropped open like a metal door. She looked over at her children. They stared back at her, their expressions demanding an explanation. Her head snapped sharply back toward Alberto. She narrowed her eyes at him. "LIAR!"

The boy's eyes popped open. "Mrs. León . . . no, he, he . . . I mean . . . it's the truth . . . or what, what I heard . . . you know, what they told me . . . ."

Raquel screeched again, her words carrying a diabolical edge, "Get . . . out . . . of . . . my . . . house . . . you LIAR!" She picked up an umbrella from the metal cylinder next to the front door and lifted it above her head to swing at him.

José María restrained her. She screeched and sobbed savagely, "No, Father! Can't you see this man is here to hurt us?" He held her until her strength gave out and carried her to the couch. All the color had left her face; her eyes were blank, her cheeks sagged like pale, wet sandbags.

Alberto stepped toward the front door to get away. Lorenzo grabbed him by the arm and yanked him back. He pulled him into the living room and forced him into a chair. He stood before him like a prosecutor. "Young man, I don't know you but you seem sincere. You say you were a student of my nephew; that's fine, I believe you. But you'll have to forgive us, because this is the first we've heard of this." He glanced at Raquel and then back at Alberto. "This is a time of many rumors, so before you say anything else, I need you to tell us how you came by this news."

Alberto swallowed contritely. "I heard it from two different people in Miami."

Raquel, sobbing into her father's shoulder, asked, "Where are his remains? Are they in California?"

Alberto opened his mouth to answer, and then closed it again. He looked puzzled. "Did you say *California?*" He shook his head slowly. "Mrs. León, I'm sorry, but I believe his remains are here in Cuba."

Everyone shouted in unison, "In Cuba?"

Alberto held his right hand out. "Mrs. León, didn't you know that Mr. León was in the invasion; that he died fighting at Girón?"

Raquel gasped and looked at her father. José María motioned to his wife with his head to take the children away. Lorenzo kept his eyes fixed on Alberto. He asked him, more calmly now, "You might know my son, Roberto León, and my nephew, Emilio Hammond." He looked over at Teresa, who was standing in the corner. "That's Emilio's mother, my sister, Teresa." Alberto bowed his head to her politely.

"Yes, of course I know Emilio and Roberto."

"Were they in the invasion as well?"

Alberto stared at his shoes, "Yes, as far as I know. My contacts in Miami told me they had joined the Brigade and took part in the invasion." Teresa gasped and fell into the couch next to José María and Raquel. She rubbed her temples and mumbled, "Oh, my God, oh my God, oh my God."

Lorenzo's mouth twisted. His nose flared. He sneered, "Son, what contacts do *you* have in Miami?"

"I'll assume I'm in safe company here, so I'll tell you. I'm in the MRR and I know who from among our ranks joined the Brigade. I was in a safe house when the G.2 and the militia began detaining people on the fifteenth, so I escaped their dragnet. I was waiting for the signal to rise up and take to the streets, but it never came."

Lorenzo took in a deep breath, pinched the bridge of his nose, and closed his eyes. "What do you know about Roberto and Emilio?"

"Nothing."

Lorenzo exploded savagely and pounced on the chair, grabbing it by its arms. He hovered over Alberto like cornered prey. "You tell me the truth! Don't you lie to me, boy!"

Alberto jerked back reflexively and raised his hands as if in surrender. "I swear on the life of my mother: I've heard nothing except that they were in the invasion."

Lorenzo backed away from Alberto. He stumbled and fell into the armchair next to him. He pressed his palms to his forehead. "I can't believe this, I can't believe this!"

Raquel went to the telephone and called Tony.

"Yes, Raquel, it's true. Goyo was in the invasion," Tony told her. "I personally drove him to the safe house from where he departed. He made me promise not to tell you; that's why I was so vague with you before. I don't know anything about Roberto and Emilio."

She balanced herself on the edge of the small table. "Is it true he's dead?"

Tony was quiet for a few seconds. "That's what I've heard, Raquel; someone I know told me that he was killed in the swamps trying to escape after the fall of Girón. But keep in mind that nothing is certain at this point. It may just be that his name hasn't been on the lists of prisoners."

"What lists?"

"The government recently started reading off the names of the captured men. The names are being announced here in Miami. Everyone assumes that those not on the lists are dead, but that may not be the case. It's all been very confusing."

"Could it be that the lists are incomplete?" Her voice had the resigned sound of a newly minted widow.

Tony hesitated. "I suppose anything is possible at this point, Raquel."

She didn't know what else to ask.

"Raquel," Tony said, "just in case the worst is true, I have a letter here for you and the children. I also have some money that Goyo left for you."

Raquel said goodbye and gently put down the receiver. Every womanly instinct told her that Goyo was now with God.

She turned on the radio and television. Her mother-in-law, Maria del Carmen, was given the news when she got to the house. She refused to believe her son was dead, declaring with her provincial drama, "I want to see a body!" Raquel was irritated by her denial. A little later, Maria del Carmen called Goyo's sister, Marta, to give her an update. Marta and her husband, Hector, had moved to Oriente to be near Hector's family.

The family all sat before the television set, watching as group after group of Brigade prisoners was taken into Havana's Sports Palace, hoping to catch a glimpse of Roberto or Emilio–maybe even Goyo. They listened in hopeful silence when the prisoners' names were read. Throughout the day, they saw Brigade prisoners whose families they knew.

Word of Goyo's death spread quickly. Throughout the afternoon, visitors came to the home to offer their condolences. It quickly turned into an impromptu wake. After a while, Raquel felt nothing. She looked around at the mourners, thinking, "This isn't real."

That night, after the guests had gone, Raquel, her mother-in-law, her mother, and Teresa went into a corner of the living room to recite the Rosary. Lorenzo and José María sat before the television set watching Castro's henchmen interview Brigade prisoners at the Ministry of Transport. The television screen suddenly went fuzzy with static. Lorenzo got up to adjust the knobs.

The sound returned first. The interviewer was asking a prisoner harshly, "Is it not true that your family was of the wealthy, bank owning bourgeoisie in Cuba?"

"No, my family operated a small family bank in Vedado that did great things for the community."

Everyone froze. Raquel's Rosary dropped from her hand.

"You come from a rich, aristocratic family! You came to take back from the people the capitalist enterprise your family lost, didn't you?"

The television picture returned just as the prisoner responded.

"No. I came to fight for God and for Cuba. I quote a famous saint, who said, 'Praise be to those who free the multitude from a tyrannical power.' And I can tell you that this Brigade came to do just that." He was much thinner and caked in dried mud. A shadow of a beard covered his face.

Raquel screeched in joyous release and fell to her knees. "Sweet Virgin!"

21

HAVANA, CUBA
TRANSPORT MINISTRY
April 22, 1961

Goyo knew there would be a price to pay for his little show. He'd manipulated his way into the television broadcast so that his family could see that he'd been in the invasion and that he was alive; but it was also to settle an old score. His hands were bound at the wrists as soon as he was off camera. He was taken back into the large room.

Paquito Vega was there waiting for him, his face like chiseled ice. "Smug and arrogant, just like a León. I should have known better than to let you trick me into putting you in front of the cameras."

Goyo said nothing. He just stared at Paquito, his expression conveying to the former bank teller that he was still nothing more to him than a witless family employee.

Paquito recoiled slightly at Goyo's look. He recovered and narrowed his eyes. He breathed heavily through his nose, his demeanor quickly taking on all the fragile danger of a schoolyard bully. "You? Looking at *me* that way? You're nothing but a *maricón*! You were the big university graduate, the member of the elite *Agrupación Católica*, the privileged heir of Don Gregorio. Well, where are you now, *maricón*?" His lips started twitching. "You're nothing, do you hear me? Just look at you, bound and powerless, just like the rest of your family!" He spat at Goyo's feet.

Goyo stood motionless and simply gave him the look again.

Paquito leaned into Goyo and whispered into his left ear. "Remember what happened to your father, *maricón*." He grabbed the right side of Goyo's head and pulled it toward his mouth. He bit Goyo's left earlobe with the ferocity of a rabid dog. Goyo screamed and spun away. He fell to the floor. Paquito stepped over and stood above him, straddling him like a victorious gladiator. He spat out the piece of earlobe he'd bitten off, blood rippling down his chin in thin, red rivulets. An army colonel came over and pulled Paquito away. "Stop! We are under orders not to torture the prisoners!" A *miliciano* standing nearby produced a towel and held it to Goyo's ear.

Later on, Goyo and a few other Brigade prisoners were put into the back of a covered military truck and driven to Havana's Sports Palace to join the rest of the captured men. He could barely see the others' faces in the dark truck. His ear was on fire. The flash of bravery he'd felt in front of the cameras had by now worn off. The sensation of emptiness and confusion that had consumed him after being captured in the swamp returned in full force. He prayed fervently that Emilio was already at the Sports Palace. Then he thought about Roberto, and his chest collapsed into his stomach; a young life snuffed out so soon. He wondered sadly how Lorenzo and Sara would react to the news of their son's death.

He felt a sob forming in his throat. He suppressed it and shut his eyes, trying to think of better times. He imagined seeing his family, laughing and relaxing on the back portico; he tried to recall the sights and sounds of the baseball stadium on game night and of Goyito's joyous expression whenever they went there; he thought about his students. An image of Pedro popped into his head. He saw the boy's intestines spilling out of his torso. He shook his head. His thoughts then uncontrollably wandered back to Roberto and the odyssey they'd endured since taking to the swamps on April 19.

* * *

Castro's helicopters had strafed indiscriminately into the vegetation all afternoon on the nineteenth. The main roads, the secondary roads, and even the narrow trails cutting through the giant swampland were crawling with Castro troops; some moved on patrol and others stayed in set posts roughly two hundred paces apart. They waited patiently for the Brigade men to be driven from the unforgiving landscape by the choppers, starvation, or dehydration.

Just before nightfall, the group with whom Goyo and his cousins had gone into the swamp decided that their chances of escape were better if they broke up into smaller units. Any hope of making it to the Escambray Mountains to continue the fight had evaporated. Survival was now their only objective. Roberto, Emilio, Goyo, Father Hidalgo, José Antonio, and Miyares continued on alone. Only Goyo and Miyares still had weapons; Goyo had two bullets left, Miyares one. They crossed through thick mangroves and swamps. That night, they drank the last of their water and slept fitfully atop sharp limestone rock nicknamed *diente de perro*, dogs' teeth, in

Cuba. A bitter cold set in, the likes of which none of them could recall ever feeling in Cuba. They started moving again in the morning. It was April 20.

Goyo and Roberto let Emilio lead. He'd had a knack for eluding capture ever since childhood. Father Hidalgo, José Antonio, and Miyares simply followed. Emilio moved slowly, racking his brain for a way to cross the militia encirclements. He knew, at the very least, that it was imperative they shed their Brigade uniforms. Perhaps they could raid an empty *bohío* somewhere and acquire some civilian clothing, he thought; that way they could pass themselves off as locals if stopped by the militia. They could then go to a town, steal a car, and drive to Cienfuegos where they had friends who would hide them. Or maybe they could simply find an unguarded stretch of road and slip past their pursuers and get to safety. Either way, they had to keep moving, probing, and looking for an opportunity. They clawed their way through thick foliage, staying under the cover of the vegetation to conceal themselves from the helicopters. Branches and thorns gashed their skin.

At around 10 o'clock in the morning, they came to a narrow trail. Emilio stepped gingerly to the trail's edge and looked around for militia. Shots rang out. They ran like madmen back into the vegetation. Bullets whizzed all around them. They heard a crash and looked back; José Antonio was lying flat on the ground. Roberto went back to him; a .30 caliber round had ripped through José Antonio's back. He was gurgling blood, gasping, "Go! Go!" His body went limp in Roberto's arms. Roberto left him and ran as fast as he could to catch up to the others. He found them crouched behind a fallen tree, out of breath. Emilio was patting his clothing.

Roberto gasped, "What's wrong?"

"He lost his last asthma puffer."

Emilio's wheezing would have been audible to anyone within twenty-yards. Roberto crawled behind him and began gently tapping on his upper back with open palms, just as Teresa used to do when he was a boy and had asthma attacks. His lungs slowly cleared. Goyo asked, "What happened to José Antonio?" Roberto silently shook his head.

They began moving aimlessly again across the thick, sweltering tropical wilderness, avoiding the militia-guarded roads and trails. Their tongues swelled from dehydration. Whatever fresh water there was in the vicinity was undrinkable, being little more than sludge. Miyares finally broke. "I can't go on without water. We should just surrender; I know they'll execute us, but it's better than dying of thirst!" Roberto shook his head, "I can't take this either." He walked a few yards away and pulled down his pants. He urinated into his cupped hands, stopping the stream every few seconds to transfer the urine into his mouth. He winced whenever he swallowed. Within the hour all of them had followed Roberto's example, except for Father Hidalgo.

They moved on, dropping for cover whenever the sound of helicopter blades roared overhead. Later that day, they began foraging the land for anything edible—small crabs, snakes, and iguanas. They ate all of it raw. By early afternoon, Goyo began hallucinating. "There! I see a telephone! And look, no militia. I can call Raquel to come pick us up; they won't stop her . . . Emilio! Listen to me! You don't know where you're going; I can call Raquel!"

Late that afternoon, they came upon an empty *bohío* in the middle of a small clearing. Castro had ordered all of the local people out of the area while his troops hunted for the Brigade. They spied it for a few minutes. There were no signs of life any-where. They went in and found no clothing or water, just a clay jar with some sour milk in it. They went back into the woods and continued their journey. An hour later, they decided to rest. Miyares sat and wiped some blood off a cut on his face. "What direction are we going in? Where the hell are we headed?"

Emilio was re-strapping his boots. "For now, we're just try-ing not to get killed. Like I said before, we'll try to find some clothes and slip past the encirclements and go to a town and see what happens." His bootstrap snapped. He swore.

Roberto said, "Listen, how long can Castro's people keep combing the area? We should just lay low in here until they give up. They can't keep this up forever."

Goyo snapped angrily, "Roberto, how can we survive out here without water? What you're suggesting is suicide!"

"Yeah, well, it's better than getting shot, which is what they'll do to us if we're captured. Even if we change into civil-ian clothes they'll probably still recognize us."

"Father Hidalgo, what do you think?" Emilio asked.

The men turned in Father Hidalgo's direction. The priest had been ignoring the conversation. He had lifted a rock out of the ground and had started digging a hole. "The ground is unusually moist under here," he whispered. "There may be fresh water further down." They all clambered over and started digging, the thought of striking water suddenly unleashing new stores of energy. They hit fresh water five minutes later.

"Praised be the Lord," Goyo declared. They dug deeper. With the ebullience of rescued castaways, they took deep mouthfuls of the water until their bellies were as swollen as Spanish wineskins. They filled their canteens and sat silently, relishing the euphoria of rehydration. As twilight descended, Emilio said, "We'll stay here for the night, near the water."

Father Hidalgo nodded. "Yes, let us enjoy this miracle for at least one night." The priest pulled out the small case he'd been carrying with him since the landings and opened it. He pulled out all the necessary materials for a Mass and then snapped some legs out of the case, turning it into a miniature altar. He spread a tiny, crisp, white linen cloth atop the case, unavoidably staining it with his muddied fingers. He placed his stole around his shoulders. In an inaudible whisper, he gave the opening prayers and delivered the requisite Latin incantations above a small container of wine and a pocket-sized ciborium. They each received Communion. It was dark by the time they made the Sign of the Cross to end the silent service.

Roberto volunteered to take first watch. He crouched on the ground next to the water hole, his only companion the nocturnal sounds of the wilderness. When the deep of night set in, he waved his hand before his eyes and found that he couldn't see it. Alone now with his thoughts, he recalled an image that had kept dancing around the periphery of his mind since early that day. He took a deep breath and allowed the image to plant itself firmly in his consciousness. It was a memory from his childhood in Switzerland. He was at the Cuban Embassy, part of a commemoration of the "Grito de Baire," the 1895 event that launched Cuba's second–and ultimately successful–war of independence. He and the children of the embassy staff were all dressed in traditional national costume: a white *guayabera* shirt, a straw hat, and a red neck-erchief tied at the front and bearing the lone star of Cuba across the back triangle. As the most erudite of the children, he'd been selected to recite a series of patriotic poems, all of which he had learned by heart. Afterward, he and the other children led the gathering in singing the national anthem and other patriotic songs. When his father took the podium later, he spoke with great pride about the Cuban children gathered before him. "They are our future, these beautiful Cuban children, whose innocent voices do such great honor to our nation. With such children, the *patria's* future is indeed bright. I am inspired by the belief that there are no limits to what Cuba can achieve." In the reception afterward, a guest commented to Lorenzo, "We can indeed be optimistic about the future with young people such as your Roberto in the vanguard of the new generation."

His whole life, Roberto had taken words like that to heart. Deep down, he'd always believed that he was predestined to play a role in fulfilling Cuba's destiny as a great demo-cratic nation. He thought the invasion was the event that would bring that to fruition. He peered into the blackness and sighed glumly, pondering the harsh reality of the pres-ent. There would be no victory march. Cuba would be for-ever enslaved and impoverished. He felt suddenly like the invasion's failure was somehow his fault. How could he ever face his father again? Shame spread inside him like poison.

Sonia muscled her way into his thoughts.

After leaving New York, he'd sworn not to think about her, deciding instead to focus all his mental energy on the upcom-ing struggle against the Communists. He'd figured they'd

The Unbroken Circle Series, Book II

have a lifetime together after the liberation. But his defenses crumbled now and his long suppressed feelings for her surfaced. He yearned for her embrace, her warmth, her sweet affection. She would understand how he felt. She would stand by him, no matter the depth of his humiliation. He vowed to marry her if he ever made it out of this mess alive.

Father Hidalgo started snoring. Roberto kicked his feet. "Quiet, Father," he whispered. The priest got up. He took the next watch. Roberto sprawled on the ground and fell into a light sleep.

The next morning, April 21, they decided to stay near the water for a while. At noon, Emilio suggested that they start moving again. They filled up their canteens and started covering the hole with twigs and leaves. Emilio noticed the mound of dirt they'd dug up the day before. "Make sure to scatter the dirt we dug up; if they come by they'll notice the mound. We'll leave some markers so we can find the water . . ."

His right hand shot up for quiet.

The group froze. They all heard the footsteps. They dropped flat on the ground, their camouflage uniforms and the dark shade from the canopy above blending them into the ground cover. The footsteps grew louder. Emilio lifted his head a couple of inches to look. He saw two Castro soldiers. He lowered his head again and grabbed a fallen branch next to his right hand. The footsteps trailed off. Emilio relaxed his grip on the branch. All of a sudden, one of the soldiers stopped. "Hey, what's that mound of dirt over there?"

They started walking toward them. Emilio squeezed the branch again. Any second now, they would be noticed. When the soldiers were only ten yards away, he sprung up from the ground and began shouting like a crazed lunatic, swinging the branch at the militiamen like a police baton. The others followed Emilio's lead, emerging from the ground like corpses springing to life in a cemetery and charging at the militiamen. The soldiers screamed in terror, turned, and fled. Emilio shouted, "Kill them! Get them with the .30 calibers!"

The cousins' group ran in the opposite direction, holding up their arms to protect their faces from the thorns and branches. In their haste and blindness, they inadvertently ran onto a narrow causeway that traversed the swamp. They stopped in the middle of the road, fear and confusion in their eyes, adrenalin rushing through their bodies. Someone in the distance shouted, "Halt!"

They turned and spotted a militia post twenty-five yards away, manned by three men. Two of them aimed rifles at the group, the other a recoilless gun. Fearing for their lives, Goyo and Miyares instinctively fired at the post with their last bullets. The recoilless gun responded. The shell landed a few feet in front of them, closest to Roberto. The concussion knocked all of them to the ground.

The militiamen surrounded them within seconds. "Stay where you are, mercenaries! Turn over! Face down!"

Goyo's head was simultaneously swirling and pounding. He lay on his stomach. He couldn't open his eyes. One of the militiamen shouted, "All of you, on your knees, fingers locked on top of your heads!"

Goyo struggled to his knees. The air smelled of gunpowder. He slowly regained his vision. Emilio was on his right, Miyares and Father Hidalgo on his left. Roberto lay motionless several feet in front of him in a pool of dark, red blood.

One of the militiamen nudged him with his foot. "This one's dead."

Goyo collapsed to his hands. He wailed, "Roberto! No! Roberto!" A militiaman strode over and kicked him in the stomach. "Mercenary! Kneel! And remain silent!" He picked up Goyo's rifle from the ground.

Goyo felt all his remaining energy give way in an internal avalanche. He struggled back to his knees and locked his fingers on top of his head. His chin convulsed uncontrollably. He arched his back and shut his eyes tightly. He tilted his face toward the sky, too frightened, too tired, too aggrieved to cry or even pray.

A fresh crew of six militiamen came up the road behind them. They carried an empty stretcher. The post commander barked out orders to them. "March these mercenaries to Girón and put the dead one on the stretcher. But first bind them and give them water." Goyo kept his eyes shut as the instructions were delivered.

The three men from the militia post went back to their station. The prisoners' wrists were bound. One of the new soldiers held his canteen to Goyo's mouth. His tone was sympathetic. "Take the whole thing if you'd like, I have more." Goyo opened his eyes and drank.

Another *miliciano* was giving Emilio water. Emilio cleared his throat between sips. Goyo looked furtively in his direction. Emilio signaled subtly with his eyes.

Goyo glanced at the militiaman holding the canteen to Emilio's lips. He had a wide girth and from behind looked to be around fifty years of age. The man turned so that Goyo could glimpse his face.

Goyo's breathing stopped. He looked to the front again. It was Horacio Lima, an employee at Belén for over thirty years. He'd been part of the school's maintenance staff and a friend. They talked every day when he came into Goyo's classroom to sweep the floors after school. "So, doctor, which of the world's problems are we going to solve today?" he'd always say when he came in. Although Horacio possessed only a sixth grade education, the affable janitor read three newspapers, cover to cover, every day and had the vocabulary to match. They would go on for hours sometimes about the political situation in Cuba, about world affairs, and about baseball. Horacio's curiosity was insatiable, and he constantly peppered Goyo with questions about history and philosophy. One day, he said, "Mr. León, I can listen to you for days and never suffer hunger or thirst! When I learn something new from you, I use it with my wife and neighbors. But I do it right away, before I forget the details. They think I'm some sort of genius!"

And now Horacio, in full militia uniform, was charged with taking him into custody.

"Boys," Horacio cried to the younger militiamen who'd accompanied him, "please, a favor for a beloved old man, a man who has treated you like nothing less than favored sons. Go to the militia post over there and fetch me a new first aid kit."

"I can get it, Horacio," one of them replied.

"No, no, all of you go and fill your canteens again; and please refill mine as well." He handed one of the boys his canteen. "We have to move quickly and it's a long march. I can keep an eye on the prisoners." He raised his rifle and aimed it at the kneeling Goyo, eyeing him along the barrel through his horn-rimmed glasses. His gray-flecked moustache twitched.

As soon as the crew was out of earshot, Horacio whispered through his teeth, "Mr. León, what are you doing here?" He kept the gun on Goyo and sighed, "Please, Mr. León, don't judge me harshly because of this . . . but you know how things are for us working people now, the pressure they're putting on us. I swear I never took part in the fight; my unit arrived here just last night. You know I'm not a Communist, Mr. León, you know more than anyone that I'm Catholic before all else."

Goyo was close to tears. His face was a mess of blood, sweat, and dirt. "Horacio, my friend," he exhaled.

Horacio looked back at his crew. It was just arriving at the post to retrieve the first-aid kit and replenish the canteens. He turned back to Goyo. "Mr. León, let me take your jewelry and anything else I can hide in my pockets. These people are animals; they're plundering the prisoners of everything, even their belts and boots. I promise, as soon as I'm able, I'll get them to your wife. Quickly, now, before they come back."

Goyo told Horacio to take the wedding ring off his finger and the St. Jude medallion Goyito had given him from around his neck. Horacio did so quickly, holding the rifle with one hand and removing the items with the other. He stuffed them into his pocket and took the rifle in both hands again. His eyes scanned the others. "My God, even Father Hidalgo is here. I'm so sorry about Roberto." He glanced at the prostrate body for a few seconds and then looked back at Goyo. "So many young people have died these past days, Mr. León, it breaks my heart." He shuddered and sighed. "Now, Mr. León, when they come back, we can't let them know that we're friends. No, No! We'll both get it for sure! So, if

I speak harshly to you, remember not to be angry with me." He looked at the others. "Let's all just get out of here alive."

When the other militiamen returned, Horacio ordered them, "OK, my good boys, let's march these mercenaries to Girón. You four," he said, pointing at four of them, "take the dead one back to Girón on the stretcher. Put him on a truck if one becomes available. The two of us will escort the others and meet you there."

The four militiamen begrudgingly picked up the stretcher by its handles. "Why do we always get the shitty jobs? It's going to take us forever to haul this corpse to Girón!"

Horacio ignored them. "Let's move," he said, "I don't want to babysit these traitors any longer than I need to!" The *miliciano* chosen to accompany Horacio was rifling through Father Hidalgo's pockets. He pulled out his stole and squinted at it curiously. He shrugged his shoulders and threw off his cap. He tied the stole around his forehead like a bandana. Then he took Emilio's Alabama flag and pinned it on his shirt.

They commenced the long march to Girón under a blazing sun. Horacio let the younger militiaman surge a few dozen yards ahead with Miyares, Father Hidalgo, and Emilio before him. Horacio stayed behind Goyo, his rifle pointed at the middle of his back. When the others were out of earshot, he whispered, "Mr. León, is there any message you want me to deliver to your family?"

"Yes," Goyo whispered back. "Tell my wife to leave the country immediately with the children. Tell her to go to Miami and to contact Tony Méndez. He has money for her." Horacio nodded. After about an hour, they reached the outskirts of Girón. The whole place was teeming with buses, trucks, tanks, regular army troops, militiamen, and foreign journalists. Off the main road, just before the edge of town and well out of the journalists' range, a group of white militiamen had tied an Afro-Cuban Brigade member to a tree with some cord. They were shouting racial insults at him and took turns punching him.

The group's arrival in Girón was noticed by a swarm of pencil-and-pad carrying newspapermen. They surrounded the group like a pack of wolves and began asking questions. Photographers started clicking pictures. Through an interpreter, a Russian reporter asked Horacio, "Where did you find this group of mercenaries?"

Horacio spoke directly to the interpreter. "A few miles back, that way." He swept his hand toward the north. Another Eastern European, his face an inch from Emilio's, said, "This one's an American, look at him. Will his fate be different?" The pack of journalists turned toward Emilio. The cameras clicked away. Emilio looked down at the ground.

"They are all Cuban, I assure you," Horacio answered indignantly.

A giddy Frenchman with a Roman nose asked the group, "Are any of you remorseful about betraying your country?"

Horacio's face flushed. He waved his hand angrily at the Frenchman. "The prisoners are not allowed to speak to anyone; no more questions, please." He led the prisoners past the journalists and turned them over to a group of militiamen guarding a few dozen bound Brigade men sitting under one of the surviving coconut trees. Other Brigade prisoners filled the half-built bungalows of the resort. Goyo's group was told to sit among the men under the tree. Horacio turned and departed without looking back.

A few minutes later, an excited commotion broke out. The journalists flocked toward a group of rapidly approaching soldiers dressed in olive green. Their attention was focused on the tall, fast-talking man in the center of the group. Goyo immediately recognized the unmistakable beard.

Fidel Castro was wearing battle fatigues, horn-rimmed glasses, a beret, and a side arm, the perfect image of the dashing guerrilla intellectual he knew his admirers couldn't get enough of. The journalists surrounded Fidel like fifteen-year-old girls would Elvis Presley. Castro, a giant cigar in his mouth, strode over to the coconut tree and stood amid the prisoners. He took the cigar between the index and middle finger of his right hand. "Gentlemen, I trust you've been treated well by the Revolution." None of the Brigade men answered him. "It seems you have been abandoned by the Americans, eh? Well, I think it's clear now that fate and history are on our side."

Fidel Castro's eyes fell directly on Goyo. His face registered instant recognition. "León, is that you? Gregorio León? Goyo, is it not?"

Goyo swallowed and looked up at his old classmate.

Castro walked over and stood silently over him for a few seconds. He looked as if he expected to have his boots kissed. Goyo turned away. Fidel said gently, "León, stand up, face me." The journalists looked on in fascination, their pencils moving.

Goyo remained seated. He and Emilio exchanged a nervous look. One of the soldiers in Castro's entourage reached over and slapped Goyo's head. "Do as you're ordered, mercenary!"

Fidel grabbed the man's hand and pulled it away forcefully. "I've said repeatedly not to harm the prisoners." The journalists cooed their approval. The soldier bowed his head in contrition and stepped back.

Fidel turned back to Goyo and ordered him to stand up with the tone of a school principal scolding a favored student. "Stand up, León."

Goyo got up and stood face-to-face with Fidel Castro. His heart was beating more rapidly than the clicks of the photographers' cameras, but he was not in the least bit intimidated, Fidel at that moment nothing more to him than a fellow Belén graduate.

"León, what were you thinking? Did you really think this scum was going to overthrow *me*? Come, Goyo, you should have known better."

"That was our objective," Goyo answered.

"You know, León, I can give the order and you'll be executed right here."

"Yes, I know, you've become a very powerful man. You're a credit to our alma mater." The subtle sarcasm was lost on the journalists, but not on Fidel.

Castro popped the cigar back into his mouth and peered at Goyo. "What was it, León? I'm curious. What made you join this ridiculous venture?"

"I came to fight against Communism. I came to fight for democracy and for God."

"For God, indeed!" Castro howled. He put the cigar between his fingers again. "You know, you people make me laugh. Listen, I know atheists who are better Christians than the hypocrites who run the Catholic institutions in this country. And as for democracy, is there an institution more autocratic than the Catholic Church? What do you say to that, León?" The journalists scratched away in their notepads.

Goyo said nothing. He wasn't going to take the bait and give Fidel a free media show. Anyway, he was tired of talking to him and wanted to sit down again. Castro huffed and waved his hand dismissively. He marched away with his entourage and media groupies in tow.

As dusk approached, the prisoners under the coconut tree were escorted into one of the half-finished tourist bungalows that had just been vacated by the last group of Brigade prisoners transported to Havana. The stench from the toilets inside the still waterless structure stung their eyes. They were unbound. Goyo sat on the floor and leaned against a bare concrete wall next to Emilio. A little later, they were brought some food: guava paste, sweetened condensed milk, and some Russian canned fish that tasted like shit. The men consumed it all, as many of them had barely eaten since leaving Puerto Cabezas.

They were allowed to talk. As darkness began to envelop them, Goyo said to Emilio, "Of the three of us, I thought Roberto was the one who had the best chance of surviving." Emilio nodded silently. He'd lost more than a close cousin; Roberto was his best friend, his brother, the person who'd come closest to filling the void left by his father's death. Goyo put his arm across Emilio's shoulders until he fell asleep. His young cousin had come to know death's devastation at far too early an age.

In the middle of the night, an official came in to inspect them. He searched their faces with his flashlight and told them that they'd be executed first thing in the morning. "But don't worry. We'll give you a last cigarette. We have American brands for you, too; that should make you happy."

The sunrise executions never occurred. In fact, not a single Castro soldier entered the bungalow until late morning, when a couple of militiamen came in, pointed to about half the men, including Emilio, and ordered them to stand. They were marched outside single file for transport to Havana. Emilio glanced back at Goyo as he followed the others out. Goyo winked at him, signaling him not to worry.

A few hours later, the men who remained in the bungalow were called out and boarded on a bus. A handful of machine gun-toting *milicianos* at the front kept guard over them. Goyo was seated next to a young man in his late teens. He was slumped forward, his drawn, sunburned face marked by deep lines of sadness. Goyo nodded a "hello" to him. The boy pursed his lips in acknowledgement. It was over a hundred degrees on the bus. The driver came in and took his seat. He closed the doors and started the engine.

Goyo got one last look at Girón, the sleepy, obscure town in Cuba that had suddenly become the center of the world. Good riddance, he thought.

The boy seated next to him began to talk. His name was Félix from the city of Baracoa, where he'd worked as a waiter. His parents had sent him to Miami for fear that he would be recruited into the army or the militia, an unacceptable prospect for them since they were not only strongly anti-Communist but hyper-protective of their only child. "And now," Félix lamented, "because of this mess my mother and father will be left childless."

Goyo searched his mind for some words of comfort, but, as he did so, the bus came abruptly to a stop in the center of a small town. A wild, Revolutionary mob rushed at them. The crowd began rocking the vehicle and pounding it with their fists, shouting in a cacophonous roar, "Mercenaries! Cowards! Traitors!" Goyo noticed an older man quietly snaking his way through the mob. He was wearing a straw hat and had a Cuban flag draped across his shoulders as if it was a cape. He held a large tote bag in his hands. He reached the bus, pulled a box of crackers from his bag, and passed it through a window to one of the Brigade men inside. Then he pulled out a couple of Spanish wine skins filled with water and passed them through the same window. One of the Revolutionaries tried to pull him away when he saw what he was up to, but the old man slipped out of his grasp. He shouted, "For the valiant men of the Liberation Army!" and handed one of the Brigade men in the bus the entire bag. It contained more food and water. He then fled, chided by the mob. A couple of Communist Youth members pursued him. The bus continued on its slow journey to the capital.

Seeing Havana for the first time since December moved Goyo to tears. It was *his* city; the city that had witnessed his birth and upbringing; the city whose every corner he knew as well as his own living room; the city where he'd received his education, met his wife, and raised his children. It was the corner of the world wherein his soul resided. The bus stopped at the Transportation Ministry building. A *miliciano* boarded and told them that they were broadcasting a live television show and that a few of them might be selected for an appearance before the entire nation. "You'll be the most famous mercenary worms in the world!" A few minutes later, a young man who carried himself with an air of authority boarded and began walking slowly down the center aisle, scrutinizing the prisoners. His hands were clasped behind his back.

As the young man's face came into focus, Goyo's heart stopped. It was Paquito Vega.

The man seated behind Goyo leaned forward. "I'll bet he's looking for the ones who look scared so they can put them on television and make us all look foolish." Goyo nodded.

As Paquito neared his row, Goyo lowered his head and started trembling nervously. He was muttering to himself in a low, shaky voice. Paquito kicked his foot. "You! Look at me!" Goyo lifted his head, his face wet with crocodile tears.

"You!" Paquito hissed, taking half a step back, his eyes nearly popping out of his head. "I can't believe it! Where are your cousins? Are they on this bus?" He scanned the rear of the vehicle.

Goyo blubbered as he spoke, "Ro-Ro-Roberto was killed in the swamp . . . Emilio is in M-Miami." His arms and shoulders shook like gelatin.

"Roberto's dead?" Paquito straightened and grinned at Goyo for a moment. "You know, I nearly captured you a few months ago."

Goyo remembered his family sitting on the front porch as Paquito's militia band tore apart his house. He felt like someone had just taken a blow torch to his head. He had to use every bit of discipline he possessed to keep up his act.

Goyo held his hands in supplication. "Paquito, please, I want to get out of here. I don't belong in this place, with these people. Is there anything you can do? I know you've had your differences with my family, but I implore you, please, get me out of here!"

"Come with me," Paquito said. He escorted him off the bus and had a *miliciano* bind his wrists. He walked him into a large room. "Listen, Goyo, you may be going on television later. If they ask you any questions, I want you to tell the people of Cuba who you are and how sorry you feel for having betrayed your country and the Revolution. I want you to denounce Kennedy and the Americans for this violation of Cuba's sovereignty in the most emphatic fashion. Then, I'll see what I can do for you."

"Yes, yes, of course, I'll do whatever you ask of me." Goyo suppressed a smirk. He knew it would snow in Cuba before Paquito did anything to help him.

Paquito called a guard over to watch Goyo and went over to confer with the man who seemed to be in charge of directing the television broadcast.

The television lights shone brightly on Goyo. "Is it not true that your family was of the wealthy, bank owning bourgeoisie in Cuba?"

"No, my family operated a small family bank in Vedado that did great things for the community."

"You come from a rich, aristocratic family! You came to take back from the people the capitalist enterprise your family lost, didn't you?"

"No. I came to fight for God and for Cuba. I quote a famous saint, who said, 'Praise be to those who free the multitude from a tyrannical power.' And I can tell you that this Brigade came to do just that."

It was past midnight by the time they got to the Sports Palace. They were taken inside the large, domed arena under heavy guard. The seats were packed with Brigade men. His comrades shouted toward him, "Hello, brother, glad you could make it!" "León, León, over here!"

Goyo was assigned to the section where the Second Battalion was seated. He felt a surge of pride at being among the men with whom he'd fought side-by-side just a few days earlier. The medical student who'd examined Pedro Vila's remains was sitting right behind him. He squeezed Goyo's shoulder. Goyo patted his hand. "I'm glad you made it out alive, Doctor," Goyo told him. The student leaned forward and said to him, "Listen, I'm sorry about your cousin, León, I truly am. It was horrible what happened to him."

"Thank you," Goyo said solemnly, "Roberto is with God now."

The man reared back and blinked. "Roberto?" He slowly shook his head. "I didn't know about Roberto. I was talking about Emilio."

"No, no, you're confused; it was Roberto who was killed, back when we were captured. I saw it with my own eyes. Emilio is OK. I was detained with him at Girón. He left for Havana before I did." He looked to where the paratroopers were seated. He scanned the faces. "I guess his group hasn't gotten here yet."

The young man turned away and sighed. Goyo glanced at the people who'd been privy to their conversation; they all pretended not to have heard anything. Goyo's intestines began twisting into a tight knot.

Girón
Late Morning
April 22, 1961

When Emilio had been called out of the Girón bungalow earlier that day, he and the others in his group were taken to the side doors of a forty-foot, eighteen-wheel truck–a *rastra*–where they were lined up with other Brigade prisoners. The official charged with loading them inside the *rastra* was no less than Minister of Public Works Osmani Cienfuegos, brother of the immensely popular 26th of July rebel Camilo Cienfuegos (In1959, an airplane in which Camilo had been traveling mysteriously disappeared and his remains were never found; many believed the airplane had been shot down on the orders of Fidel Castro.). Next to Osmani Cienfuegos there stood another high ranking official.

The official next to Cienfuegos started barking out the names of Brigade prisoners, ordering them into the truck's cargo trailer; Cienfuegos, meanwhile, stood by and hurled insults at them as they boarded. The Brigade men waiting outside looked on anxiously as more and more prisoners were herded into the truck. Emilio's name was finally called after eighty or so had gone before him. He found himself near the middle of the cargo trailer, about a third of the way from the back wall. It was a veritable oven inside. There were no interior lights. A Brigade prisoner next to him said, "Christ! Are they going to shut those doors and have us stand inside here all the way to Havana?"

Prisoner after prisoner continued to be packed inside. Emilio soon found himself pressed in on all sides by fellow

Brigade men. As the air thickened in proportion to the growing mass of humanity, breathing became increasingly difficult. Cienfuegos nevertheless continued loading men into the truck, including several injured prisoners. When the number surpassed one hundred, the prisoners inside began shouting at him. "No one else fits in here, damn you! There's not enough air! We can barely breathe!"

A subordinate told Cienfuegos, "Sir, they'll die if we put more inside." Cienfuegos famously responded, "What does it matter? Let them die! It will save us from executing them!" He signaled with his hands. "Bring me forty more pigs, now!"

The men inside the truck shouted in protest as more prisoners were squeezed in. The total number reached 149. Emilio, pinned tightly among the bodies in the middle of the truck, was sweating profusely from the savage heat and struggling for air. He became faint and started to collapse, but was caught by the man behind him, an older Brigade member called Navarro, who helped prop him up.

The *milicianos* finally shut the steel doors, enveloping the men in total, pitch darkness. The ghastly metallic grinding sound of the exterior bolts locking into place prompted a wave of panic. The *rastra* suddenly felt like the inside of a coffin. The men shouted, "No! No! Open the doors! We're going to suffocate in here!" Those wedged along the sides banged wildly on the trailer's aluminum and plywood walls in utter despair.

When the truck released its brake and accelerated, the men shifted backward, crashing against one another. The painful scenario repeated itself whenever the truck slowed down, accelerated, shifted gears, or turned; each time there were new bruises, gashed skin, and broken bones. The scorching tropical sun beating down from the outside, combined with the heat of 149 tightly packed human bodies, made the inside of the sealed *rastra* a blast furnace. Some of the men desperately ripped off their clothes in a futile attempt to alleviate the heat's effects. Many of them threw up where they stood, inundating the floor in a noxious brew of vomit, urine, blood, and, especially, sweat. They soon heard the liquid sloshing with every movement. After a few hours, the liquid began to diffuse into a mist that hung below the ceiling.

Men who had unflinchingly charged enemy positions through a hail of gunfire, who'd stood their ground through terrifying howitzer attacks, and who'd fearlessly engaged in hand-to-hand combat against a numerically superior enemy, were trapped in a battle they could never hope to win. Inside the dark truck, some cursed, some prayed with hopeless abandon, and many passed out. Soon, most of the men were lying upon the floor and on top of one another. Whenever the truck stopped–which happened with unusual frequency–those who still had the energy banged on the walls and used what was left of their strength to rock the *rastra* from side to side in an attempt to tip it over. They were blithely ignored.

Whatever oxygen had been trapped inside the trailer when the doors were bolted shut eventually ran to dangerously low levels. Some of the men used their belt buckles to scratch open tiny holes along the *rastra's* walls. Those who were close enough to them took turns putting their mouths on the tiny fissures to inhale oxygen from the outside. Some who were on the verge of losing consciousness were carried over to them. The effort saved the lives of many men, but not all of them.

Emilio made a valiant effort to hang on to life. Collapsed on the floor and leaning against Navarro, who was also now on the floor, he'd closed his eyes and thought about his childhood, about the years he'd spent with his father, about his mother, about his days in New York, about his León relatives, about his Alabama cousin, and about the many girls he had loved. He took slow, deliberate breaths, trying his best not to struggle for air; his efforts, however, simply could not compensate for the lack of oxygen. When his body began to collapse sideways, Navarro, sensing his distress, held him up and tried shaking him. "Stay awake, son! Keep breathing, we're almost there! Hang on. The doors will open in just a few minutes." The older man soon started losing consciousness himself and positioned Emilio's head on his left shoulder like a sleeping child. Every few seconds he shook Emilio, trying to keep him awake.

While leaning on Navarro's shoulder, Emilio lost and regained consciousness several times. When he first passed out, he'd entered a dream-like state and watched with great anticipation as a blurry light moved toward him across a dark landscape. Before he could make out what it was, he awoke; with every subsequent passage into unconsciousness, the light came closer. He finally saw that it was a man shrouded in a peaceful glow, but it wasn't until he was close enough to look into his eyes that Emilio recognized him.

"Papi," he muttered weakly.

"Do you see your Papi now?" Navarro said to him in a sad whisper.

Emilio's body was jolted by a tight spasm. "Yes, son," Navarro said through a sob, "you go with him now."

During Emilio's final moments of earthly existence, a fellow Brigade member reached a sweaty arm across the mass of human flesh and placed his hand on Emilio's head. He muttered:

"*In paradisum deducant te Angeli; in tuo adventu suscipiant te martyres, et perducant te in civitatem sanctam Ierusalem. Chorus angelorum te suscipiat, et cum Lazaro quondam paupere aeternam habeus requirem.*

"May angels lead you into Paradise; may the martyrs receive you at your coming and lead you to the holy city of Jerusalem. May a choir of angels receive you, and with Lazarus, who was once poor, may you have eternal rest."

His father's face was perfectly clear to him now. His gentle, loving eyes beheld his son, the message behind his expression unmistakable: he had always been proud of him, his faith in him unshakable, and his love for him unconditional. How silly it was that he could have ever thought otherwise. Emilio no longer struggled to breathe. He was lifted up suddenly by a rapturous embrace. He sensed all the disjointed parts of his soul fall into place around him, like an unbroken circle, closing him in a protective barrier.

The truck arrived at Havana's Sports Palace after more than eight hours on the road (The trip should have taken less than half that time). The *milicianos* who opened the *rastra's* doors beheld a gruesome spectacle. The men inside, many of them only semi-conscious, were twisted into a heap of tangled flesh. The pool of expelled human fluids pouring through the doors made one of the militiamen physically ill. In all, nine men asphyxiated inside the *rastra*. A tenth died shortly thereafter.

The architect of this atrocity, Osmani Cienfuegos, became a highly decorated official in the Castro government and remained for decades to come a part of the ruling, privileged elite in Communist Cuba.

GUANABACOA, CUBA
Nighttime, April 22, 1961

S onia Pérez became nauseated watching the spectacle at the Sports Palace on television. Because there were others present, however, she could give no expression to her inner turmoil. She looked around at the others in the common area of the boarding house where she'd been living for almost four months now. They all watched the television silently and with dead faces, making no comment. She wondered what was going on in their minds.

It was well past dark now, and she decided to take a long walk in the cool, April night; she knew that staying in the boarding house would make her depression unbearable. She strolled along the sidewalks of Guanabacoa, a municipality in eastern Havana where she now lived, and passed in front of the Church of Our Lady of the Assumption. For some inexplicable reason, the church always made her think about that night back in December when she believed Roberto had left her for good. She'd felt like such a fool, sitting there alone in Parque Villalón, drowning in self-pity. She stopped walking, grasped one of the iron railings running along the front of the church, and looked up at the bell tower. She smiled.

It had happened on a crisp afternoon a few weeks after she'd quit waiting for Roberto at the park. A man in his thirties, wearing sunglasses and a hat, had approached her in front of her building.

"Hello, *señorita*," he'd said amicably.

"Can I help you?"

"Yes, I have a young daughter, you see, who's interested in taking music lessons, and we've heard great things about you as a teacher."

"Oh?"

"Yes," the stranger said, smiling. He moved closer to her. "She's crazy about music, and I understand you play a beautiful rendition of 'Unchained Melody.'"

Every instinct had told her to run away. The only person she'd ever played that song for was Roberto León, at the restaurant near the University on the day they'd met. But a reckless curiosity, enhanced by desperate hope, kept her feet firmly planted.

She cleared her throat. "Yes, I know that song."

"Perhaps we could discuss the terms of the lessons," the man said. "Can we talk somewhere in private?"

Sonia's chest tightened. "Yes, of course."

They walked into a busy marketplace a block away. The smell of tropical fruit, frying pork, and freshly cut flowers hung in the air. She guided him to a small, isolated table in a corner of the eatery there and sat. He took a seat across from her, his casually staged mannerisms making it appear that they were old friends.

He spoke in a clipped tone, loud enough so that only she could hear. "You don't know who I am, nor shall you, *señorita*."

Sonia blinked. She drew a deep breath and held it.

He grabbed a napkin and began folding it, glancing at her intermittently. "I have a message for you from Roberto León."

Her face muscles contracted, but she managed to shrug with feigned indifference. She asked, "Oh, really?"

He laid the napkin down gently on the table and leaned forward. "Roberto was working with a democratic organization and his life became imperiled. He was forced to flee the country. That's the reason he has not been able to contact you."

Sonia's mouth opened slightly, a world of understanding seeping through.

"He says he wants you to wait for him until he returns." The man got up, smiled, pulled his hat tightly over his brow, and disappeared into the street.

Sonia sat frozen for several minutes, joy and hope crashing triumphantly through the layers of grief and humiliation that had settled inside her, feelings that had begun hardening into a kind of permanent moroseness. She took a deep breath and exhaled; the expulsion of air brought on a stream of tears. Emotions whirled inside her with such force she thought she'd faint.

When they began to subside, her reasoning faculties slowly returned. She felt as though the man's information was the missing piece of a puzzle, although at first she wasn't sure exactly why. Her mind started sifting through the strange occurrences that had marked her short relationship with Roberto–being stood up at the park not the least among them. She remembered Emilio suddenly showing up at the

Tropicana and Roberto having to leave with him right away. Deep down she'd never bought the story about his father being ill, especially since he'd hardly mentioned it the next time they saw each other. Did Roberto's sudden departure really have something to do with his work for a "democratic organization," as the strange man had so delicately referred to the underground?

Her recollection from that night took her back to the next morning, when her father had somehow known that she'd been at the Tropicana and that her date was from a "bank-owning family" that lived in Miramar. He'd said that someone he knew was at the club and that the person knew Roberto's family. She knew her father was lying, but she was too furious at the moment to question him about his source. But how *did* her father, a low level snitch who'd never seen the inside of the Tropicana, come by that information about Roberto so quickly? He'd never met Roberto, and she'd never even mentioned his name to him. She gasped with sudden comprehension: the militia captain her father had invited over to meet her the night she'd gone out with Roberto. Of course! He'd probably followed her and spied on her during her date—more than likely at her father's behest! The captain got Roberto's name somehow, investigated him, and reported back to her father before she woke up the next morning. Sonia's body slumped; her stomach reeled with revulsion. The blood left her face, leaving her cheeks icy. She thought slowly and deliberately. "Could the same militia captain have then discovered that Roberto was in the underground? Could he have subsequently pursued Roberto and forced him to flee the island just a few days later?"

She would never know exactly, but she was convinced of her father's complicity in the matter. Blood, boiling hot, returned to her cheeks. That was the last straw. She bolted from the marketplace, went to her apartment, packed her bags, and left before her father got home. She wanted nothing to do with him ever again. She showed up at the boarding house in Guanabacoa later that day and registered under an assumed name. She would do what Roberto had requested and wait for him until he returned. The next day she changed her University records to reflect the change of address, figuring that if Roberto did come back to Cuba he'd need to find her somehow.

Of course, now he could only return if the Castro government was ousted. Her fate was irreconcilably tied to that eventuality.

Sonia had followed the battle at the Bay of Pigs as closely as she could on television and radio. At first, when word on the street was that the invaders were winning, she became flush with hope. But now, three days after the fall of Girón and Castro's subsequent consolidation of power, she felt like a zoo animal trapped in a life of inconsolable loneliness. All hope of reconnecting with Roberto was buried in the beaches of the Bay of Pigs.

As she re-entered the boarding house after her walk late that night, she once again felt her depression close around her like a death shroud. She went back into the common area and sat at one end of a ratty old couch. There were still a few residents there watching television. Footage of the Brigade prisoners who had been rounded up in the swamps earlier ran across the screen. In one clip, the camera focused on a prisoner lying face up on a hospital bed. The announcer proclaimed with characteristic demagoguery, "And here is an injured mercenary at the small hospital in Cayo Ramona, near the battle zone. He is suffering terribly from his battle injuries, but the Revolution will provide him with the best possible medical treatment, despite his treason." The injured man had a look of total bewilderment on his face.

Her mind started clicking with recognition.

She stood and moved closer to the screen, staring closely into the young man's face. She covered her mouth in shocked horror.

It was Roberto!

Sonia looked into his eyes through the television screen, feeling that they were signaling to her. She touched the screen with her fingertips. She began to quake.

An emaciated middle-aged woman sitting at a table playing solitaire cocked her head toward Sonia. She took a drag from a long, dark cigarette and squawked at her through the small bursts of smoke exiting her mouth, "What's the matter? Do you know that worm?"

The raspy voice jolted Sonia back into the present. "No . . . I mean . . . I know his mother . . . I was just thinking of how terrible it must be for her to have a son who's a traitor." The others in the room pretended not to have heard the conversation.

Sonia couldn't contain her excitement; it was as though fireworks were exploding inside her chest. She went back into the street and started walking aimlessly, the emotion propelling her forward like a turbine engine. She muttered to herself, "My God! He was in the invasion, and he's alive!" She stopped and inhaled sharply, suddenly remembering that the government was likely going to execute all of the invaders. Her burst of elation was quickly conquered by feelings of deep gloom. She tightened her jaw and curled her hands into tight fists. She would get word to Roberto–somehow–that she was still with him, no matter what might happen. She looked around and realized she was standing before the church again. She looked up at the bell tower. "Faith," she reminded herself, "Faith."

Havana, Cuba
Miramar Section
Nighttime, April 22, 1961

Sonia Pérez hadn't been the only one watching the television late that night. The León family had remained glued to the set at Goyo's house, hoping to see Emilio and Roberto among the prisoners. Roberto's mother, Sara, had joined them despite Lorenzo's admonishments for her to stay in bed until she felt better.

When they saw Roberto's face on the screen they jumped up and screamed for joy. After their initial relief, though, they became anxious about his injuries. Sara cried in a hoarse sob, "Where was he injured? What if the doctors don't treat him?" Raquel threw her arms around her.

Emilio was now the only one unaccounted for. Teresa went outside and sat in a rocking chair on the back portico, alone, preparing herself for the worst. No one had the nerve to go talk to her.

A little while later, someone knocked lightly at the front door. Lorenzo got up. "Who can it be at this hour? I'll answer it." He opened the door and found a portly, middle-aged man with a moustache and glasses standing there. Lorenzo asked cautiously, "May I help you, sir?"

"I would like very much to see the wife of Mr. León."

"Horacio, is that you?" Raquel cried over Lorenzo's shoulder.

Horacio Lima removed his hat. "Yes, may I come in? It would be best if no one else in the neighborhood sees me here."

"Yes, of course, Horacio. Come in, come in. Please sit." Raquel motioned him inside and closed the front door.

Horacio nervously greeted the gathered family members and took a seat in an armchair. He felt like a new neighbor who'd been invited over for coffee.

"Horacio is an employee at Belén and a close friend of Goyo's," Raquel explained to everyone.

Sara asked, "Are you a teacher as well?"

Horacio shook his head. "No, ma'am, I'm one of the janitors."

"I see . . . um . . . how wonderful."

Raquel turned to face him, "Horacio, did you know that Goyo and his cousins were in the invasion?"

Horacio drew a sharp breath and made the Sign of the Cross, exclaiming, "Do I know? Praised be, Mrs. León, my militia unit was the one that marched them back to Girón after they were captured! That's why I'm here!"

The room went silent. Everyone gave each other astonished looks.

Horacio reached inside his pocket. "Mrs. León, I bring you Mr. León's wedding ring and his St. Jude medallion."

Raquel, her cheeks flushed, took up the items and pressed them against her chest. She took a deep breath and called Goyito over. She placed the chain around his neck. "Son, this is the medallion you gave your father. Don't ever take it off. When we're together again, you can place it around his neck again with your own hands." Raquel looked at the medallion closely and started sobbing. "We must pray to St. Jude every night," she said, her voice cracking and muted, "to bring Papi back to us."

Horacio pulled out a handkerchief and patted his eyes. "I'm sorry, this isn't easy for me." He gathered himself. His eyes fell on Lorenzo and Sara. "You're Roberto's parents?"

"Yes," Lorenzo said, "and we just saw him on television. They've got him in a small hospital somewhere called 'Cayo Ramona' in the Zapata Swamp. Apparently he's injured, but thank God he's alive. Of course, I'm sure you know all of this."

Horacio's eyes narrowed. "You're quite certain of this? You saw Roberto alive?"

"Just now, on television."

Horacio clapped and made the Sign of the Cross again. "Praised be! I thought for sure he was dead!" He thought for a moment, "He must have just been unconscious."

"Do you know the nature of his injury?" Sara asked hesitantly.

"Well, now that I think back, I remember his leg was bleeding very badly."

Lorenzo rubbed his wife's back. "It's a leg, dear, it could have been much worse." Sara lowered her eyes and nodded. She pulled out a handkerchief and blew her nose.

Lorenzo turned back to Horacio, "What do you know of Emilio Hammond, my nephew? He's the only one we haven't seen on television."

"I also escorted him from the swamp to the beach. The last time I saw him he was all in one piece." Just before coming over, Horacio had learned that Emilio was among the men who'd asphyxiated aboard the *rastra*. He couldn't bring himself to tell the family. Part of him felt ashamed about that, but there was nothing else to be done.

His eyes went back to Raquel. "Mrs. Léon, your husband also asked me to deliver a message to you. Would you prefer if I gave it to you in private?"

"You may give it to me here, Horacio. We're all family."

Horacio nodded. "He said for you and the children to leave for Miami immediately and to get in touch with someone called Tony Méndez. He has money for you."

Raquel could feel her father's eyes upon her. She avoided looking his way.

"Mrs. León, my rank in the militia allows me to move in and out of the Sports Palace freely. Please, if you have any message you want me to deliver to Mr. León, let me know."

Raquel sniffled and nodded her head in gratitude. "Yes, Horacio, tell him that his family's only thoughts are for him and his cousins and that we miss them and pray for them constantly." She reached out and squeezed his hand. "And please tell him how lucky we are to have a friend as valiant and honorable as Horacio Lima."

"I'll tell him the first part," Horacio said with a wave, "but the second is too great an exaggeration." He got up to leave. Raquel embraced him before he departed.

Lorenzo sighed after the door closed. "There goes a good man." He indicated toward the back of the house with his thumb. "I'd better go and tell Teresa that this Horacio fellow saw Emilio alive."

Raquel's father called her into the dining room. He motioned her into a chair. His voice was as serious as death. "Daughter, please honor Goyo's wishes. Take the children and go to Miami. He anticipated this possibility; he even left money there for you with his friend. We'll follow you as soon as you're there safely."

"No Father, no!" she said defiantly. "You can't expect me to leave Cuba with Goyo imprisoned. I need to look out for him. What if they want to send him to a prison camp in Russia? I can't leave Cuba, not as long as Goyo is here and alive."

"Daughter, you've heard about the schools. Don't you understand? Your children will be brainwashed into being Communists! Maybe *they'll* be the ones sent to Russia!"

"Father, you're frightening me . . . please stop."

"I will not stop telling you *the truth.*"

Raquel went to her room. She lay upon her bed, motionless, and stared at the ceiling until the next morning.

Bay of Pigs
Cayo Ramona Hospital
April 22, 1961

Roberto groaned sharply and looked over at the Brigade soldier lying next to him. "Where the hell are we?"

The man answered in a pained gasp, "The hospital in Cayo Ramona."

"What day is it?"

"April 22nd."

Roberto lay back and bit his fist. His leg felt like it was being held in a bonfire. He looked down momentarily and eyed the bandages. He dropped his head back down, trying to recall what had happened over the past few days. He remembered everything through the 19th clearly, but only vaguely recalled being in the swamp with his cousins and the others after that. He remembered digging a hole with them and finding some water; the rest was a disjointed collection of murky images. The next thing he remembered with any clarity was waking up to shooting pain in his leg. He was being carried on a stretcher on a road by some militiamen. When he groaned from the pain, they dropped him, jumped back, and screeched like they'd just stepped on a poisonous snake.

"Damn it! He's alive," they had shouted. One of them drew his pistol. "OK, mercenary, one word out of you and I'll put a bullet through your head and leave you here as crocodile food, understand?" Roberto passed out after that, then remembered reaching Girón, passing out again, and at some point after that being put aboard a truck with some other injured prisoners. He passed out again. His next memory was of television camera lights shining in his face and of passing out yet again.

A medic came over to change his bandages. Roberto could never have imagined such excruciating pain. His piercing scream got the attention of one of the doctors, who came over and looked over the medic's shoulder. "That still doesn't look good; send him with the group going to Matanzas tomorrow."

The next morning, April 23, Roberto was lined up along the road with a group of ten severely injured Brigade prisoners, all of them lying on stretchers, to await transport to the military hospital in Matanzas. The scorching in his leg engulfed his entire body in a sea of flames, his every nerve sensitive to even the gentlest touch. He tensed his body and squirmed against the pain. The burning sun exacerbated the high fever he was already running. When they were finally boarded onto the uncovered bed of a military truck, he used his remaining mental energy to disassociate from the pain. He shut his eyes tightly and thought about his date with Sonia at the Tropicana; he imagined giving a group of foreign tourists a detailed tour of Havana in both French and English; he tried to remember every inch of the Malecón and listed every street that emptied into it; he cataloged every feature of every room of his house in Switzerland and spelled the names of all his teachers and classmates at the International School; he tried to remember, in order, all of his birthday celebrations, the lineups of Cuba's professional baseball teams, and the roster of the New York Yankees. After roughly an hour and a half, the driver finally got into the cab with two *milicianos* and headed for Matanzas.

Revolutionary "welcoming committees" were assembled in every town they drove through. The Castro bootlicks hurled insults at them and shook the truck as if to overturn it. The outrageous spectacles distressed Roberto even more than his physical pain. He tried reminding himself that these individuals were not representative of the Cuban people, that the demonstrations were nothing more than pogroms organized by a totalitarian government. Still, the sheer energy of the vulgar mobs crushed him under a mountain of disillusion. He asked himself bitterly, "Are *these* the people I came to free? Is there a dark side to them that I never imagined?"

When at last they arrived at the Matanzas hospital, Roberto was put on a kind of gurney. His tattered Brigade uniform was cut from his body, the touch of the cold scissors against his skin stinging like lemon juice on a fresh cut. As he lay there uncovered, shivering with fever, a doctor and nurse came by to examine him. The physician took a close look at his leg; the nurse held his hand tightly. By their demeanor, Roberto could tell that they weren't Revolutionaries. When the doctor finished his examination, the nurse covered Roberto's body above his injury with a bed sheet and blanket. The doctor bent down and whispered into his ear, "Son, this leg can still be saved. Whatever happens, *do not* let them amputate it. They've already carried out amputations on Brigade prisoners that were, in my opinion, unnecessary. And be especially careful with those foreign surgeons who've been buzzing around–especially those drunken Russian bastards." The nurse squeezed Roberto's hand and nodded once.

Roberto looked at them, the word "amputation" paralyzing him with dread.

He never saw the doctor or nurse again.

The next day a different Cuban doctor came by to check on him; this one was openly antagonistic and possessed all the crudeness of a good Revolutionary. "They should have shot all of you worm mercenaries on the beach," he said as he examined the leg. "You sons-of-bitches sold out the Revolution and now they expect *me* to save you?" He huffed and shook his head.

Later that afternoon, a couple of nurses came in and wheeled Roberto's bed into a different room. In a few seconds, he realized it was an operating theatre. A moment later, one of the nurses ambushed him from behind and administered anesthesia. He jerked his body and flailed his arms to get loose, but in his weakened condition the nurse easily overpowered him. Before going under, he saw the malicious Cuban doctor entering the room, laughing along with another surgeon. The second doctor was a blue-eyed, burly man with a ruddy complexion, unkempt hair, and a Russian accent.

The anesthesia took effect quickly. Roberto's last image was of the Russian, a depraved look in his eyes, wielding a large butcher's knife over his head, ready to mutilate, ready to kill, as was his wont.

23

SPORTS PALACE
Havana, Cuba
Evening, April 24, 1961

Goyo sat like a statue for nearly forty-eight hours. A dark, mournful cloud hung over him. He spoke to no one; no one dared speak to him. Flashes of Pedro Vila's mutilated body and of Roberto lying in a pool of blood ran over and over in his mind. He felt partly responsible for their fate; still, he could take a little bit of comfort in the knowledge that, in the end, they had died fighting to save their country. But Emilio's death was nothing but a senseless atrocity. Goyo had implored the medical student to tell him what had happened soon after the young man had given him his condolences. The student had complied, leaving out none of the details. He finished by declaring, "I tell you the truth, León, for I was one of the *rastra's* survivors and I saw Emilio's dead body with my own eyes when we arrived in Havana."

Goyo now saw that Cuba had become nothing more than a place from which to flee. It no longer existed; what would emerge on this island in the years to come was a twisted perversion of a country called Cuba, but not the real Cuba. He saw nothing but repression, misery, and depravity in the future. Most of the men in the Brigade were clearly willing to fight again if they were given the chance, but Goyo knew that, in the end, the León family was done in this place. Its future lay elsewhere. He grieved the loss of his heritage and homeland almost as much as he did his cousins and Pedro. He thought about his ancestors who'd come from Spain so many generations earlier and tried to imagine what it was like for them to leave their homeland and strike out across the sea toward an uncertain future. Raquel and his children would leave Cuba the same way, he thought, shaking the island's dust from their feet. They would carry the family name to a new land and establish it there with the same dignity his ancestors had when they came to Cuba. He wanted to go with them, but, he thought dejectedly, it seemed fate had other plans.

By the evening of April 24, his mind had shifted to logistics. Did Horacio get the message to Raquel? Has she figured out a way to leave Cuba yet? Would Tony Méndez still be in Miami? Late that night, he saw the familiar image of Horacio Lima walking in his direction.

Horacio stopped next to Goyo's row and, in a harsh military tone, called his name from a clipboard. Goyo walked over and reported to him. Horacio pulled him out of earshot of the others and spoke quickly, pretending to record something on his clipboard. "I saw your family, Mr. Léon, and I gave them your things. They're OK. I'm sorry I couldn't come sooner."

"Did you tell my wife to leave Cuba, and about Tony Méndez?"

"Yes. Now, listen, I have something to tell . . ."

"Did she give you any indication about when they would leave?"

"No. But please, listen . . ."

"Did you hear about Emilio?"

Horacio sighed and paused for a second. "Yes, but I didn't tell your family about it. I just couldn't."

"Did they know about Roberto?"

"That's why I'm here. Now, listen . . ."

"How did Lorenzo and Sara take the news? Did you see them?"

"Mr. León, that's what I'm trying to tell you . . ."

"What did my wife say?"

"Mr. León, shut up! Roberto is *alive*. He was apparently unconscious, not dead."

Goyo's eyes became saucers. After a moment of stunned silence, he asked, "Are you certain?"

"Your family saw him on television; he was in a small hospital near the battle zone. I made some inquiries and confirmed the news. He's apparently very badly wounded in the leg and was taken to a military hospital in Matanzas. But, he's definitely alive."

"Will he live?"

"I don't know."

Goyo wanted to embrace Horacio.

Two militiamen started walking in their direction. Horacio cocked his head and pointed stiffly for Goyo to take his seat. He slipped the clipboard under his arm and sauntered away.

Goyo took his seat, feeling like one of the apostles upon learning of the Resurrection. Roberto was *alive*. For the first time since the end of the invasion, he felt a burgeoning hope swelling inside of him.

24

DOWNTOWN MIAMI, FLORIDA

Late April, 1961

Jimmy Strickland handed the cute little cocktail waitress a $100 bill. "Here's a little somethin' for yer troubles, sweetie." The girl gasped when she saw the money and stuffed it into her bra, even though the two of them were the only ones in the lounge. Jimmy let out a rough, drunken laugh. "Funny how good old Ben Franklin always feels right safe in there, ain't it?" He reached out and squeezed one of her tits, figuring the $100 had earned him at least that much. The waitress squealed playfully and brushed away his hand. "You're a dirty old man, you know that?"

Jimmy sank back into his stool and folded his arms. "Darling, you don't know the half of it." With that, he got to his feet and staggered toward the door.

He walked the two blocks to the Everglades Hotel. The breeze carried the scent of the ocean. He entered his room and locked the door. He sat at the small table where he'd arranged a few personal items: a bottle of Tennessee whiskey, a shot glass, a pack of Camel cigarettes, a pocket knife, and a loaded pistol. He poured himself a drink and downed it in one shot. He leaned back and shut his eyes. He was, momentarily, back in Alabama on a clear Sunday afternoon in the autumn. The cotton, ready to be picked, covered the landscape like a thick layer of fresh snow. The smell of Momma's fried chicken danced in the air, like it always did, curling around the branches of the live oak and magnolia trees. Grandpa, Grandma, and his sister were on the front porch, smiling, talking sweetly to one another. He never wanted to open his eyes again, because when he did they'd be dead all over again.

Jimmy finally sat up and opened his eyes. He lit a cigarette, the blissful, bucolic images of rural Alabama popping out of existence like a soap bubble. As he puffed on the Camel, events from the real world assaulted him. He had left Nicaragua on April 20, and came directly to Miami seeking information about Emilio. What he found there broke his heart. Wives, parents, and children of Brigade members hovered outside the offices of the Cuban exile political leadership at all hours, demanding to know the whereabouts of their loved ones and incessantly poring over updated lists of survivors. Many of the same families had marched at Bayfront Park during the invasion demanding the United States government send the promised support; they'd also held endless prayer vigils at the Roman Catholic parishes of Gesu and Corpus Christi.

Jimmy checked the lists along with them. Every time he saw that Emilio's name wasn't there, the sinking sensation in his stomach became deeper.

Earlier that day, he'd spotted an upper level CIA guy he recognized from the training camps entering the offices. He followed him inside. "Hey there, cowboy, remember me?" One of the few advantages of Jimmy's disfigurement was that no one who met him ever forgot him.

The CIA man looked perturbed. "What are you doing here? What authorization do you have to be in this office?"

"Fuck you and your God-damned authorization. The CIA don't own me."

The man bristled. "Excuse me?"

Jimmy sighed and calmed down. "Listen, I just want to know what happened to one of the guys I trained."

The man's face muscles relaxed. He jotted Emilio's name down on a piece of paper and told Jimmy to wait. He came back a few minutes later. "I've got some bad news." He told him about the *rastra,* details of which were just starting to emerge within intelligence circles.

Jimmy's face sagged. "On a *sealed truck?* Jesus. I thought only Nazis did shit like that."

Within a half hour he was at the bar tying one on.

Now back in his hotel room, he sat alone, the ugliness of life pouring over him like a bucket of raw sewage. He gulped down another shot of whiskey. He picked up his pocket knife and started scratching at the table's surface with it. He wondered for a minute if the whole encounter with Emilio had just been a dream. Maybe the whole invasion had just been a product of his imagination.

He took another shot and slammed down the glass. "How in the *hell* could they have left those men on the beaches to die? How could this government have *betrayed* them like that?" he shouted out furiously.

He took the crucifix Emilio had given him from around his neck and laid it on the table next to the gun. He stared at it. Then he grabbed the pistol and checked to make sure there was a round in the chamber. He put it down again.

He poured himself another shot and lit another Camel. He drained the glass and took a drag from the cigarette; then he snuffed out the cigarette. He picked up the gun again. He pressed the end of the barrel against his scarred temple. "Lord, forgive me."

The gunshot was heard throughout the hotel. The management immediately called the police and evacuated all the guests. Ten City of Miami police officers showed up within five minutes. They kicked in Jimmy's door and burst into the room, pistols drawn. When they saw it was a suicide, they holstered their weapons. One of them picked up the bottle of whiskey. "Looks like he took a bellyful of the strong stuff with him." Another officer looked closely at the top of the table. "Hey, look at this." A large circle had been carved into it.

25

SPORTS PALACE

Havana, Cuba
April-May, 1961

For twenty-one hours a day, the roughly one thousand Brigade prisoners were forced to sit on the hard grandstand seats at Havana's Sports Palace, prohibited even from standing or stretching. From a few hours every night, they were permitted to lie upon dirty mattresses on the arena's main floor under a full complement of theatre lights. Every now and then, a new group of prisoners arrived from Girón, late captures who had almost gotten away.

Having the Brigade in custody was a godsend for Castro, as it put into his hands a living trophy of his victory over Cuba's democratic politicians and the United States. He now sought to make his propaganda victory complete by having the betrayed, demoralized Brigade turn its collective back on its American partners. But, to do that, he needed to weaken its resolve and unity. The authorities initially tried to sow discord within the ranks, sitting the men separately by battalion, splitting them up along social class lines, and dividing them into every other grouping they thought might produce disharmony. They were equally creative with physical abuse, forbidding the men to bathe or wash, and requiring them to remain for nearly two weeks in the same condition in which they'd been captured in the Zapata Swamp. Infections became rampant. One day, Castro's people went so far as to mix *jalapa*, a powerful laxative, into the Brigade's food. Fire trucks had to be brought in to clean up the diarrhea that overflowed the toilets.

Perhaps most cruelly, in order to undermine the Brigade's spirit and reinforce whatever sense of abandonment and humiliation it was feeling at the moment, the regime continued to deride the men as "mercenaries," the most vile and shameful type of combatant. By doing so, the Cuban government also hoped to disabuse the world of the notion that the 2506 was somehow the "liberation army" it purported to be, and to try to show that its members were, instead, agents–and ultimately dupes–of foreign imperialism.

Under this intense physical and psychological pressure, the men of Brigade 2506 were asked to sign written confessions. They were also asked to petition the Secretary General of the United Nations, requesting that he condemn the United States for the invasion. Despite the coercive measures applied by the regime and the anger many in the Brigade felt toward the United States at that moment, over 90 percent of them defiantly refused to do either. They knew why they had come to fight and would not allow themselves to be used by Castro to spread his lies.

As the days passed, the men were called one-by-one over loudspeakers to interrogation desks that had been set up in the arena. When Goyo was called, he was directed to a desk occupied by a stout, red-headed man in a military uniform. He asked Goyo his age, where he was from, and what he did for a living. He inquired about his family background, what Brigade unit he belonged to, and what he knew about the role of the United States in the invasion. Then he asked him point blank: "What made you join this force to invade Cuba?"

Goyo hesitated for a moment. "I wanted Cuba to be a free and democratic country; a place where people choose their leaders and are free to think for themselves. A place where an individual can become whatever he chooses in this life."

"So you contend that Cuba under the Revolution is *not* a free country?"

Goyo remained silent. He'd said what he needed to say on television.

The man continued to bait him. "Well, maybe before the Revolution Cuba was free for the privileged class you were from–with your private schools and your priests and your country clubs–but it was not free for those of us who actually had to work for a living. It was not free for those of us who couldn't go to the best schools or attend the University because our families weren't rich."

Cuba's excellent public schools had been free and the universities had been attended by people of all social classes. Goyo stared into the stands and stayed quiet.

"So, let me see if I have this right, you wanted to come back to this country and take back what you lost: Banco León, the elitist Belén School, the Havana Yacht Club . . . does that sum it up?"

Goyo looked the man in the eyes. "No. You were not listening. I came here to fight for my country's freedom."

"Your *country*? Your country despises you as a traitor! If I let you out into the street the people would lynch you!"

Goyo knew that wasn't true. Maybe the government's mobs would lynch him. He regretted ever having said anything and wanted to go back to his seat. The man persisted. "You talk about a 'democratic country?' What kind of democracy are you talking about—the kind that produces extremes of rich and poor? The kind that allows wealthy property owners to abuse and trample the rights of the common people, all with the complicity of the nefarious political leaders they manipulate into power through some sham ballot box election? You can talk all you want about elections, but give me the kind of democracy envisioned by Marx and Engels."

Goyo yawned. He'd heard all this shit before. If this man couldn't see that Cuba was headed toward a future of complete social and political repression, economic calamity, and moral degradation, he certainly wasn't going to open his eyes at this juncture. The man would learn for himself soon enough. Goyo was sent back to his seat.

The Brigade men were put before television cameras individually to give their names and places of residence. Around forty of them—including the scions of wealthy families and the sons of exiled democratic political leaders—were selected for lengthier interviews before a panel of Revolutionary luminaries who sat at a long table. Before the table hung a sign reading, *"Vencimos,"* "We Won." They also found three wanted Batista men who'd somehow joined the Brigade and put them before the cameras as well. Fidel Castro himself visited the men in the Sports Palace one night. A contingent of salivating journalists, foreign and domestic, followed him. The cigar-puffing dictator announced that their lives would be graciously spared. Goyo deduced that Castro would barter with their lives, now that he had had his propaganda show. It seemed the Brigade was more valuable to the dictator alive than dead. It was good news on the surface, but Goyo felt not the slightest bit of optimism. Castro was a pathological liar.

During his visit, Castro began to engage the Brigade men directly. He stopped before a black paratrooper named Tomás Cruz. He said, "You, Negro, what are you doing here? Don't you know blacks can now go to the beaches with whites?" Cruz responded quickly, informing the white leader that he had no inferiority complex about his race and that he hadn't joined the invasion force to go to the beach. Castro, who was rarely at a loss for words, was silenced by Cruz's response.

After two weeks the men were finally allowed to shower. They were each given a yellow T-shirt, the color chosen to symbolize Castro's depiction of them as "yellow worms." Later that day, Goyo learned that many of the schools, Belén included, had been formally expropriated by the regime; the others were told they would be closed at the end of the school year. His only hope now was that Raquel had figured out a way to get out of the country.

Havana, Cuba
Military Hospital
Columbia Military Base

The part that tortured him the most was that it felt as though it was still there. He would stretch it, wiggle his toes, and bend his knee; but whenever he looked down, the leg was still gone.

Roberto's anguish was unbearable, despite the sanitary conditions he was accorded at the Columbia Military Base's hospital in Havana, where he'd been transferred. He carried a vague recollection about waking up during his surgery. He thought he remembered a surgical saw moving back and forth rhythmically across his leg. The memory tormented him and he tried to block it out, but couldn't. Suicide crossed his mind on several occasions, but thoughts of his parents, as well as the lack of a means, prevented him from committing the act. He would never forget that Cuban doctor and the degenerate Russian butcher. Their faces were imprinted on his mind. He'd kill them with his bare hands if he ever saw them again.

A few days after arriving at the military base, a government official came to his bedside with a file folder. "Are you related to Emilio Hammond León?"

Roberto tried sitting up. "Yes, he's my first cousin. Do you have news of him?"

"We need you to identify him for us." The official opened the folder and showed Roberto pictures of Emilio's dead, bloated face. "Is this him?"

Roberto stared at the photograph in disbelief and then looked back at the official. "He's *dead?*"

"Yes."

Roberto gave him a vacant stare. He asked, in a stunned whisper, "How?"

The man ignored the question. "So, can you attest officially that this is Emilio Hammond León?"

Roberto compressed his lips and nodded.

"Very well," the official said. He snapped the folder shut and departed without another word.

Roberto lay back and covered his face with the bed sheet. He cried for the first time since he'd been a child. The other wounded prisoners in the room looked away. When the tears dried up, he stared up at the ceiling, swollen with guilt and remorse. He wondered how he could have been so foolish as to trust those who had since betrayed them. He felt alone, isolated from the entire universe.

He thought back to the passionate, heartfelt patriotism that had compelled him to join the Brigade and all his hoopla about "liberating" Cuba. He'd even allowed himself privately to imagine future school books in Cuba explaining how the Communists and the Russians had quite nearly taken over their beloved country, but how the glorious Brigade 2506 had rescued her and preserved her freedom. He'd entertained fantasies of his descendants visiting monuments dedicated to the Brigade and proudly claiming lineage to its heroes. He glanced at the stump jutting out from his hip. He thought about Emilio's dead face in the picture. He recalled the mobs in the towns they passed through on the trip to Matanzas, those sons-of-bitches calling them "mercenaries." He was nothing but a fool, he thought. The only thing he wanted now was to get the hell out of Cuba and never return. He wanted to live out his life in peace, with his family, with Sonia, and away from all this human shit.

26

NAVAL HOSPITAL
HAVANA, CUBA
May-June 1961

I n mid-May, the Brigade prisoners were transferred to the nearly completed Naval Hospital on the eastern side of Havana. Compared to the Sports Palace, the Naval Hospital felt like the Waldorf Astoria. Fifteen to twenty men occupied each room and shared a bathroom and shower with an equal number in an adjoining room. At night, they rolled mattresses out on the floor, each of which was shared by as many as four men, their upper bodies lying perpendicular on the rectangular pad, their legs on the floor. Armed guards were stationed outside the rooms with orders to rifle-butt or kick anyone who had the audacity to stick his head out the doors.

The improved conditions lifted the Brigade's mood and added credence to the rumor that the regime was brokering a deal with the Americans for their release. Castro himself confirmed the rumor when he visited the Naval Hospital on May 18. He announced that he would be willing to exchange the Brigade for specific types of American-made tractors. They were told to elect representatives from among their ranks to travel to the United States to initiate the talks. When the elected Brigade commission left for the United States two days later, they carried with them the hopes of their brothers and their families.

One day, as the details of the tractor deal were being worked out, the Brigade prisoners were startled by a roar of voices outside the hospital. They looked out the windows and saw a crowd of thousands gathered outside. The crowd shouted and waved handkerchiefs toward the building. It took a few seconds for the men to realize that the mob was their families. The wives and mothers in the crowd confronted the guards who tried to block their way and shouted their husbands' and sons' names toward the windows. The stunned Brigade men shouted back down to their loved ones. The guards finally came in and told them that a family visitation had been announced by the regime, but far more family members had shown up than were anticipated. Most of the relatives were sent home and assigned different days to come back.

Raquel was among the relatives sent home. She had nearly strangled the guard who told her she would have to wait until mid-week. An hour later, she was back at her house. She threw down her purse and slammed the care package she had prepared for Goyo on the dining table. Her eyes burned with indignation. Goyito and Ana Cristina came barreling in from the kitchen, followed by her parents.

"Did you see Papi?" Goyito asked.

She forced herself to smile. "No, son, but I have good news. I'm scheduled to see him on Wednesday."

"Why didn't you see him today?" a vexed Ana Cristina asked.

"Well, dear, it seems so many relatives went to see the men

today that they couldn't get everyone inside the building. We were all given different days to go back."

Raquel suddenly noticed a strikingly beautiful young woman standing at the kitchen door. "Oh . . . hello," she greeted her cautiously.

José María made the introduction. "Daughter, this nice young lady came to see you. She says she's a friend of Roberto's. I said it was all right if she waited here for you."

"Of course," Raquel said. "I'm sorry, I missed your name."

"Sonia. Sonia Pérez. It's a pleasure to meet you."

"Welcome, Sonia. Please sit, you're in your home. Mamá, can you fix some coffee, please?"

Raquel smiled cautiously. She was suspicious of everyone now. She sat next to the girl on the couch. "So, you're Roberto's friend?"

"Yes . . . well, perhaps more than friends, you might say."

Raquel arched her eyebrows.

"He spoke to me about you and Goyo. He's very fond of you both."

"That's nice, but I didn't know Roberto was seeing someone."

"We met shortly before he left Cuba. I didn't have a chance to meet any of his relatives, except for . . . well, except for Emilio." She paused for a moment. "I was so sorry to hear about his passing. Roberto must be devastated; they were like brothers." Sonia had learned of Emilio's death through a friend from the University.

Raquel shifted uncomfortably on the couch and cleared her throat. "Yes, we're all grieving him. He was very much a part of our home. His mother, well, you can imagine her reaction when they came to the house and informed her. We had a quiet family service." Raquel didn't bother mentioning that Teresa had hardly spoken since then. She now spent her days on the portico talking to herself and gazing out to the sea.

"Raquel, have you heard anything about Roberto? I saw him briefly on television last month; they said he was injured. I know most of the prisoners were moved to the Naval Hospital. Is he with them?"

"As far as we know he's at the military hospital at the Columbia base."

"Is he all right?" Sonia asked, her voice quivering.

"Well, he's alive, but . . ." Raquel paused and closed her eyes for a moment. She took in a deep breath and exhaled. She looked back at Sonia. "Listen, Sonia, I don't want to alarm you, but we've been informed that they've amputated one of his legs."

Sonia's hand flew to her chest. "Oh, my God."

Raquel nodded. Adriana came in, set down the coffee, and left.

Raquel took a sip from her tiny espresso cup. "I'm sorry, but it's better that you found out now. The good news is that there's a deal in the works for the Brigade's release. They apparently want to trade the men to the United States for some tractors."

"I've heard. I hope it happens soon." She anxiously rubbed the tops of her thighs with her hands.

Sonia and Raquel chatted for the next two hours. Raquel watched her closely, studied her every move, scrutinized her every word, looking for any sign that she might be a spy of some sort. She saw none. From what she could tell, Roberto's "friend" was an affectionate, level-headed, and highly cultured young woman. Sonia, meanwhile, thought Roberto's description of Raquel had been dead accurate: a loving person with an inner core made of pure steel. Raquel reminded her of her late mother. She was relieved, too, for she'd initially thought about approaching Roberto's parents but thought they'd kick her out when they learned her address. Raquel seemed utterly indifferent as to where she was from.

Teresa came in from the portico. Raquel and Sonia stood. "Teresa, this is Roberto's friend, Sonia."

Teresa took her hand. "It's a pleasure to meet you, daughter."

"I was so sorry to hear about Emilio, Doña Teresa. I had the good fortune of making his acquaintance. He was a fine young man."

Teresa frowned. Then she waved her hand, "Ah, he was a devil." They all laughed. Raquel hadn't heard Teresa joke or laugh in weeks.

Raquel said, "Teresa, did you know that Sonia is a musician? She gives violin lessons."

Teresa smiled. "Really? Do you play the piano as well? I so love to hear the piano."

"Not as well as I play violin, but, yes, I do play," Sonia said.

Teresa motioned toward the piano in the corner of the living room, "Please, play something for me, daughter."

Sonia looked at Raquel. Raquel nodded eager approval.

Sonia played a sentimental interpretation of Bach's "Air." Teresa closed her eyes. The music seemed to transport her to a faraway place, to a happier time. The music drew Raquel's parents and children into the living room. Sonia played similar pieces for them—excerpts from Bach's Prelude in C, Beethoven's Moonlight Sonata, Chopin's Nocturne. Then she played some traditional Cuban pieces with an intonation that made the Caribbean rhythms sound like songs of lamentation, poignant farewells to something that had died long before its time.

* * *

Raquel's heart was fluttering when she entered Goyo's floor at the Naval Hospital a few days later. She looked around and spotted him across the hall. She stared at him for a long moment. It was the first time she'd laid eyes on her husband in five months. The fluttering in her heart slowed to a deep throb. He turned and saw her. "Raquel! Raquel! Over here!"

She dropped the care package and ran to him, the collision of their bodies almost hard enough to break their ribs. They held each other for several moments, a mixture of joy and sadness radiating from them like a high fever.

They broke their embrace but continued holding one another's hands. Both their faces were wet. They spoke with urgency, not knowing if the visit would last three minutes or three hours.

"How are the children? How's my mother, your parents, everyone?" Goyo sputtered.

"Everyone's just fine. The children miss you terribly." Raquel noticed that part of his earlobe was missing. She decided not to ask him about it.

"How did you weather the days of the invasion?"

"I was detained at the Blanquita, but I'm fine." She sniffled and squeezed his hands. "Do you know about Emilio?"

His mouth turned downward in a deep frown. He nodded. Raquel pressed his hand to her cheek.

"And about Roberto?"

"Horacio told me that he was alive, but that he was injured pretty badly."

"They've amputated one of his legs, Goyo. None of us have been allowed to see him, not even his parents."

Goyo looked away and shuddered. "My God." He turned back to Raquel. "Did you hear about Pedro Vila?"

"I heard he was dead."

Goyo bit his lips and nodded. Raquel kissed his fingers.

He sniffled, grunted to clear his throat, and swallowed to regain his voice. "I heard they've ordered the schools to be closed," he finally said.

"Yes, just a few weeks ago."

"Who was it at Belén? Were there any teachers on the intervention team?"

"There were only a few. The priests were asked to move out and the government took over the campus. Ana Cristina's school was shut down as well. The nuns have been told to vacate the premises within the month." She lowered her voice, "My parents are teaching the kids at home. Some of the neighborhood children have been coming, too. It's like a little academy. We can get into trouble for it, but at least for now they can keep up with their lessons."

Goyo's face turned ashen. "Hiding our children to educate them, Raquel? What happened to this country?"

"It's lost, Goyo, it's lost."

A tremor rumbled through him. Raquel felt it in his hands. "Raquel, it's time for you and the children to leave Cuba, with the rest of the family if possible. There's nothing here for us anymore. You can't hide the kids forever; sooner or later they'll come for them."

"But, Goyo . . ."

"But nothing, Raquel."

"But what about all this talk about the Brigade being exchanged for tractors?"

"No one knows how these negotiations are going to end up. We discussed this a long time ago, Raquel. Do whatever you need to do to get out. Tony Méndez has money for you in Miami. He'll help you."

Raquel swallowed.

"Listen, Raquel, we both know that the closing of the schools isn't just about the 'closing of the schools.' It means that nothing now stands between our children and the Communists. What are you going to say when they ask why Goyito and Ana Cristina haven't enrolled in one of their schools or why they aren't in a Communist youth organization? Can't you see that they want to take them away from us so they can reprogram and reeducate them to fit their needs? You'll have no choice, Raquel!"

The words "reprogram and reeducate," bounced in Raquel's mind like plague-filled vials, ready to shatter, ready to infect. She shook her head. "I don't . . . I don't want to leave you here alone, not in the hands of these people. We've been separated long enough and I won't break this family up any further." Her voice cracked at the end.

"But Raquel . . ."

Raquel suddenly blurted out, "Damn it, Goyo, I'm pregnant! Are you so blind that you can't see it?" She closed her mouth tightly, and then wiped her nose with a handkerchief.

Goyo's face froze in stupefaction. His gaze shifted slowly to her stomach.

She let out an exasperated sigh. "A couple of nights before you left Cuba, remember?" Raquel wiggled her hips and shoulders in mock sensuality.

Goyo's face relaxed into a stupid smile. "How can I forget? I've thought about that night a lot since I've been in prison."

She slapped his arm. They both laughed.

He stepped back and gazed at her belly again. "My God, how could I have missed it?"

They locked eyes, their silent expressions saying, "How in the hell did we end up *here*?"

Raquel decided not to tell Goyo about the special "visa waivers" the nuns from Ana Cristina's school had given her before they were shut down. The United States had started waiving its visa requirements for Cubans entering American territory. As far as the Cuban government was concerned, a Cuban national needed only a so-called "visa waiver" document from the United States and an airline ticket to be allowed to leave the country. The waivers, though, had to be applied for and sent by a relative in the United States–a process that cost money and could take weeks or months. However, for the past several months, special visa waivers for children between six and eighteen years of age had been quietly circulating throughout Cuba. The ready-made waivers bore the letterhead of the Catholic Welfare Bureau of the Diocese of Miami and the copied signature of Father Bryan Walsh, its director. No one in the United States had to apply for one on someone else's behalf in Cuba; parents could simply acquire one of the special children's waivers from someone on the island and purchase airline tickets for their children. The youngsters would then fly to Miami and enter the United States as unaccompanied child refugees. Catholic schools and parishes in Cuba, as well as what was left of the anti-Castro underground, kept stashes of the special waivers for desperate parents who wanted to save their children from the growing totalitarianism on the island but couldn't get out themselves. Once the children landed in Miami, they either went with relatives who met them at the airport or, if they had none, were placed in a boarding school situation of some sort. Raquel wasn't clear about the latter. At any rate, she kept the two children's visa waivers hidden in a drawer.

Raquel's sister, Conchita, had left Cuba for Miami last week with her obnoxious husband Juan José. Raquel's father had suggested a middle road that was so practical she feared Goyo would insist she accept it: she could send their children with the special children's visa waivers to Miami, where her sister could take temporary custody of them upon their arrival. Raquel could then stay in Cuba until Goyo was set free; they would then depart the island together upon his release and reunite with the children in Miami.

But Raquel wasn't ready for a three-way separation. No way. Their family would not be broken up again. She would have to find another way.

Havana, Cuba
Military Hospital,
Columbia Military Base,
June 1961

Lorenzo and Sara arrived at the Columbia base at seven o'clock in the evening. Thanks to some lingering diplomatic connections and some well-placed bribes, Lorenzo was able to arrange a private visit with Roberto. "Fifteen minutes, that's all," he was told. It was better than nothing.

When they got to Roberto's bed, which had been rolled into a private room for the visit, he was fast asleep. Sara gasped. "My God! He's so pale and thin!" She could hardly bear to look at the empty space where his leg should have been. The outline of the stump was clearly visible through the thin sheet.

Sara stood silently over her sleeping son. Her mind conjured up images of Roberto as a young boy, snuggling under the covers between her and Lorenzo, running carefree up and down the hills of Switzerland, his whole life before him. Who could have ever imagined he would end up as a Communist prisoner and amputee in his own country?

She pulled up a chair and rubbed his hand. "Robertico, son, wake up. Mami and Papi are here."

Roberto opened his heavy, darkened eyelids. "My God!" New life lit up his face.

Lorenzo ran his fingers gently across his son's hair. "Yes, son, we're here." He kissed Roberto's forehead and pressed his cheek against it. He started weeping like a small child.

Roberto threw his arms weakly around his father's neck. "Papi, I'm so sorry; I'm so sorry I put you both through this!"

"No, son, no." Lorenzo lifted his head and wiped his eyes. "There's no need to be sorry. We're very proud of you, son, very proud."

Roberto grabbed both their hands. "Have you heard about Emilio?"

"Yes, son."

"How is Teresa?"

"She's recovering," Lorenzo said. "She's suffered many blows in her life."

Roberto nodded.

"Her faith is pulling her through," Sara said. "Our faith is all we have now, and the Communists even want to take that away. But they can never take away what one carries inside." She tapped her chest with her fist.

"What do you know about Goyo?"

"Goyo is with the rest of the Brigade at the Naval Hospital. Raquel got to visit him. She says he's doing well, under the circumstances."

"Thank God."

Lorenzo asked him, "Do you know about the negotiations?"

"Yes, they've told us about them. Is there any news?"

"Not yet, but we're hopeful."

Roberto glanced down at his missing leg and then frowned at his parents. His eyes swelled. Lorenzo caressed his cheek. He fought back more tears. "Son, just remember that you have a family that loves you very much and will never abandon you."

Roberto squeezed his parents' hands and kissed them.

Sara suddenly said, "Son, there's a girl we met yesterday who has been visiting Raquel. She says she's a friend of yours."

Roberto turned his face toward his mother sharply. "What's her name?"

"She says her name is Sonia Pérez. She's a musician of some sort."

Roberto let go of his parents' hands and pushed himself up in the bed. "She's been to Goyo's house?"

"Yes, and I'm not sure what to make of it. Raquel speaks of her as if she were your fiancée or something. She's very beautiful and quite talented, but from what I can pick up her family is of the worst sort."

Lorenzo shot a disapproving look at his wife. He had explicitly told her not to bring up this issue during the visit.

Roberto's face lit up like the morning sun. "Mami, Papi, that girl is the one I'm going to marry. You might not approve right now, but believe me when I tell you that when you get to know her you'll love her as much as I do."

Sara looked indignantly at her husband. Lorenzo shook his head furtively, mouthing, "Not now." Sara glanced at Roberto's stump again and sighed deeply. She bent and kissed his forehead. "My dear son, your happiness is the only thing your father and I have ever lived for." She began weeping.

Roberto pressed his mother's hand to his lips and kissed it again. Lorenzo held Roberto's other hand. A guard came in to tell them their time was up.

HAVANA, CUBA
Miramar Section
June-July, 1961

R aquel waited for Goyito by the front window. She checked her watch every few seconds. He had beseeched her earlier to let him walk to a nearby church. He said it was to pray for his father, but she knew he just wanted to get out of the house and release some steam, away from all the adults. She rarely let the children out alone nowadays, never knowing if someone might recognize them as the children of a Girón "mercenary." Lord knows what some Castro fanatic might say or do to them on the street. Against her better judgment, she'd let him go.

She saw him coming down the street. He was running. His clothes were all disheveled, his hair mussed. She flew out the door and met him on the front porch, a few feet from the door, where he stumbled and collapsed into her arms. His face, hands, and clothes were covered in blood. Everything started moving in silent, slow motion for her. She grabbed her son's face and looked at it closely. His right eye was swollen. She regained her senses long enough to screech, "What happened? Who did this to you?"

The boy refused to talk. She took him into the bathroom where her parents helped clean him up. While her parents put him in bed, she called Dr. Mendoza on the telephone. Whoever answered told her that the doctor had left the country a week ago. Raquel hung up and stood pensively for a few moments. She should have known that the doctor would be gone. The migration out of Cuba, especially by middle class professionals, had become a flood since the invasion's failure.

Raquel went to Goyito's room and sat on the bed next to him. "Tell me, son, what happened. I'm your mother and I need to keep you safe."

Goyito couldn't look her in the eyes. She drew the story out of him in bits and pieces. He had gone to the church and prayed for a few minutes, made his confession to the priest there, and then left. There were some older boys from the Rebel Youth outside. One of them called out, "Hey look, there goes a Catholic boy. Do you think he and the priest were kissing in there?" They started making kissing sounds.

Goyito, terrified, turned away from them and walked quickly in the opposite direction. The boys ran after him and blocked his way. "Hey kid, where are you going?"

Goyito said nothing.

"Are you deaf? I asked you a question."

Goyito's knees started buckling. "I . . . I . . . I'm going home."

They laughed like a troop of monkeys. "I . . . I . . . I'm going home, to my *mommy*." One of the boys suddenly grabbed Goyito by the shirt and shoved him up against the church wall. "We know who you are. Your father is one of those mercenary worms, and I'm going to cheer like I've never cheered in my life when they execute him! Here's something to take home!" He spat in Goyito's face. The others cackled like hyenas.

Goyito turned beet red. In a rage, he thrust his knee into the boy's crotch, doubling the boy over. It would be the only blow he'd deliver. The gang pounced, raining a flurry of punches on him, sending him to the pavement. Prostrate and defenseless, they kicked him without mercy.

A woman dressed in white came out of the church. She scared off the pack, threatening to call the police. The boys laughed raucously as they fled, one of them shouting, "Say hello to your *daddy* for us." The woman in white helped Goyito to his feet. She offered to take him home. Goyito shook his head and started running.

As he finished his story, Raquel kissed him and told him to rest. She reassured him that he had not lost a fair fight and that he had nothing for which to be ashamed. He went to sleep. She stayed in his room, ruminating. How did those boys, apparently all strangers, know that his father had been in the invasion? A sense of foreboding burned in her stomach. Night fell.

A little while later, someone knocked at the front door. Raquel got up and went into the living room. Her father was peering through the window. He held his finger to his lips. "Quiet," he said softly. "Damn it! It's that Paquito fellow with a couple of *milicianos*." Raquel stood still for a moment. Her intuition kicked into high gear; it told her that Paquito's unexpected presence spelled immediate danger for her children. She said to her father, "Hide the children, quickly."

José María grabbed the children from their rooms and disappeared into the master bedroom. Raquel took a deep breath. "I'm coming, just one second."

Teresa burst through the kitchen door, her eyes burning with violence. She obviously had the same feeling as Raquel, for she was brandishing a large kitchen knife. She told Raquel, "They're not taking any more of us, Raquel. I have nothing else to lose. I swear to God I'll kill him!" She concealed the knife in her sleeve and motioned Raquel to open the door.

Raquel sent Teresa back into the kitchen. Then she cleared her throat and opened the front door. Paquito stood before her. He was smirking.

"What can I do for you, Paquito? Am I being arrested again?"

Paquito looked mildly offended. He answered her in a tone so thick with false tenderness that it almost sounded as though he was being sarcastic, "Arrested? No, no, Mrs. León. I'm here as a friend. I just wanted to see if there was anything I could do for you. I can only imagine how hard these days must be for your family. I'm certain I can help with whatever difficulties you might be experiencing."

"We are in need of nothing," she said.

"But there must certainly be something I can do for your children. Where are they? Why don't you call them out here so I can say hello?"

Sirens went off in Raquel's head. "They're in Camagüey with relatives," she said casually.

"Oh, really?" He smiled, as if amused.

In that instant, Raquel understood that Paquito was somehow behind Goyito's beating. An icy chill ran through her throat.

"What a pity. I hope they get to join one of the literacy brigades while they're in Camagüey. Send them my love." He walked to his car and drove away with the two militiamen.

José María came out of the room with the children a few minutes later. He had hidden them inside the armoire, behind the clothing. He threw Raquel a hard look. "Do you still have those visa waivers?"

Raquel said nothing, went to her room, and shut the door.

* * *

Raquel followed the negotiations for the Brigade's release any way she could. She listened to official government sources, the Voice of America, and whatever rumor was circulating around Havana at the time. Her most reliable source was a group of Brigade wives and mothers still in Cuba who had started to gather at a home in the Vedado section of the capital. There, Raquel befriended a Brigade mother in her fifties. One day she told the woman about the special visa waivers she'd received for her children, but explained that she wanted to wait to see what happened with the negotiations first. She would prefer for all of them to leave Cuba together. The woman, who was familiar with the special children's visas, told Raquel that she could procure airline tickets for the children if she decided to send them out of Cuba on their own.

By the third week of June, the tractor deal had collapsed. A second trip by the Brigade's representatives to rescue the negotiations proved fruitless. The only help they received was from impoverished Brigade families in exile, with whom they formed the "Cuban Families Committee for the Liberation of the Prisoners of War." They would try to raise the money themselves for the men's release. Despite the group's valiant efforts, Raquel knew that Goyo and his comrades now faced a lengthy imprisonment at best or execution at worst.

On July 12, Raquel was home with her parents, Teresa, Goyo's mother, and the children. Sonia was there, too. She had become a close friend and confidant to Raquel. While Adriana cooked supper in the early evening, someone knocked at the front door. José María peered outside. "Damn it! It's that Paquito Vega *again*! What in the hell does he want this time? Sonia, help me hide the children." Sonia and José María disappeared into the master bedroom with Ana Cristina and Goyito.

As José María closed the armoire door, Ana Cristina began wailing. Her grandfather pleaded with her, "Sweetheart, you have to stay quiet so the bad man outside doesn't hear you!"

That made her cry louder.

Sonia came over. "Ana Cristina, princess, if you promise me you'll be quiet and brave, I'll stay right here in the bedroom. OK?" The little girl nodded and quieted down. José María closed the door, plunging the children into total darkness.

Raquel had ordered everyone else into the kitchen under strict orders to remain silent. A few seconds later, José María came out of the bedroom, gave the "all-clear," and joined the others in the kitchen.

Raquel made no effort to disguise her contempt when she opened the door. "What do you want this time, Paquito?" He was alone and in civilian clothing.

"May I come in, please?" His tone was humble and deferential. Raquel led him into the living room. He pulled out a few canned goods, a bottle of cooking oil, and a small bag of rice from a tote bag he carried. He laid them on the coffee table. "For your family," he said.

Raquel ignored the items.

"Mrs. León, I know the negotiations have broken down for your husband's release, and I know how frightened you must feel right now. I'm here to reiterate my offer to help you."

"We have faith in God, we need no one else, Paquito."

"I see." He scanned the house. "You know, your children are missing out on some wonderful opportunities. The new youth organizations are thriving. The children of Cuba have never been happier. And the new school system will be magnificent. It will make Cuba a Mecca of progress and learning."

"I wish you luck with that," Raquel said sarcastically.

"Mrs. León, you know that your husband and his comrades are almost certain to be executed now. It's a pity to think that a good woman like you will be a widow at such a young age; and those beautiful children, orphans–orphans of a man denounced as a traitor! What kind of future awaits them in this new Cuba?"

Raquel's skull caught fire. What was this man getting at? She folded her arms and looked away.

"I can help you; I can help your children. Listen, if you made a gesture to demonstrate your devotion to the nation, I'm certain that the Revolution would be quite generous to your family."

Raquel snapped her head in his direction. So that was it: he wanted her to denounce her husband publicly. What a wonderful propaganda coup for the regime if the wife of a Bay of Pigs "mercenary" was to choose her loyalty to the Revolution over her husband–and what a career accomplishment for Paquito to have arranged it! She didn't respond, the consequences of refusing his offer slowly settling in her mind. Would they take her children away from her if she refused? Would Goyo be tortured in retribution? She felt her body begin to sway.

"You know, Mrs. León, this country is now producing a whole new breed of man—the 'New Man,' they call him— and he will be the dominant force in Cuba from now on, part of a new social vanguard. Among other things, this New Man will have the responsibility of setting an example for the boys who will become the New Men of the next generation. That's something a boy like yours can benefit from. And the New Men will also be in the best position to support and protect their children, adopted or otherwise."

Raquel reared back. Adopted or otherwise? Was he offering to pimp her off to some Revolutionary after publicly denouncing Goyo? Her body went numb.

Teresa sprung into the living room like a starved lion into a Roman arena. She pointed at Paquito. "You listen here, you good for nothing little turd!" She stepped toward him slowly, her finger still pointed at him. "This lady has a husband and her son has a father! And do you want to know something? They're bursting with pride to have such a man, a real man who risked his life to rid this island of bullies like you—resentful, insecure, little snakes!" She lowered her finger and said to him in a tone dripping with loathing, "Do you think we respect you because of your association with these delinquents? Do you think we fear you?" She laughed out loud. "How can we fear a man who needs others to tell him what kind of a man he needs to be? 'New Man' indeed." She curled her lip at him. "You're a shameless rat. Leave, now!"

Paquito was caught off guard. His face had turned five different shades of red during the diatribe. He walked to the door, held it open for a moment, and croaked over his shoulder, "You will all be sorry." He slammed the door behind him.

Everyone ran to the bedroom. Sonia was pulling the children out of the armoire. She looked alarmed. "I was watching through a crack in the door. That man is a *miliciano,* isn't he?"

"Yes," José María answered, "and apparently in the G.2 now, too. He's a former employee of the bank. He's the one who led the intervention team at the bank and chased Roberto, Emilio, and Goyo out of the country. He's caused us nothing but grief. Do you know him?"

All the missing pieces now fell into place for Sonia. Her suspicions about the militiaman that night at her father's house were truer than she'd imagined. "He's an acquaintance of my father," she said. She told them about the night she and Roberto had gone to the Tropicana and her subsequent suspicion that Paquito had spied on them and how that might have led to his discovery of Roberto and Emilio's connection to the underground. She couldn't have even imagined that he was a former employee of Roberto's family. Everyone reassured Sonia that she was not to blame.

An hour later, a rock crashed through the front window. Raquel looked outside. A mob of more than a hundred Revolutionary zealots had gathered in front of her home, no doubt courtesy of Paquito. The children were rushed back into the armoire. Raquel locked the doors, shut the drapes, and turned off all the lights. The "citizens" outside unleashed a savage barrage of profanities and chanted Revolutionary slogans, some of them right up against the windows. "Fatherland or Death!" "To the execution wall with the mercenaries of Girón!" Some of them began pounding heavily on the front door, as if trying to break it down. Raquel sat helplessly, her fingers pulling her hair.

When the mob dispersed, Raquel rushed back into the bedroom. She saw her father taking the children out of their hiding place. Ana Cristina ran into her arms. The little girl trembled with fright. Goyito stood as silently as a whitewashed Grecian statue.

José María stared at his daughter.

She nodded and went to the telephone.

Her sister Conchita answered on the other end in Miami. Raquel outlined the situation for her and explained that she needed to stay in Cuba as long as Goyo was in prison, as did Goyo's mother; José María and Adriana wouldn't leave her alone in Cuba, and Lorenzo and Sara wouldn't leave the island without Roberto. Teresa couldn't be asked to be ripped from the resting places of her deceased husband and children—even though she would if they asked her. "Conchita, can you please take charge of the children until someone else gets to Miami? It shouldn't be for too long." She paused to let a tremor ripple through her. "My sister, you're my only hope."

"Yes, my sister, yes," Conchita said right away. "These are terrible times and families must pull together. I'm sure Juan José would agree—he's always been fond of Goyo and is so proud that he served in the invasion. Send the children here and I'll pick them up at the airport. I'll treat them like they were my own. I swear it on my soul!"

When Raquel hung up, she called the lady she knew from the Vedado circle who'd promised her the airline tickets. The woman told her not to speak over the telephone and to come to her house instead. When Raquel got there the next morning, the woman produced two tickets on a Pan American World Airways flight to Miami on July 16, just a few days away. Raquel tried to pay for the tickets, but the woman refused her money.

Raquel told the children the following morning.

"Children," she said at breakfast, "guess what?"

Goyito and Ana Cristina looked at one another, and then back at Raquel. "What?"

"Well," she said, "you know how you two have always wanted to travel aboard an airplane?"

They both nodded.

"Well, soon you're both going to fly on one."

"Where are we going?" Goyito asked with some trepidation.

"You're going to spend some time with your Aunt Conchita and Uncle Juan José in Miami."

"Aren't you coming?" Ana Cristina asked.

"No," Raquel said as smoothly and nonchalantly as she could, "the rest of us have to stay here to make sure Papi and Roberto are all right. We'll join you in Miami as soon as they and the others are given their freedom. It shouldn't be too long now. Besides, while you're in Miami you can practice your English—and I want both of you as fluent as Papi when we get there. And I want you on your best behavior. OK?"

The children glanced at each other with uncertainty. Then Goyito looked at his mother and said, "We understand."

"Juan José is a grouch!" Ana Cristina squawked. She crossed her arms.

Goyito threw his sister a stern look. "But we'll do our best to get along."

Raquel looked at each of them in turn. "And another thing: do not tell *anyone*, and I mean *anyone*, outside this house that you're leaving. It could get us into a lot of trouble."

Goyito kept his eyes on his sister. "Did you hear that? No blabbing."

"I heard her. I'm not stupid, you know."

"Yeah, sure."

28

RANCHO BOYEROS AIRPORT

Havana, Cuba
July 16, 1961

G oyito felt queasy when they got to the entrance of the enclosed passenger waiting area and saw the large, glass wall separating the passengers from the rest of the airport population. Raquel told him the passenger area had been nicknamed the *pecera*, the "fishbowl." He asked his mother. "We don't have to go in there by ourselves, do we?"

Raquel stared thoughtfully into the *pecera*. "Of course not, let's go in."

A female employee with a face like a horse blocked their way. "Passengers only beyond this point."

Raquel forced herself to smile. "My dear, these children are traveling by themselves. You can't expect them to check in alone and to wait unaccompanied. I promised them that I would stay with them until they've boarded."

The woman hadn't stopped shaking her head the whole time Raquel spoke. She pointed to the area along the outside of the glass wall. "You aren't the only ones." Raquel turned and saw a large group of parents lining the outside of the *pecera*, looking at their offspring inside, all of the young- sters bound for the United States as unaccompanied refu- gee children. Some were signaling to their children inside the fishbowl; many were crying; others just stared through the glass wall with stunned, helpless expressions. One young mother had her hands pressed up against the glass, looking at her daughter; the girl stared back, her eyes popping out in silent bewilderment.

Raquel stepped back. She whispered hysterically to her mother, "I can't send them in there by themselves. Let's go home!"

Adriana grasped Raquel's wrists and yanked her aside. She looked directly into her eyes. "History and fate, Raquel, have put you in this position. Right now you face a choice. You can keep your children here, where they will be taken from you sooner or later; maybe they'll be sent to Russia, maybe they'll be taken to an indoctrination camp in the countryside, or maybe they'll just be forced to enroll in the new schools. Daughter, even if they stay with you physically, these people will find a way to separate them from you. They'll rewire their minds in every way possible, they'll turn them against you and there will be *nothing* you can do to stop it. That is the government's stated objective. Send them to your sister; at least they'll be in a place where they can have the freedom to grow into the kind of people that you and Goyo—their *parents*—want them to be, not what a group of opportunist radicals want to mold them into. Do you want the likes of Paquito Vega responsible for the formation of your son and daughter?" Adriana pulled her closer. She gritted her teeth. "Raquel, no mother should ever be asked to make this choice, but you must!"

Raquel was on the verge of collapsing on the floor; only her mother's tight grip kept her upright. She took a shallow, nervous breath. She glanced over at her children and then into the *pecera*. She turned back to her mother. With a voice faltering and choked with tears, she said, "I don't have the strength."

Adriana squeezed her wrists harder. "Daughter, put things in God's hands!"

Raquel took a deep breath and held it. She glanced over at her children again. Goyito was wearing his best suit and carried an old comic book under his arm. Ana Cristina held her favorite doll. She could have never imagined that she'd have to live through something like this as a parent. She slowly walked over and knelt between her children.

"Listen, kids, you have to go into the passenger area by yourselves." She felt an emotion swelling her throat. She paused for a moment to let it pass and took a breath. "Now, it's very simple. You just go straight to the nice people there at the desk and show them these papers." She pointed at the two government officials inside the fishbowl and gave Goyito the documents. "Abuela and I will be on this side of the glass. Now, as soon as you check in, look for us and wave to let us know everything went all right. And remember, when you get to the Miami airport you have to ask for someone called George—he's in charge of the children there. He'll take you to your aunt and uncle."

Raquel stood up and motioned for her mother to take Ana Cristina away.

She stood alone now with her son. She bent forward and grabbed him by his upper arms. She locked eyes with him and dropped her sing-song tone, speaking with a directness she had never before used with her children. "Son, listen to what I'm going to tell you, and listen well. You have to be a *man* now. You have to protect your sister. No matter what, *you have to protect her!* I don't care who it's from. And do not, under any circumstances, let anyone separate you. Ever! Do you understand me?"

Goyito swallowed and nodded.

"Son, your father wants you to be strong—strong for yourself and strong for your sister. You are now the *only one* who can be strong for her." Her eyes filled with tears, but her voice, though it trembled, was sharp and strong. "If you ever feel like you can't be strong, think of how your father and I are counting on you. Think of Roberto and all the brave men of the Brigade who are in prison and of how strong they have to be every day. Think of your cousin Emilio and how courageous he was when he died fighting the Communists. You are not alone—we are all being strong together!"

Tears flowed freely down Goyito's cheeks. He wrapped his arms around his mother. "I will, Mami. I swear it to you." Raquel rubbed his back and fought back more tears, silently chastising herself for placing such a burden on a boy so young.

Ana Cristina and Adriana came back a few minutes later. Raquel opened her purse and pulled out a pen and a piece of paper. She tore the paper in half and asked her mother, "Do you have any pins in your purse?" Adriana rifled through her handbag and pulled out a couple of small safety pins. Raquel took them. She wrote something on the pieces of paper and pinned one on each child's clothing. Goyito read his: "This Gregorio León. Please see that he is turned over to the custody of Conchita González de Fernandez or Juan José Fernandez at Miami International Airport. He is traveling with his sister, Ana Cristina León. They are not to be separated under any circumstances." She had written her name, address, and telephone number in Havana, and those of Conchita in Miami. Ana Cristina had an identical one with their names reversed.

Raquel hugged the children tightly for a long time, kissed them each on the cheek, and sent them into the fishbowl. Ana Cristina grabbed Goyito's hand. The two youngsters crossed the *pecera's* threshold together. Raquel, biting down on her index finger, watched them through a fog of tears.

Goyito briefly looked over his shoulder at his mother and grandmother. He wanted to run back to them, but his legs kept doggedly propelling him deeper into the *pecera*. When he looked to the front again, he was overcome with the feeling that his childhood had suddenly ended, left forever on the other side of the glass partition.

He thrust the papers at the attendants without a word. The man and woman at the desk scanned the documents and stamped them. The woman snickered at their little pinned notes. Then she shook her head at Ana Cristina. "I'm sorry little girl, but you're going to have to leave the doll here." Ana Cristina hugged the doll tightly to her chest. The woman narrowed her eyes angrily, reached over, and tore the doll away from her. Ana Cristina's chest started heaving. The woman thrust her right hand out, palm up. "And I'm going to have to take those earrings as well." Ana Cristina was wearing the miniature diamond earrings she'd received from her grandparents when she was a baby. She touched them and stepped back. "Either you give them to me right now or I'll call the police over," the woman snorted fiercely. Ana Cristina undid the earrings with the dexterity of a magician and surrendered them to the woman.

The male attendant spoke to Goyito. "You can take the comic book, but I'll need to take that chain I can see you're wearing under your shirt." Goyito started blinking nervously. It was the chain and St. Jude medallion his father had sent them through Horacio. The man rolled his eyes. "Look sonny, give it to me or I can't allow you to board the airplane. There's a rule now about taking jewelry out of the country." Goyito fought the urge to look back at his mother. He pulled the chain from around his neck and surrendered it to the man.

Raquel covered her mouth with a handkerchief. "Mamá, how could this be happening?"

"Courage, Raquel. We're not alone. And remember, there are people in Miami to help them off the airplane; plus, I'm sure your sister is already there waiting for them."

Goyito waved at Raquel to let her know that everything had gone well with the attendants. The two children, holding hands again, found adjoining seats inside the *pecera*. Ana Cristina sat in hers for only a couple of seconds before jumping down and squeezing into the same seat with her brother. She buried her face in his shoulder. He put his arm around her.

Raquel motioned for Goyito to have Ana Cristina turn toward her. Goyito said something to his sister and pointed at their mother. The little girl shook her head and kept her face hidden. Goyito looked back at Raquel and shrugged his shoulders.

"She's just a little scared, Raquel," Adriana said.

Raquel noticed a husband and wife arrive behind her with two adolescent boys—one was around sixteen and the other fourteen. Raquel became alive with recognition. She approached the father. "I think I know you, sir."

"Oh?" he asked. His eyes were misty.

"You're Matías Pacheco."

"Yes, I am," the man said.

"You know my father."

Adriana approached him, "Yes, you did business with him, José María González."

"Of course, of course, yes, Adriana, Raquel. How are you?" Matías blew his nose into a handkerchief. "I'm sorry, I should have recognized you."

"Matías," Raquel said, "are you going to Miami on this flight?"

"Only my boys," he said, "they're going by themselves."

"Matías, I have two little children in there traveling alone as well; they're José María's grandchildren. See them there?" She pointed at Goyito and Ana Cristina. "Do you think it's possible that your sons could sit with them in the waiting area and on the airplane? They're terrified."

Matías straightened. "Of course, yes, it would be their honor." He turned to his sons. "Boys, do you see the children at whom this lady pointed?" They nodded. "Go sit with them when you get inside. You are charged with chaperoning them on the trip to Miami and helping them in any way you can. They are the grandchildren of a man who is like a second father to me, and that makes those children family to you." The boys nodded again, obviously accustomed to deferring to their father's authority.

Matías and his wife embraced their boys and bid them farewell. The wife was an emotional wreck. They watched as the two teenagers crossed into the *pecera* and checked in. One of the boys was forced to give the attendants his watch.

When they finished, they went over to the León children. The older boy spoke to Goyito and pointed at Raquel. Goyito looked over at his mother. She nodded to him that it was all right.

"They were being pressured to join the Rebel Youth," Matías said, "and we were afraid they'd be drafted into the army. There was no way I could turn them over to the Communists. We would have all left together, but my wife and I haven't received our exit documents yet. Someone got us these special visa waivers and said we could send the boys out right away if we wanted, and that they'd be placed somewhere, maybe on a school scholarship or something." He sighed. "What were we supposed to do?"

There was some sort of delay with the flight. Hours passed without any word about when it would leave. One of the airline employees announced later that due to the large number of passengers, the luggage would be taken off the airplane and sent to Miami in a few days' time. Then they asked if any of the adult passengers would be willing to carry younger children on their laps, since there weren't enough seats for everyone. The Pacheco boys immediately indicated that they would carry Goyito and Ana Cristina.

At a quarter after midnight, the passengers were allowed to board the airplane. It was the morning of July 17. Adriana and Raquel went up to the second floor of the airport building, where there was an outdoor public observation deck. They watched, motionless, as the plane taxied to the runway. Raquel burst into tears. Adriana held her tightly.

When it took off and disappeared over the horizon, Raquel stopped crying and stiffened her jaw. "It is done."

Meanwhile, aboard the airplane, Goyito and Ana Cristina sat on the Pacheco boys' laps. The older Pacheco was called Ignacio, but went by Nacho; the younger one was Alberto, but everyone called him Berti. One of the stewardesses approached Goyito. "Are you Gregorio León?" Goyito nodded. She smiled at him. "The official at the gate asked me to give you this." She pulled out his chain and St. Jude medallion and held it out for him. He took it from her. He couldn't think of anything to say. She smiled again and walked away. Goyito stared at the medallion for several seconds. He placed it around his neck. He could feel its life force channeling into his chest. He looked out the window and watched Havana's lights fade in the distance.

A few minutes later, the pilot announced, "We are now in international air space. In a few moments, we will enter the air space of the United States of America." The adult passengers began to cheer. Some of them shouted, "Freedom!" It was as though a long dormant volcano had suddenly erupted inside them.

* * *

At three o'clock in the morning on July 17, the Brigade was roused by the militia guards at the Naval Hospital. "Come on, worms, your vacation is *over*." When the negotiations for the Brigade's release had broken down irrevocably, the government decided that the humane conditions accorded them at the Naval Hospital would have to come to an emphatic end. They were lined up outside the hospital and packed onto a fleet of buses. Many believed their hour of execution had finally arrived. The buses took them back across the bay and to the 18th century Spanish fortification and prison called the *Castillo del Principe*, the Prince's Castle.

In the dark of night, the Brigade men, still in their yellow T-shirts, were ordered off the buses. They crossed the castle's drawbridge and entered a central courtyard called the *Estrella*, the Star. They were then separated and sent into different parts of the old, musty, colonial-era fortress. A large number of men, including Goyo, were ordered to march double time down a walkway that ran into the *Principe's* gloomy depths. Guards stationed every few yards prodded them with bayonets and taunted them with cries of "traitors," and "yellow worms," their harsh, angry voices echoing throughout the dimly lit interior. As the men moved, they passed cells occupied by common criminals—thieves, rapists, murderers—who likewise insulted and threatened them. Some of the Brigade men were put into the empty cells they passed; the last four hundred, which included Goyo, were taken to the lowest level of the prison and locked inside dungeon cells called *leoneras*, lions' dens. Goyo heard the heavy, metallic sound of the iron gates and locks clanking shut behind them. He'd just been locked in Hell. He sat on the floor and leaned his back against the damp stone wall. He shut his eyes and prayed, but found no solace.

* * *

Raquel sat by the telephone waiting for her sister's call from Miami, desperate to hear the children's voices telling her that they'd arrived safely. As the lonely, pre-dawn hours crawled by, she could no longer bear to be inside the house and asked her mother to listen for the call while she went outside to get some air. She grabbed her Rosary and went behind the house to the water's edge. She felt as though her heart was being ripped out of her chest. She looked out across the moonlit water, supplicating in a low voice, "Dear Lord, may I be granted the courage to survive these desperate hours." For one of the few times in her life, prayer did not console her.

Adriana came out of the house a few minutes later and marched quickly over to Raquel. She bore a bewildered and angry expression. "Your sister just called."

"Did the children arrive safely?"

"You're never going to believe it. I don't believe it myself. *Damn* that selfish bastard and your sister for marrying him!"

* * *

Ana Cristina and Goyito had landed in Miami just before two o'clock in the morning. The man they were told to ask for–George–was there, gathering all the unaccompanied children from the flight. He took their information and gave them all bubble gum and candy. He joked around with them to help them relax. When the paperwork was completed, the children who had relatives waiting for them were separated from those going to the "camps" where they sent the children who had no family to take them in. The Pacheco boys went with the latter group, the León children with the former. Before going their separate ways, the Pachecos told Goyito and Ana Cristina to call them if they ever needed anything.

Goyito, Ana Cristina, and the other children in their group were taken to where their relatives awaited them. The León children saw their aunt and uncle in the distance. They never thought they could be so relieved to see them, especially Juan José. They were talking to a woman carrying a clipboard and pencil. Juan José was gesticulating wildly with his hands. He was shaking his head, "No, no, and no!"

The children walked over to Conchita. She saw them and hugged them tightly. "Children, you're here! Thank God!" Juan José gave them a steely, sideways glance.

"Listen, children," Conchita said, "right now, like everyone else in Miami, we're living in a little, tiny apartment. When I told your mother we would take you in, I really wasn't thinking."

"Yes," Juan José hissed, "you were *not* thinking. Doesn't your sister know how much we're suffering in this country? We have no room, no money. We can barely feed ourselves!"

The lady with the clipboard, who was also Cuban, interrupted him. "But sir, as I explained, the program can provide you with financial assistance if you take them in. It's preferable for the children, especially ones so young, to go with family rather than to the camps or into foster care."

Juan José growled, "You don't understand. We're *suffering*! We don't know where our next meal is coming from!"

"Sir," the lady grunted, "we are all suffering, not just your family."

Juan José sighed in exasperation and cast a look of loathing at the children. He said, "Look kids, you have no idea what it's like for us here. We can't provide for you, no matter what this kind lady says. They have some excellent camps outside Miami where you can be with other children. They're great places, run by priests and nuns and teachers from Cuba. It'll be great fun, just like going to summer camp."

Conchita looked at her husband scornfully. Then she turned and smiled at the children. "I promise that as soon as we're more stable, we'll bring you to come live with us."

"Conchita," Juan José huffed, "don't make promises you can't keep."

Conchita ignored him. "For the time being, I promise we'll visit you at the camp every weekend. We can go out for ice cream, or to the movies."

Juan José sighed and checked his watch.

Conchita gave the children each a kiss on the cheek and told them to go with the lady. The woman with the clipboard threw Juan José and Conchita a contemptuous look, and then told the children to follow her.

A few minutes later they were standing curbside outside the terminal, next to a large station wagon packed with other children from the flight. They checked the faces. The Pachecos had apparently been sent to a different camp. Ana Cristina and Goyito were told to climb into the tail end of the station wagon and to sit in the rear-looking back seat. A few minutes later, they set off into the dark Miami night. Goyito ripped off the little notes his mother had pinned on them and threw them out the rear window.

It was three o'clock in the morning.

THANK YOU

T hank you for reading *Freedom Betrayed,* Book II of *The Unbroken Circle* series. If you would like to be notified when the next book in the series is available, please sign up for the author's mailing list. You can send an email to victortriayauthor@att.net or info@victortriayauthor.com requesting inclusion on the email list. You may also visit the author's website at victortriayauthor.com and fill out the "Contact Information" section under the "Contact Victor" tab. Also, feel free to contact the author at the other social media locations listed at the beginning of the book. An excerpt from *The Unbroken Circle,* Book III, *On Freedom's Shores,* can be found below.

If you enjoyed *Freedom Betrayed,* please share it with your friends, family, and social networks. **You can post a review on Amazon.com and on other online review sites such as Goodreads.com.** You can also visit the author's Create Space e-store at www.createspace.com/4388424.

Please note that the book is available on Amazon.com, Createspace.com/4388424, and other retailers.

Please enjoy this excerpt from:

The Unbroken Circle,
Book III: On Freedom's Shores

To be released summer, 2014

Chapter Seven

THE BRONX, NEW YORK CITY
Monday, September 11, 1961

S ister Francesca boarded the subway train in the Bronx. She was dressed, as always, in full habit. Even though it was only 6:30 in the morning, commuters had already packed the train. Those without seats stood, balancing themselves on the handrails. As invariably occurred, one of the men offered Francesca his seat. Being a nun had its perks, she thought. She smiled at the man, thanked him, and sat down.

As the train rumbled on, many of the people who passed her nodded respectfully. One young woman actually stopped before her, bowed slightly, and recited with practiced piety, "Good morning, Sister." Francesca nodded, pegging her as a Catholic school veteran. Francesca sighed and settled in for the long ride to Staten Island, where she was to have breakfast with a group of nuns visiting from Italy.

Scanning the row of passengers seated across from her, she spotted a couple of children roughly ten feet away. They had the distinct look of having been on the subway all night by themselves; runaways, maybe, or possibly abandoned. Who knew? She shook her head and sighed indignantly, having seen it plenty of times before. The little waifs' clothes were disheveled, their hair was tousled, and a film of dirt covered their faces. The little girl was curled up asleep against the boy, who, though exhausted, kept his frightened eyes alert to possible threats, glaring suspiciously at anyone who came near them. How sad, Sister Francesca thought, that in this great city, in this great country, these things still happened. She knew she had to do something, at least find out why they were all alone and call the police or Children's Services if they were in fact runaways or abandoned. Those were awful options, but it was preferable to their present condition, especially with every sort of degenerate lurking about.

As she stood to walk over to them, she was struck by a vague sense of recognition. Peering at the children more closely, she gasped. A few seconds later, she stood before them.

The little boy looked up at her. His head and shoulders reared back in astonishment. "Sister Francesca!" He elbowed the little girl. "Ana Cristina, wake up! Look who it is!"

SELECTED BIBLIOGRAPHY

Below, please find a brief bibliography. The articles, reports, and books are listed together. It includes many of the sources I consulted, to varying degrees, for my research. I have included my own non-fiction work about the Bay of Pigs invasion on the list. In its bibliography, you will find the various interviews I conducted for that book.

"After Cuba: Who Stood for What?" *U.S. News and World Report*, December 17, 1962, 33-35.

"The Air Will Be Ours: Cuban Fighters Tell Why They Expected Air Cover." *U.S. News and World Report*, February 4, 1963, 33-36.

Ball, Ann. *Faces of Holiness II: Modern Saints in Photos and Words.* Huntington, IN: Our Sunday Visitor, 2001.

Aguilar, Luis, Introduction to *Operation Zapata: The "Ultrasensitive" Report and Testimony of the Board of Inquiry on the Bay of Pigs.* Frederick, Md.: University Publications of America, 1981.

Bissell, Richard M., *Reflections of a Cold Warrior: From Yalta to the Bay of Pigs.* New Haven and London: Yale University Press, 1996.

Carbonell, Nestor T., *And the Russians Stayed: The Sovietization of Cuba: A Personal Portrait.* New York: Murrow, 1989.

Chapman, William. "A View from PriFly." *U.S. Naval Institute Proceedings* 118 (October 1992): 45-50.

Clark, Juan. *Cuba: Mito y Realidad.* Miami: Saeta Ediciones, 1990.

Conde, Yvonne. *Operación Pedro Pan: La historia inédita de 14,048 niños cubanos.* New York: Random House Español, 2001.

de Quesada, Alejandro. *The Bay of Pigs: Cuba 1961.* Oxford, UK and New York: Osprey Publishing, 2009.

Dille, John. "We Who Tried." *Life,* May 10, 1963.

Eire, Carlos. *Waiting for Snow in Havana: Confessions of a Cuban Boy.* New York: Simon and Schuster, 2003.

Engstrom, David W. *Presidential Decision Making Adrift: The Carter Administration and the Mariel Boatlift.* Lanham, New York, Boulder, Oxford: Rowan and Littlefield Publishers, 1997.

Encinosa, Enrique. *Unvanquished: Cuba's Resistance to Fidel Castro.* Los Angeles: Pureplay Press, 2004.

Feeney, Harold. "No Regrets—We'd Do It Again." *The Nation,* April 19, 1986, 550-57.

Ferrer, Eduardo. *Operation Puma: The Air Battle of the Bay of Pigs.* Miami: International Aviation Consultants, 1982.

"For the First Time: The Story of How President Kennedy Upset the Cuban Invasion of April 1961." *U.S. News and World Report,* February 4, 1963, 29-33.

Freyre, Ernesto. *For God and Country: The Story of Ernesto "Tito" Freyre.* (unpublished manuscript, with Victor Andres Triay). Miami: 2002.

Fontova, Humberto. *Exposing the Real Che Guevara: And the Useful Idiots Who Idolize Him.* New York: Sentinel, 2007.

Gleijeses, Piero. "Ships in the Night: The CIA, the White House, and the Bay of Pigs." *Journal of Latin American Studies* 27 (1995): 1-42.

Guyanes, Eli B. Cesar. *San Blas: Ultima Batalla en Bahía de Cochinos.* Miami: Editorial Los Amigos, 2007.

Handleman, Howard. "Prisoners Tell—The Real Story of the Bay of Pigs." *U.S. News and World Report,* January 7, 1963, 38-41.

Hawkins, Jack. "Classified Disaster: The Bay of Pigs Operation Was Doomed by Presidential Indecisiveness and Lack of Commitment." *National Review,* December 31, 1996, 36-38.

Hawkins, Jack. "An Obsession with 'Plausible Deniability' Doomed the 1961 Bay of Pigs Invasion from the Outset." *Military History,* May, 1988.

Hunt, Howard. *Give Us This Day.* New Rochelle, N.Y.: Arlington House, 1973.

"The Inside Story—Kennedy's Fateful Decision: The Night the Reds Clinched Cuba." *U.S. News and World Report,* September 17, 1962.

Johnson, Haynes. *The Bay of Pigs: The Leaders' Story of Brigade 2506.* New York: W. Norton, 1964.

Lazo, Mario. *Dagger in the Heart: American Policy Failures in Cuba.* New York: Twin Circle Publishing Company, 1968.

Lynch, Grayston. *Decision for Disaster: Betrayal at the Bay of Pigs.* Washington and London: Brassey's, 1998.

Mets, David R. *Land-based Air Power in Third World Crises.* Maxwell Air Force Base, Ala.: Air University Press, 1986.

Meyer, Karl E., and Tad Szulc, *The Cuban Invasion: The Chronicle of a Disaster.* New York, Washington, and London: Frederick A. Praeger, 1962.

Momentum Miami, Miami World Cinema Center. *Stories from the Bay of Pigs Invasion: An Intergenerational Service Educational Experience,* 2011 (video)

Palmer, Eduardo, exec. prod., *Brigade 2506* (film)

Penabaz, Manuel. "'We Were Betrayed:' A Veteran of the Cuban Invasion Speaks Out." *U.S. News and World Report,* January 14, 1963, 46-49.

Persons, Albert C. *Bay of Pigs: A First-Hand Account of the Mission by a U.S. Pilot in Support of the Cuban Invasion Force in 1961.* Jefferson, N.C.: McFarland, 1990.

Rasenberger, Jim. *The Brilliant Disaster: JFK, Castro, and America's Doomed Invasion of Cuba's Bay of Pigs.* New York: Scribner, 2011.

Ros, Enrique. *Playa Girón: La verdadera historia* (Girón Beach: The True Story). Miami: Ediciones Universal, 1994.

Sandman, Joshua. "Analyzing Foreign Policy Crisis Situations: The Bay of Pigs." *Presidential Studies Quarterly* 16 (1986): 534-29.

Schlesinger, Arthur M., Jr., *A Thousand Days: John F. Kennedy in the White House.* New York: Houghton Mifflin, 1992.

Sorensen, Theodore C. *Kennedy.* New York: Harper and Row, 1965.

Thomas, Hugh. *Cuba: The Pursuit of Freedom.* New York: Harper and Row, 1971.

Triay, Victor Andres. *Bay of Pigs: An Oral History of Brigade 2506.* Gainesville, Fla.: University Press of Florida, 2001

———. *The Cuban Revolution: Years of Promise.* Gainesville, Fla.: University Press of Florida, 2005.

_____. *Fleeing Castro: Operation Pedro Pan and the Cuban Children's Program.* Gainesville, Fla.: University Press of Florida, 1998.

_____. *La Patria Nos Espera: La invasión de Bahía de Cochinos relatada en las palabras de la Brigada de Asalto 2506.* New York: Random House Español, 2003.

Valladares, Armando. *Against All Hope: A Memoir of Life in Castro's Gulag.* San Francisco: Encounter Books, 2001.

Vandenbroucke, Lucien S. "*Anatomy of a Failure: The Decision to Land at the Bay of Pigs.*" Political Science Quarterly 99, no. 3 (Autumn 1984): 471-91.

Wheeler, Keith. "Hell of a Beating in Cuba." *Life*, April 28, 1961.

Wyden, Peter. *Bay of Pigs: The Untold Story.* New York: Simon and Schuster, 1979.

AUTHOR BIO

Author Victor Andres Triay, Ph.D., was born in Miami, Florida, to Cuban exile parents. He has published three non-fiction books on the Cuban exile experience. In 2001, the Florida Historical Society awarded him the Samuel Proctor Oral History Prize for his book, *Bay of Pigs: An Oral History of Brigade 2506.* For over twenty-one years, he has been a professor of history at Middlesex Community College in Middletown, Connecticut. He resides in Connecticut with his wife and three children.